"We welcomed the
Earthwrought and their powers
to our citadel," Aumlac told
them, "to fight what grew
beneath Teru Manga."

"And what is it that dwells there?" asked
Guile.

Aumlac shook his head sadly. "A terrible
power. We hear the roar of its power in
our heads. It draws many things to it. Some
hold that it corrupted the Delvers on
Starkfell Edge, and made them its slaves,
the Ferr-Bolgan, and that many other
denizens of the deep belong to it now."

"We know of it," said Sisipher. "It does
not belong in Omara."

"It is the evil we are now sworn to
destroy," said Guile. "Anakhizer, Sorcerer
King."

ADRIAN COLE

BOOK TWO OF THE OMARAN SAGA

THRONE OF FOOLS

AVON BOOKS ◆ NEW YORK

AVON BOOKS
A division of
The Hearst Corporation
105 Madison Avenue
New York, New York 10016

Copyright © 1987 by Adrian Cole
Front cover illustration by Kevin Johnson
Published by arrangement with the author
Library of Congress Catalog Card Number: 89-92498
ISBN: 0-380-75840-7

First Avon Books Printing: July 1990

AVON TRADEMARK REG. U.S. PAT. OFF. AND IN OTHER COUNTRIES, MARCA REGISTRADA, HECHO EN U.S.A.

Printed in the U.S.A.

RA   10   9   8   7   6   5   4   3   2   1

Contents

ALTHOUGH IT IS NOT RELIABLY DOCUMENTED, it is claimed by some that the Chain of Goldenisle was once not a vast archipelago, but a ridge of low mountains pushing out from the main continent of north western Omara into the sea as a long peninsular. Little of those times has survived, and the legend of the Flood itself is now considered by most to be no more than that, an imaginative exaggeration of actual history. Yet fragments of Flood mythology abound, and there are those among the varied peoples of what is now the Chain who persist in their belief that, after the Flood, invaders came from the east (the actual word used in the native language of the surviving legends is "outsiders"), subdued the survivors of the cataclysm and founded their royal houses on the islands. It was then, these legends have it, that the Remoon Dynasty took root and apparently when the islands were given the name, Chain of Goldenisle.

The Remoon personal histories are themselves reticent on the settling (those that are accessible) with few references to violence and none to war of any consequence, although that may be a deliberate, if diplomatic, sin of omission. If there was strife, it appears to have been minimal, and in any event racial harmony does seem to have followed. One curious legend has, however, survived along with the more obvious ones. The conquered peoples not taken by the Flood, the legend goes, put a curse on the House of Remoon (in itself interesting if it is true, as it lends weight to other theories that these original peoples believed, unlike their conquerors, in some form of divine power). They cursed the House of Remoon with madness and disorder, and whether or not there was any effectiveness in the so-called curse, the history of the House of Remoon has not been exactly lacking in disorder, and while one might argue that sanity is a somewhat relative condition, it is interesting to note that more than a few members of the Remoon families have been less in possession of their faculties than other normal, rational men.

Perhaps it is this poorly documented but nevertheless

secretly acknowledged fact that has led to the quiet per-
sistence of the legend, and perhaps it explains why, in
certain circles, the royal seat of the House of Remoon is
referred to as the Throne of Fools.

> from *Goldenisle,*
> *an Anonymous Alternative History*
> (Private library of Eukor Epta,
> Administrative Oligarch to the Emperor.)

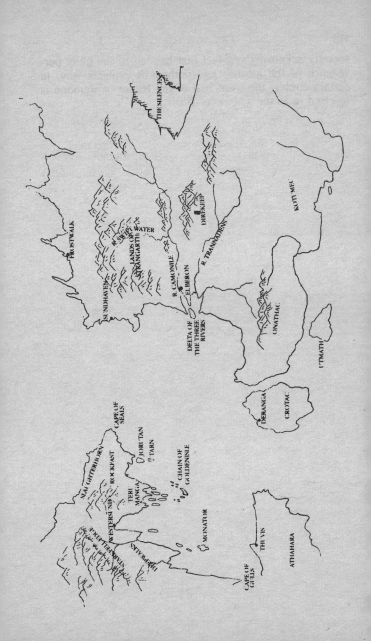

PART ONE

ENVOY

1
Snow Hunt

GUAMOK FELT as if he'd been out in the ice-fields for weeks, though in effect the young lad had been here little more than a day and a night. It had been too easy to boast to the other ice-village youths yet to be blooded that his first killing hunt would be easy, especially with a tough old hunter like Inguk to act as his seeker. The reality was different. The two of them had huddled together in a snow den for the bitter night, assaulted by a lacerating wind; it was so very different from the village, and even that was a grim place when the wind sharpened its cutting edge. At first it had been a relief to get up and creep out into the long, slow dawn behind Inguk, but after a two hour trudge through the white nothingness, featureless as oblivion, Guamok's confidence was numbed. Let the snow-seals appear soon, he whispered to the empty ice.

Visibility was not good, the light poor, and although the wind had dropped, a swirl of powdery snow danced about them. Some of the villagers would have taunted Guamok: "It is all sent to make your test worthy, Guamok. It is not just a snow-seal you are trying to best. A quick kill would mean nothing, eh?" They had made it sound easy, taking a snow-seal, but Guamok had heard from others who had made the step to manhood that it was never easy: the snow-seals were killers and they knew Guamok's people of old. If they found them, they were as ruthless as the men. Inguk was renowned for his skill, but he was an old man, Guamok had thought many times during the night. His strength must be limited.

As though he had heard the critical thoughts of his ward, Inguk stopped, head down. Slowly he swung to and fro like

3

an ice-wolf; Guamok wished they had been allowed even one of those beasts for the hunt, but the law permitted one seeker only, and even he was not allowed to use a weapon unless an emergency arose. Inguk had not, blessedly, been listening to Guamok's mind. What then, snow-seals?

"You hear it, boy?" he grunted, his eyes fixed on the ice as if he could already see the prey.

"I hear the whisper of snow, Inguk," replied Guamok.

Inguk remained very still for a few more moments, then shook his head. Guamok moved beside him and for once the old man was content to let the boy walk with him. Usually, when out hunting, the old man was lost in the work, hardly speaking, but otherwise his tongue was as energetic as that of any other of his people.

"Did you sleep?" he suddenly said, his face wrinkling into a thousand miniature crevasses.

He's laughing at me, Guamok thought. "Unexpectedly well, Inguk."

Inguk laughed, but softly, for he was too wary of his surroundings to disadvantage himself in any way. "You must learn to lie better when you are a man."

Guamok wanted to retort, to cover his flush of shame, but Inguk stiffened, listening. "Snow-seals?" the boy breathed.

Inguk shook his head. "We'll see none this day."

The words didn't come as relief to Guamok. He wanted this over. Another day? "Where are they?"

"They've been here," Inguk sniffed. "They left quickly."

"Was it our coming?"

Inguk chuckled, but there was no scorn. Patience was his strength. Age must bring that, thought the boy.

"Snow-seals do not fear men," said Inguk. "You have been told that. You must hold on to what you are told. It is not always repeated. Snow-seals kill. Few things frighten them, especially when they are in a pack." He was still again, listening.

"What do you hear?"

"Your ears are younger than mine, Guamok. What do you hear?"

Guamok tried to stretch his ears, his hearing. He could hear the wind, channelled by the chunks of ice that now thrust up like snapped bone. There was something else, quickly, then gone. The boy's eyes betrayed that he had heard the odd sound.

"Ah," nodded Inguk. "I thought I had not imagined it."

"What was it?"

"It does not belong here." Inguk's smile was gone. Now he looked slightly puzzled. There could be fewer more experienced men of the ice, Guamok knew, and yet here he was, unsure of himself. He must be very old, Guamok concluded. Does he hear as well as he once did?

Gesturing almost irritably, Inguk led them on. They moved in silence for almost an hour, but the strange sound they had heard did not come again in that time. Guamok told himself it had been the wind, which varied its voice among the scattered shapes of the ice-fields. But he thought of the snowseals, which Inguk had said had been frightened away, or so he had implied. Then again, perhaps this is the old man's way of adding to my test. Yes! That must be it. To teach me true fear, and how to overcome it. He smiled to himself, taking a little comfort from the thought, trying to keep faith with it.

It seemed a long time later that they dug themselves an icepit and burned a piece of oil-soaked munna wood, brought by the traders from the warmer northlands. With it they were able partially to cook slices of their meat ration. While chewing on it, Inguk became a little more like the imp of the village, expansive and full of tales of his past life, though had they all been true they would have filled a dozen lives.

"What was your first hunt like?" Guamok asked him.

The boy had touched a nerve: Inguk liked nothing better than to elaborate on this. "Not planned," he grinned. "Not like you young men today. No seeker for me to guide my steps. No! Life was harder, you see. Fewer of us. Lived by the spear, slept with it in your hand."

"That must have been hard for the love-making," Guamok laughed.

Inguk looked angry for only a second, then guffawed. "What do you know about such things?"

"Only what I've heard," Guamok said hastily, anxious to atone for what was obviously a mistake.

"I should hope so! Time enough for all that when you get

back from the hunt, provided all goes well. Then I daresay all the girls will want to share your furs."

"You think so?"

"Be careful, Guamok! Remember to choose your mate, otherwise one will choose you, and you may come to regret that." Inguk laughed openly, so much so that he didn't hear the sound that came quickly overhead, then was gone. But Guamok heard it, and his spear lifted instinctively into a defensive position, ready in an instant to strike.

Inguk's face fell and he groped for his own weapon. For a moment he looked old, defenseless. Then he had recovered himself, but the anger made him scowl. "What was it?" he snapped.

Guamok was as alert as an ice-wolf, but he shook his head. "Gone again."

"Well?"

"It was in the air, Inguk," said the boy, struggling to form an image. "Like a bird passing. Did you hear it?"

"I should lie to you and say I did," said Inguk. "But this is a hunt. Your hunt, Guamok. Only the truth will keep us alive. I missed it. You see how easily one becomes foolish? I did not hear it. But I will not fail you again."

"No bird could be that large," said Guamok, ignoring the old man's embarrassment; there was no time for such things.

"Sounds distort, you know that, Guamok. The snow is closing; it made a wall for the sound to build from."

"What bird would fly in this?"

Inguk did not answer. Instead he drove the point of his spear into the smoldering munna wood and raised it like a torch. The hunt was to go on. Guamok knew that they could survive many days in the ice-fields, for Inguk would see to that, and he had the extraordinary gift of his people for finding his direction no matter how bad the weather. When it was time to go back, he would find the village without effort. In time, so they had told Guamok, he would also develop this skill. It was the inheritance of his people.

Silence closed around them now, the good mood of the fireside meal gone. Whether it was fear of what he had been told, or fear at having been caught unprepared, Inguk was sullen, a rare mood indeed for him. He walked ahead as if banishing his ward to his place, and Guamok was even more determined to stay alert. Anger would not refine his awareness. I must concentrate!

When the sound came from above again, they were both ready. Something beat at the air, huge wings, and there came a strangled cry, one of pain, though that was all they could recognize in it. Inguk dropped to his knees, waving for Guamok to do the same, but the boy had already done so. A shadow passed over them, the sound rushed by, then out in the grayness they heard another cry. They remained like sculptured ice for long minutes.

"Is it seeking us?" Guamok whispered.

Inguk shook his head. He seemed, if anything, relieved. "I may be wrong, but there is distress in that cry."

They could hear now the distinct beating of wings, a thumping of the snow, still beyond vision. Inguk's spear was pointed sharply ahead, clear notice that he was prepared to use it: Guamok was not to be left to face this alone, blooding or not. Cautiously they stole across the snow like thieves, toward the sound of floundering wings. Another cry, more of a deep croak, drifted to them, much closer. In a moment the veil of snow thinned so that they could see, and both of them, even experienced Inguk, had to stifle gasps. Beyond them was a creature they had never before seen and of which no legend spoke. It was a huge bird, or so they assumed at first, for it had very long, leathery wings, one of which was crumpled up beneath it, clearly broken and the cause of its agony. Its head was elongated, and instead of the hooked beak of a scavenging gull, it had a long, pointed beak, serrated with teeth. It flung up its head, oblivious of the watchers, of everything but its pain, and a fine spray of blood drifted down about it; the snow around it was crimson. It had been in some terrible battle.

Neither man spoke, but both held their spears ready for a kill. They both studied the creature as a hunter should, wondering if it could be eaten, for here was meat that would serve the village for long days if edible. The thing thrashed about, lizard-like, growing visibly weaker. It had no feathers, its dark hide scaled, its feet not webbed like the sea birds here, but curved into sharp talons, not made for ice-fields. Inguk had heard of meat eaters in the warmer northern lands, and of how they plucked their living prey from the land. This must be one such bird, though no tale he had ever heard spoke of such a creature as this.

He motioned Guamok in. "Now, boy. Take great care. If you make the killing strike, your blooding will surpass that of all those that have gone before you."

Guamok's fear vied with his pride, but as he moved in, he thought of Inguk, the renowned hunter. He could not have many years left, but this should be his final glory. "This is an honor that I cannot deny you," he told him.

Inguk's eyes were on him for only a second before turning back to the prey. The boy means it! he thought. He does this out of respect and not fear. Inguk grinned. "The beast is yours, Guamok. But I will mark your words. You'll be a man yet."

Guamok was about to step forward and try for the exposed neck of the dying bird-creature, but as he did so it reared up, exposing its pale chest. Guamok looked, spear arm drawn back, and he could see what must be the heart, beating beneath the scales. How it throbbed! That is my target, he shouted within, releasing his weapon with all the strength he could get from his wiry body. The spear blurred as it went through the air, the point striking the center of the chest, the weapon sinking, sinking. The bird let out a scream of pain, wings buckling back, eyes glazing. Then its chest tore apart like fabric, as though the point of the spear had severed the last tendons that held it together, and blood gushed from the huge tear.

Inguk dragged the startled boy back, both amazed by the effect of the throw. This flood of matter should have been impossible, too extreme a result. There was worse to come, for something tumbled out of the frightful wound, as though the very organs of the beast had ripped from their beds and slithered on to the bloodied snow. The beast toppled to one side, its last breath gasping from its open beak. Spasms of movement shook it, and Inguk recognized them as the after-death twitches of a slain beast. He had seen enough killed prey to know that much. Even so, neither he nor the boy wanted to approach.

Long minutes after the beast had ceased all movement, they still waited. "There!" Inguk pointed. In the fallen en-trails, something stirred. Inguk lifted his spear, not wanting to use it, to spoil the boy's victory, but knowing he may have to.

Guamok thought he must be losing his mind. It was a *man*! Now on its knees, now standing, a figure rose, steam curling from it like smoke, as though it had got up from its own funeral pyre. Inguk made a choking sound, his spear wavering. Guamok pulled the weapon from loose fingers, but it was not so that he could cast it. They watched as the figure lurched forward, a step, two, two more, then, barely clear of the thick lake of blood, it fell into the white embrace of the snow. It remained as motionless as the dead bird.

Neither Guamok nor Inguk trusted himself to speak. That man had been *inside* the bird. Inside it? It was not possible. And yet, there he lay. They had seen—but what had they seen? It had been a bloody death, and one that easily confused the eye. But both men had decided on a single truth.

"How can this be?" said Guamok at last. Being a youth, his mind could more easily accept the new. Inguk, with most of his life and his experience behind him, could hardly digest the horror. He merely stared. Watching became insufficient for Guamok, who stepped forward. Inguk would have stayed him, but this was the boy's kill, his blooding. Let him act.

Guamok stood above the fallen man. He heard the gentle snow whisper around him, already filming both man and dead beast in a cloak of powder. The body before him was too filthy to be clearly recognized, but Guamok, still holding Inguk's spear, bent down. He put his free hand to the man's arm. There was a little warmth, and it was not the blood of the beast. Guamok touched the neck, feeling by instinct for the pulse. He found it.

"Alive!" he called to Inguk, who now shambled forward. For the first time, Guamok saw the old hunter as ancient, the years bowing him. He had carried his responsibilities for long enough. Now Guamok must shoulder his own, whatever the weight.

"Better come away," said Inguk dazedly, keeping his distance.

"No." Guamok was emphatic and the old man knew it. "We must help him."

"Such a vile birth," muttered Inguk. "He can only have been sent by evil."

"If he had been sent," argued Guamok, "he would not
have been dropped at our feet. See, one thrust would end
him." He held the point of the spear at the fallen man's neck.
He had no intention of killing him, and Inguk nodded.

"We must make a snow den at once. Light the munna
wood. I will begin cleaning him," Guamok went on, and
now the command was his. Inguk would not argue.

Later, walled in by ice in their snow den, heated by glowing
munna wood, they studied the man they had saved. He was
tall, well muscled, his head shaven, his features not those of
a man of the ice-fields. Inguk's people had very little geography: the man could have been from anywhere on Omara.
In spite of his extraordinary arrival, he was, it seemed, in
superb physical condition. They could not wake him, for he
seemed to be in either a deep sleep or a coma. Inguk had
seen this before, and it led, he said, to a gradual wasting and
death. Guamok clung tenaciously to the belief that the man
would survive, would come to eventually.

By his harness, now cleaned by the youth, Inguk declared
the man to be a warrior. He had no weapons, though strapped
to his belt was a long metal rod. Guamok had touched it, but
it was cold, a length of metal that could be of no discernible
use, except to beat at an opponent, or perhaps to kill a snow-
seal or whatever prey the warrior would hunt.

"How far are we from the village?" Guamok asked Inguk.

"The snows are easing. Two days if we move quickly."

"And if we take him?"

Inguk shook his head, not so much in disapproval as in
doubt. "He cannot walk. Like that, carried? A week."

The man's eyes fluttered open, which had the effect of startling both watchers into tumbling back. The head lifted, but
the eyes were vacant, seeing nothing. In a moment the man
had subsided. His lips were trying to form words. Guamok
leaned over him, but whatever he said was foreign, unintel-
ligible.

"We cannot stay here long," said Inguk. "The snow-seal
packs will be back, now that you have slain that beast. And
it is us who will become the hunted."

"Yes, I have thought of that. You must go back to the
village. Bring help."

"But you have not returned from your blooding—"

"My place is here, Inguk. I have to remain. Bring help."

Slowly Inguk nodded. "Very well. If he dies—"

The boy laughed softly. "No, he won't die. Go quickly."

Alone, Guamok found his vigil far more eerie, and more than once he felt the coming of the snow-seals, drawn to the blood of the beast in the snows. He had thought of going out to it and hacking off chunks of meat, but something told him it would be poisonous. He slept, always hoping that he would wake to find the warrior sitting up, watching him, but the man did not stir. Guamok was tempted to leave him, to go back and search for the village, but he was not sure that he would find it. He did not have Inguk's skill in that yet.

But the old man had not deserted him. Guamok had momentarily wondered if Inguk would merely write him off at the village, preferring to say the boy had failed, killed by the snow-seals, but Guamok refused to accept such a thing.

When Inguk did arrive, with a sledge and two other men, it was with a great shout of relief that the boy ran to meet them.

"Still alive?" said the old hunter, nodding at the half-buried snow den.

"Yes. He's eaten nothing, but it makes no difference. It's as though he's asleep."

The two men who had come were seasoned hunters, men in their prime, chosen by the village chief, Yannachuk, for their toughness. They did not smile and hardly spoke. In their eyes Guamok was just a boy, no matter what he had done here. But when they saw the man and later the remains of the huge bird, they spoke kindly to Guamok and told him there would be a celebration when he got home. They appeared to have taken charge, however, for they put the man on the sledge and saw to his being moved. Guamok was left to follow on foot with Inguk.

"Yannachuk did not take the news of the stranger well," Inguk explained. "While recognizing that you have acted with great honor in saving him, he is afraid."

"Yannachuk?" said Guamok, surprised. "Our chief?"

"You do not understand, Guamok. Such things complicate

life. We know very little about this man. Where he came from.''

"Then I am out of favor—''

Inguk squeezed his arm in an unfamiliar show of emotion. "Not so, boy! Though I should not say 'boy.' You have become a man. You are blooded. Yannachuk has already declared it. But you must forget the stranger.''

"Why?" said Guamok suspiciously. "Is he to be killed?''

"Not by us. But Yannachuk has sent for the Deliverers. It is for them to decide.'' And the old man spat, as if to remove a bad taste from his mouth.

Guamok shivered, pulling his skins tighter. Deliverers! The cloaked men from the mountain fort that everyone went in fear of. To *invite* them! Yannachuk must be mad, or frightened. But why should the stranger cause this? There was a mystery here, and the youth wondered if he should take Inguk's advice and have no more to do with it.

Arrol Rainword sat comfortably in the wooden chair that had been placed for him in the center of the dais. A drooping canopy overhung it, to keep the snow off, while blazing tapers sent up plumes of thick smoke at each corner of the dais. Behind him, the Deliverers waited like statues in their dark cloaks. Rainword, their leader, belched softly, pleased with the meal he had been served by his host, Yannachuk, chief of this particular village, if one could grace such a pitiful place with such a name. Word had come that the hunters would soon be arriving with the boy who would be a man, and his odd prize. Most of the village had turned out to see how Rainword would judge them.

The Deliverer prided himself on his inscrutability, although he had left all the villages in his demesne in no doubt as to how he liked to control things throughout these lands at the edge of the ice-fields. Obedience was the first law of survival here, and even Yannachuk, the fiercest of the chiefs, had accepted that. The Deliverers were not to be questioned, they were the law, and the Abiding Word that they brought was to be followed.

Rainword's face masked his deep thoughts. He was wondering if there could be any connection between the sudden appearance of this stranger he would soon be meeting and the recent messenger from the Direkeep, the principal citadel of the Deliverers, far to the north. There its ruler, the Preserver, sent out his watchdogs to keep Omara free of the dangerous belief in gods and power, punishing those who fell into the evils of such thinking. Here, deep in the southern wildernesses of Omara, Rainword had found a demesne where he would not be disturbed, where he could all but forget the Preserver, his master, and set himself up as lord. Here, the Abiding Word had long been revised to suit Arrol Rainword and his faithful Deliverers, and he had been neglected for many years. Until now.

First, the messenger. A Deliverer from the Direkeep itself had come, announcing that the Preserver was no more. There had been an extraordinary turn of events in the Direkeep, exacerbated by a man who was said to be from another world. Another world! Rainword had scoffed. Was this messenger insane? Did he not know the penalty for saying such a thing? But the man had gone on to say that the stranger, Korbillian, had proved his case, winning the support of Simon Wargallow, the Preserver's most esteemed servant. At the mention of Wargallow, Rainword began to take the messenger more seriously, for it was a name to bring a chill to the coldest of lands. Between them, this man Korbillian and Wargallow had destroyed the Preserver and revoked the Abiding Word. *Revoked* it! The foundations on which the lives of the Deliverers had been built were now pulled away, or so it seemed. Rainword was ordered, *ordered* no less, to send representatives to the Direkeep with all haste, to confirm his acceptance of the new rule. It was to be invested in Wargallow. Rainword shuddered at that. Wargallow our ruler? He would never permit Rainword his current freedom.

It had not taken Rainword long to decide. During the night his men had silently despatched the messenger, giving his blood to the earth. If Wargallow really had seized control, he would not be coming here for many a long year, if ever.

Rainword studied the falling snow intently. And now this. Another of these strangers. From another world? He would have to put down any such thinking quickly. But it would be interesting to see what this man had to say, if he could be revived. Perhaps he would die anyway, which would simplify matters.

The villagers had begun murmuring, and in a few moments they parted to let the sledge through. It stopped at the foot of the dais, met there by Yannachuk. Rainword rose and stood above them all. He saw below him the two hunters of the chief, their sledge and the man stretched upon it, covered in furs, and beyond them stood the youth and the old hunter.

"You are the two who found him?" Rainword called to the latter.

Inguk and Guamok came forward and bowed, though the face of the old man was wrinkled with hatred he made no attempt to disguise. Guamok, trying to keep his voice steady in the presence of the all-powerful Deliverer, explained what they had seen, sparing no detail. The villagers kept silent, not wanting to do anything that would incur the wrath of the Deliverer, for he had had men killed before now. Rainword listened attentively. He had no doubt that the boy spoke the truth, but the truth did not always suit him.

"A boy, not long away from his mother's side and a man who looks to be the oldest in the tribe," said Rainword coldly when Guamok had finished. "Talking of great birds that give birth to men. I see."

Yannachuk turned away, scowling. Rainword was not going to believe the youth. That was bad.

"Has the stranger revived?" said Rainword. "Has he spoken?"

Everyone looked at Guamok. He straightened and tried to look directly at Rainword, but he could not meet those deep set eyes, that frosty stare. "He tried to talk, sir, but such few words that he said were meaningless."

"He did not dare to speak of gods, or magical powers? You are not hiding anything are you, boy?"

"He speaks the truth!" snapped Inguk, staring at the Deliverer now with undisguised hatred. It had been a black day for the people of the snows when these killers had first arrived from the north.

Rainword nodded, marking the old man's stare. Here was a rebellion to trample down. If this stranger revives, Rainword thought, and talks of power, and if it is true what I have heard about the Direkeep and this man Korbillian, that power does exist, and if this stranger before me has power, what should I do? Bow to his power? If I do so, if I so much as recognize it, I will lose credibility with these scum, and quickly after that I will lose control of them. No, it is unthinkable.

"The Abiding Word speaks of the sin of power, and of those who transgress. There is no power, there are no gods."

Automatically, as they had been trained to do, the villagers repeated Rainword's quotation, obedient as children. They felt the closing of the dark-cloaked ones around them.

Rainword pointed to the prone stranger. "There is evil here. It cannot be tolerated. This is a transgressor. Will any deny it?" As he spoke, his eyes searched for the youth's, but met again the cold stare of the old man. And you, too, will perish this night, old man. Your age will not protect you.

"Give his blood to the earth," Rainword said softly, but every man and woman heard him. At once a dozen of the Deliverers stepped forward, drawing from their cloaks their killing steel, the twin bladed sickles that replaced their right hands, given to them as young men when they had first served in the Direkeep. They raised these in unison, the light from the torches flashing from them like pain as they fell. The stranger should have been cut to pieces in moments.

Instead there was a flash of light so powerful that the entire village fell to the snow, eyes dazzled by the glare. Rainword toppled back into his chair, hands over his eyes as if he had been blinded. Guamok was the first to see what had happened. The metal rod strapped to the stranger's belt was glowing as if molten; the steel of the Deliverers had struck it. Now each of the Deliverers was on his knees, gasping for breath. Guamok saw one of them beside him: his killing steel had been reduced to dripping metal, soft as running blubber, ruined. All those Deliverers who had struck at the stranger were similarly smitten. And on the sledge the man was sitting up, his eyes open like a man in a dream.

Rainword had staggered to his feet. All but three of his Deliverers had survived the explosion of light, and they stood at his back, their killing steel exposed. The stranger got groggily to his feet and stared up at the cloaked figures above him.

"Which of you," he said, his voice carrying on the night air, "is Korbillian?"

It seemed to take an age for anyone to move. Guamok was

open-mouthed, watching the stranger, while Inguk could see
the stupefaction on the face of Rainword. His men had been
brushed aside as if they did not exist, their steel hands destroyed. They were powerless!

"A sign! A sign!" shouted the old man. He shook his
spear, then pointed with it to the fallen Deliverers, some of
whom looked to be dead. The villagers began to react at last.

"Strike that man down!" snarled Rainword, holding up
his own killing steel.

But Inguk was a seasoned hunter, and he knew the weaknesses of his prey. He saw now that this was a moment he
had prayed many months for, the precise moment to strike.
Rainword was ripe for taking, and it had to be now. Inguk
thought of the boy, and of how he had offered him the glory
of the special kill. For that he would repay him. The old
hunter raised his spear and with uncanny speed he flung it.
Rainword realized what was happening too late and his effort
to knock the weapon aside was futile. It tore into his gut,
racing through him, thudding against the back of the carved
chair, pinning him like a moth. His eyes widened, his mouth
flopped open, but there was no sound. Behind him the three
Deliverers were dumbfounded, but they were far too slow to
react. A score of villagers, their hatred released like flood
waters by Inguk's act, leapt up beside them, and before Yannachuk could shout, they had cut them down, joyfully tossing
the corpses off the dais for others to kick or jab at with short
spears.

Inguk roared with laughter and clapped Guamok on the
shoulder. Nonplussed, the boy laughed too, although it was
nerves and not bravery. In all that company, only Yannachuk
seemed able to keep a cool head. He came forward to the
stranger, who still looked about him in utter confusion as if
caught up in a dream he could not explain.

"Quickly, I cannot stop this madness now. You had better
come with me, or they may kill you also."

The stranger nodded, like a man in a play in which he had
no real role. "Korbillian," he said faintly. "Is he here?"

Yannachuk shook his head, watching as his people finished
their bloody sport with the slain Deliverers. He had feared
Rainword and his grim followers, but this night's work was
well done. They had not thought it possible. As he pulled the

stranger away from the dais, a hand clawed at his feet. One of the Deliverers was not dead, but lay in the snow, gazing up through his agony.

"Spare me," he hissed, his voice hardly audible. "Spare me and I'll tell you where Korbillian can be found."

Yannachuk glanced at the metal rod of the stranger, now hanging inertly at his belt. He dared not risk this man's anger. Curtly he motioned for some of his hunters to bring the stricken Deliverer to his own hut, and they dragged the man to his feet. The villagers growled their disappointment, Inguk waving another spear he had found, but Yannachuk turned on them with a shout and they were content to let him and the stranger go. In a moment they were breaking open kegs of ale they had been keeping for their next celebrations, and toasting their new champions, Inguk and Guamok.

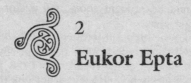

2
Eukor Epta

FROM THE WINDOW high above the stark buildings on Tower Island, the view of the city of Goldenisle was spectacular, and Eukor Epta, Administrative Oligarch to the Emperor, studied it now as he studied it every evening, enjoying the play of the sunset on the waters of the inner sea of the great island of Medallion, silhouetting as it did the higher towers of the city that could be seen across the bay in the west. Over its shadowed bulk towered the immense cliffs, protecting it like avaricious gods, emphasizing its impregnability. The city could not be approached overland: the only way to it was through the narrow northern straits into the inner sea, the Hasp, that formed the only break in the coast of Medallion Island. The ships of the Empire gently ploughed the waters of the inner sea, where a score of smaller islands formed particles in the complex structure of the city. It was on the largest of these, two miles from the shore of the mainland to the west, that Eukor Epta had made his own private retreat.

As with other evenings he had been thinking long on the strength and weakness of the Empire. Secure from external threat, it faced an inner turmoil, one that promised to come to a head before very long. Soon it would be the time of change; only the very strong would survive. Eukor Epta could smell the salt in the seas far below him, and as he turned from the window he caught the scent of something else. The city was not as it had been in its great days. Parts of it had fallen into disrepair, and they hinted at dissolution. Its Emperor, Quanar Remoon, was dying. Eukor Epta grimaced as he thought of the madman who had accelerated the decay of the proud city. He would not live for much longer. Word of his death would be brought soon, and Eukor Epta waited patiently for the event.

When the knock came on the door of this high chamber, no servant opened it. There were none up here, just a few private guards down at the base of the tower, their instructions precise. No one would pass them unless the Oligarch had sent word.

"Enter."

A young man did so, closing the door behind him and walking cautiously across the carpeted chamber. He could barely see his host, for there were two thick candles set upon the only table, and Eukor Epta stood deliberately before them. His guest bowed, eyes upon the floor. The tall figure of the Administrator did not move or speak and stood impassively. What was visible of his face was devoid of emotion; he did not believe in wasting a gesture, an expression, for he shared his mind with no one. To the majority he was a ghost, a name only, never seen, almost legendary. The shadows that cloaked him were woven from fear and he stood now like a threat.

The youth before him, Muriddis, remembered the first time he had been permitted to meet the Oligarch. His father had taken him to him when he had just passed his twelfth birthday. After a short conversation, his father had left and Muriddis, quaking, stood like a rabbit before the fabled Administrator. Eukor Epta's words of that day still came back to the youth.

"Tell me about Goldenisle," he had said, unexpectedly.

Muriddis had started to blurt out his geography and history lessons, but the Administrator stopped him with a curt chop of his hand. "Not that lip-service, boy. You know better. Tell me what your father has taught you."

Muriddis began again, talking softly about Goldenisle before the Flood, before the land sank and the sea rose, rushing in to the heart of the island to form inner waters, to create Medallion Island and the Chain.

"And the kings?" Eukor Epta had prompted. He made it sound as though he were indifferent to the boy's answer, but Muriddis had known that his entire future depended on his reply. His father had told him what to say.

"From outside. They took the islands."

"And the Remoons?" said Eukor Epta, referring to the Dynasty that had ruled the Empire for centuries.

Muriddis' father had warned him to be honest. Eukor Epta was of the Blood, he had said. Remember that, my son, when you quake before him, as you will do. He is of the Blood, as are you and I and your mother.

"Thieves," said the boy. "The Remoons are thieves."

Eukor Epta had looked hard at him then. After a long time he had said, "Remember that always, Muriddis. They are not of the Blood. The Empire is not theirs. They came after the Flood and grew fat after its ravages."

Now, standing before the Administrator in silence, Muriddis felt no less afraid of the man. He had more power than anyone in the Empire other than the Emperor, and in truth he had more say in the running of things than Quanar did. Since that first morning, Muriddis had been before him only a handful of times, but there was no getting used to his presence. Even to serve him was to know fear and doubt, for to make an error or to go beyond the bounds he set would, Muriddis was certain, lead to a swift death.

"What have you to tell me?" he asked the youth.

"The Emperor has fallen deeper into the coma. His physicians have said that it will soon be over. A few days at the most."

"When was the last ministration made?"

"Mid morning, sire. I attended to it myself. There is nothing to suggest that anyone has suspected me. The physicians have not said that it is poison. They attribute the deterioration to Quanar's mental condition and see it as inevitable. They have said that it has come more quickly than they supposed, but I have been discreet in my inquiries. If they think of murder, they do not talk of it. The Emperor is not popular, even among his own."

Eukor Epta nodded, his face betraying nothing. The poison had been brought from the southern lands of Athahara over a year ago, and the man who had brought it had conveniently disappeared long since. But the stuff had proved perfect. And this youth was to be admired for his loyalty.

"See that the word reaches me the instant the Emperor dies. Then melt into the city. We may not meet again for a long time, if at all. But you will not be forgotten, Muriddis, nor your family. Have you a wife yet?''

Muriddis swallowed hard. "No, sire. A girl—"

"She is of the Blood?"

The youth nodded.

"Good. Our work will not be over for a long time yet. A lifetime, perhaps. Patience is our greatest weapon. There will be another Emperor soon.''

"Another Remoon, sire?" said the youth, and the Oligarch noted the trace of scorn in his voice. There was a genuine contempt for the rulers in it: his family had schooled him well.

"For a while. The sword is strong, but the arm that wields it is stronger. So, go back to the city.''

There was so much more that the youth wanted to say, but a glance at Eukor Epta made him think better of it. Evidently the gaunt man was pleased. But whatever plans he had made, he would share with no one.

Muriddis bowed and withdrew.

Eukor Epta went again to the window and watched the city, his eyes drawn to the faint lights of the distant palace that rose over the dark streets and clung to the skirts of the steep cliffs. Quanar was taking a long time to die, but Muriddis was quite correct when he had said few would mourn him. His irrationality, his almost complete madness had made it intolerable to have him controlling the Empire. His removal would have been a service to any Empire, but if the Law Givers or the Imperial Killers, Quanar's private guard, suspected foul play and the hand of the Administrators, Eukor Epta would be equally as swiftly removed. Muriddis would have to be rewarded well for his discretion.

The object of Eukor Epta's thoughts had left the tower and now climbed into the waiting boat. Two of his own servants were waiting for him there and as they poled the boat from the tiny quay, the tower guards drew back into the darkness. Muriddis said nothing, unsure of his own feelings. He had been slowly poisoning the Emperor for six months, and now that he had almost completed the task, he had been more or less dismissed. He could well understand Eukor Epta's mania for secrecy. But how could he go about his life now without knowing what was happening in the greater plan? What exactly did Eukor Epta have in mind? Not revolution that was obvious. At least, it would be no bloody coup. The machinery of Empire was too wieldy to assault. But once Quanar died, who would rule? It was said by many that he was the last of his line.

Drawing his cloak about him in spite of the warmth of the early night, Muriddis sat back and let his silent servants row him back to the city. The boat was about a mile from the quays when it had to turn aside to let another, larger craft pass. There were soldiers in it, and one tall figure in the stern. It watched them keenly, although its face could not be seen. Muriddis kept his head down, out of sight. It would not be wise to let anyone know that he had visited the Administrator. Few men had set foot on Tower Island, and those that had would not speak of such a thing. Muriddis turned to watch the boat disappear, and wondered if it, too, was about to visit that most forbidden of places.

Had the youth waited a little longer, his thoughts would have been confirmed, for the boat drew alongside the same quay that Muriddis had lately left. The armored figure in the stern of the boat disembarked, stiffly saluting the guards at the base of the tower. They recognized him at once and stood aside.

Eukor Epta was surprised to hear another knock on his door. He opened it himself to find one of his guards standing there, face wet with perspiration, the man evidently embarrassed at having to race up the long flights of stairs to get here.

"Your pardon, Administrator, but you had to be told. The Acting Commander of the Armies is here, demanding an audience."

Eukor Epta's first thought was for Muriddis. Had the youth been seen? But he nodded. "It will be in order. Send him up." He went back to his room. This could only be a matter of great importance for Fennobar himself to come here. However, it would not be considered strange or out of order by any observers for the Administrative Oligarch to be visited by the Commander of the Armies, particularly with the crisis in the palace.

Fennobar entered, swiftly closing the door, and the two men faced each other like combatants. Eukor Epta was motionless, cold, but the soldier was obviously alert, restless, as if he had just stepped from a brawl. He flung off his cloak and hooked his huge hands into his belt, the pose he struck for addressing subordinates. Though he did not like the Administrator, he grunted a greeting. He needed him, and Eukor Epta had immense power and influence.

Eukor Epta studied the soldier without a flicker of apparent interest. As usual Fennobar appeared anxious, irritated or upset by something that had gone wrong. He was a fine fighting man, excellently built, strong enough to wrestle a wild bull if it came to it, but he had no patience. Everything had to be done at once with him, forcefully. There was no subtlety about the way he acted, or dressed or spoke. And if a single plan went awry, his temper would burst. Even so, such men were needed and they had their part to play in Eukor Epta's way of things.

"Another emergency?" said Eukor Epta sarcastically, though he didn't smile.

Fennobar growled, missing the jibe. "In a way, yes."

"I hear Quanar will not live much longer."

Even this didn't seem to pacify the big man, who clutched the back of a chair and leaned across it. "Elberon is dead!" he snorted. "It's been confirmed. All those tales that have been trickling back across the sea from the east were true. He's dead."

"Who told you this?" A keen observer would have seen the tightening of Eukor Epta's jaw, his roused interest. Fennobar saw nothing, only a blank stare.

"I've had ships out in force, dammit! They've sent patrols close in to the Three Rivers. You know of the place? That eastern continent is drained by three great rivers, and they empty into the sea together. I've had a ship up that delta. They're building a city there! A city, dammit!"

"I have heard rumors. But surely, Fennobar, if Morric Elberon's death is confirmed, you should be pleased. The Supreme Commander of the Twenty Armies—"

"That ridiculous title!"

"Our Emperor bestowed it upon Elberon. But if his death is confirmed, it would seem logical that his deputy should be promoted. Do you have any reason to doubt my support when the Chamber of Administration meets to decide the issue?"

"Of course not!" But the lie was quite clear to Eukor Epta. It pleased him to think that this oaf should wonder. Fennobar would have said more about loyalty, but he knew there was no point in trying to delve into the Administrator's mind. He would rather plunge his hand into a pale of serpents. "You've pledged your support, but that isn't the problem."

Though his expression never wavered, Eukor Epta felt a twinge of uncertainty. "Well?"

"Elberon deserted the Empire over a year ago, we know that. He was supposed to be on a campaign of Quanar's, seeking new lands to conquer in the east. But Elberon was gathering a rebel army of his own."

"With which to overthrow Goldenisle, yes, I am aware of that."

Fennobar pretended not to have heard. "A good many men flocked to Elberon's banner."

"He was a superb soldier."

"Aye, but he didn't intend to take control of the Empire for himself. His intention was to put Quanar's cousin on the throne. Ottemar Remoon." Now let's see you sweat on that, Administrator!

Eukor Epta did not react. "The possibility had not escaped me. Go on."

"He was here, wasn't he? A prisoner?"

"Ottemar? In a way, but he was never an official prisoner, as that could have been embarrassing politically. But he was kept in the palace, out of Quanar's way. The Emperor has a phobia about relatives, as you know. Ottemar effected an escape, the manner of which was quite remarkable. It was at a time when Quanar was still on his feet, still wandering the throne rooms, making wild decisions, threatening to cut off the heads of anyone who slighted him. And at a time, I recall it only too well, when his personal guards, his Imperial Killers, still jumped to obey him for fear of themselves being cut to pieces for the royal hounds."

"It was when that stranger was here, the lunatic who claimed to be from beyond our world. The man Korbillian."

It surprised Eukor Epta that Fennobar remembered the man's name. "Indeed. Ottemar used the so-called madman to gain an audience with the Emperor. Those responsible for allowing it were dealt with very quickly. But somehow Ottemar, always a slippery-tongued character, talked the Emperor into banishing himself and the stranger.''

"To the east.''

"Quite. But I made certain that the ship that carried them also carried men of mine. They killed Ottemar and Korbillian. The ship was destroyed in a storm, but one of my men survived. He confirmed the death of Ottemar and the so-called man of power.''

"Then your man lied.''

The Administrator felt as though a cold blade had been thrust into him, but still he did not react.

"My men are chosen carefully, Fennobar. They do not lie to me.''

"Then he was mistaken. Perhaps he only thought the two men died. This Korbillian, from what I hear, did possess strange qualities. Men feared him. Even your assassins. Your survivor probably thought they both drowned in the storm. But they lived.''

"And?''

"They met up with Elberon. My spies confirm it! After that, the story gets very confused. Instead of gathering, they split their forces. Ottemar and Elberon marched *inland*.''

"Into the eastern mass? For what reason?''

"War.''

Eukor Epta frowned slightly, a concession to surprise. "That seems extravagant, Fennobar. On whom?''

"There was some evil kingdom there that threatened not only Elberon's new lands, but those of others in the east. Other rulers joined him to go to war on this common enemy. It was during the war that Elberon fell. Many of his men with him.''

"But not Ottemar?''

"No, damn him! He is alive. My men have seen him. He calls himself something ludicrous—''

"Guile,'' nodded Eukor Epta. "Very apt. And Korbillian?''

Fennobar shook his head. "Dead. Even his supposed power couldn't save him from whatever it was he fought in the east. Not many came back from that war and they don't talk openly about what happened there. Those who did return rejoined the men left behind and now they have built a city in the

lands beyond the delta. And do you know how they have
named it?'' The soldier looked furious. *"Elberon!* They've
dared to call it Elberon!''

"And who rules this city?''

"Not Ottemar. He keeps himself to himself. No, it's a
young buck by the name of Ruan Dubhnor. Another renegade.''

Eukor Epta digested all this with a slow nod of the head.
So Korbillian had perished, that was good. There had been
an aura about him that had been worrying, and if he had
possessed the secret powers of old, he could have been extremely dangerous. And Ottemar had survived! That would
have to be attended to, and quickly.

"So when our accursed Emperor dies,'' growled Fennobar, again pacing about, "who is to be Emperor? Ottemar
may be in self-imposed exile, but he *is* a Remoon. The last
of them.''

Eukor Epta allowed the soldier to fume for a while before
enlightening him. "Not so.''

"What do you mean?''

"There's the girl.''

Fennobar looked appalled. "Tennebriel! Are you—''

"Mad?'' Eukor Epta smiled, but Fennobar felt cold as he
realized he had been about to say it.

"She could not rule! A teenage girl—''

"I agree. But Ottemar could. If he returned to Goldenisle,
many would support him. He's Quanar's cousin, the rightful
heir. History and birth are with him. And as Commander of
the Armies, even you, Fennobar, would have to offer him
your sword.''

Fennobar was trying, with difficulty, to think. He knew he
had no skill at politics and that the Administrator was far
ahead of him. But he couldn't see what the man was driving
at. "If I did support Ottemar, what then?''

Again Eukor Epta smiled. "Oh, is this a threat?''

Fennobar was silent for only a moment, but then he erupted
with laughter. It was too loud to be genuine; his fear was
evident. "It is not what you want.''

"I want only what is best for the Empire,'' said Eukor
Epta without emotion. "Ottemar is his own man. He would
be little better than Quanar. No doubt he would fall to the

same illness of mind. It is often so with the Remoons, is it not?''

"So you prefer Tennebriel—"

"She could be taught the correct way to rule. She would be glad to have the advice of the Administrators and the Law Givers. And I doubt that she would wish to interfere in military matters. No, that would be left entirely in the hands of the Commander of the Armies."

Fennobar gave it some thought, nodding.

"You and I, Fennobar, would have the responsibility of ruling."

It would be like allying oneself to a serpent, Fennobar thought. But the prize! To rule. Not just to be Supreme Commander, but to have even more power. Eukor Epta would control it all, but even so! Fennobar grinned. "Then let it be Tennebriel."

Eukor Epta smiled now, as if confiding in a close friend. "There would appear to be an object in our way."

Fennobar, the predictable buffoon, pulled out his broad sword and stroked its flat edge. "A minor detail."

Euktor Epta shook his head. "Ah, but not so minor."

"Pah! Let me take a small fleet into the delta. I'll raze this new Elberon and put them all to the sword. You shall have Ottemar's head within a month."

"Yes, I would appreciate that. But let it be attached to his body."

"You want him alive?" Why couldn't the man speak plainly!

"Yes. Kill as many of his people as you wish. But I want Ottemar alive. Bring him here, to Tower Island, in secret."

"But if I destroy Elberon and capture him alive, word will spread—"

"Then think again, Fennobar. Come now, if you are to be Supreme Commander, you must use your wits, man! You are as good a warrior as the Empire has, I know that. But to rule, Fennobar, you need a good mind."

"Secrecy?"

"Stealth, and above all think of Ottemar's chosen name. Guile. He is the enemy, I promise you. If he wins the throne, you and I will be removed. Your quarrels with Morric Elberon were well known. Ruan Dubhnor would likely be cre-

ated Supreme Commander. As for Administrative Oligarch—
who knows? Some puppet of Ottemar's. What hope would
our Empire have?''

"What do you suggest?"

"Abduction. Subterfuge. Take a single ship into the delta.
They would never expect us to abduct Ottemar. No blood
unless there's a fight. No burning. Just a simple theft in the
night.''

"Very well—"

"Don't bring Ottemar to me yourself. From now on, you
and I must not meet until Tennebriel is enthroned. We must
conduct our business apart, but we will use men we can trust.
If citizens knew that we planned together, they may grow
suspicious. What happens to the Empire must be seen as the
natural course of events.''

"I agree. I have men who will do as I ask them, and no
questions, men who have fought beside me, men whose
fathers I have honored—"

"I understand such things well, Fennobar. They are your
strength. Even so, choose with care. You are entering a new
arena now. The prize demands extreme effort and care.''

Fennobar sheathed his sword. Normally he would have
shaken hands on such a bargain, but not with this man. He
nodded. "You will have your prisoner. But why not let me
kill him?''

"Ah, but I want you to make it look as though you have
killed him. How you achieve this I leave to you. I imagine
you have men who are good enough at such things.''

Fennobar's scowl deepened. "Of course, but—"

"Those who know his true identity will consider his cause
ended if they think him dead.''

"And if I am not to have him killed?"

"I want him here, secretly imprisoned. No one would
dream that he was our prisoner.''

"But why?" Fennobar looked stunned.

"Leave politics to me, Fennobar. He is our insurance.''
Eukor Epta laughed coldly. "If it ever transpired that rebel
factions, Remoon factions, threatened us, think of the hold
we would have over them if it came to an ultimatum. But I
would not foresee such a thing. Ottemar will rot on one of
these impregnable islands.''

Fennobar grunted. "I see how the game must be played. A good strategy. Then I will have Ottemar abducted, although it will seem that he has been murdered. Already I know the men I will send to do it. Should I disguise them?"

Eukor Epta shrugged. "As long as they do not go to the east as men of Empire."

This time Fennobar's laugh was genuine. "Excellent! I have a good deal to learn about government."

Indeed you do, Eukor Epta thought. "I will be expecting a visitor then. I shall enjoy meeting Ottemar Remoon again."

After Fennobar had left, Eukor Epta summoned his closest guards. "I am not displeased that you allowed Fennobar to visit the island, but in future, no one is to be allowed into the tower unless I have given prior consent. Should Fennobar attempt to visit me without such an appointment, use force to prevent him entering."

The guards nodded. They would obey without question.

In his high chamber, Eukor Epta closed the shutters and sat in a chair. He thought in silence for over an hour, moving in his mind the pieces on the vast gaming board that was the Empire. Fennobar was useful, his ignorance vital. With Ottemar here, locked away in the tower, Eukor Epta would have a crucial hold over Tennebriel. She would be Empress, but she would be so much easier to control if she knew that Ottemar was alive, and could be brought forward as a rival at any time. Perhaps his being alive was no bad thing after all, and could be turned to advantage.

He must visit the girl soon and begin putting the seeds of unease in her mind. She was a simple enough child, with a mind that would never mature as a woman's should. Not a Remoon, but with all the weaknesses of that House. He had prepared her well, and if his plans bore fruit, she might yet prove the tool with which he could bring the Empire back into the hands of those whose legacy it properly was.

What had he forgotten? Oh yes, of course. The assassin who had reported the deaths of both Ottemar and Korbillian. In the morning he must be found and executed. And someone would have to be sent to this city of Elberon, someone who could be trusted. Someone of the Blood. Muriddis, perhaps.

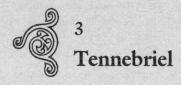

3
Tennebriel

EUKOR EPTA HAD his own private ways of visiting the many islands and islets of the inner sea of Medallion Island. Beneath each was an ancient warren of tunnels, known by the Administrator to be the remnants of the former city before the geological upheaval that resulted in the inundation of the land, when the sea had swallowed half of the island. Few of Goldenisle's inhabitants today believed the old stories, he knew, except for those who were of the Blood and kept the faith, but it suited him well, for it enabled him to keep many other truths to himself. The complex warren he now used was one of them.

It was a journey of half an hour underground from Tower Island to the heavy door where he now stopped. He set his small brand in the iron bracket and opened the door with a key from the ring beneath his cloak. Beyond the door there was another to unlock and re-lock, and in the corridor beyond this was a brand that had been set into its bracket earlier by the servants Eukor Epta had confined to this island. No one ever came to this place by boat, for it was a sheer-sided chunk of rock, thrust up from the floor of the inner sea, its top choked with vegetation, the home of a thousand bird colonies. Yet facing east, away from the city, concealed from the eyes of anyone happening to pass below in a ship, was a villa, with its own walls and cultivated gardens, a miniature paradise surrounded by verdant chaos. It was here that Tennebriel, distant cousin of the Emperor, was kept, and had been for many years since her third birthday.

The few who tended her were Eukor Epta's most carefully

selected servants. There were male guards who never entered the villa itself, posted about the isle to ensure no one came here and who had not even seen the girl. And there were the women, who treated their ward with great care and saw that Tennebriel had all that she wanted, save her freedom. As with the men, they were never allowed to leave the island.

The Administrator unlocked a final door and entered a beautifully maintained chamber. After a long climb up a spiral stone stairway he came to the villa's rooms. They opened out on to a balcony, high over the dark waters of the inner sea. Eukor Epta knew at once that the girl was awake in spite of the hour: her perfume drifted on the air. Something moved in the room and he turned, eyes not yet accustomed to the faint light from the lamps, but it was the elderly servant, Ullarga. The old woman moved back into the shadows like a ghost. Of all the servants, she was the closest to the girl, for she had once been a handmaiden to the girl's aunt, Estreen. She knew that she was alive only because it suited Eukor Epta to have her here.

Out on the balcony, Tennebriel had been staring out to sea, but she turned slowly, showing no surprise when she saw who had come. She was no longer a girl, but a tall woman, almost 19, with tumbling ringlets of black hair that would have taken away the breath of most men. Even in the poor glow from the night lamps there was a sheen to it. She wore no more than a thin gown, for the night air was warm, and it served to heighten her slim figure, a vision that would have intoxicated a thousand suitors had they been able to reach her. Eukor Epta himself felt the familiar rush of excitement at seeing her, his magnificent animal. The servants had groomed her superbly. For a moment he allowed himself the rare pleasure of seeing her outlined against the backdrop of night, bowing his head slowly.

"Tennebriel my dear," he said. "It is a joy to see you again."

"Eukor!" she said, eyes widening, her expression like that of a little girl receiving a visit from a favorite uncle who has been away. "You haven't called for so long."

It had been two weeks, but he let it pass. She knew nothing of time. What she owned in beauty, she lacked in mind.

"Pressing matters, sweet child. But tell me, how have you been? Are the servants looking after you?"

She pouted, his words her cue. "Well, yes, I suppose so. But I get so bored, Eukor. All this waiting. Sometimes I think I have been here for at least a *hundred* years."

He watched, fascinated, as her eyes changed with each word, her face alive, extraordinarily beautiful. She would make a superb Empress. "Matters of state, Tennebriel. Tedious, but so essential to those of us who struggle to keep the Empire stable. You will find out."

"When I'm Empress," she said quickly. It was a familiar statement.

He nodded. "Yes. Your cousin is very ill. He will not live for more than a few days, I am sure."

Her face lit up girlishly. "Then I can take the throne soon!"

He smiled indulgently and came closer to her, touching her hand. "Patience, my girl. It is not so easy."

She flushed, anger arching her brows. "But you said so."

"Yes, yes. But you must try to remember the difficulties."

"Tell me again."

"Very well." They sat together and it was an effort for him to ignore her beauty, to resist touching her more intimately, though he was certain she would not have resisted. She had always been pliant with him, being so simple, trusting him, believing in him as if the world could not move without a word from him. "When Quanar Remoon dies, he will be the last of the Royal House, the Remoon Dynasty."

She nodded, enjoying the story, though she had now heard it many times from him.

"You know that there are three great Royal Houses in Goldenisle: the Remoons, the Crannochs and the Trullhoons."

"Yes, and I'm a Crannoch."

"Yes." He wondered how much of this she would be able to recall. It was important for her to grasp it and so he was patient enough to go over it again and again. "Your father was Vulder Crannoch. His brother, Colchann, married—"

"Estreen!" she said as he deliberately paused.

"Good! Yes, Estreen. And who was Estreen?"

"She was the sister of—" She thought about it for a moment. "The Emperor, except that he wasn't an Emperor. He was the King because Quanar Remoon is the first Emperor."

"Exactly. Estreen was the sister of Khedmar Remoon, who was Quanar's father. Khedmar wanted to unite the three great Houses so that there would be peace in Goldenisle. His brother, Dervic Remoon, married one of the Trullhoons, and his sister, Estreen, married your uncle, Colchann of the Crannochs."

"Yes, and when I was very small, I was betrothed to my cousin, Ildar, who was Estreen and Colchann's son." She clapped her hands, pleased with herself.

"Excellent. Can you go on? What happened to all the children?"

She concentrated hard. "There was a big battle. All the islands went to war and lots of people got killed."

Eukor Epta smiled patiently. The girl never forgot about the war. He had not given her all the facts, though she would doubtless find out many of them in time. He had simply told her that she had been betrothed to her cousin, Ildar, but in fact she had been married to him when she had been 2 years old. Ildar had been 21, a hot-headed, ambitious youth, who had not the wit to keep his ambition under harness. He had been found committing adultery with Anniani, wanton wife of the King, Khedmar, and when the monarch heard of this, chaos broke out. Enraged, Khedmar had had both Ildar and Anniani executed on the royal bed. As a result, Feinnor Crannoch, head of that House, had declared war on the Remoons. It was a complete disaster for the Crannochs, for the Trullhoons had thrown in with the King.

"Nearly all the Crannochs perished," said the girl. "My father, my uncle, and my betrothed; Vulder, Colchann and Ildar. Even my grandfather, Feinnor."

"That's correct, Tennebriel. You do well to remember it. The Remoons destroyed almost all of your family. Only Estreen survived, and she lives yet, hiding somewhere in the north of the islands that were the Crannoch home."

"And me," she grinned. "Because you saved me and hid me."

"There had been enough killing. Yes, I brought you here, though many think you died. Now then—what else? You are the only Crannoch child left from their House. What about the Remoons?"

"Khedmar had three children. There were two little baby girls. I'm sorry, Eukor, I forget their names—"

"No, no. It doesn't matter. Arrani and Erinna."

"They weren't very strong and they died when they were tiny."

"Yes. A few weeks."

"Then there was Quanar Remoon, but he's always been a bit mad."

"Yes, go on."

"He succeeded his father and made himself the first Emperor, but now he's ill. Is he really going to die soon?"

"I'll speak of it in a moment. Go on."

"He hasn't got any children. He didn't have a wife." She was frowning with concentration. "And then there's, mm, the Trullhoons. I think there was one called Ludhanna."

"You're doing very well," he smiled patronizingly. "Yes, Ludhanna. She married Dervic Remoon, Khedmar's brother. Her own brother is Darraban, and he has two sons, Andric and Rudaric, but you needn't concern yourself with any of them. They are all alive, but they keep to their eastern islands and have no real claim to the throne." It was not the whole truth, for Dervic was Ottemar's father, and it was this link with the throne that had allied the Trullhoons to Khedmar in the war.

"I know the rest!" cried Tennebriel. "Ludhanna ran away from her husband with a pirate and they both drowned. Served them right. But she and Dervic had a daughter—no, a son. His name was—"

Eukor Epta leaned closer. "Think hard. It's very important. The most important name of them all."

She looked anxious. "Oh!" she snapped. "Wait—Ottemar. Ottemar Trullhoon!"

"Nearly. It's Ottemar *Remoon*. Which is why it's so important. Ottemar Remoon. Remember it."

"Is he dead?"

Eukor Epta would have said yes, but after what Fennobar had told him he had already thought hard on his next moves. "I think so. But there is a grain of doubt. I am almost sure of it, for he went to the eastern continent, a terrible place full of monsters and strange beings."

"So if he's dead, all the Remoons are dead. And I was

betrothed to Ildar, whose mother was a Remoon, so *I* am a little bit Remoon.''

"Enough, my sweet girl, to claim the throne. Yes.''

She clapped her hands in delight, but after a moment frowned again. "But what if Ottemar Remoon is alive? Won't he be Emperor?''

Eukor Epta was pleased that she had picked this up as it gave him an easy way in to his deeper control of her. "Ah, that is the question. *If* he is alive, and I am sure that he cannot be, then, yes, it is possible that he would have a stronger claim that yours.''

She looked at him petulantly as if she would strike him. "Then he must be killed, Eukor. You will have to kill him for me.''

He smiled. "Don't worry. I have men looking for him. But I'm sure he's already dead, my dear. Though if you became Empress and Ottemar did return, it could be embarrassing. You would have to step down, and we wouldn't want that, would we?''

"No! He can't have the throne!''

He patted her again. "You understand these things very well, my dear. But you know that I will protect you, don't you? You must be Empress. Ottemar is no more fit to rule than his mad cousin. If I do find him alive, I will keep him on one of my islands, eh? Where no one will ever find him. Only you and I and his guards will know he's alive.''

A wicked look came to her face. "Eukor," she said, gripping him with her slender arms so that he sucked in his breath. "Will you find a bad island? Just a cold rock, with no gardens? Somewhere where he can be tortured?''

Eukor Epta chuckled. "How very cruel! We shall see. But I really do think he's dead, child. You mustn't worry about such things. Now, I have a lot of work I must do.'' He stood up.

"Oh, must you go so soon?''

Looking down at her, he felt himself terribly drawn to her, but that must wait. In time, he told himself, I will take that, too. "I have to. But I will come again soon.''

She did not argue. "Oh.''

"Very soon. With news. Quanar will die soon.''

She nodded, watching him withdraw with wide eyes,

though she did not get up. Eukor Epta locked the door behind him and let out a gasp. By the Blood, but she was divine! How she stirred his blood. He shook his head and was about to descend the stairway, but a thought made him pause. Instead he made his way to the private rooms of the servant girls. He would not sleep this night until he had flushed Tennebriel from his mind.

Only when the keys rattled in the door to show that Eukor Epta had locked it and had gone did Tennebriel's face change. It had been an effort to maintain the facade. The smile was no longer that of an innocent, simpleminded child.

From the shadows beyond the balcony came the sound of gentle applause. "Very well played!" came a soft voice, and a man stepped down from the deep shade of a vine. Tennebriel drew in a sharp breath, not of shock but of pure delight.

"Was I good?" She reached out a hand to him as he came to her.

The man who took her roughly in his arms was in his mid twenties and in build was in direct contrast to Eukor Epta. He was not so tall, but stocky, well muscled, and to any outside eye he would have been instantly marked as a warrior. He wore only a light harness and no weapons, not even a short dirk. Laughing, he kissed the girl deeply, his hand smoothing the silk of her gown, settling on her rump as though she were a serving girl in a tavern rather than a potential Empress. She returned his ardor for a long moment, but then pushed him away with a low chuckle.

"Patience, Cromalech!" she giggled. "There are things to discuss."

She wriggled free of him, but he caught her and pulled her to him. "I didn't climb three hundred feet of slippery rock to spend the night talking—"

"Wait!"

He saw that she meant it and held back briefly, though he kept an arm about her waist. "What is so important?"

"Did the visit of the Emperor's Administrative Oligarch not interest you?"

He grinned like a wolf, tossing back his thick mane of black hair. "Are you always like that with him? A simple child? You might have been 10 years old."

"Was I convincing?"

He frowned. "Is this a game?"

"No, I'm serious, Cromalech. It is important that Eukor thinks of me that way. Is he taken in?"

"You were very good. How long have you been imprisoned here?"

"Since I was little more than a baby. Never in all that time have I let him understand me as I am. It is essential that he thinks of me as a child. I think it is because of the madness of the Remoons that he thinks I am afflicted, though there is no Remoon blood in my veins. And he knows little of women, Cromalech."

"You think not? He looked at you as a man looks at a woman he wants to bed."

"You're just jealous."

"You would use his desire?"

She grimaced. "Not in that way. But how can I achieve anything if I do not use it? You must know I have nothing but loathing for him in my heart."

"Aye! Who could love Eukor Epta? The world fears him."

"And you?" she teased.

He nodded. "A little. Only a fool would not. He has great power. Who knows how many eyes he has?"

"He believes he has control of me. I must let him think so. For the moment I need his power."

"And do you let me bed you for the same reasons?"

Tennebriel sensed his eyes upon her and enjoyed his worship, seeing in it the mirror of her own. She let her hands run down his chest, her lips brushing his face. "I am not that good an actress, First Sword of the Imperial Killers."

He lifted her gown, his hands touching the flesh beneath, and in a moment had pushed her back across one of the marble seats of the balcony with surprising gentleness. She knew instinctively that it was the concern of a man who loved her. There would be no point in trying to talk to him for now and she helped him to remove his harness. As he entered her, all thoughts of Eukor Epta vanished, and for a while she had no desire for the Empire. Afterward he cradled her head and stroked her hair as if amusing himself with a cat.

"Is it true that Quanar will soon be dead?" she asked him.

"Aye. A few days."

"You still think him poisoned?"

Cromalech laughed. "Certainly. He's been out of his head for a long time, we all know that. But someone has been administering poison, I am sure."

She looked at him keenly. "And you don't know who?"

"No. Who cares? He is a madman. We are well rid of him—"

"I care!" she scolded. "I think Eukor is killing him. If I could prove it! Are you certain that none of his servants—"

Again he laughed. "How many doctors, guards, administrators, officials, come to the palace? Scores of them. Any of them could be doing it. I can't imagine anyone not being delighted. It's not possible to find out which. No one would want to know. And be sure that Eukor Epta is far too clever to allow himself to be implicated. You should know him better."

She sighed. "Yes, you are right. Too clever."

"But it will be soon, and then you will be Empress. Then you can do what you will with the Government. Perhaps you can find a new post for the Oligarch, far to the southern continents."

She chuckled. "There are many, no doubt, who would appreciate that. But it will not be so easy. Eukor leaves nothing to chance. He thinks of me as a simple girl, easily led, and I can act the part for him. But even so, he has to be sure. He is very devious. Tell me, have you heard any news of Ottemar Remoon, Quanar's cousin?"

Cromalech frowned, surprised at the reference. "The slippery Guile. The last I saw him was as he was leaving with the strange man from over the sea. Kobara, or something."

"Korbillian."

He was surprised by her sources of information. Someone in this place must be supplying her with it. "Aye. They were banished to the east, but the ship went down, and if the truth be known, both had a knife in the guts first. Very likely Eukor Epta's long arm."

She shook her head gently. "I think Ottemar survived. I think he is alive yet."

"Oh?" He seemed surprised.

"Eukor tried to impress upon me tonight that Ottemar would still be the rightful heir if he were to return."

"Aye, he's a Remoon. First cousin to the Emperor."

"I told Eukor that he must die, if he could be found, but you heard what Eukor said. That he wouldn't kill him, but he'd bring him here, in secret, and imprison him. Now why should he do that?"

Cromalech had again become interested in her soft thighs, and he merely grunted a reply.

"Pay attention!" she chided him, gently slapping his hand away. "Well?"

"Perhaps he wants to put him on the throne instead of you," he teased her.

She shook her head. "No. Too many men would rally to Ottemar. The Trullhoons in force. No, I think he has a better reason. He could have him killed, but I think he wants to be assured of controlling me. I think he wants to hold Ottemar over my head. When he makes *me* Empress, it will be with Ottemar in his grasp. Then if I don't comply with his every wish, he'll turn and whisper to me that he'll free Ottemar. He thinks this will ensure the obedience of a simple girl."

"It won't, of course."

"No, because he won't have Ottemar on one of his filthy little islands."

"You think not?"

"Because we'll have him."

He temporarily gave up on her thighs and looked at her, seeing in her face a grim determination, a strength of will that he loved as much as her body. It gave him a pang of unease to think that her ambition was a rival for his love, though she had professed love honestly enough. "We will?"

She prodded his stomach, but her fingers met hard muscle. "You'd better find out where Ottemar is hiding."

"Me? How am I supposed to do that?"

"Start by taking a ship to the eastern continent—"

He sat up with a groan. "Are you as mad as Quanar? The east? No one has—" But he paused. "But wait, though. Wait a moment." He grinned. "I was forgetting. Stories have been coming in of strange events there. And my old adversary, Morric Elberon, late commander of the Armies, went there."

"To prepare a rebellion?"

"Many think so. But I hear he's dead. His Deputy, Fennobar, keeps insisting he must be, being keen to assume Elberon's rank himself. But the word is that a city is being built in the east, and some say it has been named after Elberon.''

Her eyes widened. ''That must be it!'' The excitement flooded her. ''Go there, Cromalech! Go to this city. You'll find Ottemar there, I am sure of it.''

''You think so?''

''Yes.'' She was nodding, gazing into the darkness as if she could already see Ottemar Remoon standing before her. ''You must get to him before Eukor's men.''

He laughed. ''My sword is already as good as in his belly—''

''No! Haven't you been listening! I want him here. *My* prisoner.''

''What use would he be?''

''Because if *I* have him, then *I* will control Eukor.''

''When you are Empress, you can have Eukor Epta—''

''I know him better. If I have Ottemar, only then will I have the Oligarch. Just think, I could even threaten to marry Ottemar—''

His fingers reached into her hair and tugged. ''Careful what you say.''

Her fingers traced his lips. She loved to tease him and watch his anger. ''Softly. You know I have other plans.''

''And so do I—''

She giggled again. ''Oh, so you think you can play Emperor?''

He shook his head. ''I know that is impossible. I know the laws. But I would be content to be your consort.''

''And shall be. But bring Ottemar to me.''

He shrugged. ''You'll give me no peace until I do it. Very well, hussy, I'll have a ship out tomorrow.''

She squeezed him as if he were an obedient dog. ''I hope, when we are married, you will not be content to make love to me for no more than two minutes before you fall asleep.''

He rolled over her. ''Am I asleep? I think you are mistaken.'' For a long time they said no more of the Empire and of their plans.

Shortly after Cromalech had gone, slipping over the balcony and beginning his perilous descent into the night, Tennebriel walked, naked, to a tiny fountain. Its water sparkled like tossed jewels in the moonlight, and though it was icy,

Tennebriel took delight in it, washing herself thoroughly. She thought of swimming in one of the ornately designed rock pools, but Cromalech's lovemaking had left her lethargic and ready for sleep. Sometimes she yearned to flee with him to some remote land, to give up this dream of empire.

"Has the pig gone?"

Tennebriel knew the voice and made no attempt to cover herself. From one of the inner chambers came yet another visitor. Misshapen by the shadows, it kept its distance as if afraid of her.

"Ullarga," said the girl with a yawn. She finished her wash and stretched her arms as if invoking the moon to be her second lover. "Your visit is timely. Cromalech has gone, but I wish you wouldn't call him that!"

"What have you promised him?" The voice was old, impatient. Tennebriel was used to it and the crone's moods. But Ullarga had been loyal to her for as long as she could recall. In a way she had been like a mother to her, fussing around her and berating the other servants if they were lax in their duties. Eukor Epta approved of her, though he did not speak much about her. Ullarga hated the Administrator, but for some reason he had made it clear to her that Estreen had his secret support. And Ullarga had worshipped her former mistress.

"Promised him?" said Tennebriel. "What can I promise him? He thinks I love him. Isn't that enough? I'm using him, Ullarga, that's all." It was hard to say if the old woman knew this was a lie, but it did not matter. Ullarga would not betray her.

"If you reject him later, you may regret it. You need the protection of the Killers, not their scorn. They are powerful in the citadel."

"He cares enough to do as I ask him. Did you know that Ottemar Remoon is alive?" She deliberately avoided turning to enjoy the effect of her words.

Ullarga was silent for a while. "You have proof?"

"No, but all the same Cromalech will go to the east to find out."

"And he will bring him to you as a prisoner? Then you are learning the game well, Tennebriel," Ullarga cackled. "But get to bed. You invite a chill."

When the old woman was satisfied that her ward was asleep under the silk covers, she put out the lamps and crossed the chamber to the outer room. As she did so, she felt a sudden stab of pain, at once trying to resist. Deep inside her she felt the stirring of the power that had lately come there, like some uninvited intruder to the island. Slowly it took a grip on her mind and she could not shake it loose. As before, it began a search of her thoughts, as a thief searches a room. She could not resist such strength and in a while she smiled, though the expression on her face was not her own. Whatever had taken her moved her to her own room and she locked her door. She got onto the bed and allowed the probing to go on, feeling the events of the night drawn from her easily as if someone was turning the pages of a book. When it was over, she felt as though her mind had been exposed to as thorough and intimate attention as the body of Tennebriel to Cromalech's love-making.

4
Orhung

IT HAD TAKEN the rider almost three months to reach the outskirts of this new city that its builders had named Elberon. He had left the ice realms, sensing the relief of the people there who were glad enough that he had been instrumental in breaking the hold of the hated Deliverers, but who preferred him gone. He had journeyed north by sled, which the ice folk had been pleased to give him, and he had eventually traded it and the dogs for a sturdy pony. On this he had crossed low, lifeless mountains to be confronted by a narrow band of icy sea. Yannachuk's people had also given him gifts to take with him on his search, and he exchanged a handful of small ivory tusks (no use to him at all) for a passage on a boat across the sea. This took him to the southern edge of the eastern continent, to Kotumec, where he traded the last of what he had in one of its poor towns. From then on his journey had been hazardous, through difficult, mostly unexplored terrain, where wild beasts beset him and huge birds dived at him from hostile skies. He found the headwaters of the Trannadens river, one of the three great rivers that wound down to the united deltas of the west coast, and he followed it to the open plains, where he had learned he would find the city of Elberon. Here, the dying Deliverer had promised him, was where Korbillian would be found, if he were alive.

Now the streets opened before him. There had been no protective walls around Elberon, just a few watch towers, but he had not been hailed or challenged. The city was young, apparently not at war, and scores of travelers were coming from the hinterlands, mostly to bring trade or to settle here.

And there were celebrations in progress. The rider had
learned from some of the many people he had encountered
in the plains that there was to be a wedding soon. Ruan
Dubhnor, military ruler of the city, was to marry the daughter
of the king of the northern forest lands, Strangarth. The match
was the talk of the country, for the girl, Agetta, was a wild,
tempestuous girl of the wildlands, as temperamental as a
mountain stream and although Ruan was a strong commander, he was no older than the girl, and thought by some
to be too polite, too refined to handle her. Even so, the court-
ship had lasted a year, and those who knew Ruan, so the
gossip went, declared that it had not lasted so long merely
because it would be good politics for the two allied states.
Some said that Agetta, for all her northern barbarism, looked
at Ruan with love, others that she'd break him in a year.

There was a central market place in the city, crammed now
with stalls and booths, and movement between them was almost impossible. The entire populace seemed to have gathered here, intent on arguing at the top of its combined lungs
over anything and everything, from the price of wheat to the
weather. The traveler found it difficult to get a room at an
inn, eventually forced to hunt in the wharf areas, although
many of the taverns here were full. The quaysides were bristling with masts, the ships bow to stern, as if everyone who
ploughed the waters of the local seaboard had docked and a
few more beside.

Once in his room, the traveler slept for a night and late
into the afternoon of the next day, and when he emerged from
his lodgings and found the bar, the inn was relatively quiet.
At this time of the day most people were out, although a few
sat at a table, gambling. The innkeeper, a large man who had
endured enough inn brawls to have become hardened to trouble, was tidying the place up in preparation for the night's
festivities, wondering how many heads would be broken tonight. The guards had given up trying to keep order in the
inns just lately. It was the fault of the visiting seamen, especially having so any of the riff-raff landing at once. In some
ways it would be a blessing when the wedding was done with,
although the innkeeper's pockets had never been so full.

The traveler sat at the bar, apparently lost in thought. The
innkeeper studied him, knowing at once that he was from

distant lands. His head was shaven, although it looked as though it had ever known hair, for it was as smooth as polished stone, darkened by the sun. His features were sharp, oddly angled as if the bones of the face had been set wrongly, and his eyes were the color of dull steel. His clothes were as foreign as his features, made of some strange material that could have been a form of worn leather, or even fine mesh. He carried no weapons, but there was a length of metal at his belt, like a rod, though it looked to have no practical use.

He accepted wine dubiously, placing coins on the table. The innkeeper recognized them as being from the extreme southern lands, Kotumec or Onathac, but guessed the man had bartered for them as he had no idea of their value.

"Here, no need to give me so much," the innkeeper grinned. "That's enough to buy a rack of wine."

"Then let it buy a little of your time," said the stranger, pushing the coins back across the bar.

Hesitating for only a moment, the innkeeper nodded, pocketing the money. "What do you want to know?"

"I search for a man called Korbillian. If you can show me the way, I will give you more coins. All I possess."

It was impossible to meet the level gaze of the man. He was not offensive, or unpleasant, but something in his alien face made others look away. There were fighting men like that, but the innkeeper had never seen an expression to match the one that faced him. It was hard, but not cruel, fascinating but not hypnotic. There was a depth of coldness to it, an indifference that he had never known before.

"Korbillian, you say?" The innkeeper leaned on the bar as if his secrets were for this man and no other. "You think he's in Elberon?"

"It is what I have been told."

"By whom?"

"A Deliverer."

The innkeeper couldn't hide his wariness. "Oh? One of Wargallow's followers, eh? Where was this? Local?"

"I do not know Wargallow. The man who told me to look here was in the south, in the ice lands of Yannachuk."

The innkeeper shook his head. "Never heard of him. Didn't even know anyone lived beyond Kotumec. You from there?"

The man shook his head. "Where is Wargallow?"

"He rules from a place called the Direkeep, a long way east of here. The Deliverers are his people. They keep order, of a sort. Used to be a bloodthirsty lot, but now that Wargallow has taken charge of them, they don't bother us. They're said to be wandering all over Omara, and some of them don't accept Wargallow as their new ruler. Pity for them when he finds them." The innkeeper frowned for a moment as if at something evil, then clicked his thick fingers. "Ah! Now I've got the name. This Korbillian—he was an ally of Wargallow in the fighting. But you're out of luck. Korbillian was killed, along with a lot of other good men. Out in the Silences, the eastern deserts."

"Killed?" said the stranger, as though the word were meaningless to him. "Nothing here could kill him. Where did he go?"

"To Xennidhum. Not many of the men who came back from that place talk about it. Sort of forbidden topic. If you really want to know about it, you'll have to talk to some of the men who survived. But they're a tight-lipped lot. Even your money might not tempt them."

"Where can I find them?"

"Tell you what," the innkeeper said softly, dropping his voice to a whisper, although the gamblers were too intent on their game to look up. "I'll send out word. I think I may be able to persuade a couple of the veterans to come and talk to you. But it'll have to be in private."

"Do it now," nodded the stranger curtly.

There was a gentle rap upon the door of the tiny room. The traveler had been stretched on the bed, not sleeping but thinking quietly. He got to his feet, lithe as a predator and opened the door. The innkeeper had been as good as his word, for two men were outside. The man gestured them in. From their bearing they were soldiers, although they did not wear uniform; both had short swords and a knife in their belts.

"We were told you are in search of Korbillian," the first of them said bluntly.

"Is he alive?"

The men glanced at each other. Already they had been told this man was not from this continent and they could see how unlike other men of the east he was. "He has friends in Elberon. Will you allow us to take you to them?"

"Is he alive?" the stranger repeated anxiously, almost as though his own life depended on the answer.

"No," said the first of the soldiers. "He died at Xennidhum."

The stranger looked appalled.

"Will you come with us?"

The stranger nodded, but he seemed deflated by the finality of the soldier's statement. Outside, there were a dozen more men waiting, but the stranger ignored them, and the fact that the soldiers had come prepared to take him by force if necessary meant nothing to him. He went peacefully, seemingly lost in private thoughts that looked from his expression to be grim and dark. He hardly saw the broad streets and fine new houses that the procession passed, nor did he pay attention to the surprised looks of citizens who assumed the man had been arrested and was to be imprisoned when they saw him pass. Only when the soldiers reached their eventual destination, up in the low hills that overlooked the city did he again look around him.

He had been brought to what was either a garrison or the equivalent of a palace, although, like the city, it had been built on a small scale. Its high vaults were lit by tall braziers, and in the gleaming glow of the flames he could see a young man flanked by more guards waiting for him. The stranger was brought before this man and only then did he seem to come alert again, studying the man closely. Although the man was young, he looked stern, hardened by the events of his past, battle perhaps. He was dressed in robes that proclaimed his high position in the city, but he wore a sword; the stranger noted that he had often used one by the callouses on his hands. The stranger was adept at measuring fighting men, and here, he knew, was a professional of the highest order.

The young man inclined his head. "My name is Ruan Dubhnor. I am in command of the city. Korbillian, who I am told you seek, was an ally of mine. Perhaps you will tell me why you wish to meet him?"

"It is highly urgent."

"I see. What is your name, please? And from where have you come?"

"I am Orhung. I am from—" But he paused, staring about him as if in some confusion.

Ruan moved closer to him. "From Ternannoc?" he said softly.

Orhung looked surprised. "Korbillian's world? No, not there. But—is he alive? He cannot be dead—"

"There are a number of guests waiting for me," said Ruan, as if changing the subject. "They are all people who would call Korbillian friend. Will you join us and give us your full story?"

Orhung nodded at once.

Ruan motioned him forward, and Orhung saw the way the guards took their positions carefully, discreetly putting themselves where they could attack Orhung quickly if the need arose. None of them realized that to have done so would have been futile.

Beyond the hallway, through a short passage, they came to a large banqueting hall where a group of people were seated at a long wooden table. They had finished an elaborate meal and were evidently in high spirits, toasting each other with goblets of wine or ale. Orhung entered and heard the doors close behind him. Ruan himself bolted them, and the last of the guards stationed himself out of sight in the shadows. There were more than a dozen of them here. As Orhung stepped to the table, he saw an unusual gathering of men and women, who seemed puzzled by his sudden appearance.

"Allow me to introduce my guests," said Ruan, and he did so. He turned to the man on his right, a huge fellow with thick golden hair and an equally tangled beard, with eyes that gleamed as a hawk's would. "King Strangarth of the northern forests." The king raised his huge goblet in a polite salute that might just have been a mock one.

"Beside him is his daughter, Agetta." The girl was everything and more that Orhung had been told. Her lustrous mane of dark hair spilled over her shoulders, her eyes blazed with life, testament to the spirit of the girl, and her mouth pouted at the young commander. She smiled at him, no more than that, but Orhung could sense the power held in check. Opposite her sat another girl, less obviously beautiful, but nevertheless arresting in her own way.

"This is Sisipher," said Ruan, and the girl did not smile, but nodded. It was as if a shadow crossed her face for a moment, but it quickly passed. Her own hair was long and smooth as silk, and her eyes drew the attention immediately. In her face was something hard to define, but it hinted at sadness, something trapped that longed for release. Behind her, stretched out on the floor, were two huge beasts which Orhung thought to be hounds, but he saw that they were wolves. They feigned sleep, but he knew they were alert to everything that happened in the room, and he knew that Sisipher had her own way of communicating with them. He understood her power at once, as though he could see it. Somewhere above, outside the building, something else stirred, some other creature that this girl could speak to.

Sisipher felt a cold breeze of uncertainty, knowing that this being read her power and she felt herself respond for a moment to something in him. At once she blanketed it off.

"Beyond her," said Ruan, "is Albar, one of my closet aides, and with him is Harrudnor, another good friend." Both men bowed where they sat. They were a little older than Ruan, but no less notable for their mien. Orhung could see that they were trained fighters.

"I had hoped for two other guests to be with us tonight," Ruan told the whole party. "Guile should be here shortly, and is late as usual." There were smiles at this. "And Simon Wargallow has left his retreat in the mountains."

This caused a gentle ripple of interest, but Orhung was quick to notice Sisipher's expression, the brief widening of her eyes.

"So I'll get to meet this man of terror yet," chuckled Strangarth.

Ruan put an arm on the king's broad shoulder, a gesture of familiarity he would once never have dared, but he and the huge king had become very close. "We have all had our reasons for wanting to see Omara rid of the Deliverers, but if we are to change their ways, it will have to be through Wargallow's help."

Strangarth grunted. "Well, if he fought with you against Xennidhum, who am I to argue! Let him come." Strangarth knew only too well the special relationship enjoyed by men who had fought together in the black war in the east.

"I have met some of these Deliverers," said Orhung. "They are men of divided loyalties?"

Ruan nodded, enlarging upon the political upheavals in their central citadel, the Direkeep. "And we, Orhung, are gathered here to plan the future of our new city. King Strangarth's beautiful daughter, Agetta," he bowed extravagantly, "has consented to marry me. In a few days there will be a feast such as the city will remember for a long time." Agetta laughed, raising with the others her glass, and Ruan gave a full goblet of wine to Orhung.

The latter hesitated, as if the drink were foreign to him, but he toasted the couple's lasting happiness. Even so, his grim appearance still cast a shadow over the gathering.

"Seems to me," grunted Strangarth, "that our guest is not as pleased with life as he might be. What's on your mind, man from the south?"

So you know that much about me, thought Orhung. He put down his glass and accepted the chair he was given. "I came in search of Korbillian, but I learn he is no more. Instead I am with his friends."

"Why did you seek him?" said Ruan and everyone studied the stranger closely. He knew how much he had soured this banquet. They feared whatever news he had brought, as they must have feared Korbillian, and as they feared death itself.

"I cannot pass on to Korbillian the news I have, so it is my duty to impart it to you. Will you give me an account of this war in the east, and of his death?"

Ruan looked around the table and there was no dissent. "Very well. Let us have your story."

"You understand Korbillian's past?" replied Orhung.

It was Sisipher who answered, speaking clearly as she looked into the past, where none of them liked to go. Although Strangarth had not himself been involved in the war at Xennidhum, he had heard the tale before, but was glad to hear it again. Sisipher talked of the Mound, the evil force that had thrust into this world of Omara when the Hierarchs of Korbillian's world, Ternannoc, had performed a ritual of power that had gone horribly wrong and polluted a score of worlds. She explained how Korbillian had been invested with the last power of the Hierarchs and had come here to destroy the power of the Mound at the city of Xennidhum, and of how he had gathered an army of Omaran followers to help him. And she spoke of how most of them had perished, including the man from another world, but of how they had destroyed the darkness from beyond.

For a while after she had finished, the others were silent, the cheerful mood of earlier now completely dissolved. Those who had been at Xennidhum reflected on its horrors, and Orhung seemed to be thinking deeply; Sisipher's words had clearly meant a good deal to him and the others could see how troubled he was, particularly on hearing of the death of Korbillian.

Orhung spoke at last. "Then you understand about the Sorcerer-Kings of Xennidhum, and of how they closed the gates, or sought to. When they discovered the Aspects, the other worlds which are a part of Omara, and what was dormant there, they sealed the gates. But their work aroused the interest of the Hierarchs of Ternannoc, whose high magic damaged the seals."

"Korbillian may be dead," said Ruan. "But he atoned for the sins of this world. The gates are sealed. The Hierarchs are no more."

Yet there was not one there who did not feel the current of apprehension flowing stronger around him. Orhung was nodding, but his face did not confirm Ruan's words. He spoke in a level voice, with little emotion, almost as if reciting lines given to him by some other, more powerful being. "Some of the Hierarchs did not render up their power at the time when it was decided to place it in the hands of Korbillian. A few fled to other Aspects while there was time."

"Aye," said Albar. "One came here and named himself the Preserver. He made the cruel laws that governed the Deliverers, the Abiding Word, until Simon Wargallow found a way to destroy him."

Orhung nodded. "Grenndak. Other Hierarchs hid themselves on worlds where they could keep a balance about themselves. There would be no need to seek them out and destroy them."

"We could not do so if we wished to," said Ruan.

Orhung did not reply, and in his silence could be read more unease.

Strangarth leaned forward. "You have still not told us where you are from." Any good-naturedness that had been in him earlier was gone. He looked ready for a quarrel. "My guess is you are not from Omara."

Orhung equalled his gaze, but there was no threat in his own eyes. "I am, and I am not."

Strangarth sat back with a growl. "Pah! He talks in riddles! In my lands, if we do not have a direct answer, we string men up over a fire!"

Sisipher calmed the king with a glance, and Ruan marvelled, not for the first time, at the effect she had on those around her. She seemed to be able to instill a sense of awe, though if you had asked men why, they could never say. She was beautiful but not stunning and she did not touch the minds of men as she did the wolves, or the birds of the air, or other creatures. But men always listened, rarely scorned her. Even Guile, secret heir to the Goldenisle throne, took her counsel without argument.

"I think it would be to our disadvantage to abuse Orhung," she said, a faint smile surfacing through her fears. "Come, Orhung. You have brought grim news. Let us have it."

Orhung nodded. "Very well. I am one of the Created, a member of the Werewatch." He could see that it meant nothing to his audience, though he had not expected it to. "The Werewatch are, or were, a company devised by the Sorcerer-Kings of Xennidhum. When they sealed the Aspects in their Chaining, they foresaw further evils." Again he paused, this time to reach out and pick up one of the few fruits remaining in one of the bowls. He pierced the soft flesh gently with a fork and a trickle of juice ran from the tiny punctures. "Just as the juice seeps from this fruit, so power can seep from a seal. Not much, but enough to harm whatever is around it before it dries up. And just as a bird may come and drink the juice, so men may feed on any leak of power, for few men can resist the pull of power, however evil."

Sisipher was nodding. It was just as Korbillian had told them.

"The Sorcerer-Kings protected their seals with the Werewatch, a company of guardians who watched over the seals for any sign of power seeping out into Omara. We did not sit beside the seals like men in a tower upon a city wall. We were put into the undersleep, which is like a deep trance to you, though it spreads out over time far longer than the life of a man. For the life of a world. We, the Created, slept, unable to wake unless power seeped from the seals.''

Agetta, who had been fascinated by his words, sat up with a gasp. "You say you were created? What does it mean?" Her eyes were wide, devouring him. Ruan grinned, though equally intrigued.

"I know nothing of the processes used. I became aware only after I was placed at my post. Before that was nothing."

Agetta screwed up her pretty nose. "So you weren't born, like a normal man? You have no parents?"

Orhung looked neither embarrassed nor hurt. "I can explain it no more simply. I am not as you are. But I am flesh. I live. I think."

"And do you feel?" said Sisipher.

Orhung looked puzzled. "Why, yes. Anxiety, fear, anger—"

"Anger?" said Ruan. "Directed at whom?"

"The enemies of Omara. My function is to make war upon those enemies."

"And who," said Strangarth, "are those enemies?"

"I am here to tell you this."

"Tell us more about the Werewatch," said Sisipher. "If you were set to guard the seals, why were you not awake when we came to Xennidhum? Power had been pouring from that place for many years. Why had it not triggered you and your company?"

"The Werewatch were not set to protect Xennidhum. The great Chaining was made there, as you know. Naar-Iarnoc was its guardian. The Werewatch were set to protect the world's other places, for it was feared that Omara would be subjected to pressures that might cause a rupture anywhere in the wall dividing it from its other Aspects. The ancient powers that the Sorcerer-Kings had stumbled upon and which they now sought to chain were impossible to gauge. How strong were they? What outlets would they use? Precautions had to be taken.

"The Created were housed in a single fortress, far in the south of Omara, inaccessible, where they would never be disturbed by the men of Omara, never stumbled upon in error as the Sorcerer-Kings had stumbled upon the old powers. In undersleep the Werewatch would each have a part of Omara to keep watch over. If evil rose in our part, we awoke and flew—"

"Flew!" cried Agetta. "How?"

Orhung did not laugh. "Each of us had a dakarza, huge, bird-like creatures, also of the Created. These were kept at the fortress and tended by the hurdas, also Created, men to watch them. The dakarza took us swiftly across the skies of Omara to wherever we needed to go. We were invested with certain powers, enough to repair damage to the Aspect wall."

"And you found leaks of power?" said Strangarth.

"A few. Only small. This was after the chaos at Xennidhum, when the great Chaining was first made good. The working of the Hierarchs had caused many ruptures to the walls of the worlds, opening many gates. Korbillian came through one of them himself, and sealed it. It was the last of its kind. Since Korbillian's coming there have been no other leaks of power, save for Xennidhum. The Werewatch have not been there. It was not our duty to go. We have watched over the remainder of Omara."

"So," put in Sisipher, "events at Xennidhum did not wake you?"

"No. They woke Naar-Iarnoc."

Sisipher's face darkened. "Yes," she said softly. "I know that well enough. Naar-Iarnoc, last of the Sorcerer-Kings, waiting to be woken by one who would come."

"Sisipher," said Ruan gently, "there's no need—"

"Down through the line of my ancestors to me. *I* woke him. And Korbillian brought the power to seal the Opening for all time."

"The Werewatch did not have such power," said Orhung. "We were no more than guardians of the outer lands. We slept through those years of upheaval, and through your war. We were not created to be a part of it."

Sisipher shook herself from her dark mood. "Yes. But you are asleep no longer. Are you?" The others saw the look on her face and the coldness of the air about them intensified as if the torches had sputtered out.

Orhung shook his head. "I have been woken."

Ruan was before him like a ghost. "There is a seeping of power? In Elberon?"

"Not here. But in Omara."

"Xennidhum?" said Ruan, the word no more than a whisper.

"No. I think that place is dead now. I have come from a place of ice and stone in the far south. The Werewatch had been in undersleep for many of your years, although there is no time for us. Less than four of your months ago, our fortress was attacked."

Again the coldness of the air intensified. No one spoke, afraid to voice the questions that had to be answered.

"Something wielding monstrous power had found us out and without warning, stormed the ice fortress. Not one of us had been triggered awake by its coming. That is itself a measure of this thing's black power. We were butchered. Our dakarza were cut to pieces, the hurdas all murdered. Flames ate at the fortress and the walls were brought down in a single night. All was smoke and blood and the ice ran in torrents from the havoc.

"I woke by some accident, sleep ruptured by the sheer ferocity of the attack. Around me, others were ripped from undersleep like babies taken from the womb prematurely. But the beings that had set upon us were terrible to see. We were dazed, utterly helpless, unable to focus our own powers. If you can imagine yourselves dreaming a nightmare, one filled with the creatures that revolt you most, then being dragged awake into the same nightmare by those creatures, even then you could not envisage what we saw. These beasts were huge, monstrous, their gaping mouths fixing on the bodies of my fellows with a demonic abandon. They were not like earthly beasts, not even like starving wolves, for they had about them a dreadful ferocity, as if their master had invested in them a pure evil. They tore at us, oblivious to any force we used against them, and even those who were caught up in the flames did not cease to attack until the fire had reduced them to nothing. It was not hunger that goaded them, or madness, but the need to destroy and crush every spark of life in our fortress.

"There were other beings with these monsters, half-men but larger than men and with half-seen faces that warned of animal cunning and feral hunger, but they, too, wanted to crush us, to drain us of life. If evil were an ocean, then our fortress would have been inundated, pounded to rubble, submerged. It is true that this force had all the elements of an ocean, the power, the fury, the invincibility.

"Those of the Werewatch who were not pulped scattered like ants. I found myself in the bedding stables of the dakarza, where other equally vile creatures were at work slaughtering our beasts. Like blind things from under the earth, they groped and tore. I reached my own dakarza by chance and we both fell among the heaped corpses of other dakarza, trodden upon, drenched in the blood of the slain, miraculously buried. Whatever these other creatures were that had come upon us, they too were filled with the evil that our creators had built us to watch for, as if molded from it."

The gathering was silent, shocked by the grotesque description Orhung had given them. Sisipher thought of her father, and of the things he had told of what dwelt deep under the earth, beings not fit to live in this world.

"Crushed by the weight of the slain, I was for a long time again in a kind of undersleep. When I woke from it, I was pinned under a wing of my dakarza and though it seemed to be dead, I could feel slight movement. The air stank of blood and the smoke was yet thick. Voices brought me to, for there were human servants of the enemy at work here. I say human, but they were not as ordinary men. They were imperfect, as if shaped hastily and without care and they fed on their hatred of us, and of all things Omaran. They gloated over their foul work, cursing, snapping like wolves, yet obedient to whatever horror had set them upon us, and they did their work with relish. It is well they boasted, for as I listened, they spoke to each other of their master and of what he planned. I cannot recall every word, for their voices were strange, but what they said was this. Their master is a Hierarch and he has been hidden in Omara since long before the war at Xennidhum, having come here after the working that went awry in his own world. He knows only too well now that the power of the other Hierarchs has been used up by Korbillian in the destruction of Xennidhum."

"Does he know Korbillian is dead?" said Sisipher.

Orhung shook his head. "Only that he used up the power. He knows also that there is no power in Omara to match his own. And he has tested a little of his power by destroying the Created. I am the last of them." Though he had described a catastrophe, Orhung had not spoken with emotion, as if in some ironic way the passing of his kind meant nothing to him personally. Yet as he watched the horror on the faces of his audience, he felt the stirring of something buried within himself, a vague sorrow that he could not share their fears, their emotions.

"What else does he intend?" said Ruan.

"His full purpose is a mystery and I cannot say what moves him, but certain things are evident. He intends to rule Omara."

Ruan turned to his companions. They were all stunned by the news.

"How did you escape?" said Agetta, fascinated.

"My dakarza was alive. I let it take me into its stomach."

Agetta blanched. "You jest!" Even her father looked appalled.

"I had no other choice. Had I mounted the beast and attempted to fly off, I would have been torn from the skies by whatever terrors beset the ice fortress. Their slaves that I had heard were dragging some of the dead dakarza outside the bedding area, preparing to cut them up for food. My own dakarza was not unintelligent and had realized at once that the trick would be to feign death. It took me into it. Later we were pulled out into a courtyard. Before they could bring their knives to us, we took to the skies—"

"And you *lived*, inside it?" said Strangarth incredulously.

"No man could have done so. But I am of the Created."

"And where did you leave this creature?" said Ruan.

"It had been badly injured. It could not go far, though far enough from the fortress to escape the weapons of the enemy. It perished out in the ice-fields and I was found by the snow people of Yannachuk."

"Why did you search for Korbillian?" said Sisipher. "You

had no part in affairs at Xennidhum. Yet you knew of Korbillian. How come?''

''I understand your suspicions of me,'' Orhung said, still unmoved by the hard looks she gave him. ''The beings that I heard spoke of Korbillian. Their master was pleased that his power was used up. As I have said, he did not know he was dead. It was my hope that Korbillian could be found, warned, and in my ignorance I had hoped that he would know how to oppose the Hierarch. I was wrong.''

''Where is the Hierarch?'' said the girl.

''I did not learn that. Nor can I tell you, for he has not come here through some fresh seeping of power. He has been here since the beginning. But he will be in some remote place, far from civilized Omaran life. It is how his servants came upon the Created without alerting us.''

''And did you learn anything of his plans to rule Omara?'' said Ruan.

''Something of it. He cannot conquer Omara yet. His first intention is to divide the nations of this world.''

Strangarth grunted. ''Then his work is almost done! Few of us are allied. Omara is a world of small states and countries. Half, nay, four-fifths of it are unknown to us!''

Ruan nodded solemnly. ''Aye and what we do know of is not likely to unite itself into a single nation, no matter what the threat from outside.''

Orhung listened to them as they discussed this. ''His main interest,'' he said after a pause, ''is Goldenisle.''

Much to his surprise, there were several grins around the table.

''A pox upon the place!'' laughed Strangarth, but his daughter gave him a withering scowl.

''Father!'' she snorted. ''My husband-to-be is from Goldenisle, and when we sail upon it and oust that lunatic who calls himself Emperor—''

''Not so quickly, sweet Agetta,'' said Ruan, smiling at her. She scowled back indignantly. ''Well!''

Ruan turned to Orhung. ''Goldenisle is the strongest Empire known on Omara. But its people are divided. Some of us have come here and built this new city. The heir to the throne is with us, and should join us this night. Strange that he is so late, but he has much to occupy his mind these days.

We make our position stronger by the day here, but no doubt in time we will go to war with the present Emperor. When we are ready," he added, with a meaningful glance at Agetta. She poked her tongue out at him.

"Then I understand more clearly," said Orhung. "The Hierarch plans to undo Goldenisle. It is the only real threat to his success. If he can see to its destruction, Omara will fall to him. Then his real work will begin."

Ruan nodded slowly. "These are bad tidings. Goldenisle has never been so unstable. The Emperor, Quanar Remoon, is mad. He will likely be overthrown from within, even if we did not attack him ourselves."

"Is war inevitable?" said Orhung. "Can you not join with Goldenisle to withstand the Hierarch?"

Ruan grimaced. "Join with him! But there is no reasoning with him, as Guile will tell you when he comes. Where can he be? He enjoys being late, but he should be here by now."

Sisipher abruptly stood up, her eyes closed, her fingers pressed to her temple. "Kirrikree!" she said, naming the huge owl with whom she communicated in her own secret way. He was circling above the palace. "There is fighting!"

A pounding of doors alerted them, and Ruan was quick to fling back the bolts. Several soldiers stood there, their uniforms bloody. One man looked badly hurt. "Sire!" cried their spokesman. "There are troops on the quay. Armed."

"Whose troops?" thundered Ruan, drawing out his sword instinctively.

"We are not certain, sire, but we think they may be men of Empire."

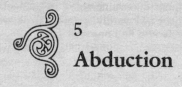

5
Abduction

GUILE STRETCHED OUT LUXURIOUSLY face down on the bed, arms draped over its sides. For the last few weeks he had been able to relax, something he had not done for a long time. Somehow the pressures of Ruan's coming wedding to the young tigress, Agetta, had allowed Guile to take a seat in the shadows. His own responsibilities in the matter were not small, but it was the young military commander who at the moment had all the worrying to do.

There was a movement behind Guile and he smiled sleepily. "Ah, there are you, Luarne. Just a little work on my shoulders before I join them at the banquet." His house was in a private part of the city, well guarded, though secretly, by some of Ruan's crack troops. Even now, few of the citizens of Elberon knew Guile's true identity, which suited him. For the time being he was not eager to declare himself and think about war. The events at Xennidhum had taxed him to the limits; the scars ran deep.

Luarne, one of the girls who was employed to keep Guile's house and who had proved to be the most gifted at massage, worked on him now, kneading his back and shoulders.

He sighed, revelling in the luxury, and the shadow of Xennidhum retreated. After a few minutes the girl ceased and withdrew.

"What—is that all? Come, I know I must go out soon, but—" Guile's voice trailed off. Someone was here, but it was not the girl. Before he could move, Guile felt something cold touch the place where lately Luarne's fingers had been. It was naked steel.

"A man of your position," said a familiar voice, "should never make himself so vulnerable." The steel withdrew and Guile rolled over awkwardly, groping for a weapon, though he knew there would be none at hand.

"No sword to protect himself?" The man who stood there wore a dark cloak, the hood thrown back to reveal himself. He was withdrawing his right arm into the long sleeve of the cloak where it could not be seen.

"Wargallow!" breathed Guile.

The Deliverer nodded, a sardonic smile on his full lips. "Yes. But I could have been your assassin. Your guards should be more alert." His large brown eyes gleamed in the lamplight, the sharp angles of his face giving him a cold, almost hostile look. He had enemies, thought Guile, who did well to fear him, and once he was my enemy. But no longer.

"I'll have them whipped in the morning," Guile avowed, grinning.

Wargallow shook his head. "No, not you. You will speak to them, but you'll not punish them. Unless you have changed in the year since I saw you last."

Guile nodded, getting up and pulling on his shirt. "I don't know if I should be glad to see you."

"I'm not here to bring bad tidings. I've come to see this fabled wedding. A good deal depends on it. The strengthening of this city."

"Yes. And you? How goes your own house?"

Wargallow shrugged. "It will be a long struggle. Even the Direkeep still has its unrest. Even now there are those who feel that the death of the Preserver was murder, and they secretly hold me to account. But they dare not raise their voices too loud."

Guile laughed uncomfortably. "Yes, I can imagine."

"You think I am too extreme?"

"Perhaps not. The Preserver's way was evil. You fight how you can."

Wargallow smiled. "Enough of politics. I came to enjoy my stay. It will be pleasant to see the others again, although I may not be made welcome by all of them."

Guile straightened. So this was why he had come to him first. He, like Guile, was not as close to the others, part of the alliance, but one that might be secretly questioned.

"We've been through far too much," Guile told him, and for a moment the awful shadow of Xennidhum, the countless ghosts, rose up, and Wargallow saw them too. They looked at each other for a moment, but Guile moved away. "Tell me, have you seen the bride to be?"

Wargallow chuckled. "No, but I hear she's full of fire."

"Oh yes! And her father, Strangarth, is like a great bear of the north. You'll have to be careful he doesn't corner you and ply you with a thousand questions about the war. It's his one great regret in life that he wasn't there. He doesn't realize—"

"I look forward to meeting him, and his daughter. But from what I hear of Ruan, he will handle her."

"Aye, he's a fine young man. Morric Elberon would have been proud of him."

Wargallow nodded silently, looking at Guile for a moment. "I am glad to see you are well. Shall we go?" They left for the banquet, Guile surprised at how easily he could talk to this man whom he had once feared.

Silently an escort of guards fell into place around them, always within reach, but not too obviously. Guile had said that if armed men surrounded him everywhere he went, people would wonder who he was. He preferred anonymity, and for the most part had achieved it.

"It's not time to start howling at the gates of Goldenisle yet," he told Wargallow when the latter commented on it.

"Is there news from across the sea?"

"A little. The same confusion, I think, though we hear from the men who yet come to us and from the traders that Quanar Remoon lies ill and may not recover."

They walked downward through the newly paved roads into narrower streets not far from the wharfs, on the way to the hill that would take them up to the main garrison where the banquet was being held. As they talked, discussing the strengths and weaknesses of the city and its forces, a number of figures suddenly moved out of the alleys ahead of them. This was one of the more unsalubrious quarters of the city, but they had to pass through it. Guile drew out his sword uncomfortably, never having been proficient with it.

"What a time to meet cutpurses!" he grunted.

Wargallow kept very close to him, watching the group of

men who were now advancing like cats on the prowl. These were no common thieves, he could see, his eyes trained to watch for men of this nature. He was certain they had come seeking him, hired by rival Deliverers. They were professionals, and they slipped from their sleeves not knives, but cudgels. Behind Wargallow there came a hoarse shout and they heard the clash of steel on steel as another group of men engaged the guards. This had been carefully planned.

Guile turned to see what was happening. His men had leapt into the street from their own cover and a fierce swordfight was ensuing. "It's a trap!" he cried. "Who—"

But Wargallow was trying to cover his front. Two of the prowlers came forward, and as they made to attack, their cudgels raised, Wargallow's right hand moved in a blur, something glinting in the pale lamp of the street. Somewhere above a woman screamed, slamming shutters, but they were the only sounds. The two men who had been closing in both toppled to their knees, and then sank on their faces. A glance from Guile showed him that both men had had their throats severed. Another pair of men rushed into the breach, more urgent now, swinging their weapons. Wargallow had revised his opinion of them. No man would attempt to take a Deliverer with a simple cudgel. They were after Guile.

Guile swung his sword, but the men evaded it easily. One of them made for Wargallow, but again the cloaked man moved impossibly fast and the man staggered back, choking. The arc of Wargallow's arm was precise to the inch, invisibly quick. The group with the cudgels was wary now, not having foreseen this obstacle. Behind them came more shouts, cries of pain as men were cut down on both sides. Guile felt himself bathed in sweat, wondering how many men were here and who they could be.

Wargallow motioned to a side alley. "If we can get in there, I'll hold them off until the guards can get reinforcements. They seem to—" A bursting shower of stars before his eyes shut off the rest, and he fell like a tree into the street, struck from behind. Guile whirled, but within seconds was gripped by strong arms. Something damp and evil-smelling was pressed to his face. He thrashed like a landed fish, but was helpless. Slowly he sank down into the waiting darkness.

When reinforcements came, they found carnage in the tiny

street. A dozen guards were dead, cut down while fighting, and about them were the corpses of as many opponents. These were dressed in ordinary clothes, none of the men recognizable as inhabitants of Elberon. The captain of the guard raced up to where Wargallow was getting to his feet dazedly, and he drew his weapon on him as if he had found one of the abductors.

"Hold your steel!" came a curt command. The captain turned with a gasp of surprise to see Ruan himself emerging from a side street. "This man is no enemy. Wargallow! What happened?"

The Deliverer pointed with his killing steel, now dripping blood, down the street. "Quickly! They have taken Guile."

At once a score of guards raced away in pursuit. Ruan had seen the blood on Wargallow's steel. He saw also the three men who had died by it. "This is not how I would have wished to meet again—"

Wargallow steadied himself on Ruan's arm, a movement which took Ruan by surprise. He would not have thought Wargallow capable of such a thing, even though he had proved himself an ally. But the killings were more like him, done without question, quickly and efficiently and without a hint of remorse.

Together they made haste after the guards, coming in time to a small square. Here there was more bloodshed, and there were bodies tumbled this way and that. Dogs barked angrily behind locked doors and faces could be seen peering from windows.

"Have you taken them?" Ruan snapped as his captain came breathlessly to him.

"I don't understand, sire. Whoever abducted Guile met opposition here. There was a fight before my men got to it."

"Where's Guile?" said Ruan.

"The men are looking."

"He must be found!"

The captain nodded and raced off, deploying his remaining men this way and that. Wargallow bent down to examine the dead men. It looked as if all those who bore cudgels had been murdered, their captive taken by someone else. He said so to Ruan.

"When we find them, we'll soon know who sent them," Ruan nodded.

"I presume they are men of Empire," said Wargallow.

Ruan grunted assent, although he had seen nothing in the dress of the dead men to confirm it.

An hour later the worst news came: the abductors had gone to ground. Guile had not been found. However, some of the dead men had been recognized by Ruan's guards, who had once been part of the Empire.

"Empire troops," Ruan told Wargallow as they made their way back to the garrison, satisfied that they could do no more this night to find Guile. The city was being watched closely, the wharfs particularly. No one would leave without being questioned.

In the banquet hall, Strangarth and the others had returned, the huge king scowling with impatience and pent-up frustration. He had brought out his war ax, but when he had been told there was nothing more that could be done for the moment, he seethed as though he would lash about him anyway. It was left to Agetta to calm him, although clearly she was also in a fighting mood, as if prepared to use her not insubstantial nails on whoever she could find that might be responsible.

"Have any of them been taken alive?" asked Sisipher.

Wargallow stood before her, remembering her at Xennidhum, and the powerful man that was her father, Brannog. "It seems I am fated to come to you in blood," he told her. "Though I would wish it otherwise."

She did not reply, instead repeating her question.

Ruan answered, seeing the tension between them. "No. But we have a mystery. There were two parties. The first abducted Guile, knocking Wargallow to the ground. The second struck soon after, killing the men of the first group and taking the spoils. The mystery is compounded by the fact that both parties contained at least one man from the Empire. Soldiers, though little is known of them. My men have not been to Goldenisle for over a year. The only man who could explain this duplicity, I fear, is Guile himself."

Strangarth came forward, his face a mask of anger, which he seemed now to direct at Wargallow. "How did these men get into the city?"

Again Ruan answered. "Men have been arriving from all parts of the continent. For the wedding. Ironically we have welcomed them. It never occurred to me that men of the Empire would come—"

"Nor to any of us," said Sisipher, with a sharp look at the king.

He grunted as if she had slapped him. "Can they get out?"

Ruan brightened. "There at least I can give you better news. I have alerted ships moored out in the delta. If any ship has left the city tonight—and I think none has—it will be stopped. In the meantime, all ships will be searched. The wharfs will not be a good place to hide, as I have many ears there. And if anyone tries to flee the city by land, word will reach me. Whoever is responsible for taking Guile, they cannot move without alerting us."

"I hope so," said Sisipher. "I have asked Kirrikree to search from the skies. Already he looks for us."

"Of all the nights!" fumed Ruan now, and Agetta came up to him and put her arms around him. "The news from Orhung, and now this!"

Wargallow had noticed the man who had been standing in the shadows, watching almost indifferently as if he were either on the point of sleep or as if he had had too much to drink. "You have had bad news?" said the Deliverer, looking pointedly at Orhung.

Ruan drew himself up. "My apologies. I should have introduced you properly. This is Strangarth—"

"And you are lord of the Direkeep?" Strangarth said to Wargallow abruptly. "We are allies, I am told."

Wargallow met his gaze and smiled briefly. "So I trust."

Ruan called Orhung forward and the man from the south came before them, though he seemed unduly listless. "You must repeat your story to Wargallow," Ruan told him.

Orhung bowed, sensing the latent hostility in the cloaked man and he could smell the blood on the steel arm that was hidden beneath a sleeve. But his cold eyes stared straight back at the Deliverer. Neither man flinched as though they were engaged in some silent mental study.

"How are you involved in this business?" Wargallow said bluntly.

Orhung again went over his story, and although Wargallow

felt a wrench in his guts at the grim tidings, he did not show it. He merely nodded. At the end, he sat back, staring off into the distance as if seeing the terrible destruction in the southern snows.

"Why did the Hierarch attack the Created?" he said suddenly.

Orhung frowned. "As a measure of his power—"

Wargallow shook his head. "I think not. You were eliminated for a reason. When a man plans war, he acts according to his best advantage. The Hierarch has alerted us, though he probably did not expect survivors. No, he destroyed the Created for a reason."

"Then I cannot give it to you," said Orhung.

"And now you say that Goldenisle is the target of this Hierarch?"

"Yes. It would be a difficult opponent if it could unite itself against him."

Wargallow snorted, almost with derision.

"Why do you laugh?" said Ruan.

"I was thinking of Xennidhum. You remember how things were when Korbillian came to us? The gathering in my own Direkeep! We were divided, all of us with our own kingdoms, or new lands. All with a cause that went against the other, more or less. Korbillian told us that if we did not put aside our own petty needs, and band ourselves together, Omara itself would perish."

"We believed him," said Sisipher. "He was right."

"Even I," grinned Wargallow. "And Morric Elberon, Guile's military genius, who had been preparing an army to win him his throne, even he had to throw in with the common cause. We were full of doubts, were we not?"

"We all had our reasons for going," said Sisipher and the others could see the conflict that must once have waged between these two.

"Of course!" laughed Wargallow. "We had come to believe in Korbillian's power. And we lusted after it. We wanted our share of it. But in the end—"

"In the end, what?" said Sisipher coldly, her eyes challenging him.

Wargallow equalled her gaze, and his steel suddenly came into the light and banged down on the table, cutting deep into it. They watched the dried blood flake from it. "In the end," he said, "reason prevailed. We did as Korbillian told us. We fought for each other."

"And now?" Sisipher's stare was remorseless.

"We must do so again. If what Orhung says is true, we have to. How ironic! Instead of making war on Goldenisle, we must woo her!"

Agetta took her arms from Ruan's and stood with them on her hips, a remarkable picture of defiance. "Who are you to command Ruan! You are not Elberon's ruler, nor are you Guile's keeper. The Empire is corrupt! It must be—"

"Silence!" came the roar of Strangarth. "Since when does my daughter give commands?" He pointed, in fury, to the door. "This is no place for you. Leave us at once!"

Agetta turned to Ruan for support, but her father took one menacing step forward. "He is not yet your husband! Leave us, I say, or I will strip you here and now and beat your backside with the flat of my ax!"

Almost bursting with anger, Agetta stormed from the room, and there were several wry grins as the door crashed to behind her.

Wargallow looked across at Strangarth. "Thank you for ending that particular dispute. It is not one I would have had the energy to prolong. Fortunately Ruan is younger than I, and fitter."

Ruan smiled briefly. "You were saying?"

"I have no wish to rule here, you know that. But I would wish to be a part of any eastern alliance. Even though the Empire appears to be responsible for this night's work, and even though you are sworn to put Ottemar Remoon on his rightful throne, dare we risk a war that would weaken us against this new power, this Hierarch?"

Orhung shook his head. "If you go to war with Goldenisle, there can be no victor. Anakhizer will destroy any survivors."

Ruan thought very hard. "Then we must plan carefully. First, we must recover Guile. As I have said, I have taken steps to see that the abductors do not pass the blockade."

"And when we have recovered him?" said Strangarth.

"I wonder if we should send the abductors back to Goldenisle, suing for peace," suggested Ruan. "They would be an embarrassment to whoever sent them."

For the first time since the abduction, Albar and Harrudnor spoke up. "With respect, sire," said Albar. "I think your plea would fall on deaf ears."

"Aye," agreed Harrudnor. "We have no recognition here in Elberon. That much is clear from the men who yet flee Goldenisle to join us. As far as the Empire is concerned, we are little better than the northern pirates, the Hammavars, and we know what esteem they are held in."

"There is a price on their heads," Ruan nodded glumly.

Wargallow considered. "Even if we mobilized all the men at our disposal, it would be rash to attack the Empire. But we have to confront it. It is true that the Empire has wronged us in this attempted abduction."

"Fire with fire," growled Strangarth. "I'm no sailor, but why not send our own secret ships across the sea and abduct the Emperor? They would never expect such a stroke!"

Ruan grinned at the impetuosity of his potential father-in-law. "Would that we all had your resolve and strength, Strangarth! But believe me, the Empire is too big for us. The city itself is ten, twenty times the size of our own Elberon. And no ship can ever pass into its inner sea without the agreement of the twin garrisons in the Hasp. It is a very narrow strip of water between towering cliffs, the only way in. A fleet a thousand strong could not get through if opposed from those forts."

"A delegation, then," said Wargallow. "Who rules Goldenisle?"

"Quanar Remoon—"

"No, I mean who is really in control?"

"The Administrators. The Administrative Oligarch, their leader, was Eukor Epta. I presume he is still there. He has been for as long as men can remember. Very few men have ever seen him. But he is the arm behind the throne. If we could reach him— But he would never agree. He would speak to us only through the lower levels of government."

"Who else is there? Palace officials?"

"The palace is run by Administrators. There are the Law Givers, but they are under Eukor Epta's thumb. The only men answerable directly to the Emperor are his own personal bodyguard, the Imperial Killers. It would not be such a wise move to attract their attention. Cromalech is the First Sword and he is his own man.''

Wargallow grunted. ''Then we have to speak to Eukor Epta, or his representatives.''

''I will go there,'' said Orhung.

No one smiled at his bluntness. ''We must choose our men with care,'' said Wargallow.

''Men?'' said Sisipher, and for the first time there was the suggestion of a smile on her lips. ''And are you men the only ones who have something to say?'' She looked straight at Strangarth. ''Or will you send me from the room, too?''

Strangarth laughed gustily. ''If you remain, I will assuredly not punish you as I threatened my daughter.''

Ruan waited for the laughter to recede. ''You would go?'' he asked Sisipher.

''Goldenisle knows nothing of Korbillian, nor of Xennidhum.''

''It's unlikely,'' agreed Ruan.

''Then I will go. And Kirrikree, if he can manage the voyage, for even he may not fly so far over water.''

Strangarth thumped his huge chest. ''I will go, of course.''

Ruan restrained him. ''I think not. No, I do not mean to insult you, sir. But the voyage would not be good for you, and besides, some of us will have to see to things here—''

''Including you,'' said Wargallow.

Ruan turned on him, but the others were nodding. ''I will go for you, sire,'' said Albar, and Harrudnor was also quick to offer himself, though both men spoke again of their misgivings.

''The city needs Ruan,'' said Wargallow. ''We can petition the Empire. Find Guile and protect him. We don't want to show our strength, such as it is. If we send no more than a small delegation—myself, Orhung, Sisipher, Albar, Harrudnor and a few soldiers, it will be enough.''

''But if you fail?''

''We will do no more than warn them against the peril that is rising against us all, offering ourselves as allies. Are they so foolish that they would not listen to reason? Are they more hostile than we all once were to suggestions of an alliance?''

Ruan sighed, pacing to and fro like some seasoned cam-

paigner. "It will not be as it was before. You do not know
Goldenisle."

"The risk has to be taken, my boy," said Strangarth kindly.
"I admit that, in war, I like to ride out at the head of my
troops and swing my ax and make a lot of noise. It is how
the men of the forests always fight. But I can see there is
more to war in your world. My methods would undo us, I
fear. Mind you," he added, the fire burning strong in his
eyes, "I'd take a good few of the vermin with me!"

There were smiles at this, but then silence for long moments.

"So when do we leave?" said Albar at last.

"As soon as Guile is recovered," suggested Wargallow.

"Very well," nodded Ruan. "I'll have a ship prepared for
you at once. And—the wedding?" He turned to Strangarth.

"I suggest," said the king, "that you waste no time in
marrying my headstrong daughter. She cannot wait to give
you a whole clutch of sons! And it will be good policy for
your people not to know that anything untoward has happened. They will know nothing of tonight, which is good.
And Orhung's story must be our secret."

"Well counselled," agreed Wargallow.

"Then you will miss the ceremony,' said Ruan.

"Never mind," said Wargallow. "You'll have enough to
think about from what I've seen of Agetta."

Strangarth roared with laughter and the others joined in.
Sisipher was smiling, glad that the huge king had accepted
Wargallow as an ally, and glad that she could accept him,
too. As she turned from them, she felt a sudden stab of alarm,
gripping a chair to steady herself.

"It must be the bird," said Ruan. "Kirrikree."

Sisipher slowly stood up, her face grim. "He has been over
the delta. There has been more fighting. A ship. Simple
cargo, or so it seemed. One of the blockade ships met it. The
inspection was routine, but there were many men in the hold,
all armed."

Ruan leaned forward. "What happened?"

"Fire. On our ship. There was fighting. The other ships
moved in, but there is thick river fog tonight. The Empire
vessel has broken through! Our ships pursue it, but they are
close to the open sea."

Wargallow was on his feet at once. "Quickly! We must get after her. Ruan—your fastest ship. If the Empire snatches Guile from us, we have no power, no credibility."

Moments later they were racing for the stables, screaming for the grooms to prepare horses.

Part Two

THE FREEBOOTERS

6
Rannovic

CROMALECH STOOD in the stern of the light trader and peered through the thick coils of delta fog, trying to make out signs of the pursuit that he knew must be closing. The ships of the city of Elberon were modelled on those of the Goldenisle fleet, and some of them were renegade Empire craft, so he knew they would close down this stolen ship easily once they had sighted it again. Well, it had served its purpose and the captive crew could soon be released. Cromalech felt the presence of one of his men, but didn't turn to meet him, his eyes fixed on the waters behind.

"So?" he grunted.

"We've lost over half the men, sir."

Cromalech swore through gritted teeth. He'd known it would be a risky venture, but he'd been glad of a chance to get away from Goldenisle and do something. He didn't want Tennebriel to think he would be happy to do whatever she asked of him, but he hadn't been able to resist the pull of this mad venture. He knew that it would not have been practical to man his ship entirely with Imperial Killers, otherwise the Administrators and that pox-cursed Eukor Epta would have been immediately suspicious. Instead he had brought no more than a dozen of his best men and had privately hired out the rest of the crew from the city docks, where adventurers could always be found, men who would take on anything for a price and keep their mouths firmly shut. He had a degree of sympathy for such men. The only trouble was, they weren't the best quality fighters, not being trained to it. Oh, aye, they were good enough in a scrap, but not soldiers. And

a long way short of being Imperial Killers. Only the very
best made that level.

"How soon do we make the rendezvous?" Cromalech
asked the captain.

"Half an hour, sir."

"Let's hope it's enough," he grinned, dismissing the man.
They had crossed the sea in a swift war galley, but had used
this old tub, a leaking trader taken by force, as a means of
getting to Elberon's docks without rousing attention, and had
succeeded. His own war craft was moored down the coast,
and he'd be glad to board her again, although there were
precious few men guarding her. If he was caught out here
now by the pursuit, he doubted that he could withstand another attack. It had only been luck that had got them through
the blockade. The fog had allowed them to move almost
alongside one of the Elberon ships before it was aware of
them, and the search by port officials had gone smoothly
enough until some idiot had shown himself and the prisoners
had been found. As soon as the fighting began, Cromalech
had the small ship's catapult dragged from hiding and sent a
flaming tar-ball into the prow of the port ship. In the chaos
they had got way with their captive, but already the other
ships were closing them down. Only the fog was keeping
them off now. Where was the war galley?

Wargallow stood in the prow of the galley, and beside him,
limned in the glow of the hurricane lamps, were Sisipher and
the brooding man from the southlands, Orhung. They had all
been studying the delta since the moment they had boarded
the hastily prepared craft. Ahead of them the fog banks were
thickening, as if conspiring with the night to confuse them.
Time was dragging by now, although at first it had raced as
they made too hasty preparations for a sea voyage.

"Kirrikree is unable to find the enemy in this darkness,
not with the fog so thick," Sisipher said, and as she spoke
the huge white owl came drifting down silently and settled
on a crossbeam above them. Some of the crew members drew
back, startled, but those who knew the owl spoke quietly to
them and no one moved to disturb the bird. Wargallow
watched Kirrikree, knowing he would understand his words.

"A number of things have been puzzling me," said the

Deliverer. "In all the haste and confusion, none of us stopped to ask a simple question."

"Why has Guile been abducted?" said the girl.

He turned to her, but she was not smiling. "Can you pull things from my mind, then?"

She shook her head. "As you say, now that we have had more time to think, it was an obvious thought. Why?"

"Ruan's men reported that there were men of Empire in both parties. But why was Guile not simply killed?"

"Killed?" she echoed, surprised.

"If Quanar is dying, as rumor persists, then Guile would be the heir, if we are to believe what we have been told in the past. He must have rivals, however removed they are from the royal bloodline. But what better course of action for them than to remove his threat to their claim? Why abduct him? And why apparent rival abductors?"

Orhung, who spoke rarely and seemed more like some watchful hound, turned to them now. "Is it possible that whoever abducted him seeks to put him on the throne?"

Wargallow scowled at the sea as if he had seen an enemy there. "Then why abduct him! Elberon is his own city, its people his followers."

"Perhaps," Orhung went on, "he is to be made a puppet Emperor, and is not to be allowed support, only the false support of whoever seeks to put him on the throne."

"That is well said," came a voice behind them. Albar had joined them. "Excuse my speaking out, but I could not help overhearing Orhung's remark."

"You think there is something in it?" said Wargallow.

"There could be. I know the rulers of the Empire. Eukor Epta, if he is still the Administrative Oligarch, is as devious a man as ever trod Omara. It would not be beyond him to have arranged this. But if so, and if he gives Ottemar his backing as Emperor, it will be under his rigid control. Believe me, if there is a tyrant in Goldenisle, it is the one they call the unseen."

"And do you have a theory about the second party?" asked Sisipher.

Albar shrugged. "Eukor Epta has many enemies. None would dare to act openly against him. He covers his acts far too cleverly. And no one knows who is in his pay."

"Then it may be," said Wargallow, "that Guile has supporters who would not only welcome him as Emperor, but would oppose this Administrator."

"Very likely," nodded Albar. "But as you have already said, it poses the question of why they did not come to us for an alliance."

"A pity we didn't take any of them alive," said Wargallow, and did not see the girl shudder.

"This affair may yet work in your favor," said Orhung. "If you recapture Guile from whoever has him and return him to Elberon, you could sail to Goldenisle without fear of reprisals. They would not risk harming you if they want him. He will be your assurance of safety."

Wargallow nodded. He turned again to the sea, but the night and fog had closed in even more thickly. His thoughts were as dark as the waters he now studied. Why had the Werewatch been destroyed? There was a possible explanation: their purpose was to see that powers did not seep into Omara through some damaged part of its "wall." Had Anakhizer removed Orhung's fellows as a prelude to opening that wall?

As the night wore on they all began to fear the worst, knowing that they were out of the delta and sailing now on the open sea. As the dawn spread out behind them, it dissolved the last of the fog banks as though they had achieved their purpose. Up on the top mast a lookout shouted, pointing to the northwest.

"A ship!"

Wargallow had not left the deck, but now he shook himself alert and ran to the side of the ship. He could see nothing. Orhung was nodding, though, as if his sleepy eyes could see great distances.

"I see it. Making for the open sea. But it is not the trader we search for. It is some other vessel. A war galley."

Wargallow turned, meeting the stare of Sisipher. "It is them," she said softly.

"Are you sure?"

She nodded. "Guile is on board. They have changed craft in the night. Kirrikree saw them."

Wargallow swore and tried to see across the gentle swell

of the sea, but the ship was too far away. "Are they moving at full speed?"

"By sail," said Orhung. "Probably their captain is confident that the pursuit has been outdistanced."

"No doubt the trader has led our other ships up the coast, or away elsewhere," grunted Wargallow. "But they are not using oars?"

Albar was beside them again. "There's a strong offshore wind. An Empire galley can move swiftly enough with such help, and there would be no need to exert the crew at the oars."

"Then use ours," said Wargallow. "Maximum speed. We must catch them."

Albar nodded. Ruan had given him strict instructions: obey the Deliverer in everything. He is in command and is not to be questioned. Though Albar was stunned at the time, he had accepted without argument. It must be, he thought, this business at Xennidhum. Those who fought there are tied to each other with bonds stronger than blood. He wished he could have shared in whatever power it was, but even so, was glad that he had not been present at the war. Those he had spoken to who had returned from the place of horror said very little about it, but their eyes spoke for them, and he had heard more than one veteran shriek out in the night in the barracks.

Wargallow's instructions were adhered to. The small craft utilized both sail and oar, and Orhung later confirmed that they were closing the distance between them and the Empire galley. Wargallow instructed the captain to pilot a parallel course. "If they see us closing, they may use their own oars," he said. "When night comes, we'll put out all lights and then cut across their prow. Sisipher, will Kirrikree be our eyes?"

She nodded. "But can we outfight them?" They were alone at the rail and she spoke so that no one else heard.

"It is a gamble. Their ship may have been well manned, but I am trying to think as its commander would think. He would have taken his strongest force ashore for the abduction and left no more than a skeleton crew on board his war galley. The reports said a good many men were killed in the battle on the river. My surmise is that they're running on a weakened crew, and they'll be battle-weary. If they do see us and use oars, they won't use them for long."

She studied him for a moment, her own expression giving nothing away. "And will you have them all put to the sword? Give their blood—"

He turned on her, his eyes momentarily blazing, but to her surprise he did not snap in anger. "You do not understand me yet. I take no pleasure in this business."

"Xennidhum should have been enough for all of us."

"Of course!" he growled, aware that others might hear. "But it is not over. Perhaps your father should have cut this from me when I asked it." He held out his killing steel to her and she kept very still, seeing the dawn light dancing on the twin curves of its cutting edge. Slowly she reached out and touched the steel with her fingers. Like some sentient creature, it both fascinated and repelled her.

"I, too, have a gift," she said, so softly he almost failed to catch the words. "Not of my choosing. I had thought Xennidhum seared it from me, but it is dormant. Alive." She drew back her hand.

"The gift of telling," he said, recalling how it had used her.

"I am afraid to use it now. Ahead I see only darkness. If I look into it, I will see only pain."

"Then don't look," he told her, and his words surprised her. Once he would have insisted. Everything was to be sacrificed if need be. "Don't search out hate."

She had no answer and after a moment turned away. Albar came to report that they were closing on the war galley, keeping a parallel course.

The second night passed slowly, and though Wargallow's ship was kept in darkness, most of those on board slept only fitfully. Few of them had fought at sea before, if at all, and they guessed that there would be blood spilled before dawn. Wargallow stood beside the pilot and watched him guide the ship ever closer to the Empire galley, which still sailed with a following wind. It had not brought out its oars and did not seem aware of the smaller ship bearing down upon it. Albar commented that it was unusually poor seamanship for an Imperial craft.

An hour before dawn they went in, on course for collision until at last they were seen by a sleepy lookout. It was far too late for the Empire ship to veer away and flee. A sea battle was inevitable.

Cromalech, who had been in a deep sleep after a long drinking session celebrating with his crew, came cursing up on to the deck. His own men, his Killers, were bitter about the deaths of their companions, not caring about the rabble of a crew they had brought with them. Cromalech had resorted to plying them with drink and promises of promotion later to keep them from starting quarrels with the men of the wharfs. Now everyone was in poor shape, and no one had expected this oncoming ship. They had believed their pursuers far behind, chasing shadows.

Cromalech stood up and laughed. "This is some toy ship, come to exchange a jest!" he roared. "Duck your heads in the water and wake up to earn your pay." There were ragged cheers, but the darkness and silence of the enemy disturbed them all.

"Pirates?" asked someone.

"Too small. From Elberon. See, they've only just shipped oars," Cromalech snorted, pointing with his sword. "They'll be too exhausted to fight, if that's how they've run us down. To arms! Prepare the catapult!"

Men scrambled to obey, but already the enemy were alongside. They did not wait for the ships to lock together, instead swinging over the side of Cromalech's ship in their dozens. In the first wave, many of his hired men were cut to pieces, unprepared as they were for a fight, and Ruan had chosen his own men carefully. Even so, as the Killers stood their ground, the balance of the battle swung back.

Wargallow and Orhung joined the fray, the latter suddenly coming to life as if from a second undersleep. Although the Deliverer wondered at Orhung's lack of weapons save his strange length of metal, he soon saw the terrible power of the rod. Orhung layed about him, and each time the rod struck an opponent it glowed gently with blue radiance. Whatever was touched by it was repelled by it, men falling in agony before it as if it burned with a molten heat. As the battle wore on, the color of the rod deepened, as if it had in some way sucked from its victims their blood. Wargallow himself fought with extraordinary speed, as the Deliverers had been trained to do since childhood. From a safe vantage point,

Sisipher watched him, the speed at which he moved his killing steel faster than the eye could follow. No sword or hook got near him, all deflected by his steel, which he turned and used to pull down a dozen assailants. He fought with no expression, as did Orhung, and the girl saw Kirrikree watching from the mast head, but for once she could not share the thoughts of the huge owl.

Cromalech, backed now to his own stern, swore violently as he fought. This entire affair was turning into a disaster! Why had he listened to Tennebriel? But he grinned as he thought of her. Why? Who wouldn't consider doing her bidding? But he frowned as he fought. Beside him were loyal Killers, some of whom had told him at the outset this trip was foolish, and the looks they now exchanged told him what he had begun to suspect already: they were beaten. Another few minutes and they would all be food for the sharks. These bastards from Elberon meant to destroy them, and how they fought! A dozen of the hired hands had leapt over the side rather than face them, and more of them were scrambling up the mast for a chance of safety. Archers in the pursuit craft shot them down in spite of the pre-dawn darkness.

"Enough!" Cromalech bawled at the top of his lungs, and the sound carried across the decks of both ships. It took a while for the ringing of steel to subside and for the last scuffle to die down. All eyes turned to the Imperial Killer. It was clear now that all his men were surrounded, grouped off. To have prolonged the fight would have been to condemn all of them. The entire battle had lasted no more than fifteen minutes.

Wargallow shouldered his way through his own boarding party and mounted the low steps up to where Cromalech had been fighting in desperation. The Deliverer confronted the man of Empire, whose face was not masked with the expected anger, but a grim smile.

"This is an act of piracy," Cromalech said, loud enough for all to hear. "The Empire is very hard on pirates."

For a moment Wargallow's face was like ice, but then it softened. "Spare me the bluff, captain," he said. "It is your cargo I want, not your ship or your men's lives. Enough of them have died, along with the corpses you have left in the streets of Elberon."

Cromalech was about to retort, but he looked suddenly tired. This was defeat and it had to be faced.

"Is he alive?" said Wargallow.

Cromalech nodded.

"Then I suggest we go below. We had better talk privately."

Cromalech hid his relief. He ordered his men to throw down their arms, and although the Imperial Killers were evidently disgusted with themselves for having to submit, they did so. Wargallow and Cromalech went below deck, with two other men of Elberon at the Deliverer's back. Cromalech took them to his cabin, locking the door behind him. Sitting in a chair, his mouth gagged, was Guile.

Wargallow went to him and gently used his steel to slit the gag and the leather that bound his hands. "Well, well," grinned the Deliverer. "Such extreme lengths to go to in order to avoid Ruan's wedding."

Guile managed a weak grin, but he had been shaken by the events of the last two days. "How did—?" he began, but Wargallow gestured for him to be silent. The Deliverer turned to Cromalech, who was making a brave effort to smother his dejection. "One question. Why?"

Cromalech stiffened, and in his expression now was the hardness of the fighting man that Wargallow recognized at once. "You have won back what I took," said Cromalech without humor. "It is all you will get."

There was a knock on the door and Cromalech unlocked it. Albar and Harrudnor entered. Both were bloody, wiping sweat from their faces.

"Our apologies for disturbing you," said Harrudnor. "But we had good reason. We wanted to confirm what we had suspected. Do you know who this is?"

Wargallow shook his head. "Enlighten me."

"Cromalech. He is the First Sword of the Emperor's Imperial Killers. Answerable to Quanar Remoon and no one else."

"How ridiculous!" snorted Cromalech.

But Guile was nodding. "It's rather pointless denying it, Cromalech. Too many of us lived in Goldenisle before we fled. I recall you and other men on this ship. They are also members of the Emperor's personal guard."

"And what of the other party?" said Wargallow. "Those who first took Guile? The men of Empire that you, Cromalech, had to kill to get what you sailed to Elberon for."

"I've no idea," said the Killer. "They stood in my way."

"But you know they were men of Empire?" said Wargallow.

It looked as though Cromalech would remain tight-lipped, but he shrugged and gave a wry smile. "I did not know it. They wore no special harness. I had assumed them to be men of your city. My time was short."

"In whose name did you take Guile?"

Cromalech chuckled. "Be content with him. You'll learn no more from me. Or my men. None of them know why I abducted Ottemar Remoon, or Guile as you prefer to call him. I had my reasons, but it was not necessary for me to share them. So spare my men any torture."

Albar nodded discreetly to Wargallow and the Deliverer knew that Cromalech had spoken the truth. He knew also that nothing would get the rest of it from him; probably even the cells of the Direkeep contained nothing that would persuade Cromalech to give up his secrets.

Another pounding on the door alerted them, and this time a breathless sailor was admitted. "Your pardon," he blurted, "but there are ships closing fast. The captain has made preparations to flee, but fears we would be overhauled."

"Ships of Empire?" said Albar.

The man shook his head. "The captain fears they may be freebooters. They show no flag."

Cromalech's face had changed at once. Wargallow had seen the concern at the mention of Empire ships dissolve when freebooters had been spoken of. It seemed that Cromalech was now attempting to cover a smile. "Freebooters?" he said. "Threatening an Empire ship? They are not usually so forward with our war galleys."

Wargallow led the way to the deck, and no one deterred Cromalech from joining him. They saw the three sleek pirate vessels at once, coming from the north, oars flashing as the dawn rose higher. Wargallow's men were ready to flee or fight, waiting for the word.

Wargallow could see the futility of flight. "We hold our

position," he said. He turned to Cromalech. "I presume these pirates are a nuisance to your traders?"

"Indeed. These eastern waters are usually safe enough, but we rarely send merchantmen out unescorted to the north."

"Do they attack warships?"

Cromalech was grinning. "There are three of them. And two of us. You seem to me to be a fighting man. Are those not favorable odds?"

Wargallow ignored the taunt. "Then it's a fight," he breathed.

"Perhaps," said Cromalech. "They have us at their mercy, but they have nothing to gain from us. I suspect that it is merely curiosity that has brought them. Why not let them make the first hostile move?"

Instantly Wargallow was on his guard. He brought his killing steel up so quickly that Cromalech could not avoid it as it rested against his unprotected throat.

"If these are your lackeys, you are already dead," Wargallow told him. He turned to Albar. "Tell Guile to keep out of sight. Get all the prisoners below. If they show any sign of dissent, kill them swiftly. Is that clear!"

"Perfectly," said Albar.

Cromalech's throat constricted, but he managed to speak. "You should be an Empire man. But these pirates are no allies of mine."

Wargallow did not answer, watching the ships move in. Two broke away and circled the locked Empire ship and Wargallow's vessel, while the third hove to fifty yards away. Her decks were crowded with men, all armed and seemingly eager to do battle. One of them swung up on to the ship's rail and cupped his hands to his mouth.

"Greetings men of the Empire!" the man called. "My captain requests that a party be allowed to come aboard. You seem to be in distress."

Albar turned to Wargallow, as did most of his men. They were all armed for a fight, certain that there would be one.

Wargallow raised his own voice, but he kept Cromalech close to him, the killing steel pressed now to his back. "You may send three men!" he called. He had no wish to provoke a fight, knowing that the outcome would go against him, but he had to know what the freebooters wanted, if anything.

After a pause and consultation, the pirate called back. "Very well. Three men only. We'll be pleased to visit you."

"No doubt," grunted Cromalech. "We're completely out-maneuvered. They could finish us with fire arrows alone from their position. It seems your victory was short-lived."

"We'll see," said Wargallow, watching as a boat was lowered. "If, as you say, it is mere curiosity that brings them, there would be no point in a fight." He saw the spokesman for the pirates and two other men climb down into the boat and in a moment they were rowing across the calm water to the side of the Empire ship. Ropes were dropped to them at Wargallow's command and they clambered up, agile as monkeys.

The man who had hailed Wargallow was first aboard, seemingly without fear, his face beaming as if he was openly delighted about something. His hair was bright red, tumbling to his shoulders in thick waves, and his chest was bare, scarred in more than one place. He bore his scars like jewelry. Round his waist was a thick belt and thrust into this was a trio of short swords.

"Gondobar greets you," he grinned, turning this way and that to study the crew before him with unconcealed arrogance. Wargallow knew the man was no fool, but he played the part cleverly.

The Deliverer had loosened Cromalech, though he had whispered to him that he would be the first to die if there was treachery. He had also told his crew to lower their arms but to be ready.

"You are not Gondobar," Cromalech told the pirate bluntly.

The latter guffawed. "I? No! I am Rannovic. But Gondobar is here, on that ship. He regrets that he could not come aboard personally."

"And who is Gondobar?" said Wargallow coldly.

"You are evidently not familiar with these waters," chuckled Rannovic. He eyed Wargallow's clothes with ill-concealed puzzlement. "Gondobar, so to speak, rules them."

Cromalech snorted. "Rules them, does he?" His usual humor had been replaced now by something close to annoyance. "I think the Emperor would have something to say about such a claim."

"The mad Remoon?" said Rannovic, aware that he could insult the Emperor with such a show of strength around him. "Perhaps. But I rather think this is not the time to dispute the matter. We watched your little affray from some distance. While we noted that this is an Empire ship, though poorly manned, we were a little unsure about the other craft? What port is it out of?"

Wargallow felt a hint of unease at the reference to the lack of numbers but he remained outwardly calm. "Elberon," he told Rannovic. "But perhaps you are not familiar with the eastern coast?"

Rannovic laughed. "Well said! But we do know of this city. Gondobar has long arms, and sees far. Are you a satellite state of the Empire? Do you pay tribute? Or are you, if you'll pardon the expression, pirates?"

"Elberon is not part of the Empire," said Wargallow.

"We had thought not, having seen the exchange of earlier. We were impressed by the efficiency of the attack. Particularly in view of the fact that this ship is crewed by the Emperor's own Imperial Killers, is that not so, Cromalech?"

The Killer scowled, his fists whitening at the knuckles where he bunched them, but he did not move or speak.

"Cromalech," repeated Rannovic. "First Sword of the Emperor's guard. A long way from home. And taken like a baby in a bath! Gondobar will be highly intrigued to know that you are here. And with so few men."

Wargallow could sense the fury growing in Cromalech. The man's dignity had already taken a blow; clearly he was no friend of the pirate, who revelled in his disgrace. "You'll forgive me, Rannovic," said the Deliverer, "if I ask you what your business with us might be?"

Rannovic turned to him, secure in his advantage. "You have a very delicate way of putting things, my friend. Business? To be honest, Gondobar is not much of a man for bargaining." The other pirates grinned at this. "Often he merely takes the things he wants. However, today he is sailing as much for pleasure as anything, being happiest when he is in open waters. But it may be that you have something that would interest him?"

Wargallow's eyes narrowed, his killing steel never more ready to strike. "Cargo? We travel very lightly, for speed."

"Yes, of course. Being warships both, although, as we have noted, also being undercrewed. There was a dispute?"

"Territorial," said Cromalech at once. "As Wargallow said, his city is not part of the Empire. The Emperor sent me to spy on it."

Rannovic's brows raised theatrically. "Spy? His First Sword? Hardly an honor, Cromalech. Had you upset him?"

"The Emperor is a man of strange moods."

Rannovic laughed, showing his brilliant teeth. "A lunatic, yes! So, you found that you had poked your head into a bee-hive, eh?"

Cromalech forced himself to smile. "Elberon is no village."

"And what are your plans?" Rannovic asked of Wargallow. "I take it you intend to hang this unfortunate soldier from the top of his own mast?"

"Is that how Gondobar deals with captive Empire men?" Wargallow replied.

Rannovic scowled, then laughed again. "But we wouldn't dare attack an Empire warship!"

"Ah, no," said Wargallow. "You would prefer a fat merchantman."

Rannovic studied him, an odd look on his face. "I think you are a man that Gondobar would understand, Wargallow."

"I am sure that when your ruler and I meet, as we surely must in time, we will have things to discuss. For the moment, I doubt it. As you see, there is very little scope for, shall we say, business."

Rannovic nodded slowly. "I take your meaning. Well put. But I think you may underestimate the situation."

Wargallow felt himself tensing; he was not out of this trap yet. "Indeed?"

"What you do with your captives is your affair, and Gondobar has no wish to interfere. Mind you, Cromalech might fetch a good price if the right people were approached."

"You are mistaken," growled the Killer. "I would be of no value, alive or dead. No one in Goldenisle would pay you for me."

Rannovic shrugged. "In which case your loyalty to the Emperor seems badly misplaced. But that does not concern me."

A good point, though, mused Wargallow. He turned to Rannovic's ship. "There is something else?"

"Well, the ship of Empire. Were you intending to sink it, or take it back with you? It would seem imprudent of you to use an Empire warship for your own purposes. It would brand you as pirates. Instead of spy ships visiting you, there would be a war fleet."

Wargallow could see precisely what the pirate was leading to. Inwardly he was pleased for it was the escape he had been looking for. "I had intended to sink the ship, naturally," he lied. "But it occurs to me that Gondobar might have a use for it himself. Presumably as, shall we say, a man in dispute with the Empire, it would not matter to him that he had utilized an Empire ship?"

Rannovic made a slight bow. "How clearly you perceive things! Even so. Gondobar would make good use of this craft, and it would be a crime to send such a vessel to the deeps."

"Then you may tell Gondobar that the ship is his."

Rannovic grinned. "Excellent." He paused, again lifting his brows.

"For my part," said Wargallow, "I will make swift return to Elberon."

"And in exchange? For this ship?" said Rannovic.

Wargallow sensed that he had not yet won free of the man. Something was not out in the open. He smiled. "I think for now your master's blessing would be quite sufficient."

Rannovic considered, then nodded, laughing a little too artificially. "It will be arranged."

"I will transfer the prisoners at once."

"There is one other point."

Wargallow felt his men tensing now. This was becoming too easy, not what they would have expected from the freebooters, who gave nothing away.

"Gondobar did ask me to look over your craft. Both of them, that is. I'm sure you understand. I have no doubt that I'll not find caskets of precious jewels in your hold, but Gondobar is rather particular about these matters. I admit that it would seem ill-mannered in view of your making a gift of Cromalech's ship, but—"

"I understand perfectly," nodded Wargallow, covering his fury. But he could not afford to deny the pirates anything.

One wrong word and they would set upon them, he knew it, even if it meant that Rannovic would be the first to die. "I will escort you myself."

Wargallow left Cromalech with Albar and Harrudnor. The remainder of the captured Empire men were transferred to Wargallow's ship and taken down into the hold, where they were temporarily chained. Wargallow, with other men at his back, took Rannovic and his two burly companions on a brief tour of Cromalech's ship. There was little to see, and no booty other than additional weapons and food, but the pirates had expected no more. Wargallow felt sure that they looked for nothing particular and were on no special mission.

They paid far more attention to Wargallow's craft, Rannovic acting out his politeness in a manner that would have, on another day, been amusing. Wargallow, however, was only too aware of the tightrope which he walked. The pirates were satisfied that there was nothing on board the ship worth taking, although Rannovic had noticed that there was enough food here for a considerable voyage. Perhaps, he thought, the ship was not merely a pursuit craft, but a patrol craft. The men of Elberon were no fools.

They came to the door of the cabin in which Guile had been hidden, and Wargallow opened it without knocking. Word had already been sent to Guile of events on deck, so that when the pirates entered, he was sitting at a table, studying some charts. Beside him stood Sisipher, attempting to look calm, although her anxiety was plain enough.

Rannovic eyed her frankly and with relish. He bowed low. "I must apologize for this intrusion," he said.

"This is Guile," said Wargallow. "His interest in maps and the geography of Omara is fabled in Elberon. And with him is Sisipher."

"His bride?" said Rannovic with interest.

She put her arm on Guile's shoulder. "Yes."

"I am mortified to hear it," said Rannovic, beaming. "You would have been a far greater treasure than both ships together." He turned to Wargallow. "I will go back to Gondobar at once and we will leave you in peace. We will, of course, meet again."

"I trust so," said Wargallow as he closed the door on

THRONE OF FOOLS   91

Guile and Sisipher. "I would like to think we could do a great deal of business in the future."

Rannovic grinned. "Oh yes. That sounds most favorable."

A few minutes later, watching Rannovic and his two men rowing back to Gondobar's ship, Wargallow and Harrudnor glanced at each other. "Can we trust them?" said Wargallow.

"Possibly. They'll be glad of Cromalech's ship. They use such craft. A good many Empire men have fled to Gondobar, just as they have to Elberon. In fact, I had a feeling that one of Rannovic's men was an Empire man once."

"You are sure?"

"As you know, I served in Goldenisle two years ago, in the army. He seemed to be staring at me at first, but he looked away. I may be wrong. So many faces. It is no matter. It is common enough for men to leave Goldenisle these days, with Quanar Remoon still in power."

Wargallow nodded, but Harrudnor's words hung between them for long minutes, like a veiled threat.

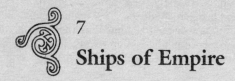

7

Ships of Empire

WHILE THE MEN of Gondobar took charge of the ship of Empire and prepared to leave, Wargallow went below the deck of his own ship to look for Cromalech. The Imperial Killer sat apart from his men, all of whom had been chained: the smell of fear was on many of them as they thought it only a matter of minutes before they would be put to the sword.

"They're taking your ship," Wargallow told Cromalech.

"And what do you intend to do with us?"

In the dim light Wargallow looked down at his prisoner, who had lost his humor. There was little fight left in him either, although the anger was close to the surface. "I see no use in killing you, although it may be better if the freebooters think that is what we'll do. No, I would prefer to take you with us to Goldenisle."

Even in the shadows, Wargallow could see the man's surprise. "Goldenisle? Is that where you are bound?"

"It is."

"Is this the wish of Ottemar? Does he assume that he can sail to the throne and take it as easily as that?"

"He is the Heir, is he not?"

Cromalech caught himself. What purpose did these people serve? They supported Ottemar, of course. But they could not seriously intend to make a play for the throne so openly. "Why, yes."

"But he has enemies," said Wargallow softly.

"No doubt."

"Two parties sought to abduct him. One of them, at least, was his enemy."

"A reasonable deduction," Cromalech grinned.

"You still have no wish to clarify your position? That would suggest you are his enemy."

But Cromalech would not answer and studied the darkness. There came a commotion on the deck above, and Wargallow was quick to go and see what was transpiring. A number of his men were gathered around Albar, who held in one hand an arrow, unrolling from it a thin scroll of parchment.

"Fired across the water at us by the pirates," he explained.

"What does it say?"

Albar began to read it but paled, handing it over to Wargallow, who was aware that the entire crew were watching him. The Deliverer scanned it hastily, cursed, then went below deck once more. Men crowded round Albar, demanding to know the worst.

He quietened them. "Our friend, Rannovic. One of his men recognized Ottemar. They have demanded that we release him to them. With one other."

"The Deliverer?"

"The girl."

Wargallow confronted Cromalech again. "Our troubles with these pirates are not over yet. I assumed I'd bought them off with your war galley, but not so. They want the Heir."

Cromalech looked puzzled. "Do they know him?"

"Evidently."

Cromalech considered. "Then you have a very simple choice, captain. Either you give them what they want and, possibly, sail away in peace, or you refuse them and they kill us all and take him anyway. It is as simple as that, believe me."

"And if I refuse them?"

Cromalech frowned. "I've told you. They'll kill us all."

"And if I release you and your men, will you fight beside us?"

Cromalech considered, aware of the eyes in the dark. "I am sure we would," he said at last. "But it would only detain the inevitable. We are vastly outnumbered and surrounded. We could all die gloriously and perhaps eliminate a good many of the pirates before we perished, but we would die. They are no rabble, captain. These are Hammavars. If that

is Gondobar out there, his men will be very good. Yes, I'll
stand beside you, if that's your decision. But it will change
nothing.''

"You would rather relinquish the Heir than fight?''

"I would rather live. A choice I have made already today.
There will be other days, other battles. I may not be outnumbered next time.''

"And what of the Heir? His safety means nothing to you?''

Cromalech grinned. "Ah, you are persistent. I refuse to
say anymore about my loyalties. But this much is clear, the
pirates have already won him. You cannot prevent that, unless
you kill him. But I would advise against that. *I* do not want
him dead, but you must already know that.''

"What will these pirates do?''

"Ottemar is far too valuable for them to kill. I believe they
will treat him well. They know who he is and what he may
become. If he were to become Emperor, they would want
concessions. I imagine that Gondobar would want full recognition for the Hammavars as an independent state, with
proper territorial rights. With Ottemar as his hostage, he
might secure such things. Killing him would be utterly pointless. There would always be another Emperor. And the Empire would bend all its power to the destruction of the
Hammavars.''

Wargallow had been listening with interest. At the end, he
nodded. "What you say holds water. And it confirms one
thing. There must be strong support for Ottemar in Goldenisle.'' He turned and went back above before the Killer could
respond. Because of this he did not see the grim smile on
the latter's face. Cromalech was thinking that Gondobar would
never relinquish Ottemar. He would promise the world, but
with the Heir in his grasp he could manipulate the Empire
into concessions. Wargallow could have no idea of the history
of the Hammavars and their place in the order of things. So
in time, with Ottemar their prisoner, Tennebriel would have
to be made Empress. She could hardly marry a man languish-
ing in a remote pirate stronghold! Which is what Eukor Epta
is probably planning, he thought. So, this was working out
far better than it was an hour ago. Wargallow, in spite of his
qualities as a fighting man, would not risk the death of all
here.

At that moment, Wargallow was with Guile and Sisipher. He held out the written message. "You were recognized," he told Guile.

"It seems I'm a popular man," said Guile. "You cannot fight, of course. They'll destroy everyone. I won't permit that."

Wargallow's lips curled in a brief smile. "You won't permit it? You have assumed command, then?"

Guile chuckled, though he felt his stomach clenching with fresh fear at his predicament. "I am the Heir. It is, regrettably, the misfortune of heirs to have men lay down their lives for them, but it would be worthless for you all to perish now. The pirates won't kill me."

"Cromalech doesn't think so." Wargallow repeated the Killer's words.

"Then I must go. But Sisipher stays with you."

"I agree," said Wargallow, looking hard at the girl.

Her anger was plain. "Spare me your gallantry! This Rannovic has already made up his mind about me. He wants me, probably as much as his leader wants Guile. I've no more wish to have anyone's blood on my head than you have. We've both seen enough of that."

"Guile would be reasonably safe," said Wargallow. "But you would not. These men—"

"I know what they are," she said quietly. "But I must take my chances. It is hardly how I would wish things, but I have no choice."

"They know you aren't my wife," Guile said, trying to lighten the mood.

"That is one pretense we can forget at once."

"There would be advantages in having you together," said Wargallow. "What of Kirrikree?"

Sisipher nodded. "He will follow. It won't be an easy flight for him, but not beyond him. He will be your eyes."

"It still seems—" Wargallow searched for a word. "Wrong. Wrong to give you to them."

"Unfeeling?" suggested Guile.

Wargallow nodded. "I am prepared to argue with the pirates."

She studied him for a moment, surprised by his words, for in the past he had shown himself to be ruthless, scorning sentiment. "No. We must both go. These pirates will not harm me, though it is easily read in their minds."

"You would be defenseless!" objected Guile.

She shook her head. "My gift tells me otherwise." She could see their questions coming, their probing of those buried powers, that inner sight. "Believe me. Any evil that I have felt ahead of me does not come from Gondobar and his men. I will go. Ironically it will spare bloodshed if I do. And you, Wargallow, must go on to Goldenisle. Let Orhung talk to them and explain about Xennidhum. We will have to talk to Gondobar. He may not care, but we have to tell him what we know."

Wargallow grunted. "This bid to unite Omarans already collapses—"

"You'll have to be more positive than that!" Guile laughed, but he could not keep the strain from his voice.

Even so, Wargallow managed a wry grin. "From you, that is odd advice. But I accept it."

"Then prepare a boat for us," said Sisipher. "They will not harm me."

Soon afterward it was done. Wargallow and his men watched the two figures step from the small boat to the rope ladder that had been dropped from Gondobar's ship, and Rannovic was there to help them aboard, gloating. He gave Wargallow an insolent wave, then all of them disappeared from sight. A few minutes later all three pirate vessels began to leave, and with them went Cromalech's sleek ship of Empire.

Orhung placed himself beside Wargallow. "This is not what you would have wished?" he said in a voice that seemed to come from far away, as if he spoke with reluctance or difficulty.

"No. This voyage is beset with the unexpected. Sisipher may have the ability to see ahead and around certain obstacles, but for the rest of us, planning is complicated. I have no idea how we will be received in Goldenisle. We have not prepared as we should have. But it may be that much will depend on you and the power of your words."

"Then you have decided? We go there now?"

Wargallow nodded. "I see no other course."

"And Cromalech?"

"I must seek to break him before we arrive, strong as he is. I have no choice. If he is an enemy, I must know it." But for once the Deliverer wondered about his own skills in such matters.

They stood together in eloquent silence, watching the pirate ships veer away to the north, while their own course took them ever westward. Wargallow also took stock of the Created, the man who was not a man. Why had his kind been annihilated? What did this Anakhizer want? There was power in Orhung, it was clear, and the girl had sensed it, responded to it. Was he, like Korbillian before him, a tool of great powers? Yet he was dormant, almost as if the life within him smoldered, in danger of going out altogether. Wargallow did not relish the idea of having such a man as a key player in his plans.

Orhung himself fought with an inner compulsion to slip deeper into the lethargy that constantly drew him. It was as though his created body had never adjusted to its premature and traumatic awakening. Yet the goal that his makers had fashioned for him, the rigid will to destroy evil from beyond his world, shone through his darkness like a beacon, drawing him irresistibly. This will, like a hunger, was slowly consuming his lethargy, dominating his thoughts. But even now he felt the undercurrents of another inner conflict, though he could not yet comprehend it fully. It was a conflict aggravated by this man Wargallow, whose own purpose was fixed, and whose companions were hardly less determined to succeed. Perhaps, Orhung considered, their human will was tempered by their doubts, their uncertainty of success. It was this, he imagined, that made them human. He himself had not had such doubts built into him, which placed him apart from them, even Wargallow. And it was this apartness that had seeded his unease with himself, though none who studied him would have known it.

After a long time at the rail, Orhung stiffened and stretched out like a hound who has the scent of something. He pointed to the horizon ahead of them.

"There are ships. Many of them. Coming this way."

"From Goldenisle?" said Wargallow. "They must be." Before Orhung could answer, he swung away and clambered down below deck.

Cromalech had been sitting in silence, almost asleep. He gazed now at Wargallow, no hint of fear on his face. Wargallow undid the man's wrists and motioned him to go above. Cromalech did so, and in a moment found himself beside the strange hairless being who had fought so grimly with the bar of steel. Orhung confirmed that a dozen warships were on the western horizon. "Ships of Empire," he added.

This had taken Cromalech by surprise, and although he hid it well, Wargallow had seen enough to realize. "Now," said the Deliverer. "Do I give you and your men to the sea before these ships arrive, or do you speak to them on our behalf?"

Cromalech felt trapped. He had guessed that these would be Fennobar's ships, come, no doubt, to find out what had happened to the ship that had carried his would-be abductors to Elberon. If Fennobar found out that Cromalech had killed his men and abducted the Heir himself, it would be disastrous, for Fennobar was Eukor Epta's man. *Curse this entire business! I should have refused Tennebriel.*

"You will have to tell me," he said, as calmly as he could, "exactly what you want in Goldenisle. I serve the Empire. You, it seems, should be enemies."

Wargallow nodded. "You shall hear our cause. We are not enemies. We are not necessarily sworn to put Guile on your throne. There are other matters we have to attend to which transcend even that. Do you know of Xennidhum?"

Something in the way this strange man spoke the name sent a cold shudder through Cromalech, as if for a brief second he had stared into the face of something terrible. "Were you there?" he said, his voice very low.

"I was." And Wargallow spoke to him then of Korbillian and of power, and of the crusade into the eastern wilderness of Omara. By the time he had finished, the ships of Empire had reduced the distance between themselves and the solitary ship drastically; they were now no more than a few miles off.

"We had thought our war to be over," Wargallow ended. "Until Orhung came to us. When you have heard him out, you will know we were wrong."

Cromalech listened intently to the words of the man of the Werewatch, knowing that neither of these men was insane or creating some bizarre fantasy with which to confuse and mislead him. Too many rumors had slipped across the ocean, too many men went in fear of mythical Xennidhum. So the place was real! And if what these men had said were true, Omara had much to fear.

"Our cause," said Wargallow, "is precisely that of Korbillian. His legacy to us. Unity. A fine word, and one which falls easily from the lips of those in power. An ideal, perhaps. But we face an enemy who will use as his greatest weapon, disunity. If he can split Goldenisle, he will go on to split Omara, be sure of it."

Cromalech watched the ships drawing to within a mile. "You would make a fine Administrator yourself," he told Wargallow.

"Quickly—you must decide. If you are to hamper us—"

"No," Cromalech grinned. "But you will understand my caution. And you will meet more stubborn men than me in Goldenisle. And more, you will learn, as you have already begun to guess, that Goldenisle has internal problems of its own."

"Such as the succession."

"Quite so. As you know, two parties sought Ottemar, and for opposite reasons. There is no time for me to speak of them now, not with these ships about to hail us. But I will not hinder you, Wargallow."

"Will you speak for us? We need an audience."

"Very well. But let there be an understanding between us. Mutual trust."

Wargallow sensed that this was to be the grounding for a bargain, but he nodded. "I accept that. Name your terms."

Cromalech nodded at the ships. "These are the ships of Fennobar. He is the commander of the armies and the fleet, the successor to your friend, Morric Elberon. Be warned, Fennobar detested Elberon. Pure jealousy, and secretly he recognizes that he is not the man Elberon was. Play down your independence, your friendship with Elberon, if you can. Now, I believe these men were behind the other abduction of Ottemar. It would be, shall I say, embarrassing for me if they knew that *I* had snatched Ottemar from their men."

"Why did they abduct him?"

"It is a complicated story. In time I will tell it—"

"Very well. Go on."

"Let us tell them that I was sent by Quanar Remoon, my master, to whom I am directly responsible, to escort a certain party from Elberon to Goldenisle. Namely, yourselves. Do not mention the Heir. If they speak of him, say that he is in Elberon. But I am certain they will not even mention him. They may have assumed that the ship sent to abduct him was destroyed and its men killed, but they will not want to admit having sent such a ship to Elberon, which would be tantamount to an act of war. I will tell my men of your intentions. There are evident scenes of battle here, and more than a few wounded, so I further suggest we claim to have had a fierce battle with freebooters, whom we beat off. Whoever commands these ships will not dare to question my right as First Sword of the Emperor to escort you to Goldenisle."

"And when we are there?" prompted Wargallow. "From what I hear of Quanar Remoon, we would be ill advised to state our case to him."

"That is true. He is ill and will not live for very long."

"So to whom will you take us?"

"I will place you under guard. For your own protection. There are those in Goldenisle who would wish you disposed of very swiftly if they knew you were from Elberon."

"Eukor Epta?"

"Possibly." He pointed. "They are coming."

"I agree to your suggestions. Go below and prepare your men."

When the longboat of the leading Empire war galley came alongside, Cromalech was ready to meet it. He and Wargallow had quickly refined their story and passed it on to the two crews. Cromalech's men were loyal to him, even his paid hands, and would not question his decisions, and Wargallow found it interesting that he should be at odds in some way with the army and navy of Empire. Did it mean that the latter did not support Guile?

The man who came aboard from the longboat was Otric Hamal, one of Fennobar's closest aides and a high ranking captain in the Empire fleet. Cromalech knew him as a disciplinarian, a loyal and reliable young man of war. He would be in Fennobar's confidence and would have to be steered well clear of the truth if he, Cromalech, were to come through this business without embarrassment.

Otric bowed, knowing that although his position in the navy put him outside the Imperial Killers, Cromalech's rank as First Sword had to be respected.

"It is a relief to meet you," Cromalech told him. "As you will have noted, we have not had an easy passage."

"A battle?" said Otric, his eyes scanning the ship like a young eagle's. He had a thin body, and did not look much of a fighting man, but he had spent many hard months in the Empire training grounds. No man made his position without a full testing.

"Freebooters. They came upon us at night, before dawn, and we would have gone to the deeps had it not been for the timely intervention of these men from the new city of Elberon."

Otric's eyes narrowed at that and he looked closely at Wargallow and Orhung, who stood beside Cromalech. "Elberon? Then this is also a timely meeting. My lord Fennobar sent us to find the city."

"Oh, for what reason?" said Cromalech casually.

"It was rumored that Morric Elberon was there. As our former Commander of the Armies—"

"Former?" said Wargallow. "Has he been relieved of his post?"

The question momentarily disarmed Otric. "Who is this man?" he said to Cromalech, making no attempt to conceal his distaste.

Cromalech introduced Wargallow and Orhung as citizens of the city of Elberon. "I had been sent to escort them and some of their men to our own city."

Otric's jaw tightened. "Under whose instructions?"

Cromalech stared at him until the younger man looked away. "As First Sword," he said sharply, "I act on the instructions of the Emperor. I should hope you are aware of that."

"Your pardon," Otric bowed, conscious of the fact that he was outranked.

"Why should Fennobar send so many ships to look for Morric Elberon?"

"We had news that he was dead. Killed in some far war."

"He was," nodded Cromalech. "The new city was named after him in his honor. These men were his allies. It has now come to light that he fought the enemies of the Emperor deep in the heart of the eastern continent. Enemies that the Emperor knew little about. We are in debt to these men.'' Cromalech said this in such a way that there was no room for argument.

Otric again bowed. ''I see. Then you must come aboard my ship and give me this news in full. Fennobar must have a report with all speed.''

''You mean to return to Goldenisle?''

''Since we have found you and since Morric Elberon is dead, it would seem best. How many of his men survived this war?''

''Far less than died in it,'' said Wargallow. ''But enough to help settle the new city, with other men of the eastern lands.''

''And who rules this new city?'' said Otric, his eyes locking with those of the Deliverer.

''It has no king, although there are a number of nations in the east who do have their own monarchs. Elberon is ruled by a military commander. Ruan Dubhnor.''

Otric's surprise was plain. ''Indeed? A man of Morric Elberon's command, as I recall. A man of Empire. Does he rule this city in the Emperor's name?''

''That,'' cut in Wargallow, before anyone else could speak, ''is what I am travelling to Goldenisle to discuss, among other things.''

''Then you are the commander's Ambassador?''

''Just so.''

''Then this is indeed a fortuitous meeting. I confess we had been anticipating conflict. We thought perhaps Morric Elberon was a prisoner in your city.''

Wargallow shook his head. ''On the contrary, there are no prisoners in our city.''

Whether Otric took the point, they could not tell. He bowed and led the way to his longboat. Wargallow had already decided that only Orhung need accompany him and Cromalech across the water to Otric's war galley. They sat beside the First Sword in silence, and it was impossible to tell what the latter was thinking. Wargallow had noticed, however, the evident tension between Cromalech and Otric. They held each other in contempt, that much was quite obvious.

Once in Otric's cabin, they sat around a chart table and Otric offered wine, though none was inclined to drink. "Tell me more about your mission," he said to Wargallow.

"With respect," said Cromalech, "I think it would be best if the Ambassador was spared the effort of having to repeat his duties to every man of Empire he meets. He has already told me, in some detail, of the east and the troubles there. When we reach Goldenisle, I will escort him to the palace, where he is expected. I'm quite certain, Otric, that before very long a full council will be called by the Administrators in the Hall of the Hundred. Then everyone shall hear of the east."

Otric's mouth tensed into a thin line as he controlled his anger at this rebuff. It had also confirmed for him that Cromalech had already won the easterner's confidence. Why had Cromalech really been in the east in the first place? The thought hit him then like a blow—was *he* the one who had foiled the abduction attempt? If so, where was Ottemar Remoon? Could he be on the eastern ship that had now become part of the returning fleet? This possibility gave Otric a sudden rush of pleasure. It must be so! And this Simon Wargallow, who was he? A traitor to the men of Elberon? And the silent man with him, the one who seemed to be drugged, who was he? Otric kept his smugness well concealed. Fennobar sent me to take Ottemar by force, and yet not a sword need be drawn. He must be *here!*

"Tell me," said Otric, relaxing, "about the freebooters. They are due for a lesson, I think. The northern waters are becoming far too hazardous with the Hammavars running amok there."

"I was on my way to Elberon," said Cromalech, "when they came on us from the northeast. There were three of them, and although we were at full strength, we were hard put to fend them off. They evidently thought that one Empire ship, albeit a war galley, would be easy meat. Ironically they had recently plundered another Empire ship, and a war galley at that."

Otric's face clouded and he sat forward. "What ship?"

"As we fought, they boasted that a ship of Empire, sailing alone, had recently been sunk by them. From what I could gather, it was a ship of the navy. Perhaps it was one you

knew of?'' Cromalech added calmly. Beside him, Wargallow
sat as immobile as Orhung, but he admired the way in which
Cromalech twisted the knife in Otric's thoughts.

Otric sat back. How best to bluff this out? The ship that
had first been sent to abduct Ottemar had been harassed out
of Elberon and had not been sunk by pirates, but had found
its way to the following fleet. Even now it was being escorted
back to Goldenisle. Why had Cromalech so obviously lied
about it? To cover his own guilt? ''A lone ship, you say?
Well, as you know, Fennobar often sends out scout craft. It
seems to me that the freebooters overreach themselves. Destroyed it! They are not usually so indiscreet.''

''They grow bolder,'' said Cromalech. He had seen Otric's
confusion, guessing that the ship had limped back to the fleet,
and glad of the news. ''They knew we had nothing worth
taking, but it was the ship they were after. My ship! And they
may have stolen it had not the ship of Elberon come upon us
before dawn. Together we beat the freebooters off.''

''But your ship—''

''Returned to Elberon,'' said Wargallow, thinking perhaps
Cromalech would not have such a ready answer. ''It was in
no state to cross the sea. Some of my own men were spared.
It will be refitted and returned in due course.''

Otric nodded. This man was going to be dangerous, he
could see that. Cromalech himself was a difficult opponent,
just as Fennobar had warned. Almost as difficult as Eukor
Epta. ''Well,'' he said, as good naturedly as he could. ''Perhaps you would prefer a cabin here?''

''That will not be necessary,'' said Cromalech. ''I will
remain with the Ambassador, although we would be glad of
an escort.''

''You shall have it, of course,'' said Otric. He excused
himself and left them for a while, saying that he would arrange the matter of the return to Goldenisle at once.

Wargallow noted that Cromalech seemed to be enjoying
himself, though he could not be sure why. His failure to
abduct Guile had not come as such a blow to him, not now
that the pirates had the Heir.

''I expect,'' said Cromalech, with a chuckle, ''that Fennobar's original ship has already blundered into this fleet.
Otric can do nothing about it. If he harms either of us, he

knows there would be repercussions. Fennobar would love to question me, but protocol does not allow him that power. I am Quanar's man. And we are no good to anyone if we are dead!''

"You were right about him avoiding the issue of the Heir.''

Cromalech laughed again. "A delightful irony! He almost certainly thinks that you and I are allied in some scheme to make Ottemar Emperor as soon as Quanar dies, and are thus hiding him.''

"Otric is Fennobar's man?''

"Aye, down to his bones! Very loyal, so I respect him for that.''

"And Fennobar?''

Cromalech chuckled and slapped Wargallow on the shoulder. "Now, Ambassador, if I told you that, you might be able to work out my own interests. And I'm not ready to provide you with that information just yet.''

"Yet you know why I am here.''

"I know what you have told me.''

"You do not believe Orhung? Or in what I have said of Xennidhum?''

"I only know what you have said. I am a cautious man.''

Wargallow gave it some thought. It was no more than he could expect. Cromalech would hardly take everything at face value. "A good deal hinges on the Heir.''

"You think so?''

"I know that Goldenisle will be the key to the war that is coming. Just as the men of the east had to unite to defeat the power of Xennidhum, so must Goldenisle strengthen itself. The men of Elberon are willing to fight beside the men of Empire. I would never have believed my own people, the Deliverers, could fight beside men of Empire, Earthwrought and others. But so great was the threat, we had to. It can be done again. But your Empire must be strong, not divided.''

"And you think Ottemar Remoon can unite it?''

"Do you, Cromalech? Will your people rally to him? Or has Eukor Epta other plans?''

Cromalech said nothing for a moment. Wargallow did seem set on the course he had outlined. "Unity? Yes, I would see Goldenisle united. It has been foundering for a long time, troubled by the ceaseless squabbles of its petty rulers. A strong Emperor could yet change things. And who would not be glad to serve a strong ruler instead of the madman who now sits upon the throne? Soon he will be dead.''

''Who will succeed him?''

''Perhaps the Hammavars will have a say in that. After all, they have the Heir.''

Wargallow frowned. ''We have to get him back.''

Cromalech grinned. ''I'm not one to run from a challenge.''

8
Gondobar

GONDOBAR'S SHIP WAS STRIPPED of everything but the essentials for a voyage, and although the deck had been polished clean, it had a lean, menacing look, the look of a craft prepared for war. As Guile and Sisipher stepped aboard, they saw the grinning faces of the freebooters, weather-beaten faces, the faces of men used to a hard life, enduring far more vicissitudes than most other men. All were armed, all like coiled springs, or hounds ready to be unleashed at a word. Guile was thinking how easily they would have swarmed over the ship from Elberon, and how Cromalech had been right: they would have taken what they wanted if they had been made to. These were dangerous enemies of the Empire, their smiles the smiles of the eager wolf.

Rannovic took his prisoners below deck, away from the stares, the open glances at Sisipher, who, for all she knew, might have been the only girl on board. Rannovic was whistling to himself, but hardly spoke to them. He took them to a cabin and ushered them in, bowing as they went by, and Guile took it to be not politeness but sarcasm. Rannovic knew Guile's status, but what did it mean to him and his ruler?

"Gondobar will see you soon," said Rannovic. "He likes to discuss things over a meal. Are you hungry?"

"It's a little early in the day," said Guile.

Rannovic's grin widened. "Ah, yes, although we have been up since well before dawn. I will return later. Meanwhile, we leave for Teru Manga at once." He closed the door, rattling a key in it, and was gone.

Sisipher sat down quietly and eyed Guile. He seemed to

be deep in thought, and for once the panic behind his eyes
had gone. In the past he had, she thought, lived near the edge
of fear, covering it with a display of humor that had not
always amused her. He had always been the one, she had
thought, who would break, and below the walls of Xennidhum, when they had all come close to succumbing to the
crawling darkness, he had fallen. She wondered now if that
would, strangely, give him the strength he would need for
whatever ordeal awaited them.

"I presume," she said, "we are in danger, whatever was
said on Wargallow's ship."

He sat beside her, nodding slowly. "Possibly. It is a difficult puzzle, this riddle of the freebooters."

"Tell me their history." Perhaps, she thought, it will calm
him, though again she noted the lack of panic.

He turned to her with a grin. "Of course, you know very
little about Goldenisle and the mad Remoons, even now. It
would take days to unravel for you, but never mind. Well,
I'll not go back too far, although when I was in the hands of
the Administrators, running errands for them, I gained access
to all kinds of information. Anyway, my uncle was Khedmar
Remoon, a powerful ruler, who had this vision of a united
Empire, an Empire in which the three great Houses, Remoon, Crannoch, and Trullhoon would come together and go
on, perhaps, to greater things. His sister, Estreen, was married to Colchann Crannoch in the western isles and his
brother, Dervic, was married to Ludhanna Trullhoon in the
eastern isles. It sounds neat and tidy, but it was the beginning
of the worst turmoil Goldenisle has seen for many, many
years.

"Let's concern ourselves with the Trullhoons, as I've got
a fair bit of their blood in me. My father, Dervic, whom I
hardly saw, was, apparently, a weak man, who would have
been quite happy to amuse himself all day on the mountains
of Medallion Island, from which the Empire is ruled. He
would have loved and honored Ludhanna, if she had let him,
but she never wanted the match. She loved and was loved by
one of the sons of another Trullhoon family, the Hammavars.
(Each House has about a score of main families.)

"The head of the Trullhoon House was Ludhanna's father,
Morbic, who had been a close ally of Khedmar's own father,

Zarubar. Morbic was delighted with his daughter's match, as he wanted nothing more than a son who would have Remoon blood, and bring the Trullhoons that much closer to the succession. Morbic's own son, Darraban—''

''Ludhanna's brother?'' said Sisipher, trying to envisage the growing tapestry.

''Yes, her brother—he also favored the match, so that the majority of the Trullhoons were supportive. Much against her will, Ludhanna lived with Dervic. And, no doubt even more against her will, she produced a son for him. Which is where I take the stage.'' He bowed, but already she sensed his discomfort. ''A year after I was born, Ludhanna's lover, Onin, no doubt horrified by my birth, abducted—if that's the correct word—my mother, and they fled Goldenisle. Onin had become the head of the Hammavar clan, and so the entire family deserted the Empire for a northern realm called Teru Manga.''

''They became the freebooters?''

''Exactly.''

''And you?''

''At the mature age of one year, I became the property, more or less, of the Administrators. A year before my birth, Khedmar had produced a son of his own, Quanar Remoon, who was later to become king and who went one better and made himself Emperor. I was an embarrassment and was hidden away in court, kept out of the way, no doubt to be produced later at some time that was convenient. But, as you know, I wriggled off that particular hook when Korbillian arrived.''

''And your parents?''

''My mother and her lover perished, ironically, at sea. Onin's brother, who had helped in the founding of a pirate fortress, in Teru Manga, became its ruler. It will no doubt amuse you to know that he still rules it. He is the same Gondobar we are about to share a meal with!'' Guile chuckled, his amusement genuine, which surprised Sisipher.

''Then he is your uncle!''

''Correct! We've never met, naturally. How touching this will be!''

Sisipher's mind raced. ''But what will it mean, Ottemar? Will he be your enemy? What will he want with you?''

"I have been trying to fathom it. It will depend, I think, on my declared position regarding Goldenisle. You see, some years after the death of my parents—Dervic died four years after Ludhanna—there was an internal war which almost destroyed the entire Crannoch House. Khedmar's wife, the queen, had an affair with his nephew (to name but one as I gather she had a penchant for young men) and he was the son of Khedmar's sister, Estreen, and Colchann Crannoch. Khedmar executed his wife and her lover, Ildar, and war broke out. The Trullhoons, now under the rule of Darraban, Ludhanna's brother, supported the king. It was because of the strength of a united Remoon and Trullhoon force that the Crannochs were so heavily defeated.

"Darraban, who still rules the Trullhoons, is a strong supporter of the Emperor, although he must know that Quanar is quite mad. He would, I am sure, support me as the Heir, being my legitimate uncle! And I am exactly what the Trullhoons wanted, am I not?"

"A mixture of Remoon and Trullhoon blood."

"Indeed. Now, the question is, what does Gondobar want?"

"Do you know?"

"Well, when I was a prisoner in Goldenisle, and I soon learned that that is what I was, I gained access to many documents and historical records as I said. It was an irony I enjoyed, for I had been made a clerk for the purpose of keeping me in ignorance and darkness, but it was through the post that I uncovered my own history! Anyway, I found out a lot about the Hammavar pirates. The latest reports I read suggested that Gondobar was not entirely happy with his position in Teru Manga. He wants, so it is believed, a reconciliation between Hammavar and Trullhoon."

Sisipher thought it over. She sat up with a smile. It was, Guile thought, the first time she had allowed herself a smile for a long time. Far too long. Her face was not meant for sorrow, or tragedy.

"Is it possible, then," she said, "that Gondobar would support you as the Heir?"

"Yes, but if he does so, he will be denouncing his brother, Onin, and admitting Onin's shame. The Hammavars would have to beg pardon, and in a family built on pride, that will come hard. Many of his young bloods will not enjoy that. No doubt they will have suggestions for him as to what he should do with me, or more specifically, my head!''

"They would rather remain independent?''

"Yes, but Gondobar's argument will be that sooner or later the Empire will come upon them in force, and when it does, they may be given a more thorough defeat than the Crannochs. They have no allies. But there is another factor, and I fear it may be the deciding one.''

Sisipher saw his face change, the muscles tighten, and knew that the fear was returning. "What is it?''

"The records are vague, but there are a number of references, or more accurately hints, that Ludhanna and Onin had a son before they were drowned at sea. It is possible, given the time span. And the son would, if he had lived, be a year older than I am. Probably living with the Hammavars even now. Perhaps under the wing of Gondobar. If so, how would he counsel Gondobar? Would he support me, his half-brother?''

"You think not?''

He shook his head. "To support me would be to admit his mother's shame. He is a Hammavar, and pride rules him, for certain. If he lives, he is the man I must fear.''

"But he may have died years ago.''

Guile chuckled. "Yes, and he may have taken a wife and sired a dozen sons by now! The Hammavars are a lusty breed, and need to be! But either way, we will soon learn.''

They fell silent for a moment, both thinking over the story that Guile had told, relating it to their position. At length he turned to her. "So I may not be as safe as others would have thought. And you are safe as long as I am useful to Gondobar, no longer. Tell me something, what brought you across the sea with them, with Wargallow?''

She broke her mood and sighed. "Some of it was impulse. But I thought of Xennidhum. Is there a day when we do not think of that place?''

"This new threat?''

"I want an end to the darkness. That is all I see before me.''

He thought of something then and looked up attentively. "What of the owl, Kirrikree?''

She smiled. "Out of sight of the pirates, but not so far that I can't find him with my mind. He whispers to me. When he knew there would be fighting, he took to the sky and has been there since, not afraid of it, but waiting to act. He has flown on and has seen the land we are seeking, Teru Manga. He will find a way of letting Wargallow know where we are. If ships come seeking us, Kirrikree will lead them."

Guile nodded, knowing the power and loyalty of the marvelous owl. But he had long sensed its distrust of him and wondered if it had voiced its thoughts to the girl. Rather than dwell on this, he changed the subject. "And Wargallow?" he said. "What of him?"

"I hated him once, as we all must have done. But not now. It is strange, but I feel in him a closeness of spirit. I think his life changed more than anyone else's at Xennidhum. It left an emptiness, having swept away his beliefs, his goals. In their place is the same darkness I see, and he, too, seeks an end to it. It goes back a long way into his past, though he never speaks of that."

Guile nodded. "Well, if I had wine to offer you now, I would raise a glass with you. An end to darkness."

The keys rattled in the door and Rannovic walked in with his usual arrogance. Perhaps, thought Guile, he has decided that neither of us is worthy of his respect after all. The pirate bowed his head, his grin no less wide than before.

"Gondobar awaits you. Will you join him?"

"Delighted," said Guile, offering Sisipher his arm. She took it automatically, averting the obvious gaze of the pirate, whose interest in her had become increasingly blatant.

They were shown to another cabin, somewhat larger and a little less austere. A man rose from behind a table there, dismissing with a sweep of his arm both Rannovic and the other men who had been with him. Guile and Sisipher were now alone with the ruler of the House of Hammavar. Neither showed it, but both were surprised, almost shocked, by the man before them. Guile knew him to be aged about 50, but he looked much older. His skin was burned dark by sun and sea, and his face was riddled with lines and tiny scars. He was not tall, but had broad shoulders, though the frame beneath them was wasted, the bright, gaudy clothes hanging limply. His eyes were set deep in his wrinkled face, his mouth hidden by a thick beard that hung like a mane to his chest, and in his ears gleamed precious stones, though on him they looked out of place. His hair had thinned to almost nothing, gray and unkempt.

He seemed to move with an effort, breathing heavily as if he had been overexerting himself. He pointed with an emaciated hand at the absurdly overladen table, which was in contrast with everything else his guests had seen on his fighting ship. "Help yourselves," he grunted. "There is wine, too. Not the best, not what would normally be placed before an Emperor."

Guile controlled himself with an effort. Had it been said facetiously? Too early to tell. He said nothing, motioning for Sisipher to help herself. She poured herself a glass of water, but took no food.

"Perhaps a little meat," Guile said at length, forking some on to a plate.

"Please be comfortable," said Gondobar, waving them to seats extravagantly. Velvet cushions had been placed on the chairs either for their comfort or to mock them, Guile could not say. The pirate watched them with exhausted eyes, saw them seated, then sat down heavily and leaned back. He prodded at a plate of rich food before him but did not eat.

"Well," he breathed. "My nephew, Ottemar Remoon." He let the words hang between them for a while, possibly waiting for comments.

"I had not thought to meet you," said Guile. "Indeed, there was a time when I had wondered if you and your people were no more than a legend."

There was no sign of a smile from Gondobar, nothing other than his massive tiredness. "It is not too soon," he said. "Another year and I, at least, will be gone. I am dying, Ottemar. You can see that."

Guile would have protested out of politeness, but he still had no idea what was expected of him.

"Just as Quanar is dying. Even as we speak, he may be dead. And you are the Heir. The first in line for the throne. Do you want the throne?"

Guile glanced at Sisipher, but her face showed nothing. "Would you believe any other answer than that I do?"

Gondobar did smile weakly. "I am sure you must. Unless you are a man after your father's heart."

Guile winced. Was this a challenge or a threat? "You have the advantage of me. I never knew Dervic."

"He was not so weak as some men thought him," replied Gondobar. "Time has shown me that. He loved the earth and all that grew in it. He preferred the clean air of the hills to the dusty courts of the palace."

"It seems to have won him many enemies."

"My brother, Onin was one. But you know the reasons. Onin loved your mother. More than peace. And we followed him."

"And now?" said Guile. It was time, he knew, to bring out the truth. To bargain, to trade, or to do whatever was necessary to compromise. "Are the Hammavars still at odds with Goldenisle?"

"We are not loved by the Empire. If you were Emperor, what then? Would you send out war fleets to avenge your name?"

"If I were Emperor?" mused Guile. "A forbidding thought. But if I were, what would you wish of me?"

Gondobar sighed. "I am dying. Before I die, I should like to know that the Hammavars were reconciled with the Trullhoons, to whom we belong. Peace, Ottemar. I want peace. Pardon for my people. And end to dispute. We will declare ourselves your men, recognising the House of Remoon."

Guile felt his heart judder at the words, which had come so quickly, so unexpectedly. But he kept calm, patient. "And Darraban, leader of the Trullhoons? He has declared openly that the Hammavars have wronged his House. What of him?"

"If you were Emperor, you could command him—no, ask him, if he would accept our offer of peace. By recognizing you as Emperor, we would be recognizing, would we not, Darraban Trullhoon? It would be to affirm the union of your father and mother."

"And to deny the rights of Onin, with whom you fled. And the Hammavars will do this? If it is true, Gondobar, Darraban will have to accept peace."

Gondobar heaved a great sigh, knuckling his eyes for a moment. He nodded slowly. "Aye, aye. It is the only way.

And not without pain. But you, as Emperor, would sanction this?''

"In spirit, yes. But there are more terms?''

"None. No hidden traps, no treachery. It is no more than we want. I speak for most of us, but not all. I have to say this now. But if you were Emperor and agreed, it would be enough, I think.''

"There would be Hammavars, of course, who would never agree.''

"I am too old and too tired to fight you, Ottemar, and so I will say more, even though you may curse me for spreading the truth out before you.''

"My life has been full of bitter truths. Go on.''

"Your mother and my brother had a child before they perished at sea. Perhaps you knew that. His name is Drogund and he is even now in Teru Manga. I, who lived to rule the Hammavars, have been cursed with impotency. Three wives I have had, and although I have loved them all as any good man can love, I cannot give them children. When I die, I leave none of my own to rule in Teru Manga. But I took Onin's son and loved him as my own. When I die, he will rule the Hammavars. And know this, nephew who would rule the Empire, Drogund hates the Empire, Remoon and Trull-hoon with a terrible passion. He would spit on me if he had heard me speak to you as I have. And he would send you back to Goldenisle in a barrel.''

Guile grimaced. "I see. Does Drogund obey you?''

"Until my death, yes, he owes me his allegiance.''

"But not me. And what do you propose now?''

"Now that you understand me, and have said you would consider my wishes, the Hammavars must be told. You must come to Teru Manga and speak to the assembled shipmasters. They must hear us.''

Guile was nodding. "Good. That is good. For there are other things your people must hear. Matters which may even persuade your rebels that we must put aside our quarrels. Far greater danger faces us than these petty squabbles over family history.''

For a moment Gondobar looked angry, and there was a hint in his eyes of the grim strength he must once have possessed. "Petty?''

"I meant no slight. But judge for yourself. Hear now of the danger that Omara has faced and must face again."

Guile spoke then of Korbillian, and of the war at Xennidhum. Many times during his talk the pirate looked horrified, or simply baffled, hardly sure whether to believe the man opposite him. Could this be another twist of the Remoon madness? But the girl spoke also, and in her words was a deadly calm that spoke not of madness, but of terrible truth.

"We had thought it over," ended Guile. "But this man from the ice wastes, Orhung, has shown us we were wrong. Omara will not be safe until this new threat is banished. And unless we are strong, we cannot succeed. If I am to rule Goldenisle, I will need the support of you all. That is what I have to tell your gathered families in Teru Manga. That they will be called upon to fight, probably, beside Trullhoons and Remoons alike. To me, that would be no small thing, Gondobar, but I have seen men of Empire standing beside Deliverers and Earthwrought and men of the east. There is an army in Elberon that would put fear into the heart of the fiercest enemy."

Gondobar's gaze was far away. Some fresh thought had presented itself to him and he examined it privately, his face mirroring the dire thoughts that followed his vision. It was a long time before he spoke, and when he did so his voice trembled, more than it had done before. It was not his ailment that made it do so. "This evil you speak of, this *power*." He said the word as though speaking of a disease.

"It is no illusion, Gondobar," said Guile.

"No, I am sure not. Where is it?"

Guile shrugged. "Hidden, as it has been for centuries. Orhung himself does not know. We will have to search for it."

"Perhaps not."

Sisipher knew then that Gondobar had experienced something beyond the normal knowledge of his people. Perhaps it had something to do with his illness. "You have heard of this power?" she asked him.

"Perhaps. My land, which we took from the few beings that lived there when Onin and I sailed into the warrens there, is called Teru Manga. It is the name the natives gave it before they fled from us and we kept it. It means 'terror below the earth.' It has never meant much to us, but our eyes have always been to the sea. To the north we do not go, for we have heard of strange things beyond the warrens, in the mountains under the Slaughterhorn. But lately we have lost men and women strangely. There are creatures we have named the eaters of flesh. We are watchful by night and are never without fire. And besides these monsters, darkness pervades the land beyond us. Fear also. This has much to do with my wish for the Hammavars to leave Teru Manga and return to the islands of the Trullhoons. We have no wish to learn what it is that broods beneath Teru Manga."

Guile looked at Sisipher. She was sitting upright, her eyes closed, and he wondered if she were communicating with Kirrikree. In a moment she opened her eyes. Gondobar was lost in his own thoughts, not seeing either guest.

"What is it?" said Guile to the girl.

"It is something I thought I had glimpsed." She referred to her inner sight, he knew that at once. "Teru Manga. Gondobar is right. A terrible darkness obscures it. Can it be that Anakhizer is there?"

Guile shuddered.

Gondobar brought both of them from their thoughts. "So you can look beyond us?" he said to Sisipher, who had already explained something of her part in the war at Xennidhum, and of how the gift of seeing had helped the army there.

"Is that why you were brought across the sea?" Gondobar went on. "Or are you Ottemar's consort?"

She felt herself bristling, but did not respond as hotly as she would once have. "I am not," she said coolly.

"Why was she brought aboard your ship?" Guile asked his uncle. "You did not bring her, I suspect, merely because you thought she was my consort."

Gondobar frowned. "No. I had not realized her place in things. It was Rannovic's request."

"What of him?" snapped the girl. "What is his place?"

"His is an ordinary enough desire," said Gondobar, unembarrassed. "He saw you and wanted you, girl. He is a Hammavar."

"And you simply agreed?" she said.

"I have to handle Rannovic with care. He is Drogund's

man. Should Drogund become ruler of the Hammavars, Rannovic will be his right arm. I have sought ways to win Drogund to my thinking. I have given his men places of honor among the shipmasters. Rannovic sails with me, itself an honor. He respects me, but his loyalty is divided."

"So when he asked for me," said Sisipher coldly, "you agreed."

"Yes."

"And what else did you agree to?"

Gondobar offered no answer.

"I will tell Rannovic that Sisipher is not to be touched," said Guile. "Or does he hold me in the same contempt that Drogund does?"

"He knows who you are," said Gondobar solemnly.

Sisipher suddenly stood up and went slowly to the table. She picked up a fruit and examined it carefully. "Very well, Gondobar. We will put Rannovic's loyalty to the test."

Gondobar looked appalled. "This is a delicate matter—"

"I understand that. We must be careful. But tell Rannovic this: if he attempts to put even a finger on me, this ship will never find its way back to your fortress."

Gondobar made to object, but Guile came to Sisipher and turned her to face him. "What are you saying?" he asked gravely.

"I have seen Teru Manga, and the pirate hold. There are a thousand cliffs, cut by as many rivers, all slicing their way through the warrens of Teru Manga. Navigating up those rivers is the most difficult of tasks and many of them lead to death. No ordinary man could find the citadel without a map or an excellent guide. And the fortress is not beside the river, it is high, high up." She swivelled to face the pirate. "Is it not so, Gondobar?"

"How do you know this!" he gasped.

"The citadel is five hundred feet from the warrens. Cut into the cliff face like the delvings of rabbits in a hill. There are rope walks and ladders—"

"How do you know this!" he said again, his face white.

"I have seen it," said Sisipher. "But I have not been there. It is my gift."

Guile also paled. "Your gift?" he whispered. "Then it did

not die at Xennidhum. Or has Kirrikree shown you these things?''

"I have seen Teru Manga," she said aloud. "And beyond it to a wall of darkness.''

"What does this mean?" said Gondobar.

Sisipher went on. "I know that you have a pilot, a man skilled in the secret ways of the warrens, just as many of your ships have one such man. Few are taught the secrets, is it not so?''

"That is so," nodded Gondobar, watching her as if it was not a woman but a dangerous predator before him.

"If Rannovic does not do as I ask," Sisipher continued, "then these ships will not find your citadel. I will touch no one. I will be content to sit in a cabin, in chains if you wish it. But your ships will not find their way.''

Guile would have protested, but it had occurred to him that this would be an ideal way to convince Rannovic and any would-be doubters that power did exist. Even Gondobar would have to be impressed. Guile turned to him.

"Believe me, uncle, she can do this," he said, but he wondered at the girl's rashness.

Gondobar's frown did not dissolve. He watched as the girl bit into the fruit, fascinated by her eyes. Then he shook himself. "Very well. We must find out. I will have the pilot brought here." He bellowed at the door. At once a huge, bare-chested pirate entered as if ready to carve into little pieces anyone that threatened his master.

"Fetch the pilot!" growled Gondobar.

Sisipher finished her fruit and wiped her lips, smiling at Guile as she did so. But her pleasure dissolved after a moment as the huge pirate returned. He stepped aside to admit Rannovic.

"You sent for me?" he asked, his grin widening as he saw Sisipher's annoyance.

"Rannovic is the pilot?" said Guile.

"Aye," grunted Gondobar. "Tell him!" he said to the girl, now shaking with anger.

Her frown slipped away to be replaced with a sweet smile. "With pleasure," she said. "With great pleasure.''

9
Teru Manga

FOR ONCE SISIPHER MATCHED the gaze of Rannovic, and this time the pirate had to look away, turning to his leader for a word of explanation.

"So you are the pilot," Sisipher said casually. "And only you know the secret way through the warrens to the citadel of Teru Manga."

Rannovic's grin returned. "That is so. Few are trained as pilots and not all our ships have them. It is a matter of great trust, and Gondobar has honored me with the post."

"Yet you abuse your privileged position by making unreasonable demands on him."

At once Rannovic scowled, glancing briefly at Gondobar, but he saw anger there. "Explain yourself, girl," Rannovic snapped.

"You had me brought here. Presumably you thought you could use me as you saw fit." Her eyes challenged him fiercely now, and Rannovic drew back a little.

He composed himself. "You have a tongue worth a dozen swords!" he laughed.

"You have a gift," she told him, ignoring his remark. "And I, too, have a gift. Gondobar would like me to demonstrate my gift." She saw fresh consternation on Rannovic's face. "Go to your post and pilot the ship. See if you can find Teru Manga. If you can, you will not find the passage to the citadel."

Rannovic looked puzzled, then grunted with impatience. "This is some foolery. Why should I not find the way?"

"Because I will prevent you."

120

Rannovic's eyes widened. "Prevent me!" He laughed. "There is a shipful of the fiercest fighters in the north around you—"

"I will sit here, in silence. Go and pilot the ship, Rannovic. You will not find Teru Manga's secret ways."

"This is absurd!" Rannovic blustered, though he was concerned. Her coldness, her sureness nonplussed him.

"You doubt her words," said Gondobar. "And so do I."

"Then if he fails," said Guile. "What then?"

Sisipher turned to Gondobar. "If I prevent him finding the way, I would ask a favor of you."

Guile felt a coldness like mist creeping upon him. What dark game was the girl playing here?

Gondobar glanced at Rannovic but nodded. "That seems fair, eh, Rannovic?"

Rannovic snorted. "If I fail! Hah! Very well. Give her the favor."

"What would you wish?" Gondobar asked.

"That he forfeit his right to take me. You agreed to his bringing me here. Rescind that agreement."

Gondobar gave it brief thought, nodding. "Aye, I will do so. But if we fail to find Teru Manga, *if* we fail—"

"I will guide us in."

Both Rannovic and Gondobar looked horrified. Rannovic's hand slid to the haft of one of his short swords. "How could you know the way? Only a chosen Hammavar—"

"There are powers that you must learn about," Sisipher told him, looking at his sword without a shred of fear. "And you will be told. Ottemar and I will speak to you all. We bring news of things that will shake you, as it shook us when we discovered them."

Gondobar nodded. "Already they have spoken to me of the land beyond our citadel. They know of the evils there."

Rannovic's eyes narrowed for a moment, but then he thought better of contesting this. "Well, we had better hear you out."

"At Teru Manga," said Guile. "Before you all."

"If that is as Gondobar wishes, so be it!" Rannovic abruptly laughed, and he strode for the door. As he reached it he turned. "But tell me, girl, if I find the way, what then? Will you come to me and obey me?"

"You will not find it," said Sisipher.

"So you say. But if I do?"

Gondobar cleared his throat, asserting himself. "If you do, she goes to your bed. That, or we stake her out for the eaters of flesh."

Rannovic's face split wide in a fresh grin. "Even I must be preferable to that!" He turned and closed the door and his laughter could be heard beyond it.

Guile raised his brows at Gondobar. "You would enforce that?"

Gondobar nodded. "Why not? The girl has promised something, and so have I. Should she fail, I am mocked. I am still a Hammavar and I have my pride. But you doubt the girl's skill?"

Guile turned to Sisipher, but she was smiling, selecting another small fruit. "No," he said. "She will do this thing." But he was thankful that Gondobar could not read his mind and the doubts there.

Soon afterward, Sisipher sat in a corner of the cabin, resting on the cushions there, and closed her eyes. Guile watched her for a few moments, remembering a stormy night in her home village of Sundhaven, far to the east, when she had first used her gift of sight before Korbillian, the man from another world. It was then that she had seen Xennidhum, and had pointed the way to all their futures.

Guile went to Gondobar and sat with him. They talked quietly for a long time, the pirate eager to know about the lands of the east and what had been found there, while Guile asked about the Hammavars and for news of the Empire.

By the time evening came, Sisipher had not moved, and Gondobar decided to leave her in her trance-like state, retiring to another cabin, posting a guard on the door. He said no more to Guile about the business of finding Teru Manga and when Guile later asked the girl about it, she was reticent.

The days passed slowly, drawn out by the calmness of the sea. Sisipher spent most of the time withdrawn and thoughtful, though she seemed perfectly healthy, while Guile spent many hours with his uncle, realizing that the man was fighting for time, his illness well advanced.

Late one afternoon, three weeks after they had boarded the ship, Gondobar came to Guile and Sisipher with his face deeply perplexed. The girl sat in silence, not long out of another of her trance-like rests.

"What is wrong?" asked Guile.

"We are off course," Gondobar grunted, staring at the girl. "Rannovic is cursing and the men are grumbling. We should have been in sight of Teru Manga an hour ago."

Guile nodded. "Perhaps Rannovic will believe her now."

Gondobar looked bewildered. He had not expected this. He withdrew. An hour later he came back and beside him, bristling with ill-suppressed fury, was Rannovic. The pilot saw the girl and made to grasp her, but Guile stepped before him.

"Do not touch her," he said, covering his fear.

"If she is doing this," snarled Rannovic, "we are in danger of going north, around the island of Tarn into perilous waters. If we are dragged into the currents of the Cape of Seals—"

Sisipher looked at him calmly. "Sit down," she said dreamily, as if she had been inhaling some exotic drug. "Sit here, Rannovic. I will find the land for you."

"This is monstrous!" Rannovic fumed, but a curt nod from Gondobar made him obey. Both pirates sat at the table, glaring at the girl, but she had closed her eyes. They had to sit with her in silence for half an hour. Guile felt his own tension mounting: there was so much about the girl that would remain a mystery. How much of herself had she kept back from them all?

Then came a hurried movement above; the door burst open to reveal another breathless pirate.

"Land, sire! Teru Manga!"

Rannovic lurched up and to the door. He swung back for an instant. "Now I shall pilot us in! And the girl will pay me dearly for this witchery!" His boots clattered up the stairs to the deck.

Gondobar's brow was glistening with sweat and he dabbed at it. He looked at Guile, his frame seemingly even smaller now than it had been when Guile first saw him. "No, he will not find the way."

Guile shook his head, now convinced. "Sisipher will not permit it," he said automatically. But he felt a fresh wave of incredulity. *Could* she control the very ship? What had happened to her? And how much further could she extend these powers? He thought of Korbillian, but his mind fled from that. Sisipher had no duty to confide in him, but there was a frightening depth to her now. And she had known at the outset she had nothing to fear from Gondobar and his men. He glanced at her, but she was motionless, like an idol.

Another hour passed, with the sun close to setting, and the mood of the ship was evident. Anxiety, fear and then panic set in. Again Rannovic came below. His face was haggard now, his thin shirt soaked in sweat, his mouth an angry line.

"You will not find the way," said Guile, convinced that it was true.

"Well?" said Gondobar in an exhausted voice.

Rannovic tried to speak, but merely shook his head.

Sisipher had opened her eyes and looked as fresh as the moment when she had sat down to begin her strange business. Calmly she rose, ignoring any threat to her safety as if it could not exist. "There is no danger to the ship," she said.

"Twice we have almost foundered on the rocks!" snarled Rannovic, finding his tongue. "With darkness coming we dare not risk entering the channels. And to anchor off Teru Manga by night would be very dangerous. The currents are treacherous—"

"I will guide us in," said the girl, as if talking to a little boy. "Let us go up on to the deck."

Rannovic looked in desperation at Gondobar. "Very well. I have to accept this madness. Something has clouded my mind. I surrender my rights to the girl. As long as she is with us, I will not so much as breathe on her!"

"Aye, and no man shall touch her," agreed Gondobar. "Well, Ottemar?"

"That seems fair. Sisipher—"

"I'm content with that. Rannovic need suffer no longer. Let him pilot the ship in." She smiled at the huge pirate.

Rannovic drew back. "I have already said!" he hissed. "I cannot."

"We will go to the deck," she told him. "And you will see." She motioned for him to lead on, and he did so. She followed with Guile, and Gondobar came behind, wheezing like a man of 80.

Once on deck, they were all greeted with hostile stares,

but Sisipher was unmoved by them. She softly told Rannovic to go to his station and he did so, though the men watching were heard muttering their misgivings. "Pilot us in," said Sisipher softly. "The cloud that was before your eyes has gone. It will be good for your men to know that you have done the piloting."

Rannovic shot a glance at her, for once his grin lost in the surf of his fury. She was sparing him further disgrace, for which he was grateful, but she had seared his pride. He turned to face the land before them. Huge cliffs loomed up, tinted by the rays of the dropping sun, which now hung low in the west. Cut into the cliffs like the workings of a race of giants, were the canyons from which the many rivers of Teru Manga rushed out into the sea, churning it dangerously. Until now, Rannovic had been unable to decide which of the countless channels to take, and when he had chosen, had done so wrongly, so that the ships had gone in only to face a furious current that had swung them round and out to sea at once.

Gulls whirled in legions above the cliff, the tallest of which were a thousand feet high, and the noise the birds made was like the demented laughter of some demonic army. Normally the pirates ignored it, but tonight they felt haunted, as if the ghosts of every enemy they had had were here to mock them. Rannovic felt a cloud lifting within himself and suddenly his way became clear. He ordered a course set that would take the ships parallel to the cliffs to the northeast. For an hour they sailed, and the crew had already noticed the calmness that had returned to him, the strong suggestion of an assurance with which they were familiar. There was little laughter but an easing of unrest.

"This is the place," Rannovic said at length, recognizing the twin cliffs that opposed each other at the mouth of another great chasm in the land mass. Skillfully he piloted the ships through the foaming narrows and the towering cliffs closed in, shutting out the last of the sun as evening began to dwindle into twilight. The crew were murmuring now about a night entry into the channel, but lights were brought forward, the flames tossing like treetops in a storm. Rannovic, however, had no fears now. He called out his commands crisply and with absolute confidence.

Guile searched the cliff walls beside them, marvelling at

their sheer height. Thousands of birds nested there, the din extraordinary as they shrieked their insults at the passing ships. For one grim moment he thought of Xennidhum, the rising walls of the plateau, of which this place reminded him. He looked at Sisipher, wondering if in her mind were the same thoughts. She looked calm, but she felt a rising terror, fighting to smother it. There were things here that she did not want to look upon. Only the distant voice of Kirrikree, cutting clear through the din of the sea birds, brought her comfort. The owl was there, hidden by the walls of stone.

Ahead of the craft the deep gorge wound on into darkness, its waters black and then silver where currents conflicted with one another, the waves roaring up against the feet of the cliffs, clawing at the stone walls. Rannovic had to raise his voice to be heard, but the ship kept its line beautifully. Guile saw that he was a master of his trade.

Sisipher had not spoken since she had first stood here. She was looking dead ahead, to the north, not seeing the gorge, locking on to some other dark destiny. Guile wanted to speak to her about it, but thought better of it. Gondobar, having assured himself that the ship was heading at last for home, had gone back below. His time, Guile knew, was desperately short.

It took the ships over an hour to find their way through the echoing gorge, the cliffs of which seemed if anything to grow higher, looming up impossibly to blot out the sky. Smaller gorges joined it on every side and waterfalls tumbled from above in a score of places along the way. There were trees above them, great hanging clumps of growths that clung tenaciously to the rock walls, trailing vines and thick roots. The sight of them, pale in the torch glow, made Guile shudder.

Rannovic turned the ship up one of the tributary gorges and then another. It was plain to see why the Empire had never uncovered the nest that was the pirate citadel. Rannovic pointed in triumph to a place high up in the cliffs, and there were dancing lights there. "It is a fine sight by day!" he called above the fury of the waters. "But tonight it is more welcome than ever before." He guided the ship under the massive overhang of the cliff face to their left, and beneath it, seemingly carved out of the very skirts of the inner cliff was a wide quay. The waves tumbled ceaselessly against it, but there were scores of men there, some bearing brands, all with ropes readied to make fast the ships. It took no more than a few moments for the men ashore and those on the ship to exchange ropes and for the craft to be made fast to the sunken stones in the quay, and a ladder was pushed ashore so that the first of the pirates danced over to their fellows, who thumped them in warm greeting. The other craft were coming in to the quayside as smoothly as Rannovic's, including the ship stolen from Cromalech. The men on board them waved at their companions on shore, and Guile could read the relief on their faces at having found the way home under Rannovic.

Once on the quayside, Guile looked up through the glow of torches to see a wide chute which seemed to have been cut like an immense chimney in the stone, going up to the citadel. A score of ladders hung down, all interlinked like some vast spider's web, from which other ropes curled out to the quayside. Men were clambering up and down with startling agility, careless of the drop below them. At once Guile's heart sank, for there was nothing he feared more than heights; he could see that this must be the only way up to the citadel, for it would not have been possible to carve steps into that monstrous climb.

Gondobar placed an arm on his shoulder. "In a moment we will go up," he said quietly as the last of his men came ashore, unloading the cargoes. Already a number of skeleton crews were preparing to take the ships out again, this time to dock them in some other hidden place with the rest of the pirate fleet. "Be warned again," Gondobar went on. "The word will have sped ahead of us. Drogund will be waiting. Let me speak for you first. Later there will be time for a longer discussion, when all are gathered. You are under my protection here and there will be no harsh acts."

Presently a wide net was lowered from the darkness above and Gondobar got into it, calling for Guile and Sisipher to join him. Though Guile was relieved, he felt a shudder of apprehension as the net was drawn up tight and closed about them. There was a crosspiece in its neck so that in effect they were standing in a cage of rope. Gondobar clung on and called out a command. In moments the net was being raised up steadily, Guile guessed by some hidden wheel or mechanism. He felt his stomach lurching and closed his eyes, turning away so that the pirate could not see his discomfort, but the old man grinned. Sisipher smiled at him, and he nodded politely, understanding Guile's predicament.

"The citadel," he whispered to the girl, "is five hundred feet above us."

"It must be a marvelous place," she nodded. Unlike Guile, the rise upward did not worry her and she watched the passage with keen interest. There were many torches set into the sheer sides of the chimney, and she wondered how such a feat had been achieved. Men, she thought, could not have hewn this fissure, nor did it seem a natural fault. But no creature could have done this. Turning from such a thought, she looked up to see tiny figures, limned in more torch glow.

At last the net stopped its rapid ascent and was swung across to a solid floor of stone, cut from bare rock. Beyond this a number of warren-like tunnels ran away into the cliff face, and beyond the lip of the chute was a vast shelf on which the citadel had been built with bricks quarried roughly from the stone. It was, Sisipher saw at once, a bizarre fusion of two cultures, for originally the cliff wall had been sculpted and burrowed by a race who must have been as skilled at their craft as the Earthwrought; later the Hammavars had come here and cut the naked rock to build houses into the cave system. Guile had opened his eyes, and now that he had mastered his balance, he came and looked about him in awe.

"Welcome to my citadel," said Gondobar proudly. He gestured to the first of the low buildings where scores of men and women had arranged themselves to greet their ruler. He waved at them and they gave a loud cheer, their attention fixed firmly on the two visitors, who did not appear to be captives. Torches were brought forward and a tall, lean man stepped in front of them, bowing briefly before Gondobar.

Gondobar turned to his guests and introduced the man. "This is Drogund."

Drogund looked briefly at the girl, paying her little attention, his eyes flashing at once to Guile, eyes which were cold but sharp, bright as an eagle's. He was clean-shaven, unlike most freebooters, his face almost gaunt, his mouth a thin line, hard. Slowly he nodded.

"And this," he said for Gondobar in a chilling voice that had no hint of compassion, "must be my half-brother, Ottemar, of the Remoon pigs." He stood with his hands on his hips, making no show of welcome. "I'll not take your hand, half-brother," he said in an equally cold voice. "But later we shall see."

"There are many things to discuss," said Guile, aware that the eyes of the crowd were upon him. He kept himself upright, knowing that pride ruled here and that a show of weakness would undo him.

Gondobar sensed the tension between the two men, the animosity of dogs, and he cut in quickly. "Tonight these people are my guests. In the morning, Drogund, I want a full gathering of the shipmasters. Ask me for no explanations tonight, and you shall hear all that there is to hear at the assembly."

For a moment it seemed that Drogund would laugh and demand that his own questions be answered, and the mood of the people seemed to be in accordance with that, but instead he put his arms about Gondobar and hugged him. As he did so, he spoke into his ears. "I hear you have brought us a witch. Let me have her."

Gondobar ignored the remark as he stood back. "Tomorrow, then," he said deliberately. Drogund studied him for a cold moment then turned and walked away, dismissing his own men who were waiting for him. The people cheered Gondobar once more, and he waved at them as they began to disperse, talking excitedly about the return of their ruler.

Sisipher and Guile were taken to a house that overlooked the river far below, itself closed in by the cliff wall and other dark walls beyond, for the top of the plateau was still some hundreds of feet above the citadel. In his house, Gondobar collapsed onto a wide divan, breathing heavily. "I cannot make many more journeys," he said. "There is so little time to put matters in order."

"Tell me," said Guile. "This assembly. How do you intend to conduct it?"

"There are laws, for even such an apparently lawless breed as the Hammavars has its rules. Firstly, I will speak. I will say who you are, though by now the entire citadel will know. The business of piloting the ship will frighten them. But you will both be given the chance to speak. No one will question you as you do so. I suggest you tell them what it is you desire, for yourself and for Omara. Let Sisipher add her words to yours. When you have done, I will give my opinions as to what I think the Hammavar people should do. Those who disagree with me will be allowed to say why. Probably a debate will follow. Then a decision.''

"By whom?" said Guile. "Yourself?"

"No, by the people. I can overrule it. If they find against you and do not wish to support you, I will overrule. You know my desires. They are bound by law to accept my ruling. But if I have to exercise my right to overrule their views, they have the right to leave the citadel and make their own way elsewhere. It is not how I would wish things to end, for my people would be divided as they were when we left the Trull-hoons.''

"Will Drogund leave?" said Guile.

"No. He has only to wait a short while and he will rule here. So he will abide by my ruling. In so doing, he will keep the balance. I doubt that anyone will leave.''

"Then Drogund will be forced to support me, but only until he takes command.''

"Aye, unless you can make the fool come to terms with Darraban Trullhoon before I die. Once that wound is healed, it will not matter when Drogund takes control.''

A girl entered and with a sly glance at Guile told Gondobar that someone was asking entrance.

"Who is it?" grunted the tired leader.

"Your nephew, sir.''

Gondobar looked irritable. "Very well," he sighed. "Let him in.'' The girl excused herself and Gondobar turned to Guile. "Be careful. He is a dangerous man, Ottemar. He will seek a quarrel with you before dawn if he can.''

"I'll not be drawn," said Guile quietly.

Drogund entered, this time not bowing. "Forgive the intrusion,'' he said. "But I felt I ought to speak before the assembly takes place.''

"Of course," said Gondobar. "But you'll appreciate that our guests are tired. It would seem diplomatic, would it not, to show a degree of courtesy to the man who is Heir to the

Emperor's throne?'' He smiled, though there was a challenge in his expression.

Drogund saw it but returned the smile. ''Naturally. I merely came to ask about the arrangements for the new ship. In these days of uncertainty, it is wise to have all ships prepared at all times.''

Gondobar frowned. ''What are you talking about?'' he growled.

''As you know, uncle, I like to fit out and man our new craft quickly. Delegating men is something I would rather not delay.''

''Yes, yes, come to the point.''

''We have a handsome new craft to fit. The one you brought with you. Rannovic tells me it was a gift from the men of the new city of Elberon.''

Gondobar's face had clouded as if a storm would burst, and his hands were white at the knuckle as he gripped the silks before him. ''Go on.''

''I gather it is a prize ship, and a fine one. An Empire war galley.''

''I think,'' said Gondobar icily, and again Sisipher was aware that once he must have been a formidable man, ''that Rannovic has presumed a little too much. The ship is not a prize, anymore than your half-brother is a prisoner.''

''Forgive me,'' said Drogund, not at all concerned at the anger he had sown. ''I understood that the ship was taken in battle. From men of Empire.''

Guile looked deliberately at him. ''It is true that I was a prisoner, but it was the men of Elberon who rescued me. Shortly afterwards Gondobar came upon us. The ship was not taken by force. I am surprised that Rannovic has not told you this.''

Drogund remained imperturbable. ''He has told me no less than the truth, confirming what you have said. Then is the ship a gift?''

''It is an Empire ship,'' said Guile ambiguously.

Drogund held his gaze. ''Ah. Of course. And yet you were a prisoner aboard her? But who held you captive? Men of Empire?''

Gondobar, who had been growing increasingly agitated, tried to speak, but Guile held his ground. ''I hardly think the politics of Goldenisle are your concern, Drogund. Or perhaps they are. Perhaps we will touch on this tomorrow.''

Drogund had no other course than to back down. "As you wish. And meanwhile what should I do with the ship?''

Gondobar waved him away. "As it is berthed, leave it. It is under Ottemar's command.''

"And does this fighting ship of Empire have a crew?''

Guile stared at Drogund, but then smiled. "She has an excellent pilot,'' he said and saw the words go home.

Drogund's mouth tightened. He bowed. "Your pardon, uncle. I merely wished to ascertain the position.''

"Tomorrow,'' said Gondobar, and Drogund withdrew.

Guile sighed gently and turned to the old pirate. "His hate is not far from the surface. This matter of the ship and of the battle for it must be explained.''

Gondobar grunted. He seemed on the point of sleep, but forced himself awake, aware of the dangers closing in on them all. "You have said little on that matter. But I know that it was Cromalech himself who held you. Will you tell me why, or would you prefer to wait?''

Guile shook his head. "I would tell you, if I knew. Two parties came to Elberon, one led by Cromalech. I was abducted by the other party, which was made up of men from Goldenisle. Cromalech also acted with men of Empire, slaying the first party. He refused to say for whom he was acting. Possibly for me, but I think not.''

"Then you have enemies in Goldenisle?''

Guile laughed drily. "What Heir does not? Not everyone would wish to see another Remoon upon the throne when Quanar dies.''

Gondobar leaned forward, intrigued. "Then who else would rule?''

Guile shook his head. "It would mean another war. The Houses would fight among themselves until someone won the throne by sheer force of arms. I've given it a good deal of thought. There's no simple answer.''

"We must avoid chaos,'' said Gondobar. "It is the only sane course open to us. I have also given it much thought.'' He stared ahead of him for many moments.

Sisipher gestured to Guile and they both rose. She came

to him with a finger to her lips. "He sleeps. And if we're to have any strength left for tomorrow, we must sleep as well."

"Aye," he nodded, aware of his own tiredness. "How long will he live, Sisipher?" He wondered if she had seen.

"Who can say? Let us hope it is long enough."

They found the rooms they had each been given and tried to settle for the night. Sisipher listened to the darkness. Somewhere above, far off as a dream, Kirrikree waited.

Guile could not sleep. He heard the distant roar of the waters, and gradually it subsided to be replaced by the loud snoring of Gondobar. This kept Guile awake for an hour, and then abruptly stopped, almost choked off. An unsettling silence followed. Restlessly, Guile got to his feet and padded out into the room where Gondobar had fallen asleep. The pirate had slumped across the divan in an awkward position. Gently Guile went to move him. As he sought to lift him, he felt a wave of icy fear break over him and bent down to listen for the sound of breathing or a heartbeat. There was none.

Gondobar was dead.

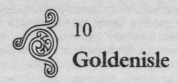

10
Goldenisle

EVENING BLANKETED THE CITY. Behind and over it the immense cliffs blotted out the sun and the shadows spread thickly over the rooftops. Impregnable, thought Wargallow, amazed by the ingenuity of the men who had built the city under those towering walls, the height of which almost defied the eye. The only way to have attacked the city would have been from the sea, and already he had seen the problem, having come through the narrow jaws of the Hasp that protected this inner sea from the ocean outside. They had almost closed over the ship as it had passed and Wargallow had felt as though the Empire had closed its fist around him and his companions, making them its own. Now, leaning on the rail of his ship, gazing up at the splendid city from its dock area, he knew that an invasion would have been futile, even with an army a dozen times stronger than the one Ruan could likely muster. Even so, it may yet come to that. He put thoughts of war from his mind, enjoying instead the view of those stepped houses with their tumbling gardens, the carefully sculpted streets and avenues. As the sun set, he saw also the signs of age, of decay, for there were parts of the city, not easily glimpsed, that had fallen into disuse, where the vegetation had taken command, smothering what man had made. The glory that the city had once been was no longer as bright, and Wargallow wondered again about its power as a nation.

During the three week voyage to Medallion Island, which he had spent on his own ship, much to the intense annoyance of Otric Hamal, Wargallow had learned a little more of

Cromalech's part in the scheme of things, although he wondered how much the First Sword had left unsaid, for the man was cunning, with a sharp brain to match his strong arm. Alone together, studying the ever-restless waves, to which Cromalech had jokingly once compared himself, the First Sword had at last spoken about the abduction of Guile.

"I am certain," he had said, "that Eukor Epta, the man who controls our Empire, was responsible for the original abduction. If he plans to put Ottemar on the throne, which is suggested by the fact that he did not simply have him killed, then he seeks to control him, just as he has controlled Quanar. Even with his senses intact, Ottemar would find it hard to rule with Eukor Epta standing at his shoulder. But the Administrator is the most devious of men. He may have other plans."

"He also has enemies," Wargallow had commented, thinking aloud.

"That is true. There are those who would wish to see an end to Eukor Epta's grip on the Empire. They would not wish to see Ottemar enthroned only to become Eukor Epta's puppet. For them, I abducted Ottemar. Guided and protected by them, Ottemar would not have been twisted to Eukor Epta's will. But I cannot name these people yet. Their safety depends on that."

"I understand that. But you would be an ally to Ottemar?"

"He is the Heir."

Otric had questioned both of them a number of times, but he had never mentioned the Heir, and Cromalech kept to his story of having been sent to Elberon to escort Wargallow, the Ambassador, to the Emperor.

As Wargallow studied the darkening lines of the city, Cromalech joined him, smiling grimly. "This business with Otric is worrying at him like a thorn in the hide of a young bull," chuckled the warrior. "I am sure that he thinks we are hiding Ottemar below decks. Anyway, I've used it to our advantage and made a compromise with him. As you know, he is in no position to prevent my going ashore with you and your companions as my wards. To challenge us openly about the abduction would be a confession of his own men's part. And political protocol forbids the interference of the army or navy in the business of the Imperial Killers, especially that of the First Sword! Even though Eukor Epta must be behind Fennobar, he cannot breach protocol. Eukor Epta is far too wily to implicate himself in anything. He will treat Fennobar's abduction attempt as a complete failure and will withdraw, to begin some fresh scheme.

"We can go ashore together, and you are under my protection. But to keep the army off my back, I've agreed to allow Otric to take charge of your ship while it is berthed here in the docks. As I've said, Otric is convinced he'll find Ottemar here, although my allowing him the ship has confused him! Let him look your ship over a dozen times! We have nothing to hide, have we?''

Wargallow smiled grimly. "Not yet. But when I am called to give an account of things in the east, men will ask about Korbillian, knowing that Ottemar left your islands in his company.''

"Tomorrow there will be a great gathering of officials and members of the Houses. You and your men will be called upon to speak. Eukor Epta himself may be there, though he rarely comes to such events in person. I suggest you give some thought tonight as to what you will tell him. My advice is, neither you nor anyone in your city has seen the Heir. Eukor Epta will know it is a lie, but it cannot be proved.''

Wargallow nodded slowly but he looked deeply concerned. "I came here, Cromalech, to win your people's confidence. The alliance is, I am convinced, vital. Yet to begin with lies, deceit, is no way to persuade men to trust us.''

"You would rather deliver the truth? Eukor Epta knows it already. No, you must play his game, as I do. Bide your time and like a good swordsman seek your opening. One will come, even against a master like Eukor Epta.''

Wargallow nodded, again watching the foreign city, aware of its size, the immensity of the task he was about to attempt. It would be as difficult as physically besieging the city walls, possibly as hopeless.

Cromalech fell silent. He had come to respect this strange man from the east, and saw in him a power not found in common men. Certainly he was genuinely afraid of the darkness that threatened Omara, and if he had lived through Xennidhum, it would take much now to frighten him. Yet how real a threat was this power? Until it showed itself, Cromalech reserved his own judgment. He had other things to think of. He knew that the men he had hired to make up his team of abductors, men who were not trained Killers, would very probably be taken secretly and tortured by Otric to get the truth out of them. But by the time Otric learned that and gave it to his master, Fennobar, Cromalech and his wards would be safely housed in the palace. Cromalech's silent fear was that Eukor Epta would now know that the First Sword acted for some other master, and although the Administrator would not know who it was, he would want to find out, and likely have Cromalech eliminated.

So be it, thought the warrior. One always has to declare oneself at some point. Eukor Epta and I will know the position in time. And I will be ready for you, and must strike the first, sure blow. It must be through Tennebriel, whom you will never suspect. And I must find Ottemar somehow. Find him and kill him.

In his tower, Eukor Epta unrolled the thin parchment that one of his servants had brought to him. Only when the man's footfalls had receded on the stairs did the Administrator look at the parchment. He sat beside the open window and looked first at the sea below, then at the city and the docks. His eyes came to rest on the ship of Elberon, barely visible in the dwindling light. He had broken all direct contact with Fennobar and his men now, making it clear to the Deputy Commander of the Armies that if any scandal did attach itself to himself over the botched abduction, Fennobar's removal would be swift.

Eukor Epta pulled his lamp close, unable to read the scrawled words by moonlight alone. The writing was hurried, and not that of Fennobar, which was far bigger and more ponderous. This was the hand of Otric Hamal, and Eukor Epta nodded to himself: the young soldier was loyal to Fennobar, a man to be trusted, although a soldier who wrote so fluently was a man to keep an eye on.

Certain men of the First Sword's crew, dock-rabble, no better, have spoken frankly to me, owing their former master nothing now that their voyage is over. It is clear our own men successfully abducted the man known as Guile, but the men of the First Sword killed them and took the prisoner for themselves. No one has been told why and I do not consider torture worthwhile. The First Sword would be too discreet to say any more than need be said to his underlings.

I am convinced he is working in allegiance with this Ambassador from the city of Elberon. Morric Elberon, I can confirm absolutely, is dead. It is common knowledge in the east. Wargallow, the Ambassador, purports to have come to us seeking an alliance. He claims that we all share a common enemy, a dark power which dwells in some unknown region, and which we must combine to defeat. This, it seems obvious, is some complicated deceit.

The Administrator stared out at the black waters far below. He had heard a little of this war far in eastern lands and of the talk of lost powers. It would be interesting to hear this man Wargallow speak.

It is virtually certain that the First Sword's perfidy does not stop at this dangerous alliance. Also implicated are Gondobar and the Hammavar pirates. I had thought Guile to be on the ship from Elberon, but it seems that Gondobar has taken him to Teru Manga. He was not taken against his will, but went in an action that was designed to look like an abduction, but which I gather had been planned.

I can only conclude that there is some plan afoot to put Guile on the throne, with the eastern rabble and the pirates as part of his support. But it is obvious that his principal ally is the First Sword.

Eukor Epta held the parchment to the flame of the candle and let it catch fire, dropping it only when a tiny corner remained. So the attempt to capture Ottemar had failed. Very well, that must be forgotten. But it had served a useful purpose. Now there was a little light where there had been darkness! Cromalech. An ambitious man, Eukor Epta had always guessed that. But something was wrong with this whole business. Why should Cromalech go to the trouble of abducting Ottemar? The suggestion in Otric Hamal's report was that Ottemar was capable of leading an invasion, or a military action. That was utter nonsense. Ottemar had only to sail openly into the islands and he would almost certainly be presented with the throne. He was the Heir, and there could be no questioning it. Of course, if he did take the throne, Cromalech would remain First Sword, and as such would become far more powerful under Ottemar than the mad Quanar. So why did he and the Heir not come openly?

There were a number of critical questions that needed an answer. How had Cromalech known there was to be an abduction attempt and not a killing and that it would be in the city of Elberon? Or was it mere chance that had sent him there? No, it could not be so, for Eukor Epta had already decided he could not be an ally of the Heir. Surely Cromalech did not intend a military coup, with himself as ruler? No, the man had far too much intelligence than to attempt such lunacy. And he had not murdered Ottemar when he had the chance.

Eukor Epta prodded at the ashes on his table, tracing sooty lines across the wood as though he would read something afresh in them. And what of the Heir now? Hiding in Teru Manga, under the wing of that old fool, Gondobar! Whatever was Gondobar thinking of? His nephew, Drogund, would be the ruler of the Hammavars within a few months at the latest: the word was that Gondobar would soon be dead. And Drogund would plunge a knife into his hated half-brother as soon as look at him!

How can I use Drogund? Is it possible? Eukor Epta played with the idea, enjoying the riddles of the game, and the more he did so, the more he thought he could find a way. The pirates were never secure in Teru Manga.

They must know that one day the Empire will tire of their rebellion and send out a fleet to destroy them all. Better for them if they capitulated and sued for peace. Well, they can have it. I shall send someone like Otric Hamal to them, and he can offer them peace, a welcome back into the Empire. But Drogund will have to bring me Ottemar. Alive. I want him alive. Drogund will be amused when he learns that Ottemar is not to sit on the throne at all. He would enjoy seeing Tennebriel take his place. How excellent that would be. With Drogund and the Hammavars as part of the Empire, Cromalech would be hard pressed to hold his position.

Eukor Epta reached for a quill and fresh paper. He did not like penning anything, but it was necessary. As he wrote, he thought of the gathering tomorrow. It would be enjoyable, with everyone wearing a political mask. Ironically it would be impossible to unmask Cromalech publicly without implicating himself in Ottemar's abduction. Eukor Epta was not, however, angry. It was a situation he relished. He sat back for a moment, again considering potential tactics.

An hour later he had finished his letter to another of his most trusted men, who would deliver by word of mouth the instructions that Fennobar was to follow. The letter would be destroyed as soon as it had been read. Eukor Epta had also decided how to deal with Ambassador Wargallow and his verminous easterners. The Empire must be seen to welcome their desire for an alliance. *We will soften them, and then when they are least thinking of it, crush them like the roaches they are.*

It was long after midnight when Cromalech satisfied himself that Wargallow, Orhung and their crew were safely settled in their apartments in that part of the palace reserved for the Imperial Killers. They were secure there, for no one entered without Cromalech's express permission, and only the Imperial Killers walked the corridors, and occasionally their women. Eukor Epta would never dare violate this particular sanctuary, and in the past, few of Goldenisle's kings had been there.

Cromalech was well aware that Eukor Epta would have his every move watched from now on. He could do nothing without exercising absolute care. He smiled to himself as he stripped off his familiar harness and shirt and changed instead into more basic clothes, disguising his rank. He wrapped a thin cloak about himself. Easing quietly down a number of flights of stairs, he came to a stable area where he knew some of his younger men were having a brief drink and preparing to go off duty. Some of them, he also knew, would be visiting certain houses in the city where a loved one would be secretly waiting: a daughter of some angry official, who did not approve, perhaps, or the wife of an unsuspecting citizen who would have been even more disapproving if he had known about the nocturnal visitor of his wife. The group called themselves the Dawn Watch, a private joke amongst the Killers, and anyone of their number who "did a spell on the Dawn Watch" had the absolute confidence of its members. When Cromalech himself joined tonight's particular band, he had already primed them to expect a certain high-ranking member, and they played their part without a wrong word. First Sword or not, the special codes of the Dawn Watch applied. Whoever their leader was visiting, they had no wish to know. All were equals on the Dawn Watch.

When the tiny company slipped out into the streets, it had absorbed Cromalech. The spies sent to watch the garrison for his exit never noticed him, disguised as he was and in such company, for the Dawn Watch invariably left the palace in the guise of drunkards, a ruse which worked so well it was still the best used.

At the harbor, Cromalech melted away from his men, who made no show of having noticed. Later they speculated wildly on his escapade, wondering whose wife he was toying with, but no word of it passed beyond the Dawn Watch. Cromalech went down a number of black alleys, reaching a deserted wharf where he hid his cloak and all but his loin cloth. Again checking to see that he had not been followed, he gently lowered himself into the water. It was not too clean here and he grimaced at it, but after a few short strokes he was out in cleaner water, diving below it. He came up, hidden by the darkness, and shook himself like a beast of the sea. It was cold but invigorating and he luxuriated in it, enjoying the thrill of the night hunt as if he were a bear up in the mountains.

After the long inactivity of the voyage, he was glad to have something to do, particularly as it involved considerable physical effort. When he reached the base of the island that rose up like a sheer tower of stone, he still felt fresh, and the prospect of the familiar climb warmed him. He had been 18 when he had first attempted it, swearing to the older lads who had taunted him that such a climb was possible. Even after he had achieved it, few of them believed him, but by then he did not care for he had stumbled across the girl, the extraordinary girl, with whom none could be compared, even though she had been no more than a child when he had first seen her. After that he had climbed the rock regularly, spying on her but not daring to speak, until one day, three years after he had first set eyes on her, he had shown himself. Tennebriel had been fascinated by him, seeing in him a young god, and they had quickly become lovers.

He swam gently around to the place where he knew the creepers reached almost to the water and he hauled himself up into the pale moonlight. Moments later he was climbing upward like a spider, and the sea dropped far below him.

Tennebriel would be sleeping by now. He would surprise her by slipping between her sheets and taking her before she knew he was there. As he thought of the act, the strength flooded back into him. He had missed her, more than he had admitted. He must be a little mad to risk this affair with her, but how many times over the years had he said that to himself? Laughing silently, he came to the parapet and swung over it, rolling with the silence of a breeze into the undergrowth that tumbled down from the heights beyond.

There was a lamp lit, but no movement. With absolute stealth he entered the hall beyond, and reached the bedchambers without being seen by any of the handmaidens, who were almost certainly all asleep. One pair of eyes did see him, but the figure was out of sight, not prepared to show itself or protest, for Ullarga had seen this visitor too often to speak out. She saw Cromalech pause at Tennebriel's door, then go in.

As he thought, she was in her bed, a single sheet half draped over her, her body naked beneath it. Her beauty did more to knock the breath from him than the cold water of the harbor. How could he have forgotten it! He went across and lifted the sheet with great care, letting it fall to the carpet. For an instant he touched her hair, then he was beside her. She woke with his arms about her and she snuggled up to him like an infant.

It was a long time before they spoke, and an hour quickly passed then as he told her of events in the east and on the seas. She listened avidly, sometimes frowning, sometimes smiling, her arms still around him.

"So you see," he ended, "Eukor Epta will know by now that I am against him. But ironically, he must assume I intend to support Ottemar! Likely he'll think I have done it to strengthen my position and weaken his, controlling the Emperor from a military base and not a political one."

"What about this man with the strange hand? Does he trust you?"

"To a point. He is far too clever to trust anyone completely. I have heard it said that he was once a harder man than Eukor Epta. I have told him that I support Ottemar, but in the name of men whose identities I cannot reveal. I think he accepts that because I have not sought to kill Ottemar."

Tennebriel got out of bed and walked up and down for a while. Cromalech's eyes followed her hungrily, marvelling at her beauty. Who could refuse to make her Empress and fight to the death to see she held her throne? Ottemar Remoon may be the Heir, but Tennebriel was like a goddess, a forbidden power that all men would have to acknowledge one day.

"So Ottemar is now with Gondobar?" she said abruptly.

"Yes, in Teru Manga, of all places! He may as well be lost in the forests of the Deepwalks in the western lands."

Tennebriel shook her head, her hair cascading around her. "No, if he were there, he'd never be found. But Eukor Epta will know where to look. As soon as he knows Ottemar is with the pirates, he'll send out another ship to find him, possibly a fleet."

Cromalech scowled. "Eukor Epta has no links with the Hammavars. Even he could not have spies there—"

"Whether he has or not, he'll try for Ottemar. He never gives up. Probably this time he will want him killed. But, no, it would not suit him."

"You should have let me kill him. It would have been very easy."

"I still want him alive," she said, her eyes narrowing. "If he dies, my path to the throne is open, but if I don't have him here somewhere, how can I hope to keep Eukor Epta under my control?"

Cromalech laughed. "Surely you aren't going to send me off to sea again? If I begin a fresh search for Ottemar, Eukor Epta will find a way to discredit me openly. I've been lucky so far."

Tennebriel was walking again. "Perhaps. What about this gathering tomorrow? What will you say?"

"That we should accept the easterners. Ally ourselves to them. Eukor Epta will do the same."

She turned to him, a vixen at bay. "You think so?" Her hatred of the Administrator was never plainer.

He nodded. "Oh yes. It's the easiest thing for him to do. He likes to win confidence, lull his opponent, then cut away his feet. It is a game I am beginning to understand."

"And this evil power? Does such a thing exist?"

She saw the shadow cross his face, but he tried to smile. "I thought it was some excuse Wargallow was using to reach us. But now I am not so sure. This city of Xennidhum casts its dark pall of fear yet. Men shudder at its very name. Strange. And Wargallow believes strongly in the power wielded by the man he calls Anakhizer."

She nodded, but seemed to have dismissed it already, her thoughts elsewhere. "You will have to get Ottemar before others do," she said suddenly. "You say this eastern Ambassador doesn't know where this evil power lies?"

"The man from the ice lands, Orhung, who moves like a being in a drug sleep (until he is fighting, and then he is a sight to behold) will speak of this. It is true, though, that they have few clues to Anakhizer's whereabouts. Suspicious."

"Then it will help us. You must insist on hunting this Anakhizer."

"I must?"

"Yes!" she laughed. "In the name of the Emperor. Take ships and go north. And while you are hunting, visit Gondobar and bring out Ottemar! What better excuse could you have than the Emperor's safety?" She jumped on to the bed, pushing him back as he began to protest. She kissed him before he could say any more and presently they made love again.

In the shadows beyond them, Ullarga watched, her gaze filled with a smoldering hate. The girl is a fool to ensnare herself with this pig! She is besotted with him, matching his lust with her own. She cannot afford the luxury of loving him! I must speak to her tomorrow. How can she be an Empress and think purely for herself and the Empire if—

But as her thoughts raged, Ullarga felt the familiar stab that came so often and so freely to her now. Its fingers held her and worked her like a doll, directing her old legs, giving them fresh strength. She opened her mouth, enjoying this possession and moved away from the lovers, no more noticeable than the scuttling of a spider in the darkness. She had her own private places to visit in the tower, guided by the power that held her, places where even Eukor Epta did not go, or indeed know of. Far down into the rock she went, burrowing like a maggot into old workings that no man of this Empire had ever seen or guessed at. Workings that had been here long before men in Goldenisle. Far below the surface of the inner sea, in halls and tunnels that stank of ages gone by, she turned into a smaller room, as sure-footed in the absolute darkness as if she could see. She lit a candle from a small supply that she had been forced to bring before, and as it flickered into life she watched it with a look of strange pleasure on her face. She took a key from its place at the wall and opened the ancient door that was outlined by the glow.

At that moment, poised for a final descent, something within the old crone's breast twisted, like some animal fighting to be free of the predator's claw. It was as if, in that one moment, her last vestiges of will struggled to find expression; what had once been her love of her mistress, her loyalty, sought its last shout. But, cruel as talons, the greater will clamped down.

Sand-choked steps were beyond, curling down into yet a further pit, an unfathomable abyss from which came the remote gurglings of water, as if waves were at play there. Ahead of her she heard voices and she raised up the light, peering intently. In a moment a number of pale creatures shifted in the gloom, hissing softly as if a nest of serpents had been disturbed.

She did not want to speak now, but to flee, but her lips were shaped by the power that had held her for so long. "Are you there?"

A figure came into the circle of light, a hand across its eyes. "Is there a message for him?" it said in a voice that few could have understood.

Ullarga did not move, frozen. Abruptly the air filled with anger at her silence. Below her, in the utter darkness where the waters swirled, the voices ceased. Light seemed to grow from nothing, coalescing into an amorphous shape. Ullarga, or whatever remained of the crone's identity, shuddered at the sight of the being which now confronted her. It wore dazzling white robes which appeared to be the source of the light around it. Yet it was the face that drew her eyes, drinking her will, her final resistance.

The only visible feature was a mouth, the lips scarlet and full. The remainder, eyes, nose, seemed to be hidden beneath a sheet of tautly pulled skin, one like a mask. The mouth moved seductively as it spoke. "You are mine, Ullarga. You are as one with me as my own flesh." Slowly a hand appeared from beneath a fold of shimmering white. Ullarga fell before it and took it in her own gnarled fingers, kissing it avidly, pressing it to her face as if it would make her youthful again.

Above her the mouth formed into a smile and where there should have been eyes there were two dark hollows.

"The Heir," murmured the crone, her lips frothing. "He is in the north, with Gondobar."

Again the lips smiled obscenely, and within moments the image of Anakhizer began to melt like wax, slithering into the pitch waters. Yet his will remained.

The gathered creatures had been listening avidly, watching the old woman, now bent like a crab, licking at something. They had not seen the frightful vision of her master, but they drank in Ullarga's words avidly. The moment she had finished they dived into the waters below and were gone. Ullarga got up, turned and began the long trek back up into the tower.

When she came to her room, little of what had happened remained in her mind. She felt light-headed, almost as if she had been drinking. She slept at once and her dreams were filled with visions of the death of Ottemar Remoon and of a huge, laughing mouth.

PART THREE

THE
STONEDELVERS

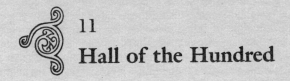

11
Hall of the Hundred

THERE WAS TO BE NO DELAY in the gathering of Goldenisle's officials to hear the words of the Ambassador from the eastern lands, and shortly after dawn the Hall of the Hundred was being prepared for the arrival of those who governed the Empire and the leading figures of the Houses. The Hall was believed to be the oldest surviving building in the city. It was huge, its walls rising magnificently, its arched ceiling supported on rows of ornately carved pillars, the marble of which had been quarried on a remote island that the sea had now claimed. Intricately woven tapestries depicting forgotten legends—strange armed giants and beasts—hung from the walls, and there were numerous carved statues and statuettes, mostly of long-forgotten heroes and dignitaries, which had survived the fables and myths that must have once surrounded them. Light streamed into the Hall from curved windows high overhead, and in some of these the glass that had been set was colored, itself etched with extraordinary glyphs and figures. In the Hall itself there were numerous rows of seats, cut from dark wood; it was said that once there had been a hundred of them, all far too large for a normal man to sit upon, but these had now been removed and replaced by far more, so that the Hall could house in excess of a thousand men. The acoustics of the place were such that a word spoken at its far end could be heard clearly at its opposite door. Between the seats, down the main aisle, ran the richly carpeted walk that itself spoke of some remote history. It led to the eastern end of the building, where a huge dais had been set. Upon this had been raised a number of smaller raised areas, each hewn from great blocks of stone, themselves carved ornately.

As Wargallow came inside the great Hall, he experienced again the sense of being closed in by the Empire as he had done on passing through the Hasp. It was impossible not to be awed by the sheer scale, for the suggestion was that the Hall had been made by giants for giants. Wargallow had not seen such quality of building before, even in fallen Cyrene. Once, he understood now, Goldenisle had been truly great. Even so, he sensed that it was in decline, as he had done when he had studied the city from the ship. He could not say what it was, but it was almost as though this place had a veneer to it that would crack to reveal the wasting beneath.

Already scores of officials and important citizens had taken their places in the vast seating area, setting up a babble that swelled as he and Orhung entered, escorted on either side by trusted men of Cromalech's guard. Cromalech himself had already taken his place in the very first rank of seats, at the foot of the great dais. As Wargallow and his escort walked down the immense aisle to meet him, the Deliverer looked ahead to the raised areas and those who sat there. There was a wide set of steps that led up to the main dais, on the left side of which five regal chairs had been placed. Each of these had been carved by the finest craftsmen, the high backs cut in the shapes of eagles with extended wings: on either end of this line of seats a warrior stood stiffly, an axe before him, the head resting on the ground. Behind the five chairs, on a higher level, was a single chair, more like a throne, which was even more splendidly carved than the five, and set, it seemed, with jewels that already caught the sunlight as it splashed down. Central to the main dais was another smaller one which rose above that of the five chairs, and on this were three seats, none of them lavish, but draped simply in green material that looked like velvet. Again, two guards stood at each end of this dais, stiff as carvings, axes to the floor. Above the three chairs rose the highest dais of all, and in the center of this was a single seat, largest of them all. It had been cut from a single block of black rock, its carvings invisible to Wargallow, and it reflected none of the sunlight. There were two other raised areas, both to the right, and each had a single chair, although guards stood at their feet. One of these chairs was occupied, and Wargallow recognized the man that Cromalech had described and had said would be there, Fennobar, Deputy of Morric Elberon, soon to be made officially the Commander of the Armies and Navies of Goldenisle. The other dais with its lone seat was for Cromalech.

Wargallow took his place beside the First Sword, who for the moment had been waiting in the front row of the Audience, as the seats in the Hall were called, with Orhung beside him. Orhung did not seem to be taking in the amazing surroundings, instead sitting listlessly in his now familiar silence, like a man whose mind has ceased to function.

Cromalech leaned over to Wargallow with a grim smile. "I trust you slept little and thought much," he whispered.

Wargallow nodded, but said nothing. He was preparing himself for the ordeal that was to come, for he could feel the weight of the Empire bearing down upon him.

Cromalech pointed to the dais on the left. "There sit the Law Givers," he said. "The five eagle seats are for the Court of Envoys, and the high seat is for the High Chamberlain, Otarus. They enforce the law of the land and also hold historical records that have to be consulted in times of great debate. Otarus enjoys quoting vast chunks of them." Cromalech's gaze swept round until he was staring at Fennobar. "And there sits Elberon's Deputy. Controller of the armed might of Empire. Both he and Otarus are directly responsible to Eukor Epta, and do little without his agreement. Only the First Sword of the Imperial Killers is not directly responsible to Eukor Epta." Cromalech grinned as he said it.

Wargallow met Fennobar's heated gaze without a show of emotion. The man was very tall, heavily built, and had a rugged face, a fighter's mien. He looked to be quick-tempered, restless, a man whose thoughts and feelings were rarely hidden, always readable on his countenance. It was clear now that he detested Wargallow and all that he stood for. The Deliverer stared dispassionately at him and Fennobar looked away, muttering something under his breath.

Cromalech was indicating the central dais. "The three seats are for the Chamber of Administration, to which almost all are answerable. This is where the real power of Empire lies. In Eanan, Tolodin and Ascanar is the greatest power vested, especially since we currently have an Emperor who is deranged. Between them, these three rule. Beyond and above them will sit their own ruler, the Administrative Oligarch, Eukor Epta. He is answerable to no one, and if he puts Ottemar on the throne,'' Cromalech added, dropping his voice still further, ''he will control him as a fisherman plays a hooked fish.''

Wargallow nodded, turning to see the last of the assembly arrive in the Hall. It was full, with lines of soldiers spread along the walls, all with spears erect, as if expecting to have to quell a riot. Cromalech stood up and turned to sweep the Audience with his gaze. Wargallow admired his coolness.

''You should be flattered,'' said the warrior quietly. ''This is the best turn-out for as long as I can recall. There are representatives from many Houses, and more Crannochs than have attended for years.'' He said no more, walking up the steps to his own place on the right hand dais beside Fennobar.

The big man leaned over and growled. ''I gather your voyage to the east was a fruitful one.''

Cromalech inclined his head with mock politeness. ''Indeed. Always a pleasure to get away from the city and see something of the world. I'm surprised you haven't found some excuse to get away yourself, Fennobar. There must be something you could do overseas.''

Fennobar's fury was written like thunder across his brow. ''There may well be soon!'' he hissed, and more than a few of the Audience heard him.

Presently the Law Givers took their seats, each of them dressed in flowing white robes and Wargallow wondered at this suggestion of purity. Their leader, Otarus, was an elderly man whose white beard flowed down below his waist. He sat quietly and with serene dignity, placing many rolled parchments beside him on his desk and studying them as though quite oblivious of his surroundings. Wargallow knew better. The Oligarchs of Eukor Epta came soon after, also wearing white robes, though these had been decorated lavishly with bright blue and red embroidery, hieroglyphs and sigils, and although these meant nothing to Wargallow, he could see that they had been deliberately designed to overshadow the simple white of the Court of Envoys. The Oligarchs also carried papers, but they set them down and gazed out at the Audience as if preparing to pass sentence.

The murmurings in the Hall died to nothing, so that silence fell. All now waited to see if Eukor Epta would come. Several minutes passed, the Audience very still, until a curtained archway somewhere beyond the raised areas opened and a single figure mounted the steps there to take the last unoccupied seat. Dressed in black, with white silks flowing from his hood, Eukor Epta ignored the throng before him and studied something on his desk. For a full minute he did not look up. No one moved or whispered and Wargallow marvelled at the control this gaunt figure had over such a gathering. Cromalech had said if Eukor Epta came in person, it would be the first time many men here had seen him. Wargallow glanced at the First Sword, but he and Fennobar both stared fixedly ahead of them. Wargallow read traces of fear in both men.

Eukor Epta sat up straight and slowly looked at the Audience. His eyes, Wargallow noted, were as piercing as any he had seen before, cold and icy, unlike those of other men. They hinted at deeper vision, and Wargallow thought briefly of Sisipher. When the eyes of Eukor Epta studied a man they were as challenging as those of a serpent, as feral but controlled as those of a wolf. The mouth was not thin, but it spoke of a fierce will, and the whole bearing of the man was a carving of power. Korbillian would have understood this and would have read it. For a moment Eukor Epta looked directly at Wargallow, but then he turned to Otarus, the High Chamberlain below his right hand, and with a mild turn of that hand gestured for him to begin.

Otarus did not rise, but when he spoke his voice carried clearly and precisely out to everyone there. He reeled off various pieces of information, all part of the preparation of the business of the day, the protocol, and Wargallow smiled inwardly. He was familiar with the type of ritual, having spent so much time in the Direkeep, where laws were strict and men were brought up to bow to them every moment of their lives.

"We have before us," said Otarus at last, "men who have traveled here from the lands of the east, lands which, until now, have been shrouded in mystery. We have little knowledge of these places, no more than gossip and mythology.

We have thought these lands wild, untamed, with a few scattered tribes and nomadic people living there. There have been rumors of strange beasts and we, in our ignorance, have gone so far as to use these to frighten our children when they have misbehaved.'' There were a few outbreaks of polite laughter. Otarus smiled. ''But we have lived in darkness. I trust that our guests will forgive us that.''

He turned to Eukor Epta, though he did not look at him. ''I would wish to move, sir, that without further discussion, we ask the Ambassador from the eastern continent to speak to us. With your approval I would wish formally to welcome him and his men to our city.''

Eukor merely nodded.

Otarus then left his seat and came down the steps to where Wargallow sat. The Deliverer rose and to his surprise Otarus held out his right hand. Wargallow paused for the briefest moment, knowing that he must not lose his head. Slowly he offered his own right hand, the blades of his killing steel muffled by the material of his robe. Otarus had not been warned, for he was obviously taken aback not to be able to clasp flesh and finger, but as he took the robe he realized. He drew in his breath and there was a murmur from those that could see, but Otarus recovered his dignity at once.

''Please come up to the dais,'' he told Wargallow, as warmly as he could, gesturing for him to do so. The Deliverer sensed in him a genuine desire to please, a need to extend friendship, but it was in glaring contrast to the reptilian silence of Eukor Epta. Wargallow wished that Cromalech had told him more about the Law Givers.

The moment had come for Wargallow to address the gathering, and he turned to them. He had spoken to large gatherings before, but now he had to draw upon every vestige of his own power to combat the atmosphere in this titanic Hall. He bowed slightly to Eukor Epta and then to the mass of people crowded into the Hall. ''My name,'' he began, ''is Simon Wargallow. I am the Ambassador of Ruan Dubhnor, who is in command of the city of Elberon on the eastern seaboard of the eastern continent.''

Already there were stirrings and at once Otarus used a golden rod to beat upon his desk for silence. It came quickly. Wargallow had expected the names of Ruan and Elberon to arouse these people. "I understand your reaction," he said. "Perhaps I should explain a little of the recent history of the east. As you know, the Commander of the Armies, the Twenty Armies, I believe—" he said with a faint smile, turning to Fennobar for confirmation.

Fennobar reddened. Quanar Remoon's insistence on the foolish title had always been extremely embarrassing. Irritably Fennobar nodded.

"Morric Elberon," Wargallow went on, "came to the east with a mission. A mission bestowed upon him by your Emperor, Quanar Remoon." Again there were murmurs, for it was widely accepted here that Morric had abandoned the Empire, possibly to mount an assault on it.

Fennobar took advantage of the murmurings to get to his feet. "May I ask the Ambassador a question?" he asked Otarus.

Otarus frowned. "It seems a little uncivilized," he said caustically, "with our guest only just warming to his task."

"With your permission," said Wargallow to Otarus, though he directed his gaze at Eukor Epta, "I am eager to answer any questions."

"Very well," said Otarus gruffly. "But I would have thought the time for questions would have been afterward."

Fennobar bowed with bad grace. "Tell me, Ambassador," he said, and few could have mistaken the contempt in his voice, "I don't understand you. You say Morric Elberon was on a *mission*? Of the Emperor's? Isn't it true that he deserted Goldenisle, taking with him a large number of ships and men—an army, in fact—with which he intended to return—"

Otarus stood up and pointed with his rod. "You are stepping outside the bounds of—"

Eukor Epta motioned Fennobar to sit down. For the first time he spoke, but not until Fennobar and Otarus were seated. "This is not a debate," he said, his voice cutting the air like frost. "I wish to hear the Ambassador, who has traveled a considerable distance to be here. He has not been brought here as a criminal. Please continue, Ambassador."

Wargallow bowed and turned back to the Audience. "Morric Elberon had his orders. He came to the east to look for new lands, lands with which to expand the Empire. He was charged with this duty by Quanar Remoon, although when he

reached the east, certain rumors followed him. It was said
that he had left Goldenisle when he would have better served
it by remaining. This was something he had wondered himself, but he had been commanded by his Emperor, and such
a command is the law." Wargallow knew that Quanar Remoon made wild decisions that had to be obeyed, just as the
Audience knew it. Eukor Epta would know his words were a
lie, but Wargallow knew that if he could sow the seeds in the
minds of the Audience that Quanar *had* insisted Morric go to
the east, he might yet convert them away from the truth.

"Morric Elberon was loyal to Goldenisle. What he did, he
did in the name of Empire. He began the building of a city
in the delta of the Three Rivers, which was at first no more
than a base, a garrison. He would have done more there, but
events overtook him. For he was forced, as were all of us in
the eastern lands, to carry war to the powers beyond us all
in the far deserts, the Silences, where the lost plateau of
Xennidhum threatened not just us, but all of Omara."

Wargallow then spoke at great length of Xennidhum and
of the powers that had dwelt there, and of the former Sorcerer-
Kings and of the Hierarchs of Ternannoc. He spoke also of
the scourging of power and of gods, and of how the men of
the east had been forced to accept that such things had come
into Omara; he spoke of the gathering of the army and of the
crossing of the Silences; he spoke of the discovery of Cyrene
under the sand and of its history, of its own wars and of its
flooding. Eukor Epta's face never changed, but as Wargallow's vivid tale unfolded, he felt as if the world had turned
on its axis. Here was the truth! Cyrene! It had been hinted
at in his books, a city in the east, flooded by terrible powers.
Its peoples had fled and in the exodus that history had forgotten, men had gone to the west. And that flood had spread
around all Omara, drowning in its wake the lands of my
ancestors, those of the Blood. And the invaders had followed
it, to usurp the islands that had become the Chain.

"Many men had come with Elberon, it is true," Wargallow was telling the Audience, dragging Eukor Epta's concentration away from the elation he felt. "Some of them heard
about the war, and it is also true that they left your city and
came to the east when they had not been commanded to do
so."

"They deserted!" snapped Fennobar.

Wargallow turned to him. "If you like, yes. They took the law into their own hands. But even if that was wrong, it is well they did, for we needed every man who could bear arms when we rode to Xennidhum. I ask you not to deride them, but to honor them for their part in that foulest of wars."

Fennobar's scowl deepened, but he did not retort.

"Your Commander fought as no other man I have seen has fought," Wargallow went on. "And he died in that black city. For every score of us that rode there, only one man came back. The new city, which we have called Elberon in his honor, was a confused place, for in going to war, Morric Elberon had gathered together not one, but several armies. He had united men who had once been bitter enemies. When the remnants came back, it was unthinkable they should renew hostilities. Thus our city has become a place of mixed races. Ruan Dubhnor, himself a man of Empire, formerly of Morric Elberon's guard, is military commander of the city, and he is well loved by its people. He is as loyal to Goldenisle as Morric Elberon was."

"Are you telling us," said Ascanar of the Oligarchs, "that this new city is a state of Goldenisle? That Elberon fulfilled his duty to the Emperor by founding it and thus that its citizens are now men of Goldenisle, loyal to its Emperor?"

Wargallow had been expecting such a question and had prepared his answer after long thought during the previous night. "It is important to understand the nature of the people of the city," he began. "To many of them, Goldenisle is almost a legend, a place they have heard of only in stories. Indeed, some of them had never heard of Goldenisle until Morric came. There are two ways, are there not, of winning such people to your banner? Subdue them in war, or woo them with friendship. They fought with Morric because we shared a common foe that had no respect for any life on Omara. There were no documents, no treaties, just an understanding that Xennidhum must perish. Afterward we remained united, but what should we be? Men of Empire? Or men of King Strangarth? Or should we be subjects of the Deliverers, my own people? There are more of us in the east than of any other nation. When the city grew, it grew as a new state. We agreed that Ruan Dubhnor should command it, as he is a worthy man, and well loved. He is soon to marry Strangarth's daughter, so he must have an exceptionally strong will—''

Again there was scattered laughter in the Hall.

''So you see,'' he ended, ''Ruan is loyal to the Empire, but the city of Elberon, while under his control, is a place of its own.'' Wargallow knew that the questions would come quickly now, so he moved on before he could be interrupted. ''Even so, my mission here is to bring my people, the new people of Elberon, closer to yours.''

Cromalech stood up and was permitted to speak. ''As you know,'' he told an attentive Audience, ''our Emperor has made more than a few decisions in his time that have puzzled us—''

This time the laughter was far louder, and Wargallow learned in that moment that Cromalech was a popular man with his people. Eukor Epta's face was totally impassive, with no hint of emotion, while Fennobar's was thunderous.

Cromalech raised his hand for silence. ''But he sees and knows more than most of us realize. When he sent Morric Elberon to the east, he did not speak of it to me, his First Sword, but that was not my business. However, he did give me a task to perform more recently. He may be ill, hardly able to raise himself on some days, but he charged me with going to the new city of Elberon and bringing the Ambassador here. So he had evidently not forgotten the task he had given Morric Elberon.'' He sat down to fresh noise. Previously he had explained to Wargallow that it suited Eukor Epta to lead people to believe that Quanar was still capable of making decisions, as any he made for him would not be questioned. Thus it was convenient for Cromalech to say that Quanar had given him direct orders.

Fennobar stared at his feet, his rage barely controlled, but he did not betray it by speaking.

Otarus now addressed Wargallow. ''These are strange events of which you tell us, for we have long held power in contempt, as have other men of Omara. It is a subject that we approach with caution, and yet it seems that a grave danger to us all has been averted by the use of power.''

''I fear,'' said the Deliverer, ''that it is not yet over. My mission here is twofold. To bring our peoples together, but also to bring news of what lies ahead.''

At this point he called upon Orhung to join him, and the Created came abruptly to life. The Hall held no terrors for him and he began at once to recite again his own peculiar story, explaining where he had come from and the purpose for which he had been designed. He spoke also of the terrible night when the Werewatch had been slaughtered and of the rise to power of Anakhizer and what he intended for Omara. While he spoke, the Audience voiced its amazement even more loudly than it had while hearing out Wargallow, often having to be quelled by Otarus, who himself was visibly stunned by many of the things Orhung said. So much of it was against the beliefs of the people, and yet they could not be ignored. The only man in the Hall who did not seem to react was Eukor Epta. Even the statuesque guards looked surprised by what they had heard.

There would have been a hundred questions afterward, but Otarus maintained order with great skill. He thanked both Orhung and Wargallow when they had sat down and he had quelled the noise. ''We have heard the Ambassador tell us that he has not merely come to ask us to accept his city but to take up arms with it against a common foe. Before we debate these issues, we must hear from others.''

He then called upon Cromalech to speak, and the First Sword rose and came to the steps before the Audience like an actor about to deliver his most prized soliloquy. ''I have spoken many times to the Ambassador on the voyage here. It is clear to me that we face a war of shadows. This evil that he speaks of has not shown itself openly, nor will it. Like the shark, it strikes from below where it cannot be seen, or like an eagle by night. It will not call us out to some field of battle, or the high seas. Where is it? It is no clearer. But I would say that we must act quickly. We must send out our ships, our warriors, to find it. Let us take the war to it, wherever it is hidden.'' This brought applause, for the Audience were in need of something to cheer after the grim words of the strangers.

Fennobar stood up and came beside Cromalech, looking down at him. At once there was quiet. The Commander held up his hand, but Otarus had to call for silence.

"As Deputy Commander," said Fennobar, "I must advise caution. A warlord does not hurl his men into the darkness without first looking very hard at the land before him."

He would have said more, but another of the Administrators interrupted him. Both Fennobar and Cromalech stood to one side, but they did not return to their seats.

It was Eanan who spoke, a tall pale-faced man with features that seemed unfamiliar with any kind of amusement. "I submit that we should not debate the question of deploying troops until later. The details are a military matter and there are other things to discuss here."

Wargallow felt a surge of unease. The urgency with which he and the army of Elberon had come together before taking the war to Xennidhum was absent here. The vast weight of Empire, its tradition, its years of thought, could not be moved so easily.

Eanan met Wargallow's gaze. "Your report, Ambassador, of events in the east, moves us to think of many things. Prime among them, as Otarus has pointed out, is the question of power."

Wargallow felt the word like an arrow. He, a Deliverer, had spent most of his life seeking out and destroying belief in power.

Eanan pressed on, coldly, efficiently. "When this man Korbillian first came to Goldenisle, he was not given an Audience here. We thought him to be insane. He spoke of power and of god-like beings. The law would have asked for his life."

Wargallow nodded. "So it was in my land."

"As you have told us. Yet it seems we were wrong about this man. You ask us to accept that he was from another world, or as you say, another Aspect of this one. And he wielded immeasurable power."

"He told Quanar Remoon as much. And the Emperor thought better than to execute him. He sent him to the east, rather than destroy him. Perhaps Quanar saw truth in Korbillian. It was a wise judgment."

Wargallow's words took Eanan by surprise, as with the assembled host, but the Administrator recovered quickly. "That may be so. But what of this Korbillian?"

"I have said. His power destroyed the darkness of Xennidhum, but his own life was forfeit."

"Quite so. Tell us, when he left Goldenisle, were there no others who went with him?"

Wargallow saw both Fennobar and Cromalech tense. The reference, no matter how oblique, to Guile, had not been expected. Was Eukor Epta about to bring that into the open? Surely he would not risk exposing himself?

"He told us that he had been banished from Goldenisle, taken by ship to a wild shore in the cold lands north of our continent. The ship was lost in a storm."

"Ah," said Eanan. "Banished. So he was not on some mission of the Emperor?" The sarcasm was delivered gently, but not lost on the Audience.

"He was banished. The Emperor would not kill what he did not understand. He sent him to as remote a region as he could think of, a land whose beasts are sometimes used to frighten your children."

Otarus had to smother a chuckle at this.

"And those with him?" persisted Eanan.

"All perished. Korbillian was a man with strength and power beyond those of ordinary men, as witness his deeds. He, alone, could have survived the icy seas of the north. He, alone, could have braved the mountains and found his way to the Three Rivers in the south. Those who escorted him to our shores never came to us."

Eanan nodded, indicating to Otarus that he had finished.

The High Chamberlain stood. "Tell us, Ambassador, what precisely does Ruan Dubhnor now want? A formal treaty?"

"He would wish the prime task to be the hunting of the enemy. Ruan prepares for war, and we already scour the east, but we do not think the enemy is there. Ruan will willingly come under one banner when war breaks."

Eukor Epta cleared his throat and all attention focussed on him. "We must thank the Ambassador for his patience with us. While he is here, he is our guest and must be treated with respect. In view of the dual nature of his mission, we have a good deal to debate and I do not see that we need detain him while we do it. Noon draws on. We will assemble again in two hours."

Orhung turned to Wargallow as the officials began to leave. "Are we believed? I thought not."

Wargallow shrugged. "The Houses believe," he said softly. "But they do not rule. Eukor Epta will only agree to our requests if they suit his greater purpose."

"And if he will not prepare his army?"

"Then we shall have to find a way of drawing Anakhizer to us, provoking an attack. Until the darkness is seen, Goldenisle may dismiss it. Even Cromalech is not convinced. Fennobar considers every word a lie, and he has support here."

"And Otarus?"

"I cannot tell. But I suspect he is a man whose concern is for the good of his people and not for his own gain."

Presently their guards came to them and asked if they would retire for food and rest. They were pleased to accept, although Orhung had already begun to lapse into his strange condition of far-awayness, as though he listened for some distant sound. As Wargallow left the Hall, he was aware of the confusion he had brought here, and he felt a constricting of the darkness. It hung about the city like a storm, but it remained unseen. It would need Sisipher's vision to penetrate it. Treachery brooded here, thick as a pall, he could at least sense that, and every wall hid a purpose of its own.

12
Otarus

WARGALLOW AND ORHUNG SAT SILENTLY in one of the more comfortable rooms of Cromalech's private quarters. He had arranged food and drink for them, but neither had taken much. Orhung looked into that unfathomable distance that no one else could see, as if removed from the world around him and all things Omaran. Wargallow had wondered more than once at his real purpose, his will, for if events went against them, what power could this being unleash? Korbillian had carried terrifying powers, wielding storms, fire, and although Orhung was probably far less gifted, he remained a mystery. Wargallow was thinking now that nothing was assured in this city. Besotted with its own power, it fought itself, its own mind unable to grasp the deeper realities outside it. Haunted by such thoughts, he waited as the afternoon sun began to slip downward toward the crest of the immense cliffs.

He would have been shocked by the mental turmoil of his companion had he been able to share it. As it was, Orhung maintained his expressionless mask. These humans, he thought, dwell in confusion. They are all threatened by Anakhizer, and yet they defy each other. Even Wargallow, who seeks to unite them, covers his hatred for some of them. I have no mechanism with which to question my own resolve, and yet, curiously, I envy these people the emotions that drive them to theirs. *Envy?* How can I think of envy when I am no more than an extension of this rod that I bear? But as he gently touched it, he knew that the rod itself was more than just a device. His fingers quickly withdrew from it as if he had touched a living being, a mind, just as his own mind shied from the thought that the rod could control him.

Cromalech returned from the second assembly. He smiled as he entered, but Wargallow still did not trust him. His motives were far too obscure. The Killer picked up a flagon of cold water and drank heartily as a trooper might after a hot afternoon's parade. He sat down opposite his guests.

"Good news, though the debate was long and in places heated."

"I would surmise Eukor Epta was not so," said Wargallow sardonically.

Cromalech grinned. "Of course not. Face as blank as a new wall. But I should like to have been inside his head. Your presence here has shaken him.

"Well, firstly approval has been given to an alliance between Goldenisle and your new city of Elberon. And it has been agreed that Elberon should be a free state and recognized." He saw Wargallow's brows raise. "Oh yes. A good many men thought Elberon should be made a part of the Empire, but it was argued that it would be better for the Empire to have an ally on the eastern continent."

"I see. How is this treaty to be formalized?"

"It will be drawn up and studied by both parties. In due course it would be signed by our officials and your ruler, Ruan."

Wargallow grunted. "In due course. We will have to consider the conditions carefully."

"You're a suspicious man," Cromalech laughed, helping himself to some cold meat that had not been eaten.

"Such is politics. But if the treaty is acceptable, it will be an important step to greater things. How soon can it be prepared?"

"These things take time—"

"Delays are inadvisable—"

"But unavoidable. Although your talk of evil powers has caused much consternation, and although Orhung's speech about the death of his fellows rocked the assembly, a good many of them were not keen to pursue the matter. You must realize that they have been entombed in this city for so long now that they have little perspective of the world outside. They hear of these disasters, black powers, other worlds even, but they respond with a shake of the head, possibly the fist, and little more.''

Wargallow grimaced. ''Is that how you respond?''

Cromalech was still smiling. ''No. I've traveled. And brushed with enough strange events to know that something exists that could harm us all. I confess to be as ambitious as any other man of Empire, otherwise I would go insane in this place. I spoke up, as did others. Fennobar, too, though he was primed, I am certain, by Eukor Epta. As a result, it has been agreed that Fennobar's ships should be partially deployed to seek out word of this power you say will threaten us all.''

Wargallow nodded. ''Ah, then that is something.''

Cromalech chuckled. ''Yes, perhaps. But Fennobar is to lead this fleet, and his prime motive will be to seek out Ottemar Remoon. It was not said, but why else would Eukor Epta agree?''

''He'll go straight to Teru Manga and the pirates.''

''Naturally! But so will I.''

Wargallow's gaze fixed on him. ''You?''

''I argued that it would be sensible for the Imperial Killers to search out this power also, and there was some opposition, but in the end it was Eukor Epta himself who condoned it. His argument was very smooth, and the assembly agreed.''

''Then he is plotting something.''

''Indeed! He knows no other way to act.'' Again Cromalech laughed, as though he actually enjoyed this intrigue, even though it was his own life that was being juggled with.

''So what did he say?''

''Simply that the Emperor would wish it. He admitted that Quanar is now so seriously ill that he has vested the power of decision in him. As he had sent me across the sea to Elberon (and I found it hard not to laugh as Eukor Epta confirmed this) Quanar would wish to have me acting directly for him again.''

''It is clear what Eukor Epta intends,'' Wargallow snorted.

''To kill me at sea? No doubt that will be part of Fennobar's orders. But I'll deal with that buffoon. When I set sail—'' He cut himself short, as if he had been about to overreach himself.

"You have a devious scheme of your own," nodded Wargallow, amused.

Cromalech smiled. "Perhaps. But there is more yet. Now that I am to go to sea, it has been decided that it would be more appropriate (a favorite word of Eukor Epta's) if you and Orhung were to be housed in the palace. The word 'detained' was not used, but it was meant."

"We are to be destroyed?"

"No, no. He is far too cunning for that. Unless he finds a good reason that the assembly would accept. Then it would be an official execution."

"Is that what he wants?" said Wargallow, appalled. "After what we have told him and your people?"

"The evil power you speak of interests him, as does any form of power. But little will be done about it until it shows itself or moves against us. It will have to be found. Unless this happens, the question of the succession will rule all our thoughts, and our plans."

Cromalech excused himself after this, going in search of a bath and rest. Wargallow cursed quietly. He turned to Orhung, whose own emotions were impossible to discern. "Then we have to play this political game, too."

"We must find Anakhizer. Since we came to this place, I have been searching. We are closer to him. I feel the darkness that draws about this island. Something moves at the edge of my vision."

Wargallow started. It was the first time Orhung had mentioned this. "Where? *Here?*"

"No. Still far away. To the north. I cannot see clearly."

Wargallow sat back and closed his eyes. Somehow the darkness thickened, closing in, and he sensed that whatever power readied itself to strike at Omara would find only a bickering rabble to oppose it. The city outside was silent, but it had become a trap, a prison. Eukor Epta would listen, but nothing would alter the plans he had already formulated.

Shortly after the sun had fallen behind the cliff wall, men came to Cromalech's quarters. They knocked politely and were given entrance, seven men dressed in simple clothes, unarmed. They bowed to Wargallow and Orhung, shown in by a lone guard of Cromalech's Imperial Killers.

The first man smiled artificially. "The First Sword has explained the decisions of the assembly?"

"I take it you have come to escort us to Eukor Epta," said Wargallow.

The man's fixed smile did not waver and he bowed again. "Indeed, sir. A place has been prepared for you both, and you'll forgive my saying so, but it is far more salubrious than these dingy quarters." It was an insult to Cromalech's rooms, but Wargallow let it pass.

"If you'll come with us, sir, we will see you to your new apartments. Eukor Epta wishes to entertain you personally."

"A great honor," said Wargallow. Where was Cromalech? "Perhaps we should thank our erstwhile host before leaving."

"That won't be necessary, sir," said the man obsequiously.

"I insist—"

"Perhaps it will be possible later."

"Your pardon," interrupted Cromalech's guard. "The First Sword is no longer here. He has duties to attend to."

"Very well," said Wargallow, sensing a betrayal. "I will see him another time."

"Of course, sir." The man bowed and led the way along the first of the corridors. Surprisingly, although it was early evening, there were no guards about. Doors were closed, and corridors and halls were empty, as if the entire garrison had been sent out into the field. Even at the gate to the street, which was a side gate, there were no guards. The only guard here was the one who had shown Eukor Epta's men in. He saluted as Wargallow and Orhung left, closing the gate and locking it behind him.

Wargallow leaned closer to Orhung in the confines of the narrow street. "I was always wary of sidestreets. Why not the main door?"

For once Orhung was not asleep. His fingers touched at the top of his rod of steel, although the escort made no move to close in, apparently casual about the walk through the quiet city. Perhaps, mused Wargallow, we are expected to try and escape. Ah, but then we would be captured and made to look fools.

From a high window above them, a face watched. Cromalech frowned down into the narrow street. In a way he was sorry that he had to relinquish Wargallow and his strange companion. But to help them and Ottemar would be to hinder Tennebriel's path to the throne. And by letting Eukor Epta have them now, he grinned, without an argument and with good grace, cooperation, it will baffle him. He'll wonder if I am part of their cause after all.

Cromalech liked Wargallow, and did not like to think of him dying. But Eukor Epta would most likely keep him hidden away, as he had with Ottemar and Tennebriel. And I will be far away, out on the seas! Already my ship is making ready, and when she sails across the inner sea, no one will pay her any heed, least of all Fennobar's wolves.

He left the window and went down to recall the guards whom he had told to keep out of sight. After that he would don the fisherman's clothes he had asked for, put on a heavy cloak and go down to the harbor to join the deep sea fishing craft that was waiting. With any luck he'd be far closer to the hidden Ottemar than Fennobar by the dawn, and no one in the city would be aware that he'd left.

Wargallow and Orhung climbed up a steep, winding street, the old houses silent, probably empty, and both men understood the antiquity of this place, possibly the oldest city on Omara. The men escorting them were like ghosts, travelling up toward the part of the city where the palace loomed over it with a noticeable air of ease. They did not seem like men bent on mischief, as if they were merely exercising a simple command and anticipated no real exertion. Wargallow revised his thoughts and wondered if this was no more than Eukor Epta's way of showing them that he did not think them worthy of a more pompous entry into the palace.

As he considered this, the shadows appeared. These men, a score of them, were far more alert, prepared, than Eukor Epta's escort. With stunning precision they had stepped out into the street and trapped each individual man in a matter of seconds. Steel gleamed in the dim glow of the lamps above, but there were no cries, no screams. Wargallow lived again the abduction of Guile in the streets of Elberon, but this was even more sudden. His killing steel slipped from his sleeve, but a voice at his ear spoke sharply.

"Peace to you, Simon Wargallow!"

The Deliverer whipped round, unimpeded, to face an unarmed man. He wore a garish mask, as did all the attackers. Already they had dragged Eukor Epta's men out of the street, out of view.

"None of them will die," said the man in the mask. "We were prepared to do battle with Fennobar's dogs, but it seems that Eukor Epta declined to send them. Perhaps he didn't want to alarm you with a show of force."

"As you have," said Wargallow, his steel hand ready to kill. Orgung was also primed to attack, but he held back.

"We have our reasons. Quickly, before we are seen! Come with us."

"I must ask why."

"Yes, of course. But not here. We must not be seen. You must know Eukor Epta is your enemy. I doubt that you would have been seen again."

"Who do you serve?"

"He awaits us. Come! It is not safe on these streets."

Wargallow had no time to deliberate. He nodded to Orhung and both men put away their weapons. At once their new escort closed in and the leader, who would not give his name, led them through a narrow door and down an old flight of stairs which looked as if it had not been used for many years. At the bottom of these the man lifted a blazing torch from an iron bracket and led them along a passage that closed in on them like the burrow of a huge worm. A number of ancient doors were set in it, and one of these was open, guarded by yet another masked man holding a brand. There were stone steps beyond.

"Where does this lead?" said Wargallow.

"To the old city. The first city," said the leader. It seemed after that that the journey went on for a considerable time, as they had to negotiate stairs after stairs, tunnels, more doorways and an arched bridge that ran over a fast-flowing river. Wargallow guessed that they must be well below the level of the sea. He knew also that these men were not going to kill him and Orhung. They would never have brought them so far just for that simple act.

Finally they emerged from a doorway into an open area, and the torches flung back shadows that raced upward to vaults of awesome size. Great arches and spans curved and interlaced across what must once have been the ceiling of a tremendous building, several times the size of the Hall of the Hundred. The place was empty now, save for great blocks of fallen masonry and other debris, dust and stone, the domain of rats and other such underground creatures. Wargallow had heard Brannog speak of the remarkable delvings of the Earth-wrought and the tunnel systems they had made under the earth, but even they could not have envisaged this. If men had made this place, they were men of power, gifted with skills beyond the dreams of any man living today. But who could they have been? Not the ancestors of the men of Goldenisle.

The masked escort led the stupefied Wargallow and his less moved companion across the immeasurable plaza to a place that might have been its mid-point. The sound of their passing, though muffled by a sea of dust, echoed back from invisible walls like the whispers of the dead. Ahead of them they saw a brand, and below it a solitary figure. As they approached it, Wargallow knew the man at once. He was not masked.

Otarus bowed gently. ''Please forgive the rudeness of your abduction,'' he said as he straightened. ''But I believed you to be in grave danger.'' He used his hands gently to dismiss the men that had brought his captives here, for so Wargallow thought of himself and Orhung. The men placed another torch beside them and withdrew into the shadows.

''This must be the time of trust,'' said Otarus. ''I hope so. Darkness draws in on us all, and I believe that you and your people are a ray of hope to mine.''

''Of which darkness do you speak?'' said Wargallow.

''The darkness within, and that without. You spoke of Xennidhum and of this creature who has either survived it or benefited from its fall by growing stronger than the Heirarchs of Ternannoc.''

''He was one of them.''

''If so, all Omara must fear him.''

''You already knew of Anakhizer?'' said Wargallow, shocked.

''No, but you have confirmed what some of us had guessed might happen. Look around you. This is the first city, or what remains of it.''

"The original Goldenisle?"

Otarus sighed. "Goldenisle had not been born when this city was old. I brought you here, to the heart of the city, for good reason. You understand history. You are a man who has had it presented to him before. You know more of Omara's past than most men. You spoke of Xennidhum, and of Cyrene, the city of wonders that perished. You have walked its streets!"

Wargallow nodded, remembering the place well, its burial beneath the desert, its terrifying unveiling by the storm brought by Korbillian. "We call it the Whispering City now, for it speaks of its past like a ghost."

"It is also the key to the mysteries of Goldenisle."

Wargallow frowned. "To this place?"

"Aye. When you spoke of it, and of the Flood, up in the Hall of the Hundred, you set ripples of wonder and terror spreading in that sea of faces. Let us speak more freely of the Flood, and of the time before this."

Wargallow was puzzled. Otarus obviously felt this to be a matter of the highest importance, and yet it was the first time that Wargallow had encountered it since coming here. He nodded. "Very well."

The old man sighed, yet even here he retained the dignity that he had shown in the Hall. "You probably know very little of the history of Goldenisle. It is a subject of intense interest to Eukor Epta, the Administrative Oligarch. It is complex and riddled with mythology—you saw the art in the Hall. No one has ever succeeded in extricating the truths from the legends, but Eukor Epta tries, of that I am sure. It is what drives him. I, too, have looked hard at the past. Eukor Epta has a library, although it is hidden on Tower Island, and even I would not hazard a guess at what is kept in it. I also have a library, some of which I repress, for Goldenisle has a guilty past, and for some men to learn of it would lead to strife, maybe war.

"Most legends concur about the beginning. That is, that Goldenisle was not a chain of islands, but a peninsular, part of a vast outstretch of land pushing down from the north. Legend has it that a terrible flood came and drowned most of this peninsular. This city in which we stand was built on a high part of the peninsular, and the people who dwelt in it were not as the men who now live above us. They had powers the like of which have not been known since in Omara. But after the Flood, when the seas rose up catastrophically, only the islands were left.

"The people of the first city, who were divided between the nobility and the workers-of-stone (as the stories put it) combined their great powers to fight the Flood, and they devised ways in which to ensure the survival of the city, locking it beneath the sea. Even so, its people declined rapidly, their powers terribly drained by their great working. When the men of the east, the men who, as you have told us, fled from the drowning of Cyrene, came here, there were grim wars. The original people were slowly destroyed, and the invaders became the rulers. They named the Chain and built their own capital above the first city. The legends spread, and it was hinted at by some that the invaders had *sent* the Flood. You have partly confirmed this, for it is clear that the Flood was part of the awesome upheavals in the east, the clash of powers at Xennidhum where the Sorcerer-Kings struggled with powers beyond them."

"And this is important to you now?" said Wargallow.

Otarus drew in his breath and nodded. "I fear so. The invaders founded their own dynasty here, that of the Remoons. History has shown that the Remoons have ruled well over the centuries, but there is a curse following them, that of insanity. It is said to have been made by the men they conquered here, the men who built the first city. A law was passed many centuries ago by the Remoons that all power and belief in gods was forbidden, for they saw only evil in such things. Other men in Omara made the same law, men who were also refugees from the eastern disasters, where the abuse of power caused such chaos. This law has strengthened over the years, has it not?"

Wargallow grunted. "Aye. You see how well." He held out his killing steel.

Otarus shuddered at the sight of the steel arm. "The guilt of the men before us was vast. And here, in this buried place, the last of the survivors, the men of the Blood, as they called themselves, knew they would be exterminated like vermin if they did not capitulate, for their own powers had been used up in keeping the sea back from their city. At last they persuaded one of the more lenient Remoon kings that they would abjure all power, leave their city and become part of the new Goldenisle.

"The Empire recognized that it had treated these people harshly, though it never admitted to usurping their lands. Yet it was agreed that the former inhabitants should have a voice in government. As a result of numerous debates, an official voice was given to them. Years went by and the Empire forgot its differences with them. In time there were no longer any differences between descendants of the men of the east and those of the Blood. History conveniently became legend.

"But there are some who clung to their past. I have not done so out of malice. I chanced upon things in the old writings. Things which explained much. You see, the Administrators have become very powerful, and apart from the Emperor himself, they hold the balance of power. Yet their history goes back to the time when the men of the first city were given a political voice. It is the Administrators, amazingly, who have evolved from those men."

"Men of the Blood, as you put it?"

"Mostly." Otarus looked about him as if he would see the throngs of the past, the ancient magnificence. He shuddered. "And I suspect that Eukor Epta is one of them. His line will trace back over the centuries. They have not forgotten, nor forgiven."

"And what is it that he wants?"

Otarus shook his head bitterly. "To undo everything! To cast out those who sailed in on the Flood. To give back the land to those who had it. And no doubt, to revive their power. It is madness! The old prejudices and persecutions ended long ago. No man of Goldenisle is now any less a citizen for his blood line. We are one race now. Our only hope for the future is to remain so."

Wargallow looked away, thinking over this in the silence that came down for a moment like a fist. He turned back to Otarus. "What of the Heir, Ottemar Remoon?"

"I believe," said Otarus, straightening, "that Goldenisle must be strong. Under Quanar Remoon it has foundered, teetering on the edge of collapse, helped by Eukor Epta. We lost Morric Elberon because of it. Oh, I know that he abandoned us! It was well spoken when you claimed he took the east for the Empire, but I knew it for a lie, as do others. Quanar is a madman, and Eukor Epta rules. We need a strong man now. You know more of Ottemar than most men do. Or am I mistaken? Do my own agents mislead me?''

''You said this was to be a time of trust. I am tired of the deceits here. Very well. I speak for Ottemar.'' Wargallow went on to talk about Guile, his part in Xennidhum, and of his eventual abduction by Gondobar. Often while he was speaking, Otarus nodded or muttered, as though Wargallow had confirmed something he had long suspected. At last, as Wargallow ended, Otarus sank back on to one of the huge blocks, using it as a seat.

''I see more clearly now, but even so, the confusion is great. Eukor Epta seeks Ottemar, but not to kill him. Then it must be to make him Emperor, a puppet, controlled rigidly from the palace. And he will find a way to force Ottemar to concede even more power to those of the Blood. You have confirmed for Eukor Epta what he has longed to confirm! That the Flood was the result of war in the east, almost as if it were sent by the men of the east. Now he will dig up the past and seek to disgrace us. Ottemar will be a figurehead. I can envisage him as he makes some royal decree that we should return the islands to those of the Blood. It must be what Eukor Epta plans.''

''And Fennobar?''

''Soon he will be declared Commander of the Armies and Navy. It will fulfill his main ambition. He is prepared to be Eukor Epta's man to secure the post. But what of Cromalech?''

Wargallow snorted. ''For a simple fighting man, he is more devious than a dozen of your Administrators. I have yet to fathom his motives. As I have told you, he is not Eukor Epta's man. He seems to support Ottemar, and claims to work for men he will not name. I hoped it was for you—''

Otarus shook his head. ''Not him! A wily one, yes. It is possible he is with some group who, like us, support Ottemar. If not, I do not understand his ambitions.''

Wargallow agreed. ''I must have been a fool to think that Orhung and I could sway the Empire into gathering itself against Anakhizer. So many factions!''

''We must find Ottemar. Before we can do anything, we

have to see that he takes his place on Quanar's throne, away from Eukor Epta. Very soon Quanar will die. Until this succession can be settled, there can be no war on Anakhizer."

"You are right. But what can we do?"

"You and Orhung must leave. We will put you on a ship and send out a fleet of our own to search for the Heir."

"In secret?"

Otarus smiled. "No, the beauty of that is that it can be done openly. The fleet, at least. Now that it has been agreed that a search can be made for this evil power, Fennobar's fleet does not have the sole discretion to look. No, it would be sensible to send all available ships. There will be volunteers. Do you know of the Trullhoons?"

Wargallow said he had been told of them.

"Their ruler, Darraban, is Ottemar's uncle," said Otarus. "He would like nothing more than to see his sister's son on the throne! And he has no love for the Hammavars, I promise you. It was Gondobar's brother, Onin, who ran off with Ottemar's mother. When Darraban 'volunteers' a small fleet to go out in search of Anakhizer, the Empire will condone it. And you and Orhung will have safe passage on Darraban's own ship."

"He is your ally?"

"He is. I have pledged my support for Ottemar secretly to him, and that was enough. He was at the assembly when you spoke, and was impressed."

"If we find Ottemar and bring him here, what then? War?"

"There may be. But I command many men who work in the city. If we have to fight, and it may be with the army of Fennobar, there are men in the city to help us. With the Trullhoons, and your people, we would take the day."

"You think so?"

"I will be honest. We will need the men of Ruan to do it. If not, it will be a grim struggle for control."

"But if Ottemar comes, surely no one can refute his claim?"

Otarus scowled. "I am sure Eukor Epta will already have thought of this. The possibility of Ottemar coming back openly, without his leave, will already have been considered. He will have a strategy for such an eventuality, be assured."

Wargallow's smile had gone. "You are right, of course.

But I must commit myself, and Ruan. We are for a settled government here. Without it, we cannot hope to destroy Anakhizer.''

Otarus watched the Deliverer. He had been stunned by this man who had dared to come out of the east and face up to the assembly so boldly. He was a man who would command great respect, a man who could possibly match Eukor Epta. "Something else troubles you?"

Wargallow nodded. "Cromalech. Something is wrong. Who *does* he serve?"

"He is well liked by the people. He would be a worthy ally. Perhaps he would even tip the scales for us. But I would not risk challenging him. He is dangerous."

"There is another possibility that neither of us has spoken of."

Otarus stiffened at this, fearing something unpleasant. "Oh?"

"We must not underestimate Anakhizer. His will is bent on undoing Goldenisle. What better way to do it than to have agents within the city."

Otarus paled, and in the glow of the torch his age hung like a yoke about him. "It would be possible. The city crawls with subterfuge."

"Could Cromalech serve this power?"

"Possibly. But if so, surely he would have killed Ottemar. With him dead, the question of succession would be even more complex. There would be even more factions. No, no, Anakhizer must seek Ottemar's death."

"Tell me, as no one else has done so, who would succeed Quanar if Ottemar was dead?"

"Quanar has no issue. Ottemar is the last of the Remoons. It would mean the end of the dynasty."

"There are no others, no distant cousins, nothing?" said Wargallow, surprised.

"Well, there was a girl, Tennebriel," said Otarus, and he explained the girl's background. "But it is most likely that she was murdered in the War of the Islands, when most of the Crannoch House perished. Her mother-in-law, Estreen, lives in exile. The Crannochs were in disgrace for years, and even now the law is immutable concerning Estreen. If she set foot on Medallion, she would be executed."

"But not the girl?"

"No. She was a babe during the war. The Crannochs live among us now, as they did before the scandal of Ildar's day, but there would be little support for a Crannoch heir." Otarus sniffed. "But this is idle speculation. She is dead. Come, let us go to better quarters. There are men you must meet."

Wargallow nodded, but he was not quite so ready to remove the Crannoch girl from his mind.

13
Aumlac

GUILE STOOD UP, trying anxiously to assess his position, for there was no doubt in his mind that the pirate was dead. He would leave them no single ally here in Teru Manga. Guile turned, and in the doorway he saw Sisipher, staring past him, past Gondobar, perhaps to some dim future. Her face was pale and he could see the open fear there. For once she had lost her composure, her sureness that had often mocked his own frailty. He went to her, touching her arm lightly and her eyes came back to him.

"We must leave," he told her softly. "As soon as it's known that Gondobar is dead, our own lives will likely be forfeit. Or worse."

She nodded mutely, as if her own thoughts were slow to gather.

Guile went back to the pirate and found it easy to move him, for the body was surprisingly light, the clothes padded to make the man seem larger than he was. Guile wondered what grim disaster it was that had so wasted him. Moments later he had dragged the body into the bedroom where Gondobar was to have slept and it was not difficult to arrange things to look as if the pirate had gone to bed and was sleeping in it.

"It will give us a little more time," he told Sisipher, as if he needed to explain his actions. She may have thought us safe from the pirates before, but no longer, he told himself.

She had been watching him sluggishly, as if her own sleep had been deep and she had not roused herself from it properly.

178

He frowned at her. "What is it?"

Again she shook herself. "Forgive me. I was thinking about flight. There are few places for us to go."

He nodded. "Aye. Not down that ropeway to the sea!" He forced a grin. He had finished with Gondobar and he closed the door on him as they came out into the hallway. "I suppose the place is guarded."

"It is," she said. "I can feel the presence of men about us."

He would have asked her to expand on that, but his heart and mind raced together. Any moment a guard might enter, and they would be trapped. He strapped on his sword and found one for her, pulling her along with him to a doorway.

Her fingers tightened in his and he could feel the fear in her. This place frightened her, he realized. Something here reached deep into her, and he was glad that he could not feel it as well. His surface fears of the freebooters were quite enough to contend with.

"No, not that door!" she whispered in his ear, and he could feel her breath on his neck. "Guarded."

They turned from the hall, searching for other doors until they found one at the back of the house. Sisipher stood by it, listening. In a while she nodded and Guile drew back the bolts. In the dark they seemed to shriek. The door creaked inwards and Guile watched the girl, but she nodded again as if she had the eyes of a cat.

Swiftly they went out into the night. They were in a narrow alleyway cluttered with sacks of rubbish. The wall of the house formed one side of the alley, while the other was the sheer stone of a cliff-like rock face. It rose up forbiddingly, lost in gloom, a place where only a spider would venture. To their left was a faint patch of light, marking a lamp set in what passed here for a street. To their right the alley sloped upward gently to pitch darkness.

Guile could see that Sisipher was listening for something, and he knew at once what it was. The owl! Kirrikree, their extraordinary ally, was here somewhere, and the girl's mind probed for him.

"Can you—?" he began, but she placed her finger on his lips.

"He's above us somewhere," she whispered. "And he's

heard us. He'll try to guide us out." She pointed to the darkness on the right. "That way."

He slipped his sword from its sheath, glad to have a weapon, and they moved on, cautious as predators on the hunt, and as silent. The darkness wrapped them as they threaded through more sacks and some rubble. The alley ended in a point, but there was a defile beyond it. It looked far too narrow, but by clambering up the sides of the rock wall they were able to squeeze through, backs to the stone. Neither of them could see anything and they moved by sense of touch, relieved to be getting away from Gondobar's house.

The angle of the defile meant they had to edge upward. "Where does this lead?" Guile asked after what he thought to be an age.

"Upward and away from the houses. There are ledges above us that will eventually bring us to the top of the plateau. Kirrikree is there and says there is thick vegetation that will hide us. But it is a dangerous climb."

"Then I'm glad of the darkness."

"There are men above us, lookouts for the freebooters. We could not avoid them by daylight."

"What can Kirrikree see? It's like tar down here."

"He sees better by night than we do by day," she told him and he thought he sensed a smile.

For some time they continued the awkward climb, partly wedging themselves into the cleft as they went up, and Guile knew they must now be a considerable height above the houses. Abruptly a number of lights were lit and voices could be heard below. There were shouts, the rush of boots in the streets, the ring of steel being drawn.

"They must have found him already!" Guile muttered.

The lights swept to and fro; they were now almost directly below, forming a great pool of yellow in which a dozen or more figures could be seen in a kind of bizarre dance. Guile gasped, seeing for the first time how near-vertical their climb had been. He was certain that men were following.

"Drogund!" said Sisipher. "And his henchmen, Rannovic. He can't wait to get his hands on me."

"Keep climbing. You know how much I detest heights, but I'm happy to make an extra effort for once."

They redoubled their attempt to climb the defile, swaying

dangerously at times, but helping each other. It was only a cautionary word from the girl that cut short the climb. "More lights!" she whispered, indicating the heights above.

"The lookouts?"

"Kirrikree sees them. Word must have got to them already. We are in the middle."

She had barely said it when torches flared above them, some hundred feet away, and by the flickering light they saw clearly the men on a ledge there, peering over it. The defile stretched up near to the ledge. It was the only way up.

"How many?" said Guile, feeling his mouth drying up.

"Too many." As she said it, the first of the men began clambering over the edge into the neck of the defile, but as he did so something gray dropped down from the darkness overhead, silent as stone. The man screamed once and fell outwards into an abyss that yawned beyond the shoulder of rock. The huge owl had seen him and had dragged him to his doom. Shouts rang back from above as the men there milled like ants disturbed in their nest.

"You cannot pass this way," Kirrikree told Sisipher, "and you are followed." His voice filled her, and with it the terror.

"Then we must fight. I would throw myself to my death rather than be taken."

"There is a way out," the owl told her, ignoring her remark. "But it is dangerous, possibly more dangerous than facing the pirates with steel. And I cannot follow."

Guile saw the great bird flash past, aware that although they were inching up the crack in the rock wall, a great darkness opened not far from them, like another chute down into the deeps below. Sisipher was pointing to it, explaining what the bird had told her.

"Down!" echoed Guile. "To the sea?"

She shook her head. He sensed that she knew more than she would admit to, but for the moment he had no wish to confront men with steel. The prospect of going down into the bowels of the earth seemed better than the heights of the plateau or the combined steel of Drogund's pack. He nodded.

Kirrikree floated down, and as Guile saw the owl come closer to them he felt a stab of emotion, for the amazing bird had played its part at Xennidhum and could never be forgotten for that. He wished for the thousandth time that he had

Sisipher's magical gift of communing with it, although there
had been times when he had thought he could read words in
its huge eyes.

"He's showing us the way down," Sisipher told him, and
he forced himself to look at the way they must go, which was
gently lit by the blazing torches high above them. Other men
were clambering down; at once Kirrikree soared upward,
readying to attack them.

Sisipher turned on her stomach and edged out of the defile
and across the bare rock. Guile swore under his breath, but
he followed. Their progress was slow, but had to be. One
slip now would mean a sudden ending far below. They
crossed a knuckle of rock and before them was nothing, a
yawning black mouth like some unguessably large denizen
readying to gulp them down. Guile could feel his body shaking, his face streaked with sweat. Much further and he knew
he would reach that terrible stage where his fear would seize
his muscles, holding him rigid, unable to move. But he heard
the pursuit and the scream of the owl as it made another kill.
Certain death came at him from behind, and only its closeness gave him the will to beat back his terror of heights.

"There's another cleft in the rock face," Sisipher was telling him. She took his hand and he squeezed. She did not
object; she knew his fear.

He would never remember how they found their way down
through the cleft, but they did so. They allowed themselves
no more than a minute's respite before struggling on, beginning a descent into they had no idea what. Kirrikree had
gone, and Sisipher thought it was because he could no longer
get at the men above; they used fire and arrows to keep him
at bay, though he eluded them with ease.

"But we are still followed," Sisipher told Guile.

"Then you lead. If anyone gets close, I'll greet him with
steel."

He heard her chuckle and it brought a surge of relief to
him, even though their ordeal was nothing like over. "You'll
be a warrior yet," she said.

"Well, I've no illusions as to that. I wonder what Wargallow would have made of this." Or Morric, he thought. He
would have revelled in this. But Guile would not allow the

gloom to swamp him, concentrating instead on the climb down.

It seemed to be almost vertical, even more so than the climb up had been. There were sounds from above them and to the side, but the glow from the torches hardly reached here and it seemed as if the pursuit was moving away, befuddled by the darkness. Down and down they climbed, getting more used to the descent, and Guile felt a degree of confidence building. He stared upward occasionally, but there was no hint of light now, and no visible night sky. He wondered if they were beneath a huge overhang, which seemed likely.

Hours later, or so it seemed, Sisipher gave a little cry, and in a moment he felt her hand stretching up to him. He took it gladly and she led him down to her. They were now standing on firm ground.

"Is it a ledge?" he whispered, and his whisper seemed to run out along the rock wall behind him, picked up by the formation there. In front of him was only the utter darkness, which could have masked yet another abyss.

"I think so," she said, and he could barely see her. Their hands still held each other. "Shall we rest! I cannot hear pursuit. And no one would see us here without a light."

He agreed, leaning back against the wall, and she rested close to his side. He thought of putting an arm about her, but knew she would rebuff him, so was content to hold her hand. "You know," he said softly, afraid that the rocks would amplify his voice and send it ringing about them in a howl, "I hear almost nothing. There is your breathing, my heart, but something is missing."

"We are far, far below the level of the citadel."

"I know! The sea. Why can't we hear the sea?"

Her grip tightened on his hand. "But—we are below it." At once she began to shudder and now he did pull her close to him. She had become like a bird, shivering, her fear almost overwhelming.

"What is it?" he breathed, feeling the awesome weight of the stone pressing in on them.

"This is a terrible place," she told him. "There is so much about it I do not understand."

"Do you know anything about Teru Manga?"

"A little," she nodded. "This is no natural ledge we have

stumbled on. It was cut deliberately from the fathomless cliff.
It is a road.''

"Cut by whom?''

"I cannot say. Brannog told me that the Earthwrought
have spread far under the earth and their delvings are far-
reaching. But it does not have their feel about it. It's hard
to explain—''

"But if they are here—''

"They may be,'' she breathed. "But so are others. I can
feel them.''

"Others?''

"The road ahead runs north. Far under Teru Manga. Teru
Manga—the fear below the earth. I have been aware of its
pull, even at sea.''

"What is this fear below?''

Again he felt her tremble as he held her, and only that kept
his own fear from rising like a tide over him.

"It is what Orhung spoke of in Elberon. It is *here*. The
evil we are set on destroying. Anakhizer. Somewhere deep
under the earth. Kirrikree spoke of it, too.''

"And we are going to *meet* it!'' he gasped, his whisper
trickling along the walls.

She pulled free of him but would not relinquish his hand.
"We must go the other way. It leads southward. We may be
able to find a way to the channels and to the coast.''

"And swim to Goldenisle?'' he grinned, but she could not
see.

She did not answer, but he gently pushed her on. "South,
then. It would be a little reckless to confront the enemy alone.
He might not take us seriously.''

She turned back and gripped him for a moment. "I cannot
see what lies below us. The nature of Anakhizer's power
escapes me. But it is strong, so strong. If we are to defeat
it—''

"Who would have said we would destroy Xennidhum?''

"We had Korbillian.''

He fell silent, glancing back impotently at the dark leading
to the north. "Aye. Well, come on girl. No despondency. We
are alive yet. Let's take each bend as it comes.''

Now it was he who took the lead, knowing that she had
used her own powers to glimpse something so dark that it

had almost brought her to her knees. Terror reached for him each step of the way in that dire place, but he would not let it push him over the lip of madness. They went doggedly on, mile after mile, until they had to stop.

The ledge ended. The stone had crumbled, the side of the rock wall had slithered down. How much of the road had gone they could not see. In despair they sank down, silent for a long time.

Eventually Guile stirred. "We must go back. As we go, we will look for a way up. Another defile. There must be others."

She nodded, but exhaustion and misery had worked on her until it seemed she would not rise. He helped her, insisting that she lean on him. She took heart and forced herself to go back with him, but it was as though she walked against a black tide, an onrushing evil that sought her out like the coming of a storm. She did not tell him this, but he had guessed it.

They had been winding their way back along the road, the abyss on their right now, for over an hour when she called a halt. Her head was lifted like that of a hunting beast, and Guile could see her outline, as though some faint glow of life sprang from the very rocks.

"What is it?" he asked her.

"Something is coming. From ahead."

He felt as though she had hit him, and his muscles went limp. "How far away?"

"I cannot say. But there are a score of them."

"We must climb!" he hissed and the rocks flung back the sound. Together they examined the wall beside them, but still there was no way up, no suitable defile. Like glass it had scorned their efforts.

"Drogund's men?" Guile asked hopefully.

He could not see her face. She was drawing back and he felt her welling horror. "No. Too big. I cannot see them, only feel them. But—they are not like men of our kind." She wrenched her mind away. "We must run!" she ended and there was more terror in her voice than even their journey had put there.

"The edge," whispered Guile. "Can we go over it and find some other way there?"

"Perhaps. But it is like an overhang. Ottemar, we must go back! Again. And quickly!" She was beginning to panic.

He gripped her hard, shaking her. "But that way leads only to the broken ledge. We would be trapped. How far away are they?"

"About a mile."

He grunted. "Come, then. Run." They did so, keeping to the rock wall, forced back to the south, all the while trying to find a way up away from the danger. They concentrated so hard on whatever nightmare was hunting them that they did not see the light ahead until too late. Round a curve in the road they dashed, almost crashing into the flaming brand that had been set into the rock wall. It sputtered and crackled, throwing out a bright glare as whatever it was burned and fizzed, the air about it thick with plumed smoke.

Neither of them could breathe for a moment. The brand had not been here before: they had passed this way.

Guile held his sword before him, pressing Sisipher to the rock wall. "Whoever put this here must know about us," he said.

"Indeed I do!" came a roar from above, and before Guile could respond, a great shape dropped from the cover of the rock above, possibly from a cave or crack that had been invisible from the road. It moved so quickly that Guile could not react as it grabbed his sword arm and swung him forward like a toy. He felt himself crushed to a thick hide, not that of a beast, but of a man. although it reeked of earth and stone.

In a moment he was pushed out and held at arm's length, like a pup being examined. Like Sisipher he was gripped by immensely powerful arms. The man who held them was not a great deal taller than a normal man, but was far wider, with immense shoulders. He looked to be more like the Earthwrought of the east, except that he was far bigger than they were. He had a thick mane of hair and a face that could almost have been hewn from stone, though his eyes sparkled, free of malice.

"Thought I could smell you, scampering about like rats!" he boomed. His manner seemed somehow far less belligerent than his looks suggested.

"Are you of the Earthwrought?" Guile asked him, aware

even now that the pursuit was closing from the road. He did
not think that this being was part of it.

"No," said Sisipher, and her lack of fear of the man confirmed Guile's thoughts. "He is a Stonedelver. Aren't you?"

The huge man snorted, but not in anger. "Well, well! Men
who speak of my earth-brothers and who know of Stonedelvers! What have I got hold of?"

"Then you are a Stonedelver?" Sisipher repeated.

The big man released them and nodded. "Aye! But what
do you know of my race and of the Earthwrought?"

Sisipher looked back. "Must we talk now? Whoever is
coming—"

The Stonedelver scowled, and his face became fearful, as
if he glowered at some already visible evil. "Ah, them! Ferr-
Bolgan. Something has stirred them up again! Hunting, hunting, all the time. In finding you I had almost forgotten that
vermin! Come! Questions later. We must flee. I'd love to take
my club to them, but I'm alone and they are many." He
turned on his heel, light as a cat, and sprang upward to where
there must be some ledge to cling to. He turned back, realizing that neither of the people below were capable of following. Grinning, he reached down and hauled up first the girl,
and then Guile. He snatched his torch from the wall where
he had set it and led the way with it into a tunnel. When they
were inside it, he did what to Guile was a staggering thing.
Speaking some soft words to the stone itself, he used his
great hands and evident strength to close up the wall behind
him. Guile could not see how he had done it, wondering if
he had used power, for the Earthwrought had gifts that others
did not.

There was no time for discussion, and the huge figure bent
down and led them quickly through winding tunnels and cut-
tings through the stone as nimbly as a rabbit passing through
it own warrens. It was a long time before he came to a halt,
declaring that for the time they were safe. He set down his
torch, which seemed to be cut from some form of fossilized
rock rather than wood and which still burned strongly. He
tested the walls of the tiny cave they were in as if to ensure
they were secure.

"The Ferr-Bolgan will be off the scent by now. For a
while."

"What are they?" Guile asked.

"Perversions!" the Stonedelver spat. "Wild things, and evil. If they had taken you, it would have been a pretty mess you'd have been in, I promise you. But you—what are you? Not pirates, I'll be bound. Mind you, even if you had been, I'd have dragged you away from the Ferr-Bolgan. Even Gondobar's rabble don't deserve that kind of doom. The Ferr-Bolgan have eaten them before now. Perversions!" He spat again.

"We were fleeing the pirates," said Sisipher. "And Gondobar is dead."

The Stonedelver leaned back and grunted. "Is he indeed? Didn't kill the old fox, did you?"

Guile explained how Gondobar had died. "And you can take it that Drogund has grasped the reins now. More's the pity."

"Aye, you've a point there. Not the best of them."

"But can we ask who you are?" Guile went on.

The huge man laughed. "You can! But Stonedelvers aren't in the habit of tossing away their life histories just like that. Firstly you'd better tell me your own names and business. You owe me that much I should think."

Sisipher smiled. "This is Guile, from the Chain of Goldenisle."

"*Guile?* That's no name, it's a title. Or a curse, depending who named you."

Guile laughed. "That's true. But my other names and my business are best kept aside for the moment."

"And I am called Sisipher," said the girl.

The Stonedelver's huge grin changed into a frown of deep thought, as if some mammoth problem perplexed him. "I know the name," he said at last. "And you knew about Stonedelvers. Tell me, who is your father?"

"He is Brannog Wormslayer, whom the Earthwrought now call King Brannog."

It was as though she had spoken some great spell, for the Stonedelver gasped and his jaw hung open. When he had recovered, his whole manner changed. For a moment a strange look came into his eyes, and to Guile's amazement he thought he saw tears there. The huge man leaned forward.

"Can this be true?" he said softly. "Brannog's daughter? You have come over the sea from the eastern delvings—"

Sisipher laughed gently, reaching out to touch the man with great tenderness. "Yes, it is true."

"Then you are revered among my earth-brethren. Does this mean that they, too, will come to us, now that we need them most?"

"It may come to that," said the girl. "Strange times are upon us all."

The great man bowed his head. "Forgive my rudeness. My name is Aumlac and I am the son of Bragorn. I am from Rockfast, where Luddac is king. Will you permit me to take you to him?"

"We will be honored," Sisipher agreed. "But before we leave, will you not tell us something of Teru Manga and what dwells here? We know so little of its history."

"You have only to ask," said Aumlac with another bow. Now that he knew her name, he was like a child with her and Guile marvelled at his respect. He had seen this in the Earthwrought, who worshipped Sisipher and her father.

While they rested, Aumlac gave them some bread that he carried in a pouch at his side, and though it was crusty it tasted as delicious as any other meal they had ever eaten. He also produced (seemingly by magic) water for them, and its taste was more invigorating than the strongest wine. As they rested under the mass of Teru Manga, they learned from their protector something of the history of its people.

"The histories of our beginnings go back so far in time that they have become confused," began Aumlac. "Once we lived in many parts of Omara. Some of our nation sprang from a branch of Delvers who lived high in the mountains above Starkfell Edge in the far west, beyond which nothing lives. Their origins are forgotten, but it is thought they were a mixture of Delvers who lived under the heights since time began, refugees who were once the workers-of-stone in the land that flooded and became Goldenisle, and others who fled from the east. From Cyrene and Xennidhum, thousands of years since. The Delvers above Starkfell Edge were fierce and became more so, their paths going deeper down to some dark power that must have been long buried under the earth, drawing them to it. My own people, who have become the

Stonedelvers of today, moved away from Starkfell Edge and
went to the range of mountains that stretched like an arm
across the north of the peninsular that was even then called
Teru Manga. The original Delvers, who had become the Ferr-
Bolgan, attacked my race, and they sought to destroy us in
our new home. But under the crags of the ice range we fought
them at the bloody battle of the Slaughterhorn. Fought them
and drove them back into the high mountains, and harried
them down into the deep gulfs below us. We carved out our
new home up on the Slaughterhorn and named it Rockfast.
It looks out over our land, and though we love the earth and
the stone below, we love the sky.also, as our ancestors worshipped it from Starkfell Edge. We are not creatures of the
dark, burrowers though we may be.

"To our citadel came Earthwrought from the east, for we
never lost contact with our earth-brethren. Few came, for
they were mostly those who fled under the endless passages
beneath the ocean. They brought word of the Children of the
Mound in the east. We took them in and made them one with
us, and their offspring are with us yet. Our own numbers had
been dwindling until they came, for we are the last of the
true Stonedelvers. We welcomed the Earthwrought and their
powers, not only to make our own nation stronger, but to
fight what grew far beneath Teru Manga."

"And what is it that dwells there?" asked Guile, although
he felt sure now that Sisipher had already named it.

"A terrible power. There are times when it is dormant,
like some awesome beast that does no more than dream, but
at other times we hear the roar of its power in our heads. It
draws many things to it. Some hold that it corrupted the
Delvers on Starkfell Edge, and made them its slaves, the Ferr-
Bolgan, and that many other denizens of the deep belong to
it now."

"We know of it," said Sisipher. "It does not belong in
Omara."

"It is the evil we are sworn to destroy," said Guile. "Anakhizer."

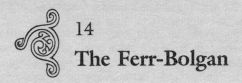

14
The Ferr-Bolgan

AUMLAC LED THEM through numerous delvings, caverns and passageways that could have been cut by underground streams or Stonedelvers, or others, it was not always possible to tell which. He carried with him an elongated club, fashioned out of stone, and had cast away the brand he had carried. His club, like the Earthwrought, glowed and cast enough light for them all to see by. When the way was too narrow to pass, Aumlac was able to work his strange powers and make a new way, although there were places where he would change direction sharply rather than interfere with the rock. He did not dwell on his fears, but Guile knew that there were certain things here below Teru Manga that kept the big man perpetually on his guard. As they moved on, Aumlac seemed to keep up an almost constant conversation with the stone around him, his voice barely audible.

They all stopped for a brief rest while Aumlac pressed his ears to a wall of stone, listening to it. He declared in a whisper that he could hear the workings of this inner world. Sisipher knew the Earthwrought could do this, like birds studying the land below them. It made her think of Kirrikree, who she could not contact from here.

"I'm sure we've gone deeper downward," Guile told her.

Aumlac turned with a grin. "Aye. That we have. This place is thick with Ferr-Bolgan. The only way to Rockfast is past them, so we've cut below. There's things above us now that I don't want us to meet. I've never seen them, but I've heard them crawling about, grinding the rock aimlessly."

Sisipher shuddered, thinking of the things her father had

spoken of, that had crawled up from below Xennidhum and invaded the delvings of the Earthwrought beneath a continent. She had seen some of them herself.

"There's a river to cross," went on Aumlac. "It's not in spate, so we can do it now. Then we go up and eventually seek out the sun. Once over the water, we'll be through the worst." He moved on, cautious but showing no fear, and Guile supposed it must be because he lived his life surrounded by danger.

They came through a cleft in the rock and found themselves in a great cavern, which looked as if it had been hollowed out by water over the centuries. Aumlac's club afforded enough dim light to see by and it picked out the bizarre carvings in the rocks, frozen gargoyles. Like some ancient glacial fault, the cavern must have wound its way through the very innards of the plateau like a gigantic intestine. Coursing down its center was a racing torrent, cut deep into the rock bed so that it sluiced down like water guided along a chute. The channel widened in the center of the cavern, where jutting stones had been arranged across its width, the only place where it looked feasible to cross.

Aumlac held his stone club at the ready, watching for signs of the enemy, but mercifully there were no Ferr-Bolgan to be seen. From the Stonedelver's description of them, Guile was not anxious to see them. He held his stolen sword before him, hoping he would not have to use it. They came stealthily to the edge of the water and it roared about their ears like thunder in its confined bed, rushing on madly to some even deeper realm.

"I will go first," Aumlac called back. "Keep close to me and have your swords ready. I can smell Ferr-Bolgan, though not too close. I have confused them enough." He frowned then in concentration, leaping out easily to the first of the flat-topped stones that poked out of the water. In a moment he had spoken to it as if saying some password, and he had moved on to the next. The stones were set fairly close together, intended at one time for smaller beings than Stonedelvers to use, so that Sisipher and then Guile were able to step across. The rocks were slippery and the furious spray chilled them as they crossed, the churning whiteness spinning around the rocks, eager to rip them from their beds.

Aumlac stared back toward the way they had come, but seemed satisfied that nothing was following. He passed on beyond the mid-point, grunting as he did so. The water this side of the stream swirled out into a calmer expanse of water, the stones now flatter, barely out of the water. As Aumlac reached the first of them, he pulled up sharply like a horse that has smelled danger ahead of it. Before he could speak, the waters beside him seemed to burst and up from out of them came a number of shapes, the water streaming from them. Neither Guiles nor Sisipher recognized them, but Aumlac swung his club at the nearest and shouted a warning.

"Strike at them!" he snarled. "Not Ferr-Bolgan, but just as evil: these are issiquellen." His club caught the first of the beings before it had risen to its full height and there was a blast of air as the heat hit it. It tumbled back into the river, knocked senseless.

Guile and Sisipher stood back to back on one of the stones, both thrusting out their swords, keeping the creatures at bay. Guile watched them as they closed in, appalled by their ugliness. They were as big as men, and indeed looked as if they had either once been men or had evolved along some similar, but aquatic line. Their skins were very pale, naked and with a suggestion of tiny scales and in places their organs could be seen through it. Their long, spatulate fingers were webbed, with a translucent membrane of skin attaching their arms to their sides like the thin folds of a cloak. They had no hair, but there were peculiar folds of flesh to their heads, and from their lower faced sprouted bristles like those of a hound. Their eyes seemed blind, opaque and empty, but they were not, watching as they did every move their victims made. They had no weapons but their fingers reached out eagerly.

Aumlac had rendered another of them senseless or dead and he called Sisipher to him. She stepped across another of the rocks and as she did so, one of the issiquellen tried to grab at her. Guile's swordpoint jabbed into soft flesh and the hand withdrew at once. Guile stepped behind the girl and chopped at another groping arm. There were a dozen or more of the foul creatures around them now, and although they were silent, their thoughts might have been words.

Guile's initial terror had subsided, for it was plain that the creatures were afraid of the weapons, particularly Aumlac's club, which seemed capable of awesome destruction. "Come along!" he bawled. "If we don't get over soon, they'll bring the Ferr-Bolgan."

The mere mention of the latter was enough to goad Guile and Sisipher on, and she was quick to jump across another stone, herself swinging steel. Guile was right behind her, and as he landed, he felt a hand grasp his foot and pull him back. He twisted as he fell, managing to avoid a ducking, but now on his knees at the water's edge. His sword banged on the rock and slipped under the water, lost. He found himself abruptly face to face with the hideous visage of his assailant.

Its awful mouth widened in a grin as if it meant to fasten on him, but it did not attack. Instead it spoke his true name, clearly, above the swirl of the water. Guile was transfixed, unable to believe what he had heard.

"Ullarga said you were here. She sees far. Come with us," the creature said softly. "Come and meet our lord."

As the creature's hands prepared to drag Guile into the water, Sisipher leapt forward and thrust her sword into its mouth. At once it released Guile's foot, gagging on its own blood, and toppled back. Guile stared at the scarlet water, mesmerized, until Sisipher tugged at him and forced him to his feet. Aumlac was beside them again, battering two more assailants backward.

"Hurry! It is as I feared, the battle has been joined." He indicated the tunnels behind them, and from these now issued a score or more creatures even more horrifying than the issiquellen. These, Guile knew at once, were the Ferr-Bolgan. Even larger than Aumlac, with long, anthropoidal arms, they seemed to lope across the rocks with uncanny ease. They were more beast than man, their faces not only intensely ugly but having about them an evilness, a wanton cruelty stamped there, that spoke of some vile twist in their evolution. It was as if the evil powers of Xennidhum had reached across the world and tainted them, molding them as it had the Children of the Mound and all their other depraved spawnings. Snarling, howling with apparent glee, the pack rushed over the rocks toward the river. Some raced into it, others leapt on to the first of the stones.

Aumlac reacted at once. He sprang away ahead, calling for the others to follow, and they did so recklessly, avoiding the clutches of the issiquellen as they went, barely getting across the water before they could bbedragged into it. Once over, Aumlac insisted on guarding their back. He pointed to a narrow passageway up into the rock wall.

"Climb there! Only room for one to pass. I'll be behind you, and if any of these filth try to get at us, they'll have a dent in their heads for their efforts."

Neither Guile nor Sisipher argued, both racing for the defile. It was uncomfortably dark within it, but anything would be preferable to a confrontation with the revolting Ferr-Bolgan. Sisipher led the way, with Guile close at her shoulder, their breathing heavy in the enclosed space. Aumlac was right behind them, cursing and growling like a wild beast himself, and already he had to use his club to beat back the first of the enemy.

The climb was a long one, and although Aumlac seemed well capable of keeping back the Ferr-Bolgan while they remained in the cleft, Sisipher and Guile became less terrified by the sounds below them. The walls rang to the snarls, making it sound as though there were hundreds of the monsters there.

Sisipher leaned back after another long climb. "There's another passage to our left. Very narrow—"

"Go through it!" called Aumlac, who had heard. "I'll seal it after us. Fortunately they are not organized and have none of the herders with them."

Sisipher wriggled through, and Guile followed. He found himself wedged, but Aumlac came up behind him and said something soft to the stone. Guile was automatically released, as if by a hand, and he tumbled forward into Sisipher. While they untangled themselves, Aumlac bellowed another challenge at the Ferr-Bolgan, clubbing them back. Then, in a moment, he was through the gap. It closed with a crack, just as though a huge door had shut. Darkness fell like a dropped blanket, and there was a complete silence, like the silence of death.

"It won't hold them for long," grunted Aumlac, invisible. "Once a herder comes, it'll be opened. We must hurry on."

"What are the herders?" said Guile.

"We don't know. Servants of the powers below. But they work with stone, and they usually herd the Ferr-Bolgan like cattle. The beasts fear them. We have never seen them clearly as they're elusive and besides, usually in the company of many Ferr-Bolgan!''

"I can't see a thing," protested Sisipher.

"We must travel in darkness now. Hold my tunic. We will go slowly, but grip each other. I will find the way. But any light will guide the herders. They will find it.''

Although it was unnerving to move in such absolute darkness, Guile and Sisipher were relieved to be out of the clutches of the Ferr-Bolgan. Sisipher held on to Aumlac's tunic and Guile gripped her hand, now holding in his other the remaining sword.

As they climbed upward again, he whispered to Sisipher. "Did you hear that water creature speak?''

"Yes," she whispered back. "They *knew* you were here.''

"They said they had been told I would be here. Aumlac, who do they serve? Who is their lord?''

Aumlac's whisper came back from the rock walls. "They have been changed by the same grim power that has made the Ferr-Bolgan what they are. In days long gone by they were a different race. They lived in cities below the waves, below Teru Manga and other such places to the north. There were great changes, floods, volcanoes. Some legends say that the issiquellen were once men who lived above the water, but that they changed when the waters rose. Once they were friends to the Stonedelvers, but no longer. Now they have become secretive, dwelling in the depths of Teru Manga. They are far more intelligent than the Ferr-Bolgan, and they have power of a sort, even though they have become servants of the greater darkness below.''

"They spoke of Ullarga," said Guile, puzzled.

"I have never heard the name before," said Aumlac.

"They were told I would be here. Could she be one of the pirates?''

"It may be," agreed Aumlac. "Though Gondobar's people have no love for the issiquellen. They hunt them for sport and have killed many of them. The issiquellen damage Hammavar ships when they can, but are not very clever at it. So I would not think them allies. This Ullarga must be some other enemy.''

"The creature said Ottemar Remoon. I heard it clearly,''

said Sisipher. "Which suggests their master wants you. Not to kill you," she added. "That would be easy enough."

"Thank you for the warming words," said Guile, and at once he felt her fingers tighten. It surprised him.

"I did not mean to—"

He chuckled. "You're right. Their master may well want me alive."

Aumlac had become very silent, hardly moving. His voice came to them as a whisper, but it had a hard edge to it now. "If you are Ottemar Remoon," he said ominously, "then you are the Heir of Goldenisle."

The silence that followed was even more absolute, as if a sentence had been passed. At once Guile realized that Sisipher had revealed his identity to the Stonedelver without meaning to. For a long time nothing moved.

"Is it true?" whispered Aumlac, and they could feel his presence now like the threat of thunder above them.

"Yes," said Guile at last.

"Then you are in even greater peril. Many of my people have only hatred in their hearts for the men of Goldenisle. They think of the long ago, when our ancestors were driven out of their lands, before the Flood took them, before the invaders came."

"And you, Aumlac?" said Guile. "Does this change things?"

"I would rather hear a man speak before I judge him. But it is well that I found this out. My king, Luddac, will have to know."

Sisipher could feel the constriction of the atmosphere, sensing that Aumlac was greatly disturbed by Guile's admission. "Aumlac," she said. "I have told you who I am. And you trust me."

"You are Brannog's daughter—"

"Then you know I am loyal to the Earthwrought, and so must be to the Stonedelvers."

"Of course, mistress, I would not question—"

"Then know this—Ottemar must be protected. His cause is your cause. Serve him as you would serve me. At Rockfast I will tell your king everything."

"If you have enemies in Goldenisle," Guile told Aumlac, "then they are my enemies."

Aumlac sighed. "This gladdens me! But we must go quickly from here. The way to Rockfast will not yet be easy. I understand why the Ferr-Bolgan have been so active of late! No efforts are being spared to find you, Guile, for Guile you must remain."

"You see how I came by the name."

Aumlac chuckled and the sound spread around them warmly as they moved on. Eventually they came up from the darkness to a new complex of tunnels, and although they could see very little, there was an odd glow to the rocks here and their eyes quickly adapted to it. As they began a fresh climb, Aumlac warned them that there were movements around them, the ever-seeking Ferr-Bolgan.

"Never have so many been on the move," he added. "They are very determined to capture you."

"Sometimes I wonder if I would have done better to have remained a lowly clerk in the inner city," Guile joked, explaining to the Stonedelver how he had once been kept hidden on Medallion Island.

"Such a life would, it seems to me, have ended with madness," suggested Aumlac.

Guile chuckled. "Hardly a precedent for a Remoon!"

Sisipher frowned at him, but he shrugged good-naturedly. "Well, there are no Ferr-Bolgan in Goldenisle at least."

Aumlac pulled up as he said this, brows knitting in thought. "There may not be Ferr-Bolgan there, but there could be issiquellen. They travel far and quickly; it is their power."

"Can they have penetrated Medallion Island?" said Guile.

"Indeed," affirmed Aumlac. "The old city lies far below it."

They thought on this as they climbed, and at last, two hours later, exhausted but with their spirits still intact, they came to a tunnel into which sunlight seeped from above. Aumlac pointed to a broken stairway on to which the weeds had begun to tumble. "There lies the way to Rockfast. Once in the sunlight, we will be safe enough."

They found fresh strength to climb the broken stair, which was unexpectedly wide, and Guile wondered who had built it and what wonders must have once surrounded it. The race that had formerly lived here must have been highly advanced to have created such remarkable systems of passages in the rock. On the upper steps they walked into the morning light and saw the sky above them, blue and inviting, cloudless as if it were always free of storms. Aumlac pointed to a ridge of mountains, sharp and snow-crested.

"We yet have a good climb, but it will be easier in the sun. By midday we can be at Rockfast, and I, for one, will enjoy a very large meal."

"I think we are in accord," said Guile.

They were laughing as they left the stair and reached the rock path beyond, although it had been overgrown. But their laughter died as they heard cries behind and below them. Looking back down the wide stair, they saw in the half-dark a swarm of movement. Countless dozens of Ferr-Bolgan had gathered there, and although they loathed the daylight, they were coming up the stairs in a tide.

"Hurry!" gasped Aumlac, taken aback by this appearance of the enemy. "They dare not venture too far out into the sun. It will blind them."

It was not hard for the fugitives to break into a run, tired though they were, and the sunlight gave them new vigor. Nothing, thought Guile, could be as bad as fleeing in the darkness below. He and Sisipher ran side by side, with Aumlac insisting on bringing up the rear. They looked back only once, to see the horde emerging from below ground. Screaming as if crazed by the light, the vile Ferr-Bolgan came on, and with them were a number of other beings, man-like but dressed in dark robes like the priests of some strange cult. They seemed to lead the pursuit, goading the Ferr-Bolgan on, shouting at them as if driving cattle.

"Herders," said Guile.

Sisipher's face had gone very pale. "Worse," she said so that he almost missed her words. "We have met them before, though I can hardly credit they are here."

"What do you mean?"

She had no chance to reply then, for they were stumbling upward. They had gone no more than a few hundred yards when they realized they could not hope to outdistance the pursuit. Aumlac knew it too. He could have sped away to safety alone, but would not. Now he would have to hold them back.

"There is the way to Rockfast," he said, pointing to a

narrow path that led precariously up the side of the mountain to their right. "Go. I will hold the way."

Guile shook his head. "No."

Aumlac was about to argue, when he saw what Guile had already seen. More Ferr-Bolgan were clambering like apes up the sides of the mountain in an effort to get to the path and cut off the flight. They were emerging like ants from their holes. The entire mountainside must be riddled with passages and tunnels. Aumlac looked about desperately, and finally saw a place where he could put up some defense. It was a cliff wall that sloped outwards, offering protection from above, and although the way to it was broad, at least they would have their backs to a safe wall. Aumlac guided them to this miniature canyon, waiting for the attack to begin. On either side were great boulders, so the Ferr-Bolgan were restricted to attacking from one direction.

Aumlac briefly examined the cliff face behind him, but it was solid and even his powers could not open it. He swung his club. "Think of one thing," he said to Guile. "They want you alive."

They waited. In a moment the first of the enemy confronted them. The dark-robed beings stood at the mouth of the retreat, then waved on the Ferr-Bolgan. A dozen of the biggest brutes rushed in madly, weaponless but terrifying, eyes almost closed against the glare of the sun, muzzles dripping with saliva. Aumlac stepped forward and two of them went down at once as his club exploded against their hides. Guile jabbed with his sword, and although it was easy to strike at the Ferr-Bolgan, he could not kill them.

"Cut at their knees!" cried Aumlac, dashing out the brains of another and it howled as it catapulted to one side, smashing into others. Guile did as he was bid, swinging his weapon in a wide arc that slashed into the flesh of two of the beasts at the knee. One of them collapsed, unable to rise, while the other lurched sideways toward Sisipher, but she avoided its clumsy movements. Guile, heartened by his success, leaned forward and rammed his sword point into the eye of the fallen monster. It fell back with a horrible scream, almost wrenching the sword from his grip. Turning, he saw Sisipher's predicament and cut downwards, hamstringing the Ferr-Bolgan that was about to grab her. As it fell back, he chopped into its throat, fueled by anger and disgust.

Briefly he leaned back, chest heaving. Aumlac had fought off the other Ferr-Bolgan, and for a moment the attack had ceased. But in front of them another wave was preparing. Aumlac stepped back beside Guile, with Sisipher behind them.

"Wait," she said. They could not stop her from pushing between them, watching her expression harden into a concentration of her every particle of being. Something had awoken in her, and she had seen glimpses in her mind of a figure who fought like a machine, directing a rod of power about him, killing all who came near it. Orhung. When she had first met him, something within her had responded, and now she could not rid herself of the same knowledge. Now, as the next wave of Ferr-Bolgan came on, she raised both her arms and directed them at the beasts, her eyes widening. Whatever force she had tapped, she now unleashed, directing it before her. It had never happened to her before, but she had known it was here, ever since she had controlled Rannovic the pilot and his ship. Here, in consternation and sheer agony, the wave of Ferr-Bolgan broke, scattering as if it had walked into a wall of flames. Three of the beasts collapsed, dead. Others tore into their nearest neighbors, clawing at them and starting frightful battles. Behind them the dark-robed herders moved back, sensing the power that had been flung at them.

"What did you do?" gasped Guile. He had never before seen her release power like this, even at Xennidhum.

Her face was like chalk, as if the release had come as an even greater shock to her than Guile and Aumlac. "I don't know. But look, it is hopeless. There are hundreds of them."

She had not exaggerated for already the next wave prepared. Aumlac raised his club. "Together!" he yelled, rushing to meet the onslaught. Guile could smell the stench of the enemy now, mingled with desperation and fear. Again he used his sword, but already it was obvious that the fight would soon be over. He felt drained, even though killing the lumbering Ferr-Bolgan was proving easy. The sheer weight of numbers was too much.

Aumlac fell beneath the combined attack of four of the

enemy; they rolled about furiously. Sisipher again discharged her power, but Guile could not get to the Stonedelver, having to cut at two more attackers. Sisipher had so concentrated her efforts that she had not realized something hovered above her in the sunlight. Now a white shape came tearing down like a missile and its claws reached out, ripping into the neck of a Ferr-Bolgan. Kirrikree had heard her struggles, and although he had failed to make her hear him, had been guided to the place where the three figures fought their desperate rearguard. Two of the Ferr-Bolgan were dead before the girl realized Kirrikree was here.

"Help comes," the while owl told her, rushing at one of the dark-cloaked figures, tearing at it so that it fell headlong off the path to its death on the sharp rocks below. From the skies now came another huge bird. It was an eagle, almost as large as Kirrikree, and with it came a score of other eagles and hawks, smaller, but no less effective when it came to attacking the Ferr-Bolgan. Like a cloud of steel they flew down, ripping with deadly talons, so that in a matter of moments the Ferr-Bolgan and their herders had again drawn back.

Aumlac was up on his feet, having brained all four of his assailants. Sisipher was spent and clung to Guile, her breath coming in great gulps. He gripped her, his sword dripping with blood, knowing that neither of them could survive this much longer. Aumlac staggered to them, grinning all over his huge face.

"It's Skyrac, Luddac's war eagle. Now we'll see a fight!"

"Aumlac," said Guile, hardly able to speak. "Sisipher and I are weak as babes. We've nothing left."

"Wait," Aumlac growled, ears cocked. "Aha! Skyrac is not alone. There is more support yet. Rockfast sends men. Ho! Stonedelvers!" he roared, and Guile staggered at the voice, which rose up like a vast clap of thunder and reverberated around the walls of the mountains.

Minutes later the Ferr-Bolgan were in full retreat and Guile saw the reason. A column of Stonedelvers was rushing forward from the mountain path, a hundred men or more, all wielding their clubs as fiercely and as effectively as Aumlac had. This, together with the continual attack of the birds, was too much for the Ferr-Bolgan, who would not hold ranks.

Lurching this way and that, blundering into each other like so many sheep, they worked their way back to their burrows. Many of them never reached them, and countless bodies littered the side of the mountain.

Sisipher heard the voice as if in a dream. "Are you well, mistress?" It was Kirrikree.

"Alive," she told him. "Thanks to you. We would have perished here." She and Guile joined the delighted Aumlac at the edge of their retreat and watched the slaughter below them. Aumlac's fellows tore into the enemy ferociously, sparing as few as possible, and their hatred of them was evident. Mercifully it was soon over. The eagles circled a few times, then were gone. Only Kirrikree remained in the sky and he flew down to perch on an outcrop beside Sisipher. She went to him and stroked his white feathers, talking softly, privately to him.

Guile approached. "Tell him," he began, but could think of no words.

Sisipher turned to him with a smile. "He understands, Ottemar. He had no love for you once, but that was long ago."

Guile stood before the bird, gazing at its huge eyes which had once put fear into him. "I wish I could speak to you as Sisipher does," he told it, and for the first time in his life, he reached out and gently stroked a white wing.

Aumlac stood agog and when Guile saw his face, he laughed. "Well, Aumlac, what do you think? How's this for an ally? Let me introduce Kirrikree. And be careful, he hears every word you say."

Aumlac came forward and bowed to the bird as if it were a king. "I am honored by his presence," he said. "Did I see him fight alongside Skyrac?"

"You did," said Sisipher. "Kirrikree fetched him and the others."

Aumlac looked amazed. "An *owl* and the war eagles! Together!"

He was interrupted by voices behind them and turned to see the first of the Stonedelvers coming up the ridge to meet them, their bloody work done. One of them came forward and embraced Aumlac.

"Stone-brother!" Aumlac laughed, and the call was repeated many times as the men embraced him. Guile had as-

sumed they were brothers, and did not learn until later that
all Stonedelvers called each other this. The men were all of
Aumlac's build, some with huge beards, others with long
manes, and all with the look of determined men, though in
them could be glimpsed a deeper suffering in spite of the
victory today.

Aumlac introduced Sisipher and Guile, but was mindful to
say as little as possible about Guile's true identity. Guile was
glad to shake the hands of these people, whose power coun-
terbalanced the evils he had experienced under Teru Manga.

"We must hasten back to Rockfast," said their leader, Brod-
gar, a huge fellow who was even larger than Aumlac. "Even
now the Ferr-Bolgan are trying to come again. We have never
known such determination in them before. And so many
herders!"

Sisipher's face clouded, but she said nothing as the Stonedelvers led the way quickly up the path. They treated the girl
with reverence, and he overheard the name of Brannog several times, wondering where in Omara his friend might be.
Aumlac had to help him up the steep incline, grinning like a
child, apparently not at all tired.

"A fine scrap!" he chuckled. "My club has rarely seen
such sport."

"You enjoyed that fight?" Guile said.

"Well," Aumlac confessed sheepishly, "a little. But it did
cross my mind that it would be my last. Are you well?"

"I don't know—I can't feel anything," Guile laughed.

"Rockfast will put you right."

They went on quietly, and an hour later they saw the Stonedelver's citadel. Both Sisipher and Guile gasped. The place
seemed to teeter on the very brink of the mountain top, cut
from sheer rock walls that fell away for thousands of feet to
the valleys in the cloud below. The rock had been beautifully
shaped and sculpted, fused almost by hands that must have
had tremendous power to do it. Unlike the Direkeep, where
unnatural forces had been used to contort the rock into agonized formations, here Rockfast was a monument to the understanding of man for stone. The wills of both had been
blended and had produced a structure of unsurpassed beauty.

"Well?" said Aumlac, bursting with pride as if he had
personally built the place.

"Magnificent," said Guile, and Sisipher nodded.

"Wait until you get inside," said Aumlac, further enthusing.

They went on more easily now, the vision of the citadel and its towering heights an inspiration to them. High above it, under the snow-covered peaks of the Slaughterhorn, the eagles were like tiny dots, and they saw Kirrikree rise like a white cloud to join them. For the first time since coming to Teru Manga, Sisipher and Guile felt as if they might be safe. But Sisipher turned briefly back to the valleys.

Guile saw her expression change as she did so. "What is it?"

"The herders have been trained," she said so that only he could hear.

"Anakhizer controls many forces."

"So I have seen. But the herders have been made what they are by others we thought destroyed. Anakhizer rules, but with him are a few of the Children of the Mound."

15
Rockfast

AUMLAC HAD NOT EXAGGERATED the inner beauty of Rockfast. Even though the place was cut from naked stone, its
furniture, its floors, there was a warmth about it, and although there were many windows, some of which looked out
on dizzy vistas, neither the wind nor any cold draught found
its way into the remarkable structure. The powers of the
Stonedelvers contained such things, so that both Guile and
Sisipher felt, as they were taken to a place of rest, that the
stone itself was alive and had sounded them out and accepted
them. Sisipher in particular had been utterly spent when she
had arrived here, her extraordinary feat with the Ferr-Bolgan
having taxed her to limits she had not endured before. The
working of the power within her began to frighten her, as if
it might use her when she could not control it, but the stone
here seemed to calm these fears. She was shown to a room
where a bath had been sunk into the stone, and in its hot
luxury she had revived amazingly quickly, almost as though
the water had infused a new magic into her. Guile also felt
revived, and later, when he and the girl had eaten the food
given to them by Aumlac's folk, he felt as healthy as he could
remember.

Now, sitting in the council room of the king, Luddac, they
had begun to expand their reasons for being in the mountains.
Luddac, a huge Stonedelver who dwarfed many of his companions, had a thick beard and brows that met like thunder-
clouds beneath his wide forehead. He sat as if cast from the
stone around him, his face drawn into a deep frown, although
Aumlac had said that he was always thus. Luddac rarely

smiled. Beside him, about the stone table, sat his warlords, for so they called themselves, considering themselves now to be at perpetual war with the denizens of Teru Manga. They were polite but as fierce in their expressions as Luddac, as if little news that reached them ever cheered them. Even so, they had greeted Guile and Sisipher with patience and generosity.

As Sisipher spoke of Xennidhum and of the war there and of the history of the Earthwrought and the coming of Korbillian, Luddac's frown deepened, and he nodded. The girl had spoken for over an hour when she at last paused. There were murmurs about the long table and the king raised a huge fist for silence. It fell at once.

"Many of the things you have told us," he said in a voice that rolled like the promise of a storm, "we have suspected, having heard rumors. More than once we have welcomed fugitive Earthwrought into our ranks. There are many here in Rockfast, some of whom you will meet, Brannog-daughter. It would seem that the Stonedelver nation owes you and your companion a great debt. It is a matter of great regret to me that my people were not able to fight beside you at that unspeakable place in the east."

The warlords banged the table with their fists in a gesture of unanimous agreement, and Guile found himself thinking that they would have made a marvelous addition to the army. Wargallow would have been even more stunned by them than he had been by the Earthwrought.

Luddac nodded. "My people have been hunted since we left the mountains above Starkfell Edge and what have become the drowned lands, and here, under the Slaughterhorn, we made our stand. Nothing has moved us since. But our numbers are thinning. We have been glad to take our earth-brothers to us, and we are glad to see you, Brannog-daughter."

It had annoyed Guile at first that Luddac would not call Sisipher by her name, but he had come to realize that the king held her in very great regard, and thus used a title for her out of deference. Brannog, it seemed, was revered here as a mage might be, and Guile wondered what the girl's father had been doing with his newly chosen people to earn him such respect.

Luddac turned to him. "And now we would hear the words of your companion."

Guile bowed. "I have taken the name Guile, sir, to keep my real identity veiled. But I am Ottemar Remoon, son of Dervic, who was brother to the former king, Khedmar. I believe I am the Heir to Goldenisle."

There was instant murmuring, and beneath it a note of shock, even hostility, which Luddac stilled at once, his face even more clouded. "Let him speak! Remember courtesy!"

Guile then went on to talk at length as Sisipher had done, of Xennidhum and of the new danger, the evil below Teru Manga and of the power behind it. "It is certain," he said, "that these Ferr-Bolgan and the issiquellen have become a part of Anakhizer's plans."

"Our sorrow deepens," said Luddac. "We know war is fomenting and on a far greater scale than we had guessed. But you, Ottemar Remoon, what is your goal?"

Each eye in the room was upon Guile. He managed a smile. "It is not as it was at Xennidhum. Before that war I was intent on sailing to Goldenisle to wrest an Empire from its mad Emperor, and that above all else. I turned aside from that cause and fought for Korbillian, for all Omara. I will not pretend that I did so unselfishly." He turned to Sisipher. "Brannog's daughter knows my heart. She knew that I sought power for myself, too. Many of us did so, but I cannot excuse myself on those grounds. But I learned my place. I hope that some of my greed was replaced by compassion."

Luddac was surprised by this statement, for he could see that it was a plea, not so much to him, but to the girl. Did this man, then, love her? But that was a private matter.

"It is not for us to judge you on that," said the king.

"What he tells you is true, Luddac," said Sisipher. "Xennidhum changed us all. I spoke of Wargallow, the Deliverer. To see the change in him would show you just how deep-reaching such things can be."

"We have heard of this Simon Wargallow of the steel hand. Had you not spoken in his favor, we would have held him to be an enemy, and would have wished him slain. But tell us, Ottemar Remoon, of your goal now."

"It is the reverse of what it was. Now I must win the

throne of Goldenisle first, and then make war on Anakhizer.''

"And why is that?''

"Goldenisle is the one power that can threaten Anakhizer.
He seeks to break up the Empire, and having done so will
isolate the people of Omara and conquer them one by one.
But if Goldenisle became strong, drew into it all the peoples,
then Anakhizer can be defeated.''

Several fists banged down on the table, mostly in anger at
this. There were murmurs of dissent and suggestions that
only a fool would expect to control all the peoples of Omara.

"You misunderstand me—'' began Guile.

Luddac stood up, his face difficult to read, but as he did
so, two men entered the chamber from a stairway beyond
him. One was a Stonedelver, very old, yet tall and heavily
built. He carried a long staff in place of a club, though it was
cut from stone and not from wood. Beside him was an Earthwrought, taller than most, with a gray beard and eyes that
fixed upon what they watched like arrows. Sisipher knew the
latter to be an Earthwise, a lore-master of the little people.

"We have heard,'' said the Stonedelver, his voice deep,
rich, and in those three words he had somehow instilled a
wave of calmness. He came forward with his companion and
at once the Stonedelvers got up and offered them seats at the
table which they accepted graciously.

"I am Einnis Amrodin,'' said the Stonedelver. "Stonewise
of Rockfast. This is Ianelgon, Earthwise of the Earthwrought
who are our brethren below the Slaughterhorn. We have been
listening, for the walls do not hide sounds from us. We did
not wish to intrude, but felt that it was time to come to you,
reading as we now do the disunity. The stone is always pained
by such things.''

"The warlords were stung by Ottemar Remoon's statement
that he wished to rule the peoples of Omara,'' said Luddac
bluntly.

"That's not what I meant,'' gasped Guile.

Einnis Amrodin smiled, again infusing calmness into everything about him. "I understand that. But let me tell you
something of our own history, Ottemar. Perhaps Aumlac has
already spoken of it?''

Aumlac bowed. "I have.''

"You see, Ottemar, our history goes back far beyond that of men. Our legend tells us that many of us came from the lands that have become Goldenisle. There were mountains there, before the Flood. After the Flood, men came from the east and conquered the survivors. Other ancestors of ours had already fled from the high mountains in the west, and together, homeless, we made our home here.

"Stonedelvers have no love of the Chain now, nor of the men who usurped those lands. By history, you are our enemy."

There were nods at this, but no one dared make a sound. The stone itself seemed to be listening.

Guile also nodded. "I understand this, of course. By history I am your enemy. But I speak of tomorrow, not of yesterday. I spoke of Xennidhum, where many people who, *by history*, should have cut out each other's throats, but who turned instead upon the evil that threatened all Omara.

"I have no wish to rule Omara! No wish! But if we are to defeat Anakhizer, we must stand beside each other, as equals, again. When that is done, then we shall have a place, each to his own land."

"What is your plan?" asked Ianelgon quietly, as if anger or impatience were unknown to him. "How would you set about rallying the peoples?"

Slowly, carefully, Guile explained as best he could how he would bring together the various forces that could oppose the Hierarch. He gave voice to things he had barely thought of in detail, surprising himself by the clarity of the things he now foresaw. He may have imagined it, but he thought he sensed a softening of the Stonedelvers' attitude toward him. Surely they realized he had no wish to rule them.

When he had finished, he slumped back, very tired. The stone did not come to his aid with strength.

Einnis Amrodin broke his silence with a gentle cough. "I cannot deny the wisdom in what you say. We know the dangers that beset us. How strong our enemy is, that we do not know."

"Another thing is clear," said Ianelgon. "We are in grave danger here in Rockfast. Already the Ferr-Bolgan are closing in on us. We have known they were becoming even more restless, turning their attention to us as if making ready for war. But now they have another goal. They seek Ottemar Remoon. This Anakhizer is bending all his will to finding him. Why?'' He flung this last out as a challenge to the Stonedelvers and they were taken aback.

''Why?'' Ianelgon repeated. ''Because he fears the Heir! Fears him because he is the one who can thwart his intentions—by uniting his enemies.''

''It is true,'' agreed Einnis Amrodin. ''We are surrounded. Rockfast is soon to be besieged.''

''Then I must leave at once!'' said Guile. ''I cannot be responsible for your peril—''

''Well spoken,'' said Einnis Amrodin. ''Yet, it seems to me that we have to think of our own responsibilities. And I believe we should protect you. What is it that you wish of us?''

Although surprised by these words, Guile answered quickly. ''I must get to Goldenisle swiftly. I have enemies there, and unless I can overcome them, the Empire will be on the brink of a civil war that will bring it down. I must prevent that. I do not ask that you send me an army, nor that you send men with me. Help me return, that is all. Then, when it is done, I will return to Teru Manga in force, and I will reverse roles with Anakhizer: it will be me who is the hunter.''

The Stonewise turned to Luddac. ''Well, my lord? Is that such an unreasonable request?''

Luddac's frown did not break. He studied Guile unflinchingly, and while he was doing so, there came a beating of wings at the window ledge. Skyrac appeared, seemingly twice as large as he alighted, and his fierce eagle's eyes seemed to glare at Guile equally as intensely as his master's. A moment later there was another rush of wings, and a huge white shape appeared beside the war eagle. It was Kirrikree. Together the birds watched, their wing feathers brushing. Behind them, towering over everything like the sword of the forbidden gods, the Slaughterhorn range split the clouds.

The effect on the Stonedelvers was startling. There were gasps of surprise and some of them even stood. Guile caught a glimpse of Einnis Amrodin's face, and he, too, looked shocked. Quickly Guile stood up and went to the window, aware that the eagle still studied him as if it might attack him. One sweep of its talons would kill him easily.

Gently Guile stroked the white feathers of Kirrikree, and then, his body trembling, he stretched out his fingers to Skyrac. The huge bird dipped its head, and for an instant Guile thought its beak would snap his fingers in half, but instead it allowed him to stroke its neck. Very slowly he turned back to the gathering. "When I return to your mountains," he told them, "I will be yours to command."

Einnis Amrodin sat back with a great sigh, and Ianelgon smiled as though a victory had already been achieved.

Luddac came forward and put his massive hand on Guile's shoulder. "It is time to think of tomorrow and put away our history," he grinned.

As he said it, the Stonedelvers banged their fists down upon the table, but this time it was not done in anger or dissent. Guile looked to Sisipher, and she, too, looked as if she had passed through an ordeal and survived it.

All over Medallion Island the bells were tolling. One huge bell tolled dolorously above them all, and Tennebriel could hear it clearly, although she could not see the city from her high balcony on the island where she was kept. Yet she knew with certainty what the cacophony of bells meant. Quanar Remoon had died at last.

She smiled, watching the play of moonlight on the waters, far below. Soon, she thought, soon. I will be Empress, and I can throw aside this false Tennebriel, this fawning girl, this simpleton. And Eukor Epta will come to me for favors and do what *I* ask of him. Soon.

There was a rustling behind her and she turned like a cat to see Ullarga standing before her. The old hag bowed so low that her head almost touched the floor. There will be much of that in court, Tennebriel thought. After all the years wasted here, I will see to it.

"Well, old one? Have you come to gloat at our triumph or are you frightened that I won't have room for you now?"

Ullarga cackled, but the old woman was obviously nervous. "I hope you will not forget me now that you will have a thousand better servants."

Tennebriel softened. "No. You've been good to me, Ullarga. A hard teacher, though," she laughed.

"For your own good, mistress, or should I say, Empress?"

"Who would have thought such gloomy bells could have sounded so melodious!" But how much happier I would be if I had Ottemar under my thumb! Damn him, where is he hiding?

"You are pleased, mistress," said Ullarga, coming forward. "But not completely so. Is there something else that would make your happiness complete?"

Tennebriel started. It was almost as if the old woman had read her mind. She had that strange look on her face, a knowing look, that had been there often in recent weeks, as if the crone had developed a sudden fresh intelligence, waking from years of drudgery. Perhaps it was just the thought of Tennebriel's future that made her so. "Why do you say that?"

"Ah, my dear child, now that you will be Empress, you will find the world outside is full of enemies. Some you need have no fear of, for they will do no more than talk behind their hands. But others, ah, they will plot. All rulers have such enemies."

"And you know of my enemies already?"

"A little. I hear much that goes on in the islands of the Chain."

"Oh?"

"One enemy you will have. A man whom many had thought dead. A great threat to your succession."

Tennebriel felt herself stiffen. What did Ullarga know? "What are you talking about? What enemy?"

"You have been taught your family history well. You know it better than most, but no better than Eukor Epta. You know the story of Ottemar Remoon."

Tennebriel went cold at the sound of the old voice speaking the name of her enemy. "Of course I do."

"He is alive," said Ullarga flatly. "Or did you know that?"

"And?"

"He is the true Heir. Before you."

Tennebriel's eyes blazed and she towered over the old woman, fists clenched. "Come to the point!"

"I have no wish to see him steal your throne. And there are others who would see him perish."

Eukor Epta for one, thought Tennebriel. She tried to remain impassive, but how much did Ullarga know. Had she overheard her and Cromalech? Had they been careless? Ullarga had sworn never to speak of Cromalech to anyone, but what had she heard? "Who are these others?"

"It is time to show you, mistress, now that Quanar has died. You are not alone. There are many who would serve you. Already there are those who would become your allies, once you take the throne."

"I don't understand."

"You will, mistress. Just as you have been kept here in secret, so other forces have gathered in secret, readying for the time to reveal themselves. In the north, deep in the mountain lands, is a power as strong as that of Goldenisle. The ruler there knows of you. His people are oppressed, and he seeks to win free of his oppression, and by binding himself to you, the Empress, be strong."

"Who is he?"

"Anakhizer. He has promised to support you if you will consider aiding him in his time of need."

Tennebriel's eyes narrowed suspiciously. Was this no more than rambling madness? Ullarga spoke of things she had never even hinted at previously. Why should Tennebriel seek the alliance of some far-flung monarch? "It would depend," she said. "What would this monarch do? How could he support me now, being so far removed?"

Ullarga's voice dropped as if she feared the wind might carry it to listeners in the night. "Ottemar is even now lost in those far mountains. Soon Anakhizer will have him. Many seek Ottemar, but it will be Anakhizer who takes him. And he will destroy the others, and any who oppose you. Think of that, mistress?"

"This is all nonsense! How am I to believe it, Ullarga?"

"There is a way, mistress," Ullarga cackled, delighted now to have captured her mistress' interest.

"Which is?"

"Anakhizer's servants reach far to the south of his lands. They even come here. I have spoken to them more than once. Tonight I am to speak to them again. Say you will help him, mistress, and he will give you the head of Ottemar Remoon. His servants will bring it to you."

Tennebriel flinched. Could this be the Ullarga she had known for so long? Ottemar's head? She would rather have had him alive. But if that had become too risky, then his death would be better. "Has Ottemar allies?"

"Indeed, mistress. They search for him as we speak."

"Then he must die."

"Mistress, will you come with me for a while? Come and meet with Anakhizer's servants."

Tennebriel looked about her uncomfortably. "Where are they?"

"Far below us. We will not be discovered."

Tennebriel thought for long moments, eventually nodding. She must find out more. Quickly she wrapped herself up, careful to strap a dagger to her belt, though she was mindful not to let the old crone see that she had done so.

Ullarga then led her by secret ways down into the depths of the tower, and thence to even deeper places. She carried a slim brand that kept off the crowding shadows, skipping like a child down the winding stairways. Tennebriel kept her hand on her dagger hilt, amazed at the complexity of the old tunnels and passageways. At last these debouched into a wide cavern, deep below the tower's foundations, and Tennebriel could hear the wash of waves as they slapped against solid bedrock far below. Ullarga motioned her on, and they climbed down the final flight of stairs, mindful of the slippery weed. Before them was a lake, though it seemed to be part of the sea. Tennebriel was sure that they had come below the level of the sea, though.

They stood in silence and Tennebriel shuddered, knowing that her life was in the hands of the old woman, who could easily have been crazy or plotting with her enemies. Yet her curiosity proved stronger than her fear and she waited. Presently Ullarga held aloft her brand. There were voices beyond its light, from the water's edge.

"Who comes?" hissed one of them.

"It is I, Ullarga. Come forward!" snapped the crone.

Out of the water broke three shapes, and as they came closer to the light they shielded their faces from it. Tennebriel could not make them out clearly, but they were not human.

"What are these?" she whispered, shocked.

"They are issiquellen, mistress. Servants of the one I spoke

of. They travel far below the ocean waves. Listen to me!''
Ullarga called to them. "There is good news for your master
in Teru Manga. The Emperor is dead.''

The three shapes murmured to each other, understanding
what they had been told. Tennebriel was glad of the dark,
which masked her disgust.

"Tennebriel stands before you. Mark her! She is to be
Empress. Tell your master that she looks forward to an alli-
ance. But he must do what he has promised. He must destroy
Ottemar Remoon. You are to bring his head to us.''

"It will be done,'' called the first of the creatures, just as
though a man had spoken.

"Tell your master to begin the destruction of Tennebriel's
enemies where he can. All those who support Ottemar Remoon must be dealt with.''

"It will be done,'' came the voice again.

"Wait!'' called Tennebriel, seeing the shapes about to sink
down into the inky depths. They paused, swimming closer.

"What is your wish?'' Ullarga asked her.

Tennebriel had felt the onrushing of events, the too-easy
fitting together of pieces. She sensed also the manipulation
Ullarga seemed to be exercising. If there was to be control,
it must be her own.

"Do these creatures know where the First Sword is?''

The creatures spoke to themselves, but had no answer.

"What do you want with him now? You have had your
pleasure with him,'' growled Ullarga irritably, and there was
an anger in her eyes, a fierceness that Tennebriel had not seen
before. How dare she! To speak of Cromalech as if he were
a plaything, and to reduce what we have done to an act of
self-indulgence.

"He is loyal to me,'' the girl retorted, but yet guardedly.
"I will not have him harmed. If your master wants an alliance,'' she told the creatures, "then not only must you bring
me the head of Ottemar Remoon, but you must see to the
safe return of Cromalech. He is searching for Ottemar. Bring
him back, safely.''

"Is this necessary?'' snapped Ullarga.

Tennebriel turned on her angrily. "It is. If Cromalech is
harmed, I will be without mercy in my vengeance. Under-

stand that well, Ullarga. Your own loyalty to me I prize highly. Should I not reward Cromalech as I do you?''

The old woman nodded to the issiquellen. "Do as she commands.''

Moments later the creatures were gone. Ullarga gestured for Tennebriel to go back up the steps. "You are a fool to think of tying yourself to such as Cromalech," she complained. "He is ambitious. He will seek to control more than his private assassins.''

A fool! She dares to call me that, Tennebriel thought. This is a sudden change. "I have said he is loyal," she replied coldly. "See that you are.''

She saw now that Ullarga eyed her suspiciously, almost brazenly, and again the girl had the feeling that some deeper evil worked in the old woman, one that had not shown itself before. Then she had turned and was scurrying up the steps with surprising agility. Tennebriel followed, glancing back at the shadows, thinking hard on the events of the last hour. She watched the old woman's back. How much did Ullarga know? Had she made a point of listening to Cromalech and her as they plotted? Impossible. But so much was uncertain now— her ears were sharper than they should have been. Where was her real loyalty? She certainly had no love of Cromalech, even despised him, and she might even slip away and speak to those revolting sea beings and countermand Tennebriel's order to spare him. The thought of Cromalech's abandonment and death went into Tennebriel like a sudden spear and she caught her breath. What have I done! I have sent him away repeatedly on my errands, and yet if I win the throne without him, what use is it?

The more she thought of this, the more she knew that Ullarga posed a serious threat. She had never interfered until now, but if this strange alliance with the north bore fruit, she would become more dangerous. She would be able to hold Cromalech over her, a poised sword, going to Eukor Epta with word of the affair—

As they climbed toward the place where they would join the tunnel complex of the lower tower, Tennebriel felt her world spinning in giddy confusion. The word back to this power in the north could not be stopped now. Ottemar would die and Cromalech would return safely. Ullarga must be prevented from changing that; she must be kept aside. Imprisoned? Or even killed? But Tennebriel recoiled at the grim thought, as if something or someone dark had planted it within her. The thought appalled her.

As though she had heard this thought of murder spoken, the old woman stumbled, and for a second it seemed as if the brand would topple over the steep stairs into the abyss beyond. The old woman grabbed at it, holding the ledge with a curse, calling for help. Instinctively Tennebriel bent over her, reaching down. As the fingers gripped her, the girl knew at once that something was wrong. For as long as she could remember, those fingers had tended her, soothed her, seen to her dress, but now they were alien, those of a stranger. The moment Tennebriel knew this, the face of Ullarga changed: the eyes blazed, then became two dark pockets in a face without features. The lines and wrinkles of age vanished as if a sheet of flesh had been pulled taut, smooth as silk and a growl half of pain, half of anger, issued from the abruptly open mouth.

Ullarga's grip tightened, far too powerful for the crone that she was and Tennebriel tried to free herself. It was impossible. Her eyes locked with the horrific, unfinished face and by a supreme effort of will she pulled the dagger from its place with her free hand and drove it hard as she could into the exposed throat. The mouth widened as if to engulf her and a howl of rage burst from it. Again the eyes fixed her, baleful and malefic. Blood gushed from the wound but still the creature hung on. Tennebriel snatched at the fallen brand, using it to strike at the hand that gripped her. Ullarga screamed, releasing the girl and trying to grab her ankle, the knife still in her throat. Again Tennebriel swung the fire, this time into the face and a moment later Ullarga had gone over the edge. Tennebriel knew she must die on the rocks below if the awful knife stroke didn't kill her first.

Tennebriel drew back, shaking and feeling slightly nauseous. She leaned on the wall and fought for breath. Ullarga: What had happened to her? That *creature*—it could not have been her. Tennebriel shrank back, fighting away tears of remorse. Ullarga! What have I done? I should have saved you from this.

She lurched to her feet, shuddering. And yet something

foul had been destroyed. What had it been? An agent of this
northern power? Perhaps it was better that Ullarga was dead,
released from its nightmare grip. Tennebriel ran up the stairs
as fast as she could, eager to be in her rooms again. There
she plunged into cold water, cleansing herself of this night's
evil work. Her mind sped to the imagined landscape of the
north and the terrors it must hold for her lover.

Far below the halls of Rockfast, in secret caverns where few
of the Stonedelvers had cause to wander, a dim light grew in
an ancient passageway. Two large shapes moved cautiously
along the tunnel, one holding a glowing stone rod, the source
of light.

"How much further?" grunted the second of the shapes.
He had been protesting steadily for half an hour. It had been
a long walk.

"I hear the waters now," said the first irritably.

They confronted each other, their faces haggard, and their
eyes looked away from each other guiltily.

"We have come this far," said the leader. "Do we go back
and forget why we came? Or are we decided?"

There was a long pause, but the second being nodded.
"No. We go on. It is for our people. And for Rockfast."

The first nodded. Then he turned, hearing the coming of
yet another being. Limned by the glow, it waited ahead of
them.

"Men of Rockfast," it whispered, its voice trickling along
the walls that were the roots of the citadel. "Strange allies
for the issiquellen."

Both Stonedelvers looked angry. "What we do, we do for
Rockfast. We have no wish to see your master set his armies
on us."

"As long as you have the Heir to Goldenisle in your tower,
the Ferr-Bolgan will amass. And when they come for him,
Rockfast will crumble."

"That must not be," said the first of the Stonedelvers.
"We have no love for this man! Nor his hated Empire. It
stole our lands, after it had flooded them. Too many of us
have fallen to sentiment, including the Stonewise."

"Aye. But we will not sacrifice our home for the Remoon."

"Then give the Remoon to us," said the issiquellen.

"We do not have him. He is too well guarded. But there is a way. He is to leave Rockfast soon. He goes back to Goldenisle."

The issiquellen hissed in annoyance. "That will not do!"

"No. But we have the route. He is to be escorted by Stone-delvers. They go north and west, then down to the coast. There will be a ship at the village of Westersund."

"The details," said the watcher, and they spent long min-utes in discussion.

"And the witch?" said the issiquellen. "She goes with them?"

"Aye. She has many allies above us. She is the daughter of Brannog, a king among the Earthwrought, though he is a man. We are Stonedelvers, and not all of us are glad of the Earthwrought among us. Let Goldenisle fall, and let the Stonedelvers be Stonedelvers."

"I understand," nodded the issiquellen. "Very well. I will see that Anakhizer is told of this. The siege will be stopped. Rockfast will be safe."

"Then we are content."

The Stonedelvers saw the issiquellen leave and for a while they stood in silence, unable to move.

"It is a cruel business," said the leader.

"Aye," nodded his companion. "But Teru Manga crawls with evil. We must secure Rockfast, otherwise there is no hope for us. We must use what skills we can, no matter how unseemly."

"It would be madness to ally ourselves with Goldenisle! We would become its slaves. Better death than that."

"Aye. Death and a clean grave here in the mountains."

They walked from the caves together, but there was no gladness in their hearts at what they had done.

PART FOUR

THE HEIR

16
Westersund

GUILE AND SISIPHER SPENT the afternoon and night of their stay in Rockfast sleeping, and neither of them could remember having slept so well and so deeply before. When they woke, shortly after sunrise, their heads were clear and the aches and pains of their long journey across Teru Manga were gone. There was a new vigor to them and Guile felt for the first time a degree of the earth and stone power that must have fed Brannog and his daughter. He dressed himself cheerfully, for a moment confident that the darker power that gathered around the stronghold could be bested. He stood by the window and watched the rays of the sun stretching out like fire over the peaks of Teru Manga, and far in the distance he thought he caught a glimmer of sea. His thoughts as he stood there turned to the girl, Sisipher, with whom he now had shared so much. At once he found himself in turmoil. He had always thought her beautiful, a girl apart from those he had known in Goldenisle, where the courtesans strained to be attractive to men of power, or those who had access to them. Sisipher was natural, unspoilt by any such false graces. Guile had offered her a place beside him once, but it had been done in fear, at a time when the cruel power at Xennidhum had warped his reason. She had forgiven him for it, but he could never tell how deep her forgiveness was. She had been linked to him since by circumstances, that was all.

He turned his back on the view and such thoughts and left his private room. There was a small hall near where he had spent the night and he found Sisipher already up. She sat at a table, eating some warm bread, and he caught his breath

223

as he saw her, for she was more beautiful than ever. Two
Earthwrought sat with her, talking eagerly, and Guile saw the
flush of pleasure in her face, mirroring that of the strange
men. They rose as he entered, not as at ease with him as
they were with the girl, but he bade them a cheery good day
and sat beside them. Aumlac appeared soon afterward.

"I trust you are well rested," he said, putting his club
down beside him. Guile assumed he was never without it.

"I feel reborn," Sisipher laughed. "There is great power
here."

"Great goodness," nodded Guile. "It is as if our journey
here was a bad dream."

"But I trust you had no evil dreams," said Aumlac.

Guile shook his head. "None." He accepted some bread
that the Earthwrought offered him. "Well, what plans have
you made for us, Aumlac?"

The Stonedelver grinned. "I am pleased to tell you that
Luddac has honored me with your charge. I am to take you
from here with all haste. The Ferr-Bolgan and their master
will not be expecting you to leave us so quickly."

"Excellent. But where are we to go?"

"North and west. There is a narrow coastal plain and we
can reach it by crossing the mountains. We do not need to
go below, where our enemies wait. On the plain there is a
small village. The people there are not hostile, and although
Stonedelvers have little traffic with them, they will not take
offense if we go to them. Especially," he grinned, "if we
take them a few things they will be glad of. Supplies and the
like. You will have to retain your disguise. You can say that
you were wrecked by the freebooters. Gondobar's rabble are
not loved along these coasts, for they have raided, or exacted
tolls where they have been unable to coerce the villages into
supporting them."

"Is this village loyal to Goldenisle?"

"Neutral I should say. But the men will not be averse to
helping you across the sea. We will pay them handsomely."

Guile nodded. "I will not return to Medallion, not yet. I
have to know what transpires there first. I may not be welcome!"

"We have to find Wargallow," said Sisipher. "Although
he may be in Goldenisle by now."

Guile again nodded. "Aye. We'll be sailing blind, but we'll just have to become simple travelers once more."

Aumlac looked thoughtful. "The mood here is good. At first Luddac was not sure. We have become so isolated that it is not easy for us to give our trust. And you know from our history how wary we have become of your lands. But there is a greater hope here now. If you are to fight here in Teru Manga, the Stonedelvers will be with you. I would like to see that, for there are yet a few among us who are not content. They would rather you had not come. For myself, I know that Rockfast is in great peril. The Stonewise has counselled us more than once that we may have to leave it and either go to the northern wastes, or find a new home elsewhere. Our people are divided. Some would agree, others would rather die defending Rockfast."

"And you, Aumlac?" asked Sisipher.

"I love Rockfast as much as any man does. Perhaps if war broke, I would stand here. We must see."

Soon afterward they were taken to visit Luddac. He seemed as deep in thought as ever, with his clouded brow and sombre expression, but he welcomed them. They spoke for a while of potential futures, of war with the Ferr-Bolgan. Neither the Stonewise nor the Earthwise appeared, and before long the journey had begun. Aumlac had been given an armed party of twenty of the sturdiest Stonedelvers, picked by Luddac himself and privately verified by Aumlac. Men, he told Guile, who would die before allowing the Ferr-Bolgan to take him.

They set out from Rockfast, gazing back along the narrow mountain path at the splendid fortress, reluctant to leave it and its compelling power. Guile could not imagine such a place falling to the wickedness of the enemy, but he knew now the scale of the threat to it. Aumlac also looked sad, and Guile had the impression somehow that the Stonedelver sensed a grim future, just as Sisipher had once looked ahead into pain and fury. On this, however she ventured nothing. Kirrikree swooped down from overhead, and Guile saw Skyrac wheeling away, as if the two great birds had bid each other goodbye, much as men would have done. The owl flew on ahead, and for the remainder of the day was always in sight.

They moved quickly and surprisingly easily over the rocky

terrain, and although they were thousands of feet up in the mountains and had to wind along many precipitous pathways, Guile did not feel the fear of heights that usually assailed him. He was amazed by the scenery and often paused to admire some plunging view. Sisipher, laughing softly, had to coax him along, prodding his ribs, or pushing him in the back. Each time she touched him he felt a stab of joy, telling himself not to be a fool. Yet here in the mountains, where the air was pure and filled with a unique magic, she had changed and become as he had never seen her before; she was happy, her face bright, her dark mood lifted for once, and although it gave him pleasure to see this, it made it more painful for him, knowing that deep inside she could never forgive him for the past. Even so, he took great joy from the day.

That evening they camped under the snows of the Slaughterhorn range, the Stonedelvers lighting a fire and roasting wild goats they had caught. They surrounded their charges, mostly out of sight, blending with the exposed rocks. Sisipher, Guile, Aumlac and three others sat by the fire, delighting in its warmth, for once the sun had fallen, the air became crisp, threatening a snow flurry. Aumlac, however, said there would be none tonight and Guile knew better than to ask how he knew such things. Sisipher had spoken to Kirrikree, who slept high above them on a rock ledge; he had reported that he had seen no movement around them in the mountains, save for other goats and for the rabbits he had taken for his own food.

"Another day," said Aumlac, "and it may be that we will have fooled the Ferr-Bolgan. This speedy retreat was well thought of."

Sisipher said nothing. She had felt something stirring in the land far below, but she had put it down to her imagination. She did not have the Earthwrought power to look into the stone, although she wondered what limits there were to her powers at times. The business with the Ferr-Bolgan still puzzled her, and she thought again of the man from the ice fields, the Created.

There was no attack that night and the following day was much as the first. They journeyed on across the high ridges, just below the snows of the long range, and every step away from the eastern peaks gave Guile more hope. Kirrikree flew down to them often, but again confirmed that there was no overland pursuit and that he had seen nothing in the valleys or in caves that he had found there.

It took them four days to reach the mountains above the village of Westersund, and they could see it clearly below them on its green strip of land, like the model of a child. Aumlac pointed, his face split in its customary grin, and Guile felt a wave of relief as he saw the open sea beyond. The view from here was stunning: to his right the mountains spread out and went on to join an even mightier range whose white peaks towered upward in the west as if they would go on to even loftier heights. Aumlac said that Starkfell Edge began there, high above that range, while beyond the Edge itself, real mountains began. Guile simply could not imagine the scale. His eyes turned to the sea, which ran from left to right, sweeping out to the horizon, beyond which, to the south, the Chain would be found.

They began the descent, passing through the last of the foothills after midday and reaching the green fields which the men of Westersund tended and where their cattle grazed. Word had already been sent to the village, and a party of its men came out to greet the Stonedelvers on the trackway that served as a road up to the forest, where they cut their wood. They were hardy-looking men, and at once Sisipher was reminded of the fishermen of her own village of Sundhaven. They said little, but welcomed the party, saying that a room had been prepared for the "merchant" and his wife who had been unfortunate enough to fall foul of Gondobar's men.

"They were lucky," said Aumlac to Thunfinn, the headman. "We Stonedelvers don't often pay much heed to Gondobar's foolishness at sea, but it happens that Guile here is an asset to us. He brings us certain goods and has not lacked bravery in finding us! Speaking of goods—" And he went on to point out to the villagers the items that Luddac had had packed for them, and they went to them eagerly.

Aumlac's Stonedelvers would not be staying in the village, but took up posts close at hand. They eyed the plump cattle hungrily, but Aumlac warned them that if they took so much as a leg, he would brain the man responsible. Meanwhile, he joined Thunfinn, who took his guests to the place that had been made ready for them. They went into the village, which was nothing more than a score of houses, made from the logs of the forest, and which had been set close to the shore, with a number of wooden piers running out to the deep water, a natural harbor for the fleet of small ships. It would have been very difficult to defend such a village, which seemed hardly equipped to hold back the worst of any winter weather.

"A ship leaves at first light with the tide," Thunfinn told Guile gruffly. "It is small, but sturdy, and may not be as grand as what you are used to. You are from Goldenisle?"

"One of its many outer islands," said Guile. "We like to be a little independent. The Emperor rarely casts his eye our way." He winked.

For a moment he thought he had said the wrong thing, for the frown on Thunfinn's face equalled that of any Stonedelver, but then the headman grinned.

"Should I find my way home safely," Guile went on, "I will add to the gifts the Stonedelvers have brought you, that I promise."

Thunfinn grunted, pleased. "Your business is your affair, sir. We will leave you. A man will call for you as soon as the ship is ready to leave." He bowed and took his men with him.

"It seems very straightforward," said Guile.

"There is another night ahead of us yet," replied Sisipher.

Aumlac turned to her at once. "What is wrong?"

"I don't know," she said, shaking her head. "The villagers are honest enough. I'm sure they can be trusted. But we have slipped away from our enemy far too easily. Don't you find that odd?"

"Well, we will be vigilant," growled Aumlac. "I will leave you, as I must watch my own men. Keeping them away from those cattle will not be easy. And the villagers will not be comfortable with so many of us about. But I promise you, you will be safe here. And I will be back when you leave." With a last grin, he closed the door.

Guile adjusted the lamp and studied the room. "So you are fated to be my wife again," he said, not looking at Sisipher.

"In name," she replied, turning back the sheets on one of the beds.

He was about to say something else but thought better of it. They had had a good journey; better not to spoil it. He went to his own bed and stretched out on it, arms behind his head. He felt tired now, and wished again for the balm of Rockfast. Overhead he heard the flutter of wings, guessing that Kirrikree had alighted there. He stole a last glance at Sisipher. She had her eyes closed as if in thought and he knew she was speaking to the bird. His own eyes closed. The silence was complete.

The tapping broke it, startling him. With a shock he realized he had fallen into a deep sleep. Sisipher was already up and crossing to the door. She spoke softly to someone outside and turned to Guile.

"It is dawn," she told him with a smile.

"Already!" he gasped, jumping from the bed. They opened the door to find the promised villager beyond.

"The tide is about right, sir," said the man.

Guile and Sisipher collected a few things to take with them and came out into the freshening breeze. It was colder here than it had been in the mountains, and the sky had clouded over ominously. The wind came from off the sea, bringing with it the taste of salt.

They walked through the sleeping houses beyond the single street of Westersund and were quickly joined by Aumlac and a number of his men. They looked cold, as if the sea wind chilled them.

"How are the cattle?" whispered Guild beside Aumlac.

Aumlac growled. "A close thing! I had to send a good many men up into the foothills on scouting parties just to keep them out of mischief. They saw no Ferr-Bolgan, though. Our ruse has worked."

"Where are your men now?"

"Posted about the village. But we won't be attacked now." He walked with them to a long landing stage, a rickety structure that looked in need of repair. The tide had swelled up just beneath it, slopping over it as the waves moved, and a few small craft bobbed up and down on the swell. Aumlac's face was screwed into a grimace of distaste.

"Water," he said, trying to smile. "Rivers and small lakes we have no fear of. But there are too many things buried in our memories to make us love the sea! The Flood. So, I must say goodbye here, from the land.''

''I understand,'' said Guile, suddenly realizing what it was that had so set the big man on edge. He held out his hand and Aumlac's great ham swallowed it, but his touch was gentle, full of warmth. Sisipher abruptly reached up and kissed the big man on the cheek. He looked extremely embarrassed, but the men who stood with him looked serious, and did not smile.

''You honor me, mistress,'' Aumlac said.

''We will meet again,'' she told him. He bowed. The seamen had arrived and were anxious for their passengers to get along the landing stage to the boat.

''Have you seen another meeting?'' Guile asked the girl as they walked down the stage.

She shook her head. ''No. But I cannot imagine not seeing them again. Can you?''

''No.'' He turned back and returned Aumlac's wave. His face set, his hand dropped and he looked resolved, hardened. ''We cannot allow Rockfast to fall into the hands of the Ferr-Bolgan.'' His hands had become fists. ''We cannot,'' he breathed.

Sisipher saw the look in his eyes; she knew what he had been through under the earth. Since she had first met him, he had changed. The whimsical fool who had unsuccessfully tried to jest his way through chaos had gone. He still had his humor, a strength in him, but he had learned so much.

''Quickly, mistress,'' came the voice of the villager beside her and she was wrenched out of her thoughts. She gripped Guile's hand and together they approached the plank up to the ship. It was not easy to turn away from the watching Stonedelvers.

At that moment the waters below seemed to boil. Foam surged brightly in the pale dawn and shapes heaved up from the sea. Guile leapt back, thrusting Sisipher behind him, and pulled out his sword. A dozen issiquellen had dragged themselves up on to the boardwalk. They were unarmed, but they meant to smother Guile in one swift assault. On the boat there were shouts of dismay, and the air hummed as an arrow was loosed. At once one of the issiquellen stiffened, the arrow in his throat, and the creature toppled back into the sea.

Sisipher screamed as hands reached for her. She beat at them but felt herself being dragged to the edge of the stage. Behind her there came a bellow of rage and she was wrenched around to see Aumlac racing over the landing stage, his fear of the sea put to one side. Guile used his sword with instinctive sweeps now, far more proficient with it than he had ever believed possible of himself. Two of the sea creatures shrieked as the steel bit into their bellies and they flopped down. Another skidded on their blood and Guile was quick to drive home the point of his sword.

Aumlac came rushing forward like a man demented, his stone club flailing about him and several of the issiquellen were immediately sent spinning to their deaths. Sisipher was almost on the brink of the sea when Aumlac brought his club down on the head of her assailant, and with his free hand the Stonedelver dragged the girl clear. He and Guile closed ranks and a furious battle ensued. Almost a score of the sea creatures ringed them, but the fishermen were firing into them, picking them off with their unerring accuracy with the bow. Guile felt hands ripping at him, but he knew these beings did not want him dead. Desperately he cut at them, yelling his defiance. Sisipher was too stunned by the speed of the attack to use the terrible power she had used on the Ferr-Bolgan.

By the time Aumlac's companions had braved the narrow landing stage, the battle was over and the issiquellen that had not been killed had dived into the sea and disappeared. Aumlac raised his club in a final gesture of fury and cried out some curse upon them. He turned to Guile with a laugh, but as he did so the planks beneath him snapped with a loud report. The huge man lurched sideways, flung by his own momentum into the sea. He went under the waves like a rockfall.

"Aumlac!" shrieked Sisipher. "He'll drown!"

Guile acted at once. He flung aside his weapon and plunged into the water. Sisipher and the villagers from the boat crowded the landing stage, horrified.

"Guile!" Sisipher called. "You imbecile! The water."

A number of the fishermen had their bows ready, arrows strung, searching the water for a sign of the issiquellen, but for a minute there was no movement. Then Aumlac's shaggy head broke surface in a burst of spray. He sucked in air and yelled in terror, but Guile was under him.

"Keep still, you bear!" Guile spluttered into the Stonedelver's ear, fighting to keep the terrified man from dragging them both under. He tried to work him to the side of the stage, but they went under again. None of the fishermen dared leap into the water, knowing that the issiquellen might be coming back in strength.

Again Aumlac broke surface, sagging now, and weighing impossibly. Guile shut his mind to the coldness of the water, filling his lungs with air as he sank beneath the Stonedelver, thrusting with his feet at the huge man's back in an attempt to propel him toward the stage. He could feel Aumlac going downwards and pulled at him, but it was like hauling at a net filled with boulders. Anger flared in Guile and he kicked out with all the strength left in him. Above him, through the blur of the water, he saw hands groping for him. Aumlac bobbed upward and with another heave, Guile got him to the hands. It took six fishermen to get a hold and heave the man above the water. Aumlac coughed and spat out mouthfuls of salty water, but an arm flung out and gripped the broken boards. It was enough. Minutes later he had recovered enough of his strength and used his own terror of the sea to propel himself out of it. The fishermen pulled him to safety. But there was no sign of Guile.

Sisipher ignored the huge man, searching the water frantically. If the sea creatures had not fled, Guile would now be an easy victim. She concentrated, trying everything in her power to search under the water with her mind, but she encountered only darkness.

Guile's head broke surface, fifty yards away. He began stroking for the landing stage, fighting the tide with fading strength. As he came to it, hands reached down. As he gripped them and was swung upward, two of the issiquellen finally appeared, rising from the water on either side of him, their spatulate hands grabbing for him. A dozen arrows tore down into the bodies of the sea creatures, every one hitting an organ, and at once they sank from view. Guile crawled on to the landing stage and retched.

Sisipher stood over him, watching him with a mixture of anger and anxiety. He stared at her, eyes streaming, face drawn. He was about to make a rude comment, but the coughing fit took him again.

"Get this lunatic aboard at once!" Sisipher snapped and the fishermen around her did as she bid quickly, still amazed, lifting Guile and carrying him into the boat. Aumlac had staggered to his feet, held up by his companions, who looked just as winded as he was.

"This," gasped the bedraggled Stonedelver, "was well done."

"It was reckless!" said Sisipher.

Aumlac shook his head, trying to see into the boat. "This will be spoken of for many years, and for as long as Rockfast stands. I would have died. I will not forget Ottemar Remoon."

Sisipher's face softened. "You must go back, Aumlac. We will sail at once. before these things come again."

Aumlac bowed and Sisipher turned to climb the plank on to the boat. The fishermen pulled it aboard after her and in a moment the boat had left the stage. Aumlac stood very still, watching it as if mesmerized. Only when it was far out to sea where he could no longer see it did he at last move; he turned away from the water without a word and went back to the land. There he was met by his other men.

He spat out more of the brine. "Those who believe Goldenisle to be our enemy will think hard on these tidings when we report them."

"A man worthy to be Emperor," said one of his men. "And more than an ally."

Aumlac glanced back at the graying sea. "Aye. More than that."

As he and his Stonedelvers took their leave of the village, Guile had recovered enough to insist that he be allowed to go on deck. A cup of boiling grog warmed his hands as he gazed seawards.

"What course, sir?" asked the man who skippered the craft, Garrond, a cousin of Thunfinn. This man was no merchant, he thought, not by the way he fought.

Guile put an arm around his shoulders. "Your men are handy with their bows, Garrond. I owe you my life."

Garrond, not a man to smile often, broke his habitual

sternness now with a gap-toothed grin. "Always a pleasure to see those see pigs stuck, sir."

"Think they'll come again?"

"They'll not board us, not if we watch. Where to?"

Sisipher stood beside them now and Guile nodded to her. "South," he said. "The western arm of the Chain ends in a cluster of islands. The largest of them is Tolkerrin. You know it?"

"Aye, though I've not landed there," said Garrond.

"There's a smaller isle to its northwest, Skerrin. Very few men live there, and they have no great regard for the main islands, being of Crannoch stock. It would suit me to land there for now."

"Very well, sir. You'll get no more questions." Garrond grinned again, then went off to see to his ship, calling out orders as he went.

Sisipher came closer to Guile. "Have you lost your senses?"

He shrugged. "Perhaps it is the Remoon madness. But when I saw Aumlac fall, I had no choice. I know how he must have felt. I have visited that place myself."

Her hard look softened. "Well, it was a worthy deed, Ottemar. Not one you would have considered once."

He turned, an angry fire suffusing his cheeks, and at once she drew back. "I—I am sorry," she stammered. "That was not fair—"

He looked again at the sea. "It is true, though. Once I would not have considered helping. Anyway, it's done. Aumlac is alive. So am I." He laughed. "Come! Enough sour looks. We are bound for sanctuary. On Skerrin we will be safe. Then we can find out where our steel-handed friend is hiding. No doubt he has fared well. I expect he's found a position for himself in the royal court!"

"It would not surprise me," she grinned, glad to be able to relax with him again. Somewhere high above she saw a flash of white and knew Kirrikree to be there.

"Is he well, mistress?" came his soft voice.

She answered that he was.

"He has found power of his own now. That which was turned in on himself, he turns outward. There is more strength

there than his friends would know. I would not have called
him friend once.''

"Nor I.''

Behind them, along the rocky shores of the coast they had
left, a small group of beings were gathering in a cove where
the waves beat incessantly, cutting a natural cavern out of the
soft rock strata there. Painfully, one of the beings dragged
itself from the water and hung over a rock. One of its arms
was pierced by an arrow, and in its side was a deep gash
which bled freely. As the being slumped down, the others
came to it and pulled it free of the clutching sea.

"Well?'' growled the biggest of the rescuers dispassionately.

The mortally wounded issiquellen gasped as the hands
tightened on its arm. "Disaster. We attacked when they were
not expecting us, and away from the land, out of reach of the
Stonedelvers. The seamen had bows.''

"So? They always have bows, we know that! You had speed
and were numerous. Where is the Remoon? *Where!*'' snarled
the leader.

"The Stonedelver took us by surprise. He came to the
water.''

There was a stunned silence at that. "He *what?*''

"He ran to defend the Remoon. Together they beat us off,
them and the bowmen. Many of us were killed.''

The leader snorted. "See to him!'' he snapped to his subordinates and turned away. There were others waiting for him
and among them a being draped in dark clothing, a man not
of the sea but of the land, a herder of the Ferr-Bolgan.

"They have failed,'' said the issiquellen.

"How is that possible?'' came the voice of the herder, and
the sea creatures felt it like a slice of the wind from the high
lands.

The issiquellen leader explained. "Now the Remoon is
sailing away from us. We can try for the ship, but the men
of Westersund are adept at repulsing us when we seek their
craft. I doubt if we could do it at sea.''

The herder considered this. "A setback,'' he agreed. "But
I have better news. There are many ships at sea now, most
of them from the Chain. Curiously they sail from different
places, but all are coming here to Teru Manga. And all seek

the Remoon. Some of them are his allies, but we have learned that he has enemies among them, too. First among these are the ships of the navy, commanded by Fennobar himself. It is to him you must go.''

''To Fennobar?'' The issiquellen leader looked appalled.

''Yes. You must find a way of leading him into the path of the Heir. Since we cannot bring him here as our prisoner, let Fennobar have him. He is Eukor Epta's man. And the Administrator will put Tennebriel on the throne. This suits Anakhizer very well. The Remoon will either be killed or imprisoned, far from the eyes of men. Civil war is bound to follow. So, lead Fennobar to the Heir and our work will still be done. Tell the Commander of the Armies that Ottemar sought refuge in Teru Manga but that we would not support him, fearing reprisals.''

''I will attend to this myself.'' The issiquellen turned, called to his companions, and minutes later all had disappeared into the sea, leaving the corpse of their former companion floating in a pool with the weed. The herder had not even glanced at it.

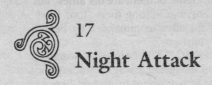

17
Night Attack

RANNOVIC SCOWLED at the darkening skies, smelling a storm. There had been an ugly turn in the weather lately and it matched the grim mood of Drogund and the freebooters as they searched for the escaped Remoon. Not for the first time Rannovic thought of the girl, Sisipher, whose eyes haunted his sleep. Ah, but had she not escaped she would already have been his, now that Gondobar was dead. But Rannovic could not afford to dwell on the delicious possibilities, not with this cursed hunt still on. It had been almost three weeks now and there was still no sign of the two who had got away. It was impossible to believe anything other than that the evil beings under Teru Manga had taken them, in which case they would be long dead, probably eaten alive by those horrors. Still Drogund insisted on a thorough search, almost obsessively, wanting to be sure. He would be glad to know that his half-brother was dead, but Rannovic was more interested in the girl. He turned away from the open sea and studied the barren coast line of Teru Manga. They could not have found a way here and then stolen a boat. They must be inland if they were alive. Pah! Impossible.

"Sail! Sail ho!" came a shout from the mast. Rannovic raced to the prow, shielding his eyes. He had the vision of a hawk and in a few moments he made out a sail to the south, surprisingly heading toward him.

"What is it, a fishing craft?" He knew that many trawling fleets braved the waters east of Teru Manga as the seas there were rich in fish, and the freebooters exacted a minimal toll from them.

"Fishing craft it is, Rannovic," came the reply. "Alone, moving quickly."

"Fetch alongside her. We'll see if she has any news of merit."

Soon afterward they closed with the craft, a large, sleek vessel. Rannovic studied her with a grin. He had his suspicions about these lone craft, wondering if they were in actuality spy craft from Goldenisle. This one looked built for speed, hardly a requirement of a deep sea trawlerman. He took a party of armed men with him and accepted a request that he go aboard.

On the decks of the boat from the south he saw evidence of much hard work, and the catch had proved excellent. His suspicions were mildly softened as the captain came to him, a huge muscled man who looked well capable of handling his craft and surly crew. And he was a fisherman, he could not have acted the part so well.

"I am Krebarl, out of the Chain," he said. "Are you Gondobar's man?"

"Indeed I am," bowed Rannovic extravagantly. He was not yet prepared to confirm the death of his ruler. "You seem to have a heavy catch, captain. Yet you sail north. The Chain and your market is to the south."

Krebarl grunted with false humor. "I've fish enough, but I have a passenger who seeks your master."

Rannovic chuckled. "A good many men seek Gondobar. What have you got? Another renegade from the Chain? A fresh man for our ranks?"

A figure emerged from the stairway to the hold. It was cloaked, but as it came on to the deck it tossed aside its hood. Cromalech laughed as he came forward. "Well, well. Rannovic the abductor."

Rannovic's hand went straight to his sword. A trap! his mind yelled. This ship must be full of Killers.

Cromalech's own empty hand came out in a gesture of peace. "No need for your sword. I have none of my men with me, just Krebarl's fishers, and they have few weapons. I did not come to fight." He walked closer to Rannovic and nodded to Krebarl, who withdrew at once.

Rannovic realized then that Cromalech was at his mercy. He relaxed.

"I have to see Gondobar," said Cromalech bluntly.

"Ah, yes. No doubt you are anxious about a particular guest."

"I'm well aware that you knew who he was when you abducted him," Cromalech grinned.

His easy manner alerted the pirate, but he feigned ease himself. "The Remoon. Aye, my men recognized him. But the girl—who is she?"

"One who has captured your interest, I fancy."

Rannovic scowled, but then grinned again. "I have to say that she intrigues me. She is not Ottemar's wife, nor his concubine."

"Tell her she is and see the answer for yourself! But she is a close ally of the Heir." They had moved to the prow of the boat out of earshot of the rest of the men. The fishermen took little notice of the pirates, working on their nets and tending to their tackle, eager to be sailing home. Rannovic could see this and thought if this were a trap, it was superbly concealed.

"I imagine you were in no position to give me the truth when I boarded your ship," he said to Cromalech. "I had the feeling you were in some difficulty."

"Indeed I was. Your arrival was timely, otherwise I would not be here."

"Enlighten me."

"That's why I'm here," Cromalech chuckled. "Some wine while we discuss it? I have an excellent vintage aboard."

"A fine idea."

Cromalech gestured to Krebarl's men and they arrived a few minutes later with two goblets and a small wine cask. Rannovic tasted the wine and pronounced it to be excellent. He recognized it as having been made from the grapes of the Trullhoon islands, once Hammavar lands. Cromalech had not chosen it randomly, knowing that such wine was no longer available to the men of Teru Manga.

"Now," said Cromalech. "The truth of the matter. I was sent to the east to abduct Ottemar Remoon, or Guile as he calls himself. Not by the dying Emperor, Quanar, who was comatose when I left the Chain some two weeks ago. The fact is, there are two contenders for the throne."

"Only two?" grinned Rannovic, enjoying the wine.

"By birth. Ottemar is the prime Heir, but there is also the Crannoch girl, Tennebriel."

"Crannoch?" said the pirate, surprised. "I'd thought their high Houses wiped out long ago."

Cromalech explained Tennebriel's lineage. "She is well enough. And there are many who would have her as Empress."

"Including yourself."

Cromalech bowed. "Yes. I am in her confidence. And more to the point, the Administrative Oligarch, Eukor Epta, wants her on the throne."

Rannovic's brows contracted. "Is that so? Power indeed. The spider at the heart of the web. And he is for Tennebriel?"

"Aye, but the law is for Ottemar."

"So you went eastward to abduct him? And who are these easterners, these men of Elberon?"

"They support Ottemar. Even now they are in Goldenisle."

Rannovic stared out to sea. He could take his wine, so his mind was not clouded by it, and he was wary of deceit, being one of the laws he lived by. "Tell me, as you found Ottemar why did you not kill him?"

"We wanted him in Goldenisle, as a prisoner. Eukor Epta knew that if he had him, he could use him to keep Ottemar's supporters under his control."

"Ah. Politics. But you were thwarted."

"As you discovered. Wargallow, the leader of the easterners—"

"Yes, an interesting man. And a dangerous opponent I would surmise."

"Be sure of that!" Cromalech laughed. "A man I have to confess I admire. But dangerous—yes, he is that. And bold! Having watched you sail away with his prize, he abandoned his plans to return to Elberon."

"Why did he not kill you?"

Cromalech laughed, and Rannovic's men watched uneasily. "I had to use my tongue as I use my sword! Somehow I convinced Wargallow that I was not Ottemar's enemy. I said nothing of Tennebriel. Merely that if I had been Ottemar's enemy, I would already have killed him. I doubt that Wargallow was fully convinced by me; he wouldn't trust anyone. Instead, he set sail for the Chain itself! On our way there we sailed into the fleet of the navy, Fennobar's lackeys. Fennobar is Eukor Epta's man to his boots, and he will, therefore, support Tennebriel.''

"Is that so? Then the odds seem to favor this girl.''

Cromalech nodded. ''Wargallow went to Medallion Island and had the nerve to stand before the Hundred. He spoke eloquently enough, mostly about the recent war in the east and of the terrible powers that he claims threaten Omara. He told us we must forget all political differences and unite. Eukor Epta himself presided over this assembly. It was stirring stuff, Rannovic, but you can see now that everyone is saying one thing and doing another!''

"Including yourself?''

Cromalech poured more wine, enjoying himself. ''Naturally! But I promise you, I support Tennebriel.''

Rannovic shrugged. ''There's no reason for me to doubt that. But I have to ask the obvious. Why are you here?''

"There will be war, I am sure of it. Nothing is open yet, for no one admits that Ottemar is alive. No one has declared for him, mainly because he cannot be found! But I suspect all parties must know by now that he's in Teru Manga. You Hammavars will have to declare your ground.''

"You think so?''

"I think you have no choice now. You see, if Tennebriel takes the throne, she will grant Gondobar a full pardon and welcome him back into the Chain. All harbors will be open to you, and you will be given lands.''

Rannovic looked impressed. ''Well, that's inviting bait. Presumably to earn this we have to make our ships available if the war begins?''

"Think of the rewards. But there is something else.''

"Ah, now you sound like one of us!''

Cromalech smiled. ''No trick. Give me the Remoon. Just his head will suffice.''

Rannovic paled. Here was an opportunity at last to strengthen the Hammavars, to bring them back into the Empire with honor, and yet the Heir was lost.

"I'm no politician,'' Cromalech went on quickly, pressing his advantage as he read it in the pirate's eyes. ''I've no time for more blunders. I should have killed the Heir when I had him. I have no wish to imprison him; it will only give his supporters fresh hope. He must die. We may even prevent a war, though I doubt it.''

Rannovic again studied the sea. He emitted a long sigh, shaking his head. "Sometimes I think the Hammavars accursed. It would have been so easy."

"Why should it not be?" said Cromalech, frowning.

"Two things. Firstly, we do not have the Heir. He and the girl, the witch who can twist a man's mind when she chooses—"

"Are you so smitten?"

"You misunderstand me. She has power, Cromalech." And he explained.

"Where are they?"

"They escaped us," said Rannovic describing events at the citadel.

"Then they may yet be alive?"

"Perhaps. This gift she has—But there are things below Teru Manga that we do not even speak of. The only way the Heir could have got away was by going under the earth. They must be dead. They must be!"

Cromalech looked troubled. "Perhaps. But if they survived, where could they go? They could never hope to find a ship and steer it."

Again Rannovic paled. "Had you seen my ship struggle to find our home, with the witch promising to thwart me, you would question that."

"Where could they go?" repeated Cromalech. "Not to the Chain."

"Not openly. But perhaps," Rannovic said, looking about him, "they could have concealed themselves in a fishing vessel."

Cromalech groaned. "Of course! Are there fishing villages?"

"Not on this coast. West of Teru Manga there are a few."

"Could the Heir be there?"

Rannovic shook his head. "No, they'd never reach them, not by land."

Cromalech nodded dubiously. "You said there were two things—"

"Aye. The second is worse news for you. Gondobar is dead. He had been ill for a long time. Now he has been succeeded by Drogund. The son of Onin."

Cromalech sat back against the rail and thought hard, feeling a sudden closing of a trap. He forced a smile. "Onin? Was he not the lover of Ludhanna, Ottemar's mother? Of course! But this is better news."

"Explain yourself." Rannovic knew full well that Cromalech knew his history and that Drogund, more than Gondobar, was the sworn enemy of the Chain.

"Ottemar has sworn to rid these waters of the Hammavars if he takes the throne. He would stop at nothing to avenge the abduction of his mother, even though we all know she was not exactly carried away screaming. Drogund is a stain upon Ottemar's family. Think of it, Rannovic. Tennebriel is a Crannoch. The Remoons almost wiped out her House. She owes them no favors."

"Aye, but you seem to have ignored the fact that the Trullhoons helped the Remoons destroy the Crannochs. With a Crannoch on the throne, the Trullhoons would not fare so well. And exiles or not, we Hammavars are yet Trullhoons."

Cromalech smiled. He had his man now. They had their pride, their honor, these Hammavars. "Exactly! Tennebriel would pardon the Hammavars, as I have said. The Trullhoon ruler, Darraban, would be made to accept the word of the Empress. He would have to sit on his pride, his House's curse on you Hammavars. The roles would be reversed. A nice irony, don't you think?"

Rannovic smiled. "Indeed. With the Hammavars in favor, the Trullhoons would look to us to keep the Empress sweet! Even Drogund would enjoy that. Perhaps Darraban could have Teru Manga as his home?"

"In the war, Darraban will clearly not turn away from his own nephew. His great dream has always been for a Trullhoon to rule the Empire, and although Ottemar is a Remoon, he has as much Trullhoon blood in him."

"Oh aye, Darraban will be for Ottemar. More reason to find the Heir now! Then we must hasten to Drogund. He is searching the land for his half-brother. His temper is evil, Cromalech. Perhaps your news will change that, though not if Ottemar eludes us!"

After this, Cromalech went aboard the pirate ship, dismissing Krebarl's craft. The first Sword allowed himself to be taken below where he could not see how the pirate citadel was reached, and he spent the time in further discussions with Rannovic until the pirate was needed to pilot the ship through the tortuous channels of Teru Manga to the citadel. Once there, Cromalech was taken, blindfolded, up into the heights, and kept in a locked room. He did not resist or argue, anxious to see his plan through to the end, determined to secure the alliance of these fierce northern fighters. He had known he would be in danger on this voyage from the outset, but had expected to be dealing with Gondobar, whom he was certain he could win over, but Drogund would be a different man. He had a reputation for being a cold-blooded warrior, a merciless enemy of the Chain. He would not be so easy to reason with as Rannovic had been. Had Rannovic been the pirate leader, Cromalech mused, the future of this enterprise would have been assured.

The lamp in Cromalech's room had burned low by the time he was sent for. Rannovic fetched him, the pirate's face lined with fresh anxiety. "The hunt goes badly," he whispered as they walked up the street to Drogund's base. "No sign of the fugitives. Drogund is in a vile humor."

Drogund awaited them within, the room bare and stark. A number of men stood around Drogund, all of them tired, faces like thunder. Drogund looked up from his charts angrily as if annoyed at being disturbed. As Cromalech entered, Drogund made a point of spitting into the dust as he studied the First Sword.

"You must be tired of life," he said softly to Cromalech. "What sympathy do you expect here?"

Cromalech looked evenly at him. "Has Rannovic not told you?"

"He told me I should hear you," Drogund cut in before Rannovic could answer. "He said something about an alliance, a new place in the Empire for the Hammavars." He spat again. "Now you tell me."

Cromalech did so, and as he spoke, calmly, never wavering, for that would be the way to ruin, he saw that Drogund's face never altered. At the end, Drogund sat back, examining his nails. He studied Cromalech for a long time.

"Well," he grunted at last. "A pretty story. The Empire is full of barking hounds, all about to set at their own throats. And you want me to add my own hounds to the battle. If I do not? What if I wait until your Empire is in tatters, then sail in to her harbors and put them to the torch? Take Medallion for myself?"

"You don't have the strength," said Cromalech coldly.

Drogund's eyes narrowed. "You think not?"

"My information is good. You would not fare well, whoever takes the throne, if you attack them after the war. If Tennebriel is defeated by Ottemar, he will seek you out, and if not him, his House. If Tennebriel wins, as she must, the Crannochs will grow in power."

"With the Trullhoons as renegades?" said Drogund with heavy sarcasm.

"Possibly. But the Hammavars would be even more isolated. You would have no support, from the throne or from the Trullhoons. Your position here is not what it was. I hear strange tales of these lands and the evil here. You would do better to leave them. You could have your old homes—"

Drogund looked as if he would leap up, but he must have thought better of it. He turned to his men and saw them looking down at the map, their eyes confirming their interest in Cromalech's offer. Teru Manga was no place to live, not now. And since the hunt had begun for Ottemar, they had found things they would rather not have found. Drogund's lips pursed in a cruel line.

"Tomorrow, at first light, I will call the shipmasters together. You tell them what you've told me. If they agree, we'll consider supporting this Crannoch bitch, under our own terms."

Cromalech stiffened, but nodded.

"And when we find Ottemar, if he's alive, you can have him." The pirate rose with a final glare at the First Sword. "As an act of faith, you can behead him yourself, before my people." He walked past Cromalech and Rannovic without another glance at them. His men followed him and in moment only Rannovic and Cromalech remained.

"How will your people vote?" said Cromalech.

"Many of them will wait to see Drogund's hand. If he goes against you, so will they."

"He must know I speak the truth! They would be fighting for their old lands—"

"Aye, but when we broke from the Empire, it was to support Onin and his rebellion. That is past, but even so, many of the older men remember it and have sworn to stand by Onin's son. His father's honor still comes first for them."

"And you, Rannovic?"

The big pirate looked away. He was about to say something when there came a frightful shriek from outside. At once Rannovic was through the door, Cromalech at his shoulder. They saw a number of men struggling with other shapes in the lamplight. One of the men was down, gurgling, his throat ripped. Rannovic's sword leapt out and he was cutting at an opponent with great agility. Cromalech found himself set upon from behind, and as he whipped round he confronted a being the like of which he had never seen before.

"Flesh eaters!" came the cry and more pirates rushed into the street to help. Cromalech had no sword but he ducked down and slammed his fist into the thick hide of the being that had groped for him. It seemed part man, part beast, and although he had never heard of the Ferr-Bolgan, he had heard strange rumors of the denizens of Teru Manga. Its breath was foul, its eyes ablaze, and only the fact that it moved awkwardly and clumsily saved the First Sword in the confined street. He punched at its soft belly twice more and it sank back, winded, and as it did so he put his hands together and swung them like a club at its neck. There was a dull snapping sound as its vertebrae pulped under the awesome blow and the beast fell to one side. At once another three came out of the darkness.

Cromalech leapt back and found himself hemmed in by pirate swordsmen. Rannovic was nearby, cutting at the attackers, and Cromalech saw there were scores of them in the citadel, swarming like a nest of ants from whatever dark holes they lived in. The ring of swordsmen forced the way to a doorway and the men struggled through it, slamming and bolting it from within. Outside they heard the howling of the Ferr-Bolgan.

"There are scores of them!" gasped Rannovic wiping his blade free of blood. He found a spare sword and tossed it to

Cromalech. "Here! You'll need this. Hammavar or not, we're all the prey of those monsters," he grinned.

"What are they?" said Cromalech. "Is this what Wargallow spoke of?"

"We know of them," said Rannovic, listening to the frightful blows upon the door. "They are always skulking about us, usually far below. They've never come here in force before. This is something fresh."

"We've stirred them up," said another of the men. "Since we started looking for the Remoon. There's hundreds of them below us, and now it's just like they're hunting too."

"The Remoon?" said Cromalech. "How can that be?"

"Who knows?" grunted the pirate. "Something's got them moving. I've seen other creatures with them, cloaked, more like men. And there's worse in the seas. Fish-folk. Just as dangerous. They've been gathering lately as well as the flesh eaters."

"There's a way out at the back!" someone shouted, and the men made their way through the abandoned house, squeezing through a narrow window into another alley. Cromalech had just entered it as the front door shattered. Rannovic guided him to a tiny square where the main party of Drogund's men had already rallied to their leader.

"It's worse than we thought," said Rannovic.

"I don't know if we can hold them!" Drogund called. "We can't tell how many there are. Get everyone to the ships. Women and children, everyone!" He marshalled his men well, Cromalech saw, as the pirates prepared a good defense of the ropeways that led down to the ships at the quayside far below. Already scores of Ferr-Bolgan were swarming out of the night.

"We believed our citadel safe!" said Rannovic, using his sword to keep back a fresh assault. Beside him Cromalech welcomed the chance to use his sword arm, and many of the beasts fell to him. They were easy to kill, but he knew it would be impossible to defend the citadel with so many of them breaking into it as if they had poured from the living stone itself.

"Who commands these things?" he yelled to Rannovic.

"No one knows. Nor their numbers."

Again Cromalech thought of Wargallow's warnings. How

far did this evil extend? What did it plan? But he had no time
for deliberation, the battle now becoming furious. The Ferr-
Bolgan seemed to have no set purpose other than to overrun
the citadel and kill anyone in their path. The pirates were
prepared for an evacuation, and had been for months, it being
part of their precautions against discovery here in Teru Manga
by their many enemies. Cromalech was impressed by the
way they got their women and children to safety, losing none
of them, although a good many of the pirates fell. He saw
for the first time the herders that moved among the Ferr-
Bolgan, beings who never put themselves within reach of the
swords of their enemy, but who goaded the lumbering beast-
men on. Only the confines of the streets saved the pirates
from annihilation.

At last the pirates made their own retreat, and Cromalech
stood with Rannovic, Drogund and a score of others who
were the last to use the ropes. Drogund spared the First Sword
one glance, and even now there was not a glimmer of respect
in it. Rannovic knew that Cromalech was a superb warrior,
and was glad of it, even though any man would have fought
for his life against such an uncompromising enemy.

The Ferr-Bolgan tried to follow the last of the pirates down
the ropes and nets, but by doing so made themselves easy
prey for the swords below. When the last of the pirates had
started the ape-like climb down, the cloaked figures urged
the Ferr-Bolgan on to new deeds, trying to sever the ropes.
Some men were lost because of this, but for the most part
the evacuation was successful. There was, however, a fresh
battle below. Most of the pirate ships were brought to the
quay in relay, taking on the people of the citadel, but from
the water came wave after wave of issiquellen, with more
Ferr-Bolgan erupting from the stone tunnels beyond the cave.

Cromalech stood at the foot of the immense chimney only
to be embroiled in another furious sword fight. Some of the
Ferr-Bolgan wielded crude weapons, but the main enemy now
was exhaustion. Many of the pirates fell because they no
longer had the strength to lift their sword arms quickly
enough, so furious was the attack.

Drogund looked about him in horror, knowing that a third
of his people had already been wiped out. The remainder
were almost all aboard the ships. High overhead he could see

flames licking the walls of the cavern and a pall of smoke
rising even higher. The citadel would be gutted and never
used again. How had this happened?

He was still wondering as he leapt on to the last ship to
leave the quayside. Two craft had been sunk by the swarms
of issiquellen, many of whom were dead, their corpses floating about the hulls. Never had so many of them been seen
before. In the past their attacks had been random and isolated, but this was a concerted effort, and they were clearly
allied to the Ferr-Bolgan. The talk of evil powers under a
single command came back to Drogund now, and he could
no longer dismiss it. He swung round, chest heaving with
effort. Cromalech faced him, equally exhausted.

"You cannot fight these things alone," breathed the First
Sword, watching the quayside where the enemy had gathered
in terrifying force and howled its united fury at the fleeing
ships. "None of us can."

"We're free of them," snapped Drogund, wiping blood
from a deep gash at his brow.

"Where will you go?"

"Around the coast, to the west."

Cromalech nodded. "I cannot believe that Ottemar has
survived."

Drogund scowled at the smoke high in the night sky. Like
a dark stain it blotted out the stars. In one short hour the
world of the pirates had been ripped asunder. Drogund moved
away, too tired to give voice to his fury.

The fleet moved slowly through the canyons toward the
open sea while the men licked their wounds and saw to their
wives and children.

No one prevented Cromalech joining Rannovic as he piloted the ship through the narrow channels. The pirate looked
on the point of collapse. "We are lucky to be alive," he
panted. "Any longer and you could have forgotten the Hammavars. I think I must owe you my life several times over."

Cromalech smiled grimly. "And I owe you mine. You fight
like an Imperial Killer."

Rannovic coughed. "I was about to tell you that you fought
like a Hammavar."

They fell silent, spent now, listening to the slap of the
waves. After they had reached the openings of the sea, Dro-

gund gave the order to sail into open water before moving south and west. He had no wish to find anything else moving on the coastal heights.

Three hours later, at the first hint of dawn, there was a shout from the mast.

Drogund came to the sleeping Cromalech and woke him roughly with a kick. "Up, you filth!" he snarled.

Baffled, Cromalech got dazedly to his knees. "What is it?"

"A fleet!" snapped Drogund. "Brought here by you, no doubt."

"Who—?"

"I understand your game now! Ships of Empire!" spat the pirate. "So here's your answer, son of the streets!" He set the point of his sword at Cromalech's throat. Out on the water Cromalech could see many ships, and he recognized them at once. They were indeed Empire war ships, though he could not see their colors in the poor light.

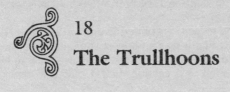

18
The Trullhoons

WARGALLOW AND ORHUNG WERE TAKEN by the men of Otarus through yet more tunnel systems and up again into the city. They were given thick cloaks to don so that when they came out into the open air they were able to cross the quayside nearby and slip clandestinely to the place where a ship waited for them. Men were standing apparently idly by, but as Orhung and Wargallow came to them, it was evident that they expected them and they played their parts well enough. Quickly they took the two men on board as the men of Otarus slipped back into the darkness of the alleys.

The ship was a large fighting vessel, that much was clear to Wargallow, and he could tell that she was ready for sea. Soon after he and Orhung went below decks they felt the ship move, already preparing to leave the harbor. There were men here, armed as if for war, and Wargallow noticed the eagle device on their shields and the emblem sewn on their tunics: these were Trullhoons. The guards took them to a cabin, knocked softly and then ushered them inefficiently.

Inside, Wargallow and Orhung took off their cloaks and found themselves in the company of a single man. He had been watching the quay from a port, but now turned to them. He was tall, about fifty Wargallow thought, and had a thick red beard. Something about him spoke of the sea, as if he could never be far from it, and as he nodded by way of greeting, Wargallow recalled the few things he had already heard about him and his reputation for being a hard man.

"Welcome to my ship," he said. "I am Darraban Trullhoon, master of the Trullhoon House."

Wargallow and Orhung both bowed. "It is an honor to meet you," said the Deliverer. "Otarus has spoken well of you."

"Has he indeed?" grunted Darraban, but he smiled. Wargallow saw that it was an honest smile and not one that was used for convenience. "He tells me that you are to be trusted. You'll pardon my caution, but Goldenisle faces difficult times."

Wargallow nodded. "We are setting sail?"

"We'll be in the Hasp shortly. Then the open sea. Fennobar will not be far behind us. They tell me you know my nephew, Ottemar. I heard you speak in the Hall of the Hundred. If what you told us there is true—"

"I'm afraid that it is. It was no trick to fool your nation. Omara is in serious peril."

"Otarus seems to think so, too. He spends enough time with those grimoires of his that he won't let anyone else see! We must talk of these things as we sail. Tell me now, what of my nephew?"

Wargallow spoke then of the abduction in Elberon and of the subsequent flight and of Guile's going to Teru Manga.

"Gondobar!" Darraban said with a patient scowl. "The old fox of the north. He won't harm Ottemar."

"You think not?"

"No!" Darraban laughed. "He's a tired enemy and if what I hear is true, ill with it. He was never entirely happy with the exile of the Hammavars. If you ask me, he'll see this as a chance to talk."

"And you?"

Darraban's eyes gleamed. "The Hammavars are Trullhoons! Onin Hammavar shamed us by taking Ludhanna. They deserved their banishment. Still, if they have Ottemar, we must be wary."

"How do you mean to take him?"

Darraban eyed the Deliverer. He had been told of this man and of the relentlessness of his purpose, and he could feel it in his gaze. "How would you take him?"

"Assuming I could find him?"

Darraban laughed. "Aye! But the Hammavars can't hide forever. I've never sought them before and certainly no fleet such as mine has bothered to look for them. I've a hundred ships in the northern islands, waiting for us now. I'll find the Hammavars!''

"How is it that you have such a fleet? Is it a part of the navy?''

Darraban gave his guests a suspicious look, but after a moment he grinned. "Perhaps you are not over-familiar with our history. There was a war not so many years ago, the War of the Islands, when Trullhoon and Remoon almost removed the House of Crannoch from Omara. Since then it was agreed that there should be one navy for Goldenisle, made up principally from the other, lesser Houses. It is how Fennobar's fleet has been built up. The Crannochs have a fleet now, as we do, but the official business of the Emperor is conducted by his navy. My fleet is far larger than the Administrators know.''

"So you'll take your nephew by force?''

"If I try that, they'll hold a sword at his neck, eh? Wouldn't you? How would you defend him, or yourselves, from a fleet like mine? They'll not match it, fine sailors though they are.''

"I would defend with words, not swords.''

Darraban shrugged. "Not the customary Hammavar way. Not the Trullhoon way! But Otarus tells me I am too bellicose for my own good. He also tells me,'' he said sternly, leaning over the table, "that I ought to be guided by you.''

Wargallow smiled. "Indeed? Well, I should say that it might be better to put aside your arms this time. Ottemar's safety is paramount. We must secure him upon the throne.''

"Aye, I'll pledge my sword to that, even if I'm not to use it! Here, we'll toast that in ale. The finest! You'll not know what ale is until you've had your belly filled with Trullhoon brew. Or if you prefer wine, we also make the best.''

"We will drink as you do,'' said Wargallow.

Darraban grinned hugely. He opened the door and bellowed a command. Footsteps quickly receded outside. Shortly thereafter, two young men entered the cabin, one with two fistfuls of tankards. These he banged down on the table, slopping a fine head of froth onto its surface. Darraban swooped on a tankard and held it aloft.

"Here! Take a drink with the Trullhoons!'' he boomed, and Wargallow lifted a tankard, Orhung doing the same, though he did not relish the thought of drinking. The two men also held their tankards up in a toast.

"These boys are my sons, Andric and Rudaric. Anything you wish to say can be said before them," said Darraban proudly, quaffing his ale.

"Then I drink to the health of you all," said Wargallow. The ale was superb and he said so.

Darraban almost emptied his tankard and laughed, wiping froth from his beard. His sons were like him, tall and red-haired, though both were clean-shaven. They looked as fit and muscular as hunting cats and carried themselves like seasoned fighting men, which both Wargallow and Orhung had seen at once. They had the same look of mischief about their eyes that was in their father's, for all his sternness, and it was clear from the way the big man looked at them that they were his world.

He gave them a wicked grin. "This man from the east wants us to go and shake Gondobar's hand!"

Andric scowled. "His hand? There's another part of his anatomy I'd rather shake, aye, and pull it loose!"

Darraban guffawed. "And you, too, Rudaric? Not in the mood for an exchange of political views?"

Rudaric grinned at Wargallow. "I'll shake his teeth loose if you wish."

"You see!" Darraban laughed again, finishing his ale. "And this is how my fleet will be, dogs on taut leashes, eager to get at the throats of the Hammavars."

"They may be wild dogs," said Wargallow with a smile. "But you are still the Houndsmaster. They obey you."

"Hah! That they do! Well, boys?"

"We are no longer boys, father," said Rudaric rather curtly.

Darraban's face changed at once and he leaned toward his sons like a huge bear about to crush them. "Then behave like men," he said coldly, his humor gone. "Boys blunder in. Men do not."

"Surely, father," said Andric more reasonably, "we can flush out the Hammavars easily enough. They cannot dictate to us."

Darraban softened. "That is true. But you must listen to

our guests. I have told you what I heard in the Hall of the
Hundred. Now hear all of it.''

Both Andric and Rudaric were amazed by what Wargallow
and Orhung told them for the next two hours, particularly by
the news of what faced them in the north. Darraban listened
equally as attentively as his sons, and at the end sat back with
a gusty sigh.

''I had sensed the movement of something evil more than
once,'' said Darraban. ''When you spend as much time at
sea as I do, you hear strange tales from many lands, some of
which men of Goldenisle have never been to. We had heard
of the east, of course, and we hear also of the west, where
no man has ever been and returned, where the endless Deepwalks spread under Starkfell Edge. So, what are you sug-
gesting, Wargallow? That we offer peace to the Hammavars?''

''Goldenisle is our one hope against Anakhizer. When he
strikes, we must be ready, as one army, or should I say,
force, since it seems our great strength is naval!''

Andric grinned. ''Goldenisle has a fine navy under Fennobar, even though there are very few Trullhoons in it. But
my father's fleet is a match for any.''

Wargallow nodded. ''How much stronger would it be if
the Hammavars were a part of it?''

Both youths looked sharply at their father. He was stroking
his beard thoughtfully. ''I wish to see Ottemar Remoon on
the throne. It may mean sacrifices.''

''Honor, father?''

Darraban stiffened. ''I have thought of this, many times.
But the Hammavars also have their honor to think of. If, *if*
Gondobar is prepared to sue for peace with us, and to support
Ottemar, then honor would demand that I accept.''

''And should he hold Ottemar over us and make other demands?'' said Rudaric.

Darraban sighed. ''Wargallow has explained what that will
mean. We will be falling into the hands of this Anakhizer.
He seeks to drive a wedge between us all.''

Wargallow pushed aside his empty tankard, which had been
filled more than once. ''There is a way.''

''Then let us hear it!'' said Darraban.

''An amnesty. Until we have settled things with Anakhizer. Tell Gondobar that your own disputes with him can be settled later.''

"He'd expect a trap," said Andric and Rudaric was nodding.

Darraban sat up. "Well, we've time enough to plan it. But for the moment, the keg is near empty."

They had argued as they sailed north. Darraban had brought his captains to meet Wargallow and Orhung, and the discussions had gone on, often for hours at a time. The longer they did so, the more Darraban became resigned to the fact that Wargallow was right. It would only be possible to defeat Anakhizer if they settled their internal disputes first. Otarus had said so at the outset, and now many of Darraban's Trullhoons were coming round to his way of thinking. The unknown quantity was Gondobar.

When they finally reached the coast of Teru Manga, they sailed up its eastern side, knowing from past reports that the freebooters had their warren somewhere there. Two weeks after the fleet had set sail from Goldenisle, with dawn barely breaking, they saw a great plume of black smoke rising inland. Drawn to it, the leading scout ships reported vessels at sea, a small fleet of them.

Darraban stood beside his guests and they studied the horizon together. "I don't believe it!" he gasped. "It's the Hammavar fleet. Not only their swiftest craft, but others, too. Unless this is some bizarre trick, we are seeing a migration. Can they be going to seek other lands, in the east, perhaps?"

"No, father," said Rudaric, who had been gathering reports. "They sail this way, southwest. And it is all of them, for they have their women and children with them."

"Have our ships armed. But we are *not* to attack."

Rudaric bowed and raced off.

"Something's wrong," said Wargallow. "Inland."

Orhung, who had been almost completely silent and withdrawn for days, wore now a strange look, one of both sharp awareness and alarm. "It is," he said, his voice like a cold wind from the north. "I have come to know what is here as we approached it. Anakhizer is already at work. His servants crawl throughout Teru Manga as maggots infest a carcass. They are innumerable. We must not go ashore. It is why the

Hammavars flee. They have been attacked and that smoke was their home." Orhung shuddered and closed his eyes, but he would say no more, even when pressed.

"Then the Hammavars are at our mercy," said Darraban.

Wargallow stood close to him. "The very word," he said softly. "Mercy. Spare them now."

Darraban grunted, but Wargallow knew him for a reasonable man. Even so, Darraban gave the order to bring his fastest ships around the freebooter fleet, fanning his ships out in a semi-circle from which the pirates could not break free. As dawn came up, the movement was completed.

It was as this naval maneuver began that Cromalech found himself kicked awake by Drogund. The pirate glared at him now, sword point an inch from his throat.

"Well?" snarled Drogund. "You have a minute to explain before I give you to the crabs."

"Whose ships are they?" said Cromalech, trying to hide his shock. "Those of Fennobar, or others?"

"What does it matter!" Drogund spat. "They are *Empire* ships! And we are too exhausted to outrun them. They are surrounding us."

"If they are Fennobar's ships, they are not here to destroy you. They want the Heir. They are Eukor Epta's lackeys and support the Crannoch girl."

Drogund was almost too tired to consider it, having lost a lot of blood. His sword point wavered. He called out to men at the mast, but the enemy had still not been identified. Drogund turned back to Cromalech, who was now on his feet.

"And if they are not Fennobar's men?"

"They may be men of Elberon, in which case they are also looking for Ottemar. They'll know you had him, but you'll just have to tell them the truth."

"Or they may be here to sink us, brought by you, Cromalech. And did you have a part in that massacre as well?" Drogund nodded toward the plume of smoke.

Rannovic stood close to his shoulder. "He couldn't have," he told Drogund. "He did not lie about that."

"I would not have come to you alone if I had wanted to bring a fleet in!" said Cromalech.

Drogund spat, not satisfied, and it seemed as though he

would run Cromalech through. Rannovic reached out to touch his arm, to whisper something. Cromalech had waited for the hint of an opening. He wrenched himself aside and as he did so, Drogund lunged instinctively. Cromalech felt the cutting edge of the pirate sword along his shoulder as he drove his fist hard under the pirate's heart in a blow designed to kill. He felt something snap inside Drogund, who folded up and almost took Rannovic over. Other pirates had seen the sudden move, but as they came forward, Cromalech was already up on the ship's rail. Before a single sword could cut at him, he was gone, swallowed up by the dark seas in an instant. A dozen men watched, but none of them could make out a sign of the First Sword.

Drogund was gasping painfully, his face gray as Rannovic stretched him out on the deck. He bent over him, trying to catch the words of the man. "Forget him, Drogund!" he told the agonized face. "He has no chance of surviving out there. And if he gets ashore, he's finished."

There was blood seeping from Drogund's ashen lips. "Aye."

"Those creatures were not his allies—"

They were interrupted by a shout from the mast. "A flag! Truce! They seek a parley."

Men rushed to the ship's prow, and in the excitement, Rannovic was left alone with Drogund, who tried to raise himself.

"The eagle sails!" came a cry. "Trullhoons! And the flagship of Darraban is there!"

Drogund's face filled with fury now.

"You must accept this truce," Rannovic told him. "That or they will sink every one of us."

Drogund shook his head, words coming from him in a ragged whisper that was like the curse of a risen corpse. "And foul our honor for ever? No! Pick up your swords! Even though we die here, Rannovic, we will teach these bastards—"

Rannovic looked about him, sure that no one had heard. Then he put his hand on Drogund's throat, so that it looked as though he was ministering to his leader.

When men finally came to him, he stood up. "We have no

choice," Rannovic told the men. "We must accept the truce."

"Is it Drogund's wish?"

Rannovic put his arm on the man's shoulder for support and looked very tired. "Drogund does not command here now. The blow of the Imperial Killer has killed him."

Although he had agreed to a truce, Rannovic argued over the method of holding talks, which was the Hammavar way. He had been given the task of leading the Hammavars now that Drogund was dead, and the people were only too glad to have a leader who could make firm and positive decisions for them at a time when their world was falling about them. Rannovic refused to accept an offer to go aboard the Trullhoon flagship, just as he was refused a request that Darraban should come to his own craft. In the end both leaders agreed to send out longboats and meet between the fleets, and this seemed to satisfy honor.

Both craft were filled with armed men, neither party trusting the other, and anxious eyes watched the two boats from both fleets, all ships prepared for a sudden engagement. The longboats were secured together and at last Rannovic faced Darraban and his sons. He saw that Wargallow and the strange man from the southern ice were here, bowing to both with a grin.

"Where is Gondobar?" was Darraban's opening question. "I have not come here to talk to spokesmen."

"Gondobar is dead," said Rannovic. "And so is Drogund, who was our ruler after him. I, Rannovic, am the head of the Hammavar House, and I speak for us all."

Darraban looked stunned by this, but did his best to remain calm. "Then I am sorry to hear that Gondobar is dead. And what of my nephew, Ottemar Remoon? Is he also dead?"

"Is that why you are here?"

"I'll have an answer first!" snapped Darraban.

Wargallow stepped to the edge of the longboat. "Rannovic, this is of vital importance to us all. Is the Heir safe?"

"Why do you ask?"

"Quanar Remoon will soon be dead," said Wargallow. "Ottemar will succeed him. If you have him, what do you intend?"

"What are your own intentions?" persisted Rannovic.

"To see Ottemar safely upon the throne," said Darraban.

"Who attacked you?" said Wargallow, pointing to the smoke over Teru Manga.

Rannovic's face darkened. "What do you know of them?"

"I think I know who sent them," said Wargallow.

"Are these the things you have fought before, Ambassador from the east? Oh yes, Simon Wargallow, I know more about you than you realize," said Rannovic, recalling the details of Cromalech's revelations. He had been sure the First Sword had not lied.

"Then I admit that I know these evils. Where is the Heir?"

Rannovic's grin faded. "We have lost him."

Darraban looked appalled. "What? Dead?"

"We cannot say. He and the witch-girl fled us. They went deep into Teru Manga. Do you think they could have survived that? You cannot know what lies there."

Wargallow and Darraban exchanged glances. "Then they may yet be alive," said the Trullhoon. "How are we to find them?"

"Say what you want of us," said Rannovic. "We have no home. Nor can we give you what you seek, though if we had the Heir, we would give him to you." And side with you? Rannovic thought. In spite of Cromalech's offer? But the First Sword would speak up for no one, not now. And besides, if the Heir was alive, the girl would be too.

"We do not seek your blood," said Darraban. "It is, after all, Trullhoon blood."

Rannovic and his men felt a stab of hope in this. "Then— will you let us pass by?"

"Where do you sail?"

"West," said Rannovic. "Few lands are safe to us. You know how well we would be received in the Chain!"

"The Empire is changing," said Darraban. "There may be war."

"We have heard of this. Ottemar has enemies, I am told. There is another who would wish to sit upon the throne of Empire."

In spite of their shock, neither Wargallow nor Darraban let their reaction to this show. "That is so," nodded Darraban.

"It is said," went on Rannovic, himself eager for the truth, "that Fennobar himself supports another cause. A Crannoch cause."

Darraban stiffened visibly, but he felt Wargallow's hand on his arm.

"Tennebriel?" said the Deliverer, and the word hung between the boats like a threat.

Rannovic nodded. "So I hear."

"Otarus spoke of her," said Wargallow. "Then it is this girl who is our enemy."

"You say you know of this?" Darraban asked of Rannovic.

"Aye, and of those who support her. Eukor Epta himself, so my spies give me to believe."

Darraban's horror was clear and he swore under his breath. "You are extremely well informed."

Rannovic laughed. "Well, Tennebriel's agents have already been to us. They gave us truce, as you have. And they wanted the Heir, or to be more precise, his head."

"If you have given them this—" began Darraban, speaking now with a terrible, controlled fury, his fists clenched.

Again Wargallow drew him back, sensing an explosion of violence. "Who was this agent? Who came to you?" said the Deliverer.

"A man whom I should have little reason to doubt. A man who told me that if we fought for Tennebriel against you and her enemies, she would pardon the Hammavars and give them back their islands in the Chain."

"Tennebriel would do this?" said Darraban. "A Crannoch! And you believed her man?"

"Drogund doubted it. He said, 'since when did a Crannoch offer the hand of peace to a Trullhoon?'"

"And yet," cut in Wargallow, "a Trullhoon can offer the hand of peace to a Hammavar."

"Is that what you offer us? If we take arms with you against the enemies of Ottemar, we are to have a place in the Empire?"

"Aye," said Darraban, though he did not smile. "Though Ottemar is a Remoon, his mother was a Trullhoon."

"Tennebriel's man told us that if enthroned, Ottemar would put all Hammavars to the sword," said Rannovic. "Ottemar has not forgotten that his mother abandoned him to take flight with Onin Hammavar.''

"Ottemar was a babe at the time!" snapped Darraban. "He has no wish to prolong that shame now."

"Ah, but you were no babe, Darraban," said Rannovic. "And she was your sister."

Darraban swallowed hard, aware that every eye was upon him. "We must end our dispute here. And satisfy honor. Drogund is dead. Has he no sons, no daughters to carry his name?"

"He took an oath before the shipmasters," said Rannovic quietly. "He swore that he would be the last of the line and that no Remoon blood should linger in Hammavar veins." As he spoke, he looked at the sea, thinking of how he had ended Drogund's life, for the good of the Hammavars, and he felt a rush of shame for his act.

Darraban had been moved by his revelation. "Drogund did this?"

"Aye," said Rannovic, stiffening. "So I ask you now to recognize him as your nephew. Recognize him as a Trullhoon first, before a Hammavar."

Darraban turned to his sons and to those who were in the boat. "Then hear me! I offer this to the Hammavars: come under my banner and oppose the enemies of Ottemar Remoon and I will accept Drogund as a Trullhoon. By this act will I absolve any breaking of the Trullhoon honor committed by Onin Hammavar."

Rudaric looked across at Rannovic. "No daughter of the Crannochs could offer you that."

"Then I will swear before the shipmasters," said Rannovic, "that the Hammavars will sail with the Trullhoons. Although first I must see to the sea burial of Drogund."

Darraban again looked surprised. "Burial? Has Drogund only lately died?"

"Aye, killed after the flight from the citadel."

"Then you must allow me to attend his burial with you. It will make our vows here the stronger."

Rannovic bowed. "You do us honor, Darraban."

Darraban reached across and offered his hand and Rannovic took it warmly. Darraban's stern features at last broke into a semblance of a smile. "Although your House has suffered evil this day,'' he said, "this is a moment of joy to me. It has been too long in arriving.''

"Gondobar would have echoed you,'' said Rannovic.

After a moment, Wargallow drew closer to them again, like a grim shadow of the events that gathered about them all. "Who was this agent of Tennebriel? How did he come to you?''

Rannovic nodded. "The girl chose well. The man had the nerve of a shark. It was Cromalech.''

Wargallow smiled grimly. "I had wondered. Cromalech. I should have known sooner.'' He explained to Darraban. "He held things back from me, I knew that, but I could not fathom what they were.''

"Well, he's likely dead now,'' said Rannovic, pointing to the sea. "As we sighted you, he struck Drogund down and dived into the sea.''

"Then Drogund died by his hand?'' said Darraban.

"Aye. He is gifted with great speed, though Wargallow knows this.''

"Indeed,'' said the Deliverer.

"I have wondered what he would have done if it had been Fennobar who came to us,'' Rannovic went on. "He said we would have been safe.''

"Then Fennobar is for Tennebriel?'' said Darraban.

"Aye. Eukor Epta's man.''

"This much we knew,'' said Wargallow. "I think, though, we should spare no effort to find Cromalech. A man like him may yet survive. Whatever he knows, we must exact it from him.''

Darraban grunted. "May as well torture a stone.''

Wargallow and Rannovic looked at the sea together, both thinking of the First Sword, the thought of his death disturbing to them both.

"So,'' said Rannovic. "We look for him and for Ottemar. The Heir may have gone to the western villages, if he survived. It is why we chose to sail that way.''

Darraban nodded. "We go together, as Trullhoons.''

By midday, after the formal sea burial of Drogund, the combined fleets were sailing around the southern tip of Teru Manga, although there was still a certain amount of wariness

about the new alliance. There had been no sign of Cromalech
and Wargallow had reluctantly had to give him up for lost. It
seemed unlikely that he could have survived, extraordinary
athlete though he was. Wargallow gazed landwards, regret-
ting the loss. If he could have yet persuaded Cromalech to
join him, he would have made an invaluable ally.

Wargallow's thoughts were broken by a cry from the deck
and as he went to see what the commotion was about, his
heart leapt. Circling the boat, white wings beating the air as
he dived, was Kirrikree. The huge owl gave a shrill cry that
had half the men on the ship gaping at him in amazement.
An owl at sea was a strange enough sight, but one so huge!

"Kirrikree!" called Wargallow and at once the great bird
swept down and perched close to him on the rail. The bird
looked exhausted but yet held its head proudly.

"Fetch meat!" called Wargallow to the startled men. "Do
it!"

Darraban came to him, stunned by the bird. "What is this
magnificent bird?"

"Magnificent is right," said Wargallow. "I have never
been more glad to see him. This is Sisipher's companion.
She speaks to him and he to her."

"A bird? How is that possible?" said Darraban suspiciously.

Wargallow shook his head. "I wish that I could exchange
words with him now. He would have been near to them in
Teru Manga."

Rannovic, who had come aboard Darraban's ship to discuss further plans, gasped when he saw Kirrikree. "The bird!
It is the one that sent more than one of my men to his death
above the citadel!"

Kirrikree's great eyes met those of the pirate, unblinking,
and Rannovic drew back.

"Then he was protecting the Heir and Sisipher," said Wargallow. "When they went below ground, where did the bird
go?"

"The bird? Up into the skies. We never saw it after that."

Wargallow turned to the bird in desperation. Once it would
have been content to kill him, and indeed had killed his men.
Had it erased those cruel days from its heart? "Kirrikree. Do
you know where they are?"

A soft but acutely clear voice answered from behind him, so that for a moment Wargallow thought that the bird had answered him. But it was Orhung who had spoken. "He does."

Darraban and Wargallow swung round to face the Created, whose eyes were wide, and who seemed unusually vibrant with life. "He speaks, but you do not hear him. I understand a little of what he says."

"You hear him!" gasped Wargallow. "What does he say?"

"The Heir did get across Teru Manga to a village with the girl. They were taken out to sea by a fishing boat. They went south."

"When?" said Wargallow anxiously.

"About two weeks ago. It was a slow journey, the boat being small and there was a storm. Three days ago they were met by a fleet of ships."

Darraban gasped as if stabbed. "Fennobar's vermin!"

"Yes," nodded Orhung, watching the owl. "He was there. And the Heir was taken with the girl. They sail now for Goldenisle."

Darraban was doing some frantic mental calculations. "A small fishing boat? How long were they in it?"

Orhung closed his eyes, listening to the owl. "Eleven days."

Darraban scanned the sea. "Eleven days? It would take them as long to sail from the villages to a point as far south as we are now, longer in bad weather. And three days in Fennobar's hulk? Very well! We'll set a course and show the Imperial Navy what sailing is! I'll wager this ship to a keg of ale that we'll better Fennobar."

"What is your plan?" said Wargallow.

"To meet them in open water, before they are in sight of the Chain. They'll not expect to be set upon."

"Can it be done in time?"

Orhung answered before Darraban. "Kirrikree says it is possible."

Darraban laughed aloud. "Then this bird is not only an omen, it is a prophet, and a wise one!"

Orhung envied them their laughter, unable to share it: he withdrew to the shadows. A prophet! I would gladly seek one. His fingers touched again his rod and he felt its warm life, knowing it grew as the weapon came northwards. It had been fashioned to destroy evil such as Anakhizer, but there was a fresh fear in Orhung's mind. If Anakhizer had the power to wrest control of the rod—but such a thought was dangerous, foolish. I was Created for one purpose. Doubt is a human failing. I reject it.

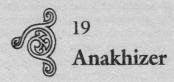

19
Anakhizer

CROMALECH FOUGHT TENACIOUSLY for consciousness as the strong currents that raced along the shores of Teru Manga sought to drag him down. Already he was exhausted by the events of the night and it took all his reserves of strength, all his warrior training to keep him afloat. As he struggled, death waiting below him with grim certainty, he saw in the breaking waves tumbled images of the future, possibilities that taunted him with the knowledge that escape from a watery doom would only prolong his freedom for a brief period. He had cast aside his mantle of deceit before the Hammavars and offered them an allegiance with Tennebriel. But it was evident that the freebooters, driven from their nest, would be captured by the fleet racing up from the south. It was likely that Drogund would die from Cromalech's blow, and if Rannovic became ruler of the Hammavars, which way would he go? Very likely he would throw himself on the mercy of whichever fleet it was that approached: he was skillful enough to win mercy from either camp if he agreed to capitulate. Cromalech grimaced at the thought. Either way, his own ambitious cause would no longer be a secret. Whatever the outcome of his present plight, he would be forced to declare himself. There would be war now, he was certain of it. And if Tennebriel lost, there could be no hope for him. Aye, he could still return to Goldenisle, if he could find a way, and perhaps even yet marry her, but they would either be imprisoned or exiled. As he tumbled among the waves, rising up for the dozenth time, he knew he would prefer even that to losing her.

Of course, if she won—but he had no more time to dwell on it. Something grazed his knee and he clutched at a submerged rock. The waves heaved about him as if eager now to be rid of him, having punished him enough, and he was tossed across a matted expanse of weed which itself tugged him forward to a bed of rocks. Choking, he clambered on to it waiting for another wave and allowing it to push him further to safety. He tumbled forwards in the foam and there was sand beneath him. The dawn light splotched a path of it, wending ahead of him to darkness. He had made the coast.

For a while he was unable to move, but he knew that if he gave in to sleep here he would likely be drowned. On his elbows he wriggled up the sand, wallowing like a seal. The noise of the sea was in his ears, now somehow distant. He moved on, at last reaching the relative safety of the rocks. A cliff face loomed ahead and he knew he would have little chance of scaling it, but for the moment he was living by inches. The will to survive was strong in him, his body used to physical labor: many lesser men would have perished.

He slumped over the rocks, beyond which there was a deep pool. Its contrastingly calm waters were black, as though like a mirror they reflected not the dawn sky but the starless emptiness of space. Cromalech gazed at it wearily, and it seemed that it called to him, offering comfort and relief. He was too tired to move another inch. His hands flopped down, his body hugging the rocks like a child clinging to its mother after a nightmare.

As he lay there he felt the stirring of the earth as though a great heart beat far below him. His body instinctively responded, as if drawn by some force, reacting in spite of itself. He shook his head as if to be free of an unwelcome dream, feeling himself sinking into the rock, being absorbed by it as if it were a peat morass or some unheard of creature devouring its prey as he had seen certain plants do. But he was powerless to move and the illusion persisted. The ring of darkness tightened.

He felt as though he was being drawn through some translucent substance, down through layers of it into a place where the sea was far away. He could no longer hear the surf, nor feel its spray. He was floating, in a void and yet encased in rock, drawn through it. He tried to clear his mind of the vision but could not, for whatever force it was that pulled him to it, he had no strength of will to resist. He was aware that other things around him were also being drawn to this force, living things in the rock and growing things. Everything seemed to be channelled impossibly toward the center of that power, which was like some underground whirlpool, sucking into its maw all that came near it.

There was no sound, no voice in his mind, but Cromalech sensed an unspoken command and wondered idly if this was like the unknown instinct that drew birds across the face of the world from one climate to another, or guided the shoals of fish and eels from coast to coast. It had no language, no name, but it could not be disobeyed.

The darkness below became lighter. He was conscious still of drifting ever downward, somehow travelling across vast gulfs, like being high above the world. At length the sensation of movement ceased and he became abruptly aware of the rock beneath him, which had not changed. His first thought was that he had been dreaming or hallucinating, for his immediate environment had not altered. He could no longer see the dark pool before him, but he could see very little. The powerful call had also ceased.

He moved his fingers, then raised his head. The view took his breath away and he shut his eyes at once. This was an illusion yet! He felt the rock under him, his entire body pressed to it just as it had when he had crawled from the sand. How could I have come under the earth? All the talk of power: was this how it worked in Teru Manga, if this was Teru Manga?

It occurred to him briefly that he hadn't survived the sea but had drowned after all, sinking now to some oceanic afterlife, but part of his reason refused to accept that. He opened his eyes, craning his neck. Before him was an immensity of emptiness, vaguely lit, as though he had come to rest on the brink of the world, overlooking the very heavens, and yet no moon shone here, no hint of star, no sun. Steeling himself, he pulled himself forward, looking over the drop. It fell away, lit by an invisible light source, its hues unlike the hues seen in the skies of Omara above him. The light seemed to leak from the endless cliff face below him, like blood from a wound in the wall of the world.

As he stared downward, he saw that the cliff was not sheer; cut into it were shelves, eroded out of the bands of strata by some force, and he guessed that it was on one of these shelves that he had come to rest. Turning on to his back, he was about to look upward, but he was overcome by such a powerful wave of nausea that he quickly turned back on to his stomach. Whatever was above him, he was not meant to see. He looked again over the cliff.

Silence reigned there, absolute as death, and beyond the drop was the vastness of forever, as if something had eaten a hole through the very stomach of the world. As he thought of this, a wave of coldness lapped at him, for he thought also of the things he had been told by Wargallow, the easterner. He recalled the story of the working of the sorcerers that Wargallow had spoken of, men from another world he had said, who had inadvertently opened a gate between their world, Ternannoc, and Omara. And the cost of closing the gate, sealing it, had been terrible. Was this some nightmare vision of that gate? If such things existed, this must have been their guise, Cromalech thought, an endless, infinite void. Yet it could not be real. Power had been used to close the gate at Xennidhum: all the power that the Hierarchs of Ternannoc could render up, and the power within the countless people who had been sacrificed at Xennidhum.

I am dreaming this. Or I am dead.

The light strengthened. Below him, on one of the wider ledges some hundred feet down, Cromalech saw a solitary figure. It appeared to be robed in dazzling white garments that reflected the light that made the figure pulse with fire. Instinctively Cromalech knew that the figure watched the abyss before it, and did so expectantly like a man facing some forbidden god. Not only was it relaying whatever power it had—and Cromalech knew with absolute certainty that this figure possessed vast power—outwards, it was also drawing power to itself. In a moment it came to Cromalech what that power was. *This* was the Hierarch, Anakhizer, that Wargallow had warned of. Here, deep below Teru Manga, or far beyond it, Anakhizer was sending out the power that summoned all who heard it. All those strange beings that polluted Teru Manga, the Ferr-Bolgan, the issiquellen, and many other, unseen horrors, all were being drawn to this one focal point, Anakhizer. The very rocks were bending to permit the demands of his will! Cromalech's mind tried to tear itself away from such madness, but it clung to this one image, that of a sorcerer drawing in his nets like some awesome fisherman.

Around him, on the ledges of the measureless cliffs, the call was being answered. Milling like ants, the denizens of this grim world gathered, unable to resist the call. There were thousands of the Ferr-Bolgan, all of them mesmerized, worshipping the robed figure as if it were a god. Such things may have been forbidden, but in the Hierarch the creatures of Teru Manga had found one. Cromalech could not draw back, still held rigid by the deep spell. It had not been meant to trap him, probably unaware that he had been on the rocks above, or so he told himself, but he could not free himself from it, forced to watch the unfolding of the ritual. So there's a chance, he thought, that my presence here is unknown.

In spite of the numerous creatures on the cliff face, the silence remained fixed, so that Cromalech still clung to the hope that this may yet be a dream. He had to watch, unable to take his eyes from the figure of Anakhizer. Distance blurred its size, its features, and he saw no face, only the open mouth. It spoke, breaking the silence, addressing not its slaves but the void before it. Its language was meaningless to Cromalech, and yet through those strange syllables he was able to glimpse meaning, visions that flickered and danced across the vaults before him. From these turbulent scenes, these violent snatches of war, of catastrophe, he was able to discern something of the terrible purpose of the Hierarch.

The abyss hid something vaster than anything Cromalech could ever have dreamed of. His mind was unable to grasp what it was, but again he drew on the extraordinary revelations of Wargallow and his companion, Orhung. Some shapeless power, some remote reservoir of energy, once dormant, dreaming in the limitless wastes of the infinity in which it floated, had been awakened. And it had been the events at Xennidhum which had awakened it, focussing its awareness. The events had been like a dream to it, a part of the cosmic tapestry of dreams that it wove for itself. Amused, perhaps, for a while, it had fed on these dreams before turning to other stranger cosmic canvases. Yet it had not been allowed to turn away. Anakhizer, who had been a party to the working that had aroused the power, the terrible working that had gone so tragically astray for the sorcerers of Ternannoc, had seen the power and had yet schemed to pursue it. It had made him a renegade, an outcast, and he had hidden deep under Omara before the gates to it had been sealed by men with the safety of the many Aspects paramount in their own designs.

In his refuge, Anakhizer had retained enough knowledge to seek out the forbidden things that dwelt outside the Aspects of Omara, the many phases of the world. He had done enough to win back the attention of one of those denizens.

Cromalech drew back from the cliff face, staring in fresh horror at the abyss as if it were a plague pit. He knew what it was now. It was no gate to another realm, not another Aspect. It was the sleeping mind of this power. Anakhizer sought to wake it.

As surely as he realized what was before him, Cromalech understood how the Hierarch intended to pursue his course. He meant to feed the dreaming mind with power, the power of *life*. Omaran life! It was for this reason that he had set himself up as Omara's would-be conqueror. Yet it was suicide, Cromalech knew at once. Sheer madness. And yet, detached from it as he was, he could see beyond the madness. Anakhizer had begun by attempting to control this power from beyond, and although it slumbered, it had responded. Even while dreaming, it was channelling him. Its own hunger, its formerly unconscious whim to take physical form, had already clouded Anakhizer's reason. He had become its weapon, and was even now no more than the lens that would focus its power here on Omara. And it would take from Omara all the power that it could drain, a living world. It would become Omara.

Cromalech saw all this and more, pulling the visions from the air like a conjurer, yet unable to stop them. He did not want them, and would have shrieked out his rejection of them, but he could not. Whatever power had dragged him here still gripped him, albeit unknowingly. But a final knowledge was yet to be imparted to him.

Again he looked down. Anakhizer had finished his long ritual. It had been filled with promises, a swearing of fealty, of the carnage to come, the plunder of a world. Now he drew back and delivered up his sacrifice. Cromalech watched in horror as all the victims of the recent battle above were given to the abyss, all the fallen, man or beast, all the dead. It was these victims these slain, that were given to the sleeping power, and as their corpses toppled out into the well of light, Cromalech's terror reached a peak, for he guessed that he was indeed slain also. How else could he have come here?

His head swam as he watched, his eyes blurring, but he was powerless to stop the renewed tug. All light quickly faded, and he was gathered up by the arms of darkness, his scream throttled before it could escape.

He must have slept. He opened his eyes to see daylight above. Under him was the familiar rock, and before him the rock pool, brightened now by the early morning. He still found it difficult to move; he began by flexing his fingers. As he did so, he thought once more of the nightmare. No, it was no dream! But neither am I dead. Being alive *saved* me. He tried to grin, but it was harder than moving.

In time he reached down and scooped a handful of water into his eyes, realizing he was not only alive but hungry. At last he sat up. He had been lucky to escape the Ferr-Bolgan by reaching this bleak stretch of coast, a narrow cove chiselled from the cliff walls of Teru Manga. The only way out was up, unless he was prepared to swim around to somewhere easier to climb. But he wasn't ready for that kind of effort yet.

He stared at the pool. If I get away from this haunted place, what am I to do? I must warn them in Goldenisle. No one, not even Wargallow, can guess what Anakhizer has unleashed. Anakhizer must be found! If he could be killed before this power got out of control, it could yet be foiled. And Wargallow was right about one thing, a war would be playing into the hands of the enemy. Goldenisle had to be strong, and not decimated by internal feuding. Cromalech laughed hollowly. How am I to tell my haughty Tennebriel? How could she set aside the throne? But his laughter died: what hope had he of warning anyone?

As he looked to the sea, his heart froze. Emerging from the waves were a dozen shapes, familiar from the battle of the night. They were issiquellen. Instinctively Cromalech reached to his side for his sword, but his fingers met only air. Behind him the water of the pool broke, and from them erupted three more of the water people. They gripped Cromalech's arms with ease, his resistance almost spent.

He glared at his captors as they took him to the beings from the sea, suddenly twisting and breaking free. But they had him down in a moment and one of them dealt him a heavy blow behind the ear which sent him into immediate darkness, this time free of visions.

The leader of the sea dwellers leaned over him. "The last of them," he grunted.

"Is he to be taken below, or left for the sea?" said the being who had felled him.

The other bent down and examined Cromalech's face. "Wait. This is the man we were told to watch for by Ullarga. It is Cromalech. He is wanted elsewhere." He turned to his subordinates and called brief commands. At once they dragged the unconscious warrior to the sea's edge.

It was the cold that woke Cromalech. The rock was no longer under him and instead he was stretched out on something that shifted as he moved. Sand. He tried to clear his head, but he felt as though he had come to after a colossal bout of drinking. Water rushed around him and he could taste its salt. He pushed himself up and leaned on his arms for a moment. He was in darkness, although his head seemed to be full of light. The roaring, rushing sounds that had been there were gone. Slowly the flashing lights went too, leaving only the dark, the cold, and the gurgling of water.

He struggled up from the shallow water, which was barely ankle-deep, and moved up the gentle sand slope to dry ground. After he had gone a short way, he found a roughly cut ledge like a tiny quay and sat there. He was ravenous. And he thought it would be impossible to feel any more exhausted, as if his entire body had been pulped.

Where in Omara am I? he kept asking himself. He recalled the water dwellers, but wondered now if they had been a dream. He had been in the sea again, though. There was no one else here now. Even so, he couldn't think of getting away, not yet. He would have to rest, even though it might be dangerous. Behind him was a wall, and he dragged himself to it and leaned back, closing his eyes.

It may have been minutes or hours later when the light came. He saw it dancing above him, a torch that threw the stairway into relief, the flame carried by a darkly robed man, and with him came several others. They stood above Cromalech, apparently recognizing him.

"Who are you?" he croaked, his voice almost failing him. "And where is this place?"

"You are in Goldenisle," said their leader, leaning down to offer his hand.

Cromalech gasped. "How? How did I come here?"

"Perhaps you can tell us," said the man. Two of his robed companions put their arms around Cromalech. It was clear to them that he was as weak as a child. Slowly they ascended the stairs with him, and although he wanted to shout a dozen questions, he found himself sinking into the dark once more.

When he next woke, he was in a bed, and was strong enough to take some broth before falling again into sleep. After that his time was spent waking, eating, drinking, then taking a little exercise in his room. He saw no one and could not make anyone hear him, locked as he was in here. They brought food when he slept. Gradually his strength came back to him and he was eager to leave, desperate to impart his knowledge, to speak of the dangers he had stumbled upon.

His captors, if captors they were, saw the change in him and their spokesman came at last to him and sat with him, though the door was yet locked.

"How did I get here?" Cromalech asked.

"It is as much a mystery to us as it is to you, First Sword," said the man with seeming indifference.

"But this is Goldenisle?"

"Indeed. You did not recognize the island when you came to it?"

"No. Which is it?"

"It has no name. but you have been here before, I think."

Cromalech felt his hair crawl at this. "Who do you serve?" he said icily. It would have been easy to throttle this man, but it would avail him nothing with the door locked.

"We serve the same one you serve, Tennebriel."

"She is here?" said Cromalech, unable to resist asking.

"It is her island."

"Then I must speak to her at once."

"That will not yet be possible—"

This time Cromalech reached across and took the man by the folds of his robe. "Make it possible! I have come from the north, and I must be heard. It is vital."

The door swung open and a shadow fell across the room. An Administrator stood there, one of the underlings of Ascanar, and with him were two armed guards. They came into the room as Cromalech released the man. The guards were alert for any sign of hostility from the First Sword. He did not know them, but he knew their breed: a wrong move and they would hamstring him.

"Why are you here?" he growled to the Administrator.

"I was about to ask you that, First Sword," replied the man blandly.

"Where is Tennebriel?"

"No longer on this island."

What did they know? his mind screamed. "I must see her."

"We understand from her servant that you have spoken to her many times. Yet you are First Sword to Quanar Remoon, the Emperor."

"I found her here by chance She is loyal to Goldenisle, as am I."

The Administrator shook his head. "Urgent matters are pressing the Government of Empire. Matters of deception must be clarified—"

"Deception?" *How much did they know?*

"If you'll come with me." The Administrator turned on his heel and left the room without another word. The guards motioned Cromalech to follow, and as he entered the corridor outside, he found six more of the guards waiting. Again he knew it was pointless to resist.

The Administrator led them to a bare room, the only feature of which was a marble slab fixed across two square cut stones. Spread out on the marble was a small corpse, draped in black. A twisted arm hung from under it like the withered limb of a tree. The Administrator pointed to the body. "You will recognize her, I think."

Cromalech was prodded forward at sword-point. He found himself looking down at the broken body of Ullarga, her face contorted so grotesquely that she must have died a grim death.

Her eyes stared out on the beyond as if it held profound terrors for her.

"Before she died," said the Administrator, "and the ocean alone knows how she lived so long with the broken bones she has, she spoke to me." The man shuddered as he thought of it, and Cromalech noticed his disgust.

The Administrator saw again the awful spectre of Ullarga, crawling toward him across the floor like a maimed insect after her fall. What was it that moved the woman? How could she live so long? She had come up from the deeps below the tower, covered in her own blood, a knife in her! And she had said enough to the men who had found her to bring him, the Administrator, to her. He had watched in horror as she spoke, like a puppet being worked by the unseen hand of darkness. Cromalech, she had said, is your enemy. He has been to Tennebriel many times and has sought to pervert her away from Eukor Epta. He has wooed her simple mind. Think no ill of the girl, the crone had said, the words squeezed from her by the invisible fist of her purpose. But the First Sword defies you all.

"How did she die?" came Cromalech's voice.

The Administrator recovered himself. "Tennebriel stabbed her and cast her from the stairs that lead to the place where we found you. Ullarga told us you would be brought there. I was sceptical of her ramblings. She spoke about sea dwellers. They would bring you up from the deeps, from Teru Manga, she said. Gibberish, from the mind of a crazy old woman."

"Of course it is," said Cromalech.

"Oh no. It was not. You were seen being pulled from the sea below us."

Cromalech understood then what had happened. The issiquellen had brought him here! But why? What possible reason could they have had?

"Why did they bring you?" said the Administrator.

But he knew why, and could not say so. Ullarga must have commanded it, or the power that had worked in her, for her eyes betrayed that possession. She had had him brought here to betray him, her last act of vengeance before she died. But had she also betrayed Tennebriel? Would that suit her master?

Cromalech shook his head. "I have no answer."

"A pity," said the Administrator. "Eukor Epta will want one. As will Tennebriel."

"Where is she?"

"Safe enough, in the palace."

"The palace? And the Emperor?"

"Dead."

Cromalech nodded. It had come, then. Then Eukor Epta must have declared himself for Tennebriel. Had he seen to her enthronement?

The Administrator gestured for the body of Ullarga to be removed, and from the shadows two men glided in silence, taking the gnarled corpse from the room. "You need not concern yourself with these matters," said the Administrator.

Cromalech turned to him then, his only course of action a direct one. "Listen! I have been in the north, in Teru Manga. I have to speak to your master. It is essential that he hears what I have to say."

"Ah, yes. Your strange aquatic allies—"

"They are not my allies—"

"Then why have they brought you here?"

"I don't know! But they are no allies of Goldenisle. They serve Anakhizer, who seeks the downfall of us all. Look, if you will not take me to Eukor Epta, then hear me out."

"Gladly." The Administrator made no sign of moving from the chilling room, waiting as patiently as a snake. He listened expressionlessly while Cromalech spoke of what he had done in the north, of the pirate citadel and its sacking, of his own escape and of his experiences under Teru Manga. He spoke of Anakhizer and reminded the Administrator of Wargallow's words before the Hall of the Hundred.

"War of any kind," he ended, "would be disastrous. The north makes ready. Divided by our own war, we would be an easy prey."

The Administrator waited patiently until Cromalech had finished. "I would not have expected such eloquence from a man of arms. You have the imagination of a balladeer."

"Do not joke—"

"Joke!" snapped the Administrator. "This is hardly the time! But you, who were sworn to serve Quanar, went behind his back to consort with Tennebriel, and now wish to profess sympathy for Ottemar Remoon also. The outcast Hammavars as well!''

Cromalech glared at him. "Take me to Eukor Epta. He must be told what gathers in the north."

"I will speak to him." He left at once, gesturing for Cromalech to be taken away. The guards removed the First Sword to a cell and locked him in. There would be no escape from the place, it being like a tomb. Cromalech thought of Ullarga's corpse. She had wrought her evil well enough. He stared into the darkness in despair, even more desolate here than he had been in the north, where a glimmer of hope had fed his spirit enough to keep him alive. Here, far below Goldenisle, he did not expect to see daylight again. How much had the old crone told Eukor Epta's lackeys? Did the girl still maintain her act of simpleness?

20
War Fleet

GUILE HAD NOT SLEPT and although the dawn was beginning to break in the east, he did not feel tired. His only emotion was anger. He stared at the bare cabin wall, his mind going over again the events of the previous twilight.

The fishing boat out of Westersund had been making its laborious but determined way southward, hampered by several squalls but sufficiently away from regular trading routes to go unnoticed. At that time there had been no reason to suppose that anything would stop it from reaching the chosen harbor of Skerrin. As the sun slipped away, the seas rolled, heavy but not difficult for the boat and the tough northern crewmen handled the craft easily and without a hint of fear. They had their nets out for a last haul, having been told by Guile to put the voyage to good use if they could. It had given them work to do, otherwise they would have chafed, he was sure of that.

Sisipher had been the first to warn him. He had been below, sharing a meal with the captain, when she came to him, her face lined with anxiety. "Kirrikree is far from us, but he has warned me of ships coming. Many of them, and they are from the Empire."

An hour later they had known that this was no chance meeting. They were being hunted, as if the oncoming fleet knew who sailed in the fishing boat. They had decided to keep up a pretense of being simple fishers from Westersund, knowing they could not have outrun Fennobar's swift war ships. Gradually these had closed around them like sharks around a kill. Garbed in sealskins, Guile and Sisipher had helped with the nets in an act of innocence, but their boat had been hailed and quickly made fast to Fennobar's own flagship. As Guile and Sisipher had been taken aboard, the girl had whispered that Kirrikree had seen and would do what he could to find help.

Yet now, sitting in the bare cabin, Guile had concluded that it would be hopeless. He knew Medallion Island and its city too well, recalling his time as a prisoner there. This time he would not be allowed to get away from it.

Again he grimaced as he thought of the brief reception given him by Fennobar the night before. The Commander of the Navies had looked him over curtly, almost scathingly. "Ottemar Remoon," he had said. "Your fisherman clothing becomes you."

"There has been some error," Guile had told him. "I am not the man you seek."

Fennobar had leaned close to him, face twisted with unexpected hatred. "When you and your sorcerer, Korbillian, fled from Goldenisle, I had a young nephew on your ship. And you and your friend murdered him and the crew. I recognize you, Ottemar Remoon. You are finished."

"Haven't you slept?" said a voice close to him now.

He snapped his attention away from the visions of last night and looked across to where Sisipher was stretched on another bunk.

He shook his head at her.

"You'd think more clearly if you did," she said.

"This is Eukor Epta's doing. But how did Fennobar know where we would be found?"

Sisipher sat up, stretching as if she had enjoyed a deep sleep and Guile marvelled at her freshness. "I think I can guess. Issiquellen. They guided the ships to us."

Guile made no attempt to mask his horror. "They are *in league* with Fennobar?"

"Possibly, but I think it was little more than spite. They wanted you for their own master, but having failed at Westersund, betrayed you to your enemies instead."

He studied her. "Well, you seem surprisingly cheerful about it!" He looked abruptly more serious. "Any news of Kirrikree?"

She shook her head. "No. But we are not in Goldenisle yet. How long a journey is it?"

"Two weeks, perhaps less. Why?"

She shrugged. "I don't think we should despair."

Suddenly he began to chuckle. "Ah, then have you regained something of your gift for telling? Have you seen a better day for us?"

She tried not to frown. Even now the thought of seeing ahead was painful to her, knowing that it had been a bane in the past, using her darkly. "No, I can promise nothing. But we must think."

"I've done much of that already! I thought of confronting Fennobar, talking to him about the future. But he's committed, and will not waver, I'm sure. Eukor Epta has him in his palm. And the navy are loyal to him."

"Try to sleep."

Wargallow was in conference with Darraban and Rannovic when the news came. Fennobar's ships had been sighted at last.

"Perfect!" exclaimed Darraban as he stood on the deck and squinted at the southern horizon. "A week out from the Chain in open water. Now we'll put our ships to the test."

Wargallow stood beside him, unable to see as clearly as the Trullhoon, but knowing that Fennobar must be close with his fleet. "It would be best achieved without conflict," said the Deliverer.

Darraban laughed and clapped him on the shoulder. "You can still say that? After being kept on a taut leash for so long, the men are like hungry dogs scenting food."

"Every man that dies weaken us against the north."

"Can't be helped," snorted Darraban. "But I'm willing to reason. If Fennobar is, too, and I doubt it, we may yet have a bloodless day."

Behind him motionless as a statue, Orhung stood facing the sea. His hand gripped his metal rod, though the others did not notice, nor did they see the sudden flare of blue light within it.

By midday the two fleets had closed and Fennobar's men knew they were being pursued. Fennobar watched as the Trullhoon ships reduced the distance, sending out flanking craft to his east and west. "What's that fool Darraban playing at? Showing off because he thinks these waters belong to the Trullhoons?" Fennobar growled to himself. "*Flanking* us? What kind of stupidity is this?" It was only then that the thought occurred to him that Darraban knew who his prisoner was, and for a second it chilled him, but he pushed the thought away. No reason for the Trullhoons to know.

However, as the Trullhoon war fleet completed its maneuvers, now seen to be threatening, Fennobar's worries increased.

"Sir," panted one of his lookouts who had come shinning down a mast to deliver his message personally, "Darraban has closed around us. His ships are escorting us."

"Escorting us! This is lunacy! Send word to the impudent pig. I want him here." Fennobar stormed below, but not before he had warned his captains to arm themselves. There could be no mistaking the suggested menace in the Trullhoon formation.

An hour later, drinking in his cabin, Fennobar was approached by Otric Hamal, who looked unhappy at the news he brought.

"Darraban will not come aboard," he told Fennobar.

Fennobar hurled his tankard aside and swore crudely. "I did not expect him to! Well? What does he want?"

"I have been across to him."

"I know that! And?"

"The eastern Ambassador is with him."

Fennobar's knuckles whitened and his face reddened with fury. "What! That sorcerer!"

"There is worse news. Not only has Darraban given Wargallow his protection, but he has many of the Hammavar freebooters with him, including their ruler, Rannovic. There are Hammavar ships in the Trullhoon fleet, and they are not prisoners."

Fennobar gasped. He whirled about like a bull and stormed up on to the deck. He pushed aside his waiting men and stood at the rail, glaring at the Trullhoon fleet as if he could wither it away. Otric joined him.

"Hammavars!" snarled Fennobar. "Traitors!" He began to breathe less heavily and turned back to Otric. "Then they have shown their colors. They are the enemies of the Empire.''

''And they are here to fight, sir,'' Otric told him.

''What have they told you?''

''They have declared themselves for Ottemar Remoon.'' Otric leaned forward and said, so that only his Commander could hear, ''And they know we have him and the girl below. If we give them up, there will be no fighting.''

Fennobar's scowl deepened and he trembled with fresh fury, but then he threw back his head and laughed. ''Is that all they want!'' He spat over the side of the ship. *''That* for their demands!'' He gripped Otric by the shoulder. ''You go back to them. Tell them that if they fire a single arrow or raise one sword against us,'' and he lowered his voice so that only Otric heard him, ''I will slit the throat of both the girl and the Heir. Tell them that!'' He leaned back and laughed again.

Otric looked even paler. ''Sir, I fear they will not be deceived.''

Fennobar was thunderous. ''Deceived! You think I am jesting! Ottemar may as well die now. I know Eukor Epta wants him alive, but he'd be better dead. I'll kill him if I have to.''

''Wargallow does not believe you will,'' said Otric. ''He told me to tell you that Ottemar is too valuable. He knew you would threaten his life.''

Fennobar swore vehemently, drawing his sword. ''Is that so? We shall see! Bring him here.''

''Sir,'' cautioned Otric. ''If we fail Eukor Epta—''

Fennobar's eyes blazed as if he would strike Otric, but he turned instead to the sea, then brought his sword down with a tremendous chop so that it bit deeply into the wood. If it had been a man, he would have been sheared in two. ''Curse the Administrator!''

''Sir,'' breathed Otric at his shoulder. ''Can we not turn this to our advantage?''

Fennobar glared at him as if ready to strike at him next, but he nodded. ''Well?''

''By making demands upon us, the Trullhoons insult the Empire. We are the law here. Dare they attack us? When the news reaches Goldenisle, the Trullhoons will be discredited.''

Fennobar grunted, his temper cooling. "Aye, man, but we have the Heir. And we cannot declare it openly. Tennebriel is likely the Regent by now. When the Trullhoons get word to the Chain that we have the Heir and are not to put him on Quanar's throne, then *we* shall be discredited. We could deny it, but too many of our own enemies would believe the Trullhoons." He nodded slowly at the Trullhoon ships. "You see what this means? War. It begins here. The time of subterfuge is past. Eukor Epta will not be pleased, but it is unavoidable."

"Strangely," said Otric, "it is the one thing that Wargallow seeks to avoid. He yet speaks of the evil in the north, and Rannovic confirmed that some dark power gathers there. They urged us to support the Heir and sail with him to the Chain, setting him upon the throne."

Fennobar scowled at the sea. "Just like that? They think I would calmly accede to their ridiculous demands? This talk of northern evils! Powers greater than any we know of! It's just an attempt to divert us."

"And the water beings, sir? What of them?"

Fennobar again pictured the strange beings that had come up out of the sea, giving him the information he had needed about the whereabouts of the Heir. He had not understood their motives. "We should fear fish-men? The seas are full of such creatures. If they belong to Teru Manga, they were glad to rid their shores of the Hammavars and any men of Empire, Heir or otherwise. Which is why they betrayed him to us. No, Otric, this talk of power is a deceit. Think! If we gave Darraban the Heir, or if we discarded our support for Tennebriel and put Ottemar on the throne, how long before the navy would be reorganized? How long before Darraban Trullhoon became Supreme Commander? And what of the Hammavars? And these eastern renegades? A pox on them all! If they want a fight, they must have it. And if we aren't men enough to sink them, they can have the Heir. But he will be in pieces, I promise you that."

Otric bowed. "Then I shall return to them—"

"No! They'll likely slit your throat for refusing them. Go and fetch the girl."

This command took Otric by surprise, but he did as bidden, relieved that he had not been asked to bring Ottemar here on deck. To kill him would, as Fennobar had said, have been the easiest solution, but Eukor Epta wanted him alive. Otric went below to where the guards stood beside the cabin door of the prisoners. Taking a key from his belt he unlocked it and pushed it open gently. He could see the figure of Ottemar, apparently asleep on his bunk. The girl stood up, looking straight at Otric as he entered.

She was beautiful in some strange way, he thought, with eyes that were unique, cold and yet riveting. No one understood who she was, though most assumed she was Ottemar's mate, some girl he had chosen for himself in the eastern lands. It would be a pity to kill her, but Otric guessed this was what Fennobar intended, as a gesture of defiance to the Trullhoons that would show his willingness to do battle.

"You are to come on deck," Otric told the girl, reaching for her hand. As he did so, a bolt of pain raced up his arm as if he had placed it in molten metal. He screamed and staggered back through the open door behind him. At once the guards entered, swords ready, but there was a crackle of blue light that seared the eyes; something slammed into the men and they were tossed back through the door like puppets.

"The door!" shrieked Otric through waves of agony. One of the other guards kicked it shut and hastily locked it. Another sprawled on the floor, the life burnt out of him. Otric whimpered like a child, bending over his arm, and the stench of charred flesh came up to the men who were now racing down the stairway to him. They gathered about Otric and in a moment Fennobar shouldered them aside.

"What is happening!" he roared.

Otric fought for breath, eyes streaming. "Don't go in there," he gasped. "Sorcery. Something—"

Fennobar snarled commands and more of his men came forward. They unlocked the door and waited, their faces masks, but their eyes full of fear.

"The girl," said Otric, staggering to his feet. "She has power—"

"Come out!" roared Fennobar. "Or I'll have your head!"

"Send in your men, Fennobar," said Sisipher calmly. "Or come yourself."

Fennobar made to wave his men forward, but then changed his mind. There was a deeper evil here than he could have expected. Instead he kicked shut the door and had it locked. "Bring more locks," he called. "Seal them in. Whatever this power is, it must be contained." He turned to Otric and saw with horror the ruined arm.

"Fire," said Otric. "Liquid fire." His face whitened like chalk and he slumped to the floor.

Inside the cabin, Sisipher had fallen back on to the bunk, her face drained. She had not wanted to use this frightening power, but she had seen what Fennobar had planned for her. Guile was mercifully asleep, and had done no more than groan before turning over during the flash of power. She did not want him to know what she was capable of, though she was not sure herself. She knew only that, somehow, the nearness of Orhung was connected with this power, but she also knew that it could not be sustained. If the guards came in numbers, she could not keep them off for long.

As she shrank back, she heard the remote voice of Kirrikree and she made a great effort to reply.

"Mistress! I heard you cry out—"

"I live yet, Kirrikree," she told him. "But you must tell them to begin. Ottemar and I are safe for a while. Time enough for Fennobar's fleet to be dealt with. Where are you?"

"On Darraban's ship."

"Poor bird. Are you exhausted?"

"Never mind. But I'll be glad to get back to land where I can feed properly. I have no love of unfresh meat, or fish. But mistress, you are sure it must be battle?"

"Yes, Kirrikree. Fennobar will kill us both rather than give us to the Trullhoons. He is Eukor Epta's right arm, spurred by his own greed. Tell them to begin."

She felt the bird leave her, experiencing the pang of regret she always did at this. Now she had to fight to keep awake, watching the door, although she could hear the men beyond it nailing fresh wood in place to secure it.

Wargallow looked hard at Orhung. For long minutes the silent man of the Werewatch had been sitting with eyes closed as if listening to some far off words, speaking possibly with the huge white owl, which itself perched high up at the masthead. There had been moments when Orhung's steel bar had glowed with its faint blue radiance, not the first time that

Wargallow had seen this happen, but he had not asked about it. He merely waited, knowing that Orhung would speak when he was ready. His purpose, the reason why he had been Created, had never been fully explained and Wargallow was certain that the man did not have the answers himself. Wargallow recalled only too vividly the way in which Sisipher had been used by powers beyond her understanding.

When Orhung did speak, it was to confirm what Wargallow had feared and what Darraban had promised. "Sisipher has closed herself and Ottemar off from their captors for a while. They will not be released to us. She tells us to begin. Kirri-kree has said this."

As the word was passed among the Trullhoon and Hammavar ships, there were whoops and cheers. Rannovic had already gone to prepare, uppermost in his own mind the safety of the girl. Darraban's sons were likewise in battle position. Wargallow stood with Orhung and they waited as the Trullhoon fleet closed in. Already a rain of fire arrows and fireballs showered down upon the Empire ships of Fennobar as the sea battle commenced. Smoke billowed up from damaged ships in ever-thickening palls, combining to spread a black cloud across the entire scene.

"How many ships are here?" Wargallow asked Darraban.

"Almost two hundred. The pride of the Empire's navy and the entire Trullhoon war fleet. This will be a day to remember for many a long year. And with the ships of the Hammavars among ours, we will carry the day. They fight like tigers! It is why we never bothered to harry them in the north. Too costly."

Wargallow watched a number of contests as opposing ships locked and their men leapt at one another in droves. He saw all this as if from afar, or as if in a dream, and his detachment from it made him cold. Nothing could be achieved here without great loss: already a dozen ships were sinking, a score more burning. Lives were snuffed like candles, reduced in seconds, just as the lives went out at Xennidhum. Each side was well matched, and there would be no easy victory. Wargallow noticed Darraban's face from time to time, and the grim pleasure he saw written there appalled him. Once he, Wargallow, had served a master as grim as death, Grenndak the Preserver, and had rooted out and sacrificed his enemies, but it had been with a sense of duty, not pleasure, however misplaced that duty had been. Now, seeing the carnage before him, Darraban took a kind of pleasure from it, like some reveller at a feast.

The afternoon sped on, with more ships disappearing beneath the waves, both fleets seemingly totally entangled so that it was impossible to say which had the upper hand. All the controlled moves that had opened the engagement seemed to Wargallow to have been broken up, but Darraban insisted that his fleet had a stranglehold on Fennobar's. He kept abreast of the action, listening to every report, issuing orders ceaselessly. Again and again he swore that the day would fall to his ships. At last, late in the afternoon, he pointed ahead to where a large warship defended itself against an attack from either side, where two smaller Trullhoon craft were threatening to ram it.

"Fennobar's flagship!" Darraban roared with delight. He had been clutching a curved sword for the duration of the battle, and now he waved it as if about to use it. "We attack. Once we sink that overweight hulk, the day is ours! Give the order to ram her."

"Ottemar and the girl!" protested Wargallow.

"Hah! We'll have them off before she sinks. Trust me! And we'll have Fennobar's head for our masthead yet." He leapt away to prepare for the fighting before Wargallow could stop him. Beside him, Orhung gazed expressionlessly at the mayhem, as he had done all day. His ears had heard the screams, the cheers, the crackle of blazing mast and hull, the slap of waves across sinking craft, but he had said nothing, as if his mind had gone on a far journey, away from this scene of horror.

Wargallow felt oppressed by the weight of Xennidhum's madness, although its terrors had been far worse. Now he watched as Darraban's sleek ship bore down on that of Fennobar. He gripped the rail hard as her nose and pointed ram drove into the front of the Empire ship with a splintering crash that shook every timber in both ships. At once there was a uniform howl of glee from Darraban's men, all eager for the affray; they had waited until now to enjoin the battle and were yet fresh. Fennobar's tired men defended with animal ferocity, knowing they would die if they did otherwise.

Neither Wargallow nor Orhung moved from their vantage point, though no one expected them to.

"Is Ottemar aboard?" Wargallow asked.

"Still locked in the cabin," nodded Orhung.

"We'd better look for them, in case they are forgotten in this madness." Wargallow drew out his killing steel, hating it but knowing he must use it now. Orhung raised his own steel weapon and the two of them made their way to the rail and dropped easily on to the leaning Empire ship. It would sink before long, and already many of its defenders had jumped over its far side into the sea, some of them crushed against the hull like insects by the Trullhoon warship that pressed in for the kill on that side.

As Wargallow fought, relying on instinct to keep steel away from him, he found his mind still apart from this slaughter, as though he cut down not men but cattle. Xennidhum had sickened him, but this numbed him, severing him from his emotions as if he moved like Orhung, more machine than man. He envied the Created his isolation.

Darraban and his men were making short work of the remaining defenders, butchering them until after a while a cry went up for mercy. At once Darraban howled for an end to the killing, for he was no madman after all, for all his ferocity in battle.

Wargallow abruptly found himself standing among men dazed by the fighting, men spattered with blood, men of both sides. They all seemed, briefly, ashamed of their acts. Then the men of Empire dropped their weapons and looked askance at the victors; Darraban's men were no less exhausted. The sudden calm had a chill to it.

"Where is Fennobar?" said Wargallow, but the beaten men about him offered no reply.

Darraban strode up, his chest heaving, a long cut across his shoulder weeping blood. "Long gone," he grunted. "Once he knew we had him, he used the smoke to run for home. A good few of his ships have gone with him."

"But the Heir—"

"Abandoned!" Darraban laughed. "He's bought Fennobar his life."

Moments later Wargallow saw two figures emerging from

below. Guile was gently leading Sisipher through the debris and the crushed bodies.

Wargallow went to them at once. He wanted to grip them both, but instead they all gazed at one another as if they had met in some dark afterlife.

"Get us away from this charnel house," said Guile softly, and Wargallow saw the revulsion in his eyes at what was around them. He nodded in silence and together with Sisipher they left the crippled ship and returned to Darraban's craft. Soon it had pulled free of its broken victim, leaving it to drown slowly, a smoldering coffin for the hundreds who had died on its decks.

Darraban confronted his guests in his cabin soon afterward. "Fennobar's men have surrendered. The fighting is over." He bowed to Guile. "Sir, I am honored to present to you my sword, my fleet—"

Guile put a hand on his shoulder and looked at him wearily. "I am pleased to have you at my side, Darraban. Today has been a triumph, but I have to be honest and tell you that it is not how I would have wished to take my throne."

Wargallow studied him and the girl. They looked dreadful, and he wondered if they had suffered at the hands of Fennobar, but Sisipher spoke as if she had heard his thoughts.

"They didn't harm us. They wanted us alive, for all their threats."

Orhung shook his head. "You were to die," he told her. "It was in Fennobar's mind to kill you."

Darraban banged the table with his fist. "Then we'll fetch him back, and all his rabble—"

"No," said Guile. "Let him run to his master. Goldenisle will learn of this day. I have put aside my mask. I am Guile no more. I must be Ottemar Remoon to all men. When I sail into the Chain, it will be openly."

"But sir, the war has just begun," said Darraban. "If we take Fennobar now, we will ease our task."

"There may be no war now," said Guile.

"I think you are mistaken in that," said Wargallow. "Eukor Epta has committed himself. Word has come that Tennebriel is Regent, and soon will be made Empress. War is unavoidable."

Guile nodded solemnly. "If you say so."

"May I suggest," said Darraban, "that we sail to my islands! We will be safe there for the time. No one would
attack us there."

"I am indebted."

Sisipher rose and at once the company got to its feet. She
said nothing, but went out to the deck and no one followed
her. They saw her at the rail, with the white owl beside her,
and they knew that the two of them conversed in secret. Even
Orhung did not hear their words.

Guile turned to the gathered men. "It is true what Orhung
told us before. I've seen the enemy in the north. While we
turn our eyes to the throne, Anakhizer gathers his strength.
We have allies in Teru Manga, but this war will leave us
open."

"We must prevent it at all costs," said Wargallow.

"It is possible," said Darraban. "It will mean a show of
great strength. If we are able to prepare an invasion of the
Chain on such a scale that they know we are too strong for
them, they may yet capitulate."

"If they do," said Guile, "I will spare them all. I want
no more of this carnage."

"You will need a silver tongue to convince them you mean
it, sir," said Darraban, but no one laughed.

"You took the Hammavars to your side," Wargallow reminded him. "Let them see that as an example of our intent."

Darraban nodded politely. Aye, but you see, Eukor Epta
is a fanatic. Now, kill him and you will have a peaceful settlement. Otherwise it will be the War of the Islands again,
and worse, far worse."

Wargallow considered this. Darraban was right. They had
to risk showing their full strength, pulling every ally they
could to their banner. But if they had to fight, how many
would die? How much weaker would they be when the power
in the north came seeking them?

Guile turned to him. "Then we must get word to Ruan and
to all our allies. We have to gather them."

Wargallow nodded slowly and in his ears he heard the
screams of the fallen at Xennidhum, though as he listened
they turned to scornful laughter.

PART FIVE

SIEGE

21
Assembly

EUKOR EPTA SAT in customary silence before the gathered Hall of the Hundred, his eyes taking in the faces below him like those of a bird of prey surveying its killing ground. Interesting, he thought, that not a single Trullhoon sits before me. Equally interesting was the fact that for once most, if not all, the Crannoch representatives were here, and not just the minor Houses. With Tennebriel now declared Regent, their position had changed. In spite of the empty seats, the Hall was in turmoil until silence was called for. Eukor Epta did not allow his mental exhaustion to show: he had spent most of the night awake, thinking deeply, planning how this day must go. He was pleased with his conclusions, and he let his pleasure buoy him. Now that Ottemar had shown himself at last, the real game could begin. Tennebriel was hidden safely out of the way where she would take no part in the coming discussions, which would only confuse her. She managed quite well during the tedious ceremony that had made her Regent. By the end of the day, Eukor Epta felt confident, she would be confirmed as Empress.

Otarus, High Chamberlain of the Law Givers, rose as the last of the murmuring died down. He, too, had passed a sleepless night, but his strain showed, and he pulled himself together with an effort, sensing the power that sat above him, poised there like the hand of some lost god, readying for a stroke that would crush without mercy. But Otarus knew that he must remain cold, his own mask fixed. Soon there would be private orders to give to his men and now was not the time to falter. He must play by Eukor Epta's rules.

"There is unsettling news abroad," Otarus told the gathering. Many of the Audience would have heard rumors, he knew, and some had already formed their own opinions. "Since we sent our ships northwards to look into the question of these so-called powers, many things have come to light. While we understand little of—"

"Your pardon, Administrative Oligarch," cut in Tolodin, sitting directly below Eukor Epta and turning to address him. "As there is some urgency about this matter, could I respectfully move that direct evidence is brought forward? Can we hear the report of our Supreme Commander, Fennobar?"

Eukor Epta turned to Otarus. "Perhaps it would be appropriate."

Otarus bowed and sat down. Moments later Fennobar appeared, his left arm bandaged. It was well staged, Otarus thought. Fennobar's manner was as belligerent as ever. His defeat at sea had shaken him, but he was too experienced a warrior to let this be seen and as he stood to speak he carried himself as if he had come fresh from the field of victory. Eukor Epta had warned him privately that he must do so.

"It is true that I sailed north in search of the evil powers that were discussed here. True also that I found them!"

There were brief mutterings from the Hall, but they quickly subsided as the gathering strained to hear the news.

"Fortunate indeed that I sailed! I uncovered a thick blanket of intrigue and treachery, and I hesitate to bring you the name of the one at the heart of it."

"You must speak openly," said Tolodin. "We must hear what you found. The facts."

"Very well. I found that Ottemar Remoon, cousin of the dead Emperor, is alive."

This time there were several outbursts in the Hall and it was many minutes before peace could be restored.

"This should have been good news," Fennobar went on. "But I fear to say, it is not. Ottemar had been banished to the eastern continent by Quanar Remoon, and I know now what occurred there. We have been deceived by these eastern Ambassadors! Ottemar was preparing a rebellion against his cousin, the late Emperor, and it was Morric Elberon who supported him. Aye! We heard from Wargallow how Elberon saved the Empire. But he would have served us cruelly had he lived and not fallen in some eastern squabble. Ottemar's plans to overthrow Quanar had to be rebuilt, and this was done, with the aid of a number of allies, all hostile to Goldenisle.

"The city of Elberon is ruled by Ruan Dubhnor, himself a renegade from this city, one of many who fled to Morric Elberon's traitorous cause. Wargallow is his ally, not ours. Oh, there was a war in the east, for I have heard enough reports of it to know that much is no lie, but after this war, Wargallow and his own Deliverers, who were aided in the war by Elberon, became the allies of Ottemar, sharing his city. They had the audacity to name it Elberon! A taunt to us if ever there was one and flaunted before us in this very Hall! You will recall how Wargallow told us that it would not consider itself part of the Empire, but would retain its independence. His part of the black bargain!"

Otarus took advantage of a pause to ask a question. "Your pardon, Fennobar, but I have to ask this. Ottemar was biding his time, and why should he do so? As Heir to the throne, it seems strange to me that he did not come to us openly. Why did he not come to this Hall and make his case? None of us here would have been his enemies." Otarus avoided the eyes of Eukor Epta and his Administrators, looking instead at the Audience, who had taken his point. Many of them were nodding, surprised that Ottemar should have found it necessary to indulge in such intrigues.

"Your questions," said Fennobar with a smile that disturbed Otarus, "are ones that I myself had asked. Why should the Heir hide abroad? It is evident that he did not find favor with Quanar Remoon, but the Emperor's whims were well known. Well, I found the answer when I sailed north. It lies in the truth concerning the evil power there. Such a force does exist, and I have seen its terrible servants, and how they work." He described the issiquellen and spoke of other mythical beasts that roamed Teru Manga, though he drew on stories whispered by his men and not on facts.

"Somewhere at the heart of that black land lies the sorcerous ruler of these creatures. What powers he has I cannot tell you. But he does have the power to corrupt. I doubt that he has the extravagant powers that Wargallow spoke of—yet another lie! You see, Wargallow and this evil power are allies. And they have corrupted the Heir. I suspect that they have twisted Ottemar's mind with their deceits.''

This brought uproar, as Fennobar had known it would.

"What proof do you have of this?'' cried one of the Audience, many of whom were on their feet and shouting similar things.

Fennobar remained calm, and again Otarus felt deeply disturbed. The warrior was too much in control of himself, too assured. He acted like a man who knew he could not be beaten.

Fennobar gestured for silence, itself a mark of his confidence. "Aye, I understand how my words appal you. But I have seen proof enough. But look about you now. Is there a Trullhoon who will challenge my next words?''

Eukor Epta's face showed nothing, but he was surprised at how well Fennobar was managing his part of this. He had been expecting to have had to cut him short, but there was no need.

"Save your eyes the task of searching. There are none!'' Fennobar went on. "They are with the Hammavars! Yes, I hear your voices, your disbelief. But it is so and I have a thousand men outside who will tell you so and who will show you their wounds." He held up his own arm. "In Teru Manga the Hammavars became servants of this evil power. And now Darraban Trullhoon himself has joined them. And who stands beside the ruler of the Trullhoon House? Who stood on his flagship as it bore down on my fleet? Wargallow! The man we thought had come to warn us. Corruption!

"The Trullhoons are not with us. They have defected, just as the Hammavars defected when Ludhanna Trullhoon betrayed her House and family and fled to mother a Hammavar bastard. Aye, and Drogund, that same traitorous bastard, sailed with them until he was cut down. Darraban has deceived us for years. Loathe his own nephew? No! Waiting for the chance to draw him back into the Trullhoon fold, and now of course, to raise the banner of his other nephew, Ottemar, Ludhanna's firstborn.''

Otarus shuddered inwardly. This argument could not be fought, not with the Trullhoons absent. But Darraban must know what he was doing. If he had chosen now to show his support for Ottemar, he must feel that the moment was the right one. Otarus wished that his line of contact with the Trullhoons had not been severed, but he dared not risk being associated with them. Where were they now? What were they planning? How best to act to help?

Eanan spoke beside Tolodin. "You say you found Ottemar Remoon. Did you speak to him?"

Fennobar managed a passable expression of embarrassment. "To my shame I have to say yes. Shame because I had him in my grasp. There was a conflict at sea. Ottemar and his she-witch—"

"She-witch?" said Eanan at once. "Please explain this."

Fennobar nodded. "Her name is Sisipher. A girl from the east, that land of evil we already know of. I call her a witch, for she uses power in a way that you shall know more of. Otric Hamal, one of my captains, has felt that power and will speak of it after me. Sisipher is the constant companion of Ottemar, probably his lover, and it may be that through her Wargallow controls him.

"I had him, you see. Both of them! They were sailing with ships bearing the Trullhoon device, and I captured them both. Ottemar said little to me as I brought him before me, but I could see that something strange worked in him. Sisipher used her dark power to keep my men at bay, killing more than one of them. I had to keep her and Ottemar imprisoned in their cabin so that they could be dealt with on arrival here. But we were set upon by the war fleet of the Trullhoons, assisted by the Hammavars. In spite of the size of the fleet— and mark that, why should it be so vast?—we may well have won the day had they not used power. These sea creatures, the issiquellen. Many of my men claim to have seen them in the sea where we fought. Their evil workings contributed much to our defeat." This was a blatant lie, but Fennobar had enough men who were prepared to avow that it had been so, and many others had begun to believe it.

"Those of us who escaped were fortunate. But we lost Ottemar to his allies. It was only when we saw the size of the forces ranged against us that we realized just how powerful an alliance it is. Wargallow was there, conducting the battle, with Darraban his puppet. And Wargallow himself is corrupted! He was a Deliverer, and he stood very high among them!"

"And just what are these Deliverers?" said Eanan, though he knew very well.

"Fanatics based in the east who are devoted to the rooting out of power. They punish belief in power or in gods by sacrificing their victims, or transgressors as they call them, to the earth. They give their blood to Omara."

"Then they believe, as the teachings tell us, that power is not to be tolerated?" said Eanan.

"Just so. But their ruler, the Preserver, was murdered in his citadel, the Direkeep. By Wargallow, who has become the slave of this power in the north. This shows the measure of its evil, that it can so corrupt a fanatic like Wargallow! Now it uses the she-witch, and all the others. The man from the ice lands, Orhung, who also uses powers better left untouched."

Fennobar sat heavily, clutching a large goblet of water that had been placed near him and he drank thirstily. He watched as the Audience argued and shouted before him. It was Eukor Epta himself who called for silence. He turned to Fennobar and in his face there was no hint that he had spent almost three hours with the Commander the night before.

"Many of the things you have told us are greatly disturbing," he said. "They demand serious debate. But can you tell us one thing more. What is the purpose of this evil power and those who appear to have become its servants?"

Fennobar tossed back his water and stood up stiffly. He turned to face the Hall, unable to meet the calmness of the Administrator. "Its plan is simple. To make Ottemar Remoon the new Emperor. He is the Heir, even now. But if he sits upon the throne, who will control him? The she-witch? Or Anakhizer himself? How long before all of Goldenisle would fall to his will?"

Otarus stood again. "You paint a bleak landscape for us, Fennobar. I have never before heard you speak so thoroughly. But I would be ill-mannered and naive to mock your words. But you talk of control, of one being exerting power over others. How much of this is fact? Do you speak of things you know exist, or of things you *think* exist?"

Fennobar was about to make some angry retort, as Otarus had hoped, but he was forestalled by Ascanar, the third of

Eukor Epta's Chamber of Administrators. He had seen the perfect opportunity to bring his own carefully prepared report into the open.

"Perhaps we can discuss what Fennobar has told us in greater detail a little later," he said sharply. "Meanwhile I have some further information which will, I feel, add more light to this dark terrain, as the High Chamberlain puts it. May I?"

Eukor Epta gestured for him to continue and Otarus sat down, feeling the trap closing in. This was too well orchestrated to be anything but Eukor Epta's work. Then he must have found a way to discredit Ottemar and intended to move that he be opposed as Heir.

Ascanar pointed to the seat where the First Sword normally sat. "Not only are the Trullhoons absent today, but you will note that Cromalech's seat is unoccupied. He is here, far below us, in chains."

Otarus came out of his chair quickly, indignantly. "Why has he not been brought here! If he is with us, he has the right to speak—"

"The order to chain him was mine," said Eukor Epta. "I will take full responsibility. Continue, Ascanar."

Ascanar bowed and Otarus had no choice other than to sit.

"One of my responsibilities," said Ascanar, "for some years now has been to see to the education and well-being of the daughter-in-law of Estreen, Tennebriel, whom this Hall has recently made Regent while the legal matters surrounding the throne of Goldenisle and the succession are resolved. As you are fully aware, Tennebriel has lived in seclusion since she was a child, protected from possible harm, her mother-in-law having been exiled after the War of the Islands."

Again the Hall became a hive of noise. The many Crannochs that were here were eager to talk of injustices to their House.

"While Estreen has remained in exile, the House of Crannoch has remained a part of the Empire."

"And rightly so," said Fennobar loudly.

"It seemed politic and just to shelter Tennebriel, however. Initially the order was given by the Emperor Quanar himself, and although his wish was to imprison the child, everything has been done to make her life comfortable. In my work as

her guardian I rarely came into contact with her, not wishing
to distress the child with officialdom. Instead I was permitted
to appoint another guardian for her, and I chose the woman,
Ullarga, an old retainer of Estreen's. Quanar Remoon would
not have approved of this choice, I am sure, but I wanted to
know that whoever tended to the girl would be loyal to her.

"Ullarga was that. In spite of her great age, she acted like a
mother to Tennebriel. She carried out her tasks with love and
great tenderness, and not once did I have cause for doubting
her. On the few occasions when Tennebriel has been questioned
by me or men of my office, it has been clear that the girl has
not suffered for being isolated from most of the world.

"However, even Tennebriel was not safe from this strange
power that gathers about our Empire. Fennobar has spoken
of corruption and of deviousness. Of control. It seems to be
the method by which this evil power works. Tennebriel was
well concealed, but not well enough. She was visited by a
man who sought to force himself upon her." Ascanar paused
to allow this outrage to sink in. "Somehow this man had
found out that Tennebriel lived and he sought her out, then
stumbled upon her. Ullarga knew of this but was too frightened to speak of it to me or my men. At first she thought the
man wanted no more than to amuse himself in conversation
with the girl, but she began to see that he had stronger
ambitions. The man was Cromalech.

"It was after the last great gathering here that Ullarga finally brought the news to my men. She admitted that Cromalech had been to Tennebriel in secret, climbing the very
tower in which she resided. She refused his lascivious ad-
vances, although Ullarga said that she sensed a particular
magnetism about the First Sword, something odd which the
girl responded to. Some strangeness, Ullarga said, mark that.

"As many of you know, Cromalech disappeared shortly
after we heard the eastern Ambassadors speak to us. Fennobar went north, as did Wargallow, who slipped away without
warning just as he was being invited to the palace. The likely
truth is that he was taken north by Cromalech. Fennobar's
captain, Otric Hamal, was the captain who brought Wargallow to us initially. And he will speak of how he had noted
the apparent friendship that had sprung up between Wargallow and Cromalech on the voyage here.

"Cromalech disappeared. Perhaps Fennobar noted him at the sea battle?"

Fennobar had been told how to answer. "If he was there, neither I nor my men saw him."

"No," said Ascanar. "I believe he was elsewhere. Firstly in Teru Manga, consorting with whatever it is that lurks there. Ullarga overheard Cromalech tell Tennebriel that he would go north, to friends. He told her he would return, Ullarga said, and bring great power with him. Ullarga was very frightened by now and only this gave her the courage to speak to me.

"Prepared as I was for Cromalech's return, I was not able to prevent tragedy. Cromalech did return, and in the way that Ullarga had promised. He came from *the sea*. Not by ship, but from its deeps. He was brought by the same vile allies that Fennobar has described, the issiquellen. Ullarga watched for him and he came suddenly, up from the very waters below us, deep under the tower. When he saw her fleeing, he killed her at once, guessing that she would betray him at last. But my own men were already waiting for him. They found him with the body of his victim.

"He was imprisoned and word was sent to the Administrative Oligarch, who viewed him and gave immediate orders that he be chained." Ascanar turned to Eukor Epta with a bow and sat.

Eukor Epta saw every eye switch to him. He cleared his throat, nodding curtly at Ascanar, who had remembered every word expertly. "There was little I could do with Cromalech," he said. "Whatever grim power had corrupted him had made him part of its web and had wrought changes it is difficult to describe. Physically he is the First Sword, but he has changed in other ways. These issiquellen, sea dwellers, spawn of the north, are beings with which he has some unnatural link. How else could he move in the deeps of the sea, or scale the tower where Tennebriel was kept?"

"And what is his part in this supposed plan of Anakhizer's?" asked Otarus, though his tiredness could be seen clearly.

Eukor Epta gave a slight shrug. "It seems that Cromalech had two intentions. One was to bring Tennebriel under his sway, both physically and mentally. She is a simple girl, not experienced in such things. How could she be?"

"And Cromalech's other intention?"

"Not his own, I think. He was to be another puppet."

"But," persisted Otarus, thinking that perhaps he had found a loophole in Eukor Epta's elaborate arguments, "I thought Anakhizer was working through Ottemar? Does he not wish to rule Goldenisle through him?"

Eukor Epta nodded, no sign of alarm on his face. "Yes, that is the conclusion that seems most likely. But of course, such a power, set as it is upon the destruction of Goldenisle, would use any advantage it could take. To control both Ottemar and Tennebriel would place it in a position of unlimited power, would it not?"

"Aye! But we were warned by Wargallow of war—"

"Yet he brings it to our very walls."

Otarus could say no more in the shouting that followed. He knew that peaceful negotiations with Ottemar were impossible. He would have to resort to the strategy of stealth yet again, to play Eukor Epta at his own game, a game at which the Administrator was unsurpassed.

A member of the Audience rose and called out loudly. "May I be permitted to ask of the Supreme Commander what plans he thinks Ottemar has now?"

Fennobar was given permission to answer. "It has already been said. War. Anakhizer will urge Ottemar to bring all his forces down upon us. We will be given two choices, to submit and place Ottemar on the throne, or to make ready for a siege."

"A siege!" returned the spokesman, who was one of the Crannochs. "Only a lunatic would attempt to besiege Medallion Island."

"Quite so," nodded Fennobar.

"Will there be an ultimatum?" said another, more sober voice.

"When you see Ottemar gathering his allies, will you need one?"

"We must be certain that he means war!" cried Otarus, but no one heard.

Eukor Epta stood up, something he never did unless quitting the Hall. His movement had the desired effect, silence falling like a stone. "Hear me," he said. "We can discuss this for days, and we can bring before us a hundred witnesses to verify the facts as we have heard them. While we are doing that, Ottemar Remoon and whatever dark forces sail with him move against us. To me, his intentions are clear. We do have a choice. Either we accept him as the Heir, or we defy him. But if we give him his birthright, into what new era of darkness are we descending?''

"We must act now!" cried Fennobar, but no one shouted him down as out of order. Otarus could see that the Hall was ready to erupt, fueled by fear. He would not argue now, knowing that if he did he would be one of the first to be secretly removed.

Someone in the Hall stood up on his seat and raised his fist to the vaults high above. "Death to the traitor!" he yelled. "Death to Ottemar Remoon!"

Again there was silence, but suddenly other voices echoed that wild shout, until there was a chorus. The Crannochs gave full vent to the cry and Otarus saw, with growing coldness, that there were many Remoons here who also called Ottemar traitor, seeing Ottemar now as a stigma, like the legendary curse on the Remoon House. At the debate of the succession, many Remoons had been content to support Tennebriel as Regent.

Eukor Epta sat down, seemingly impassively, but he had recognized the youth, Muriddin, who had been schooled well into leading the shout for Ottemar's death. His father should be proud of the boy.

"We must make speedy arrangements for the defiance of the Empire," said Eukor Epta when a semblance of order had been restored. "I take it that this Assembly is in agreement?" The reaction was loudly unanimous. "Otarus? This is a hard decision to make. What do the Law Givers say? Dare we consider caution and delay?"

Otarus stood as steadily as he could, though he felt his strength slipping away from him. He must be seen to conform. "The Court of Envoys would wish to avoid conflict, but for the safety of the Empire, we must agree."

"Very well," nodded Eukor Epta. "We will hold a meeting of military commanders today." Without another word or glance, he walked from the Hall and the noise he left behind him was deafening.

Through the empty corridors beyond the Hall Eukor Epta went now, making for one of his many private towers. Already he had drawn up his plans of defense, having been certain that the gathered men of the Empire would support his decision. Darraban Trullhoon had played into his hands.

Eukor Epta opened a desk and pulled out the scroll of parchment, scanning the letter he had already written in the night. He detested the risks involved in committing pen to paper, but this was the time of risks, now that all he had planned for was coming to fruition.

The letter was to Estreen, exiled on the isle of Skerrin. She knew his hand and would respond to no other. He had been in contact with her for a long time now, promising her that her daughter-in-law by her marriage to Ildar would be Empress. Although many of the Crannoch families of old were scattered and weakened, she could rally them. She saw this potential war as a chance to redeem the Crannoch House, and now that the war was about to be confirmed, she would come to Medallion in force.

Eukor Epta permitted himself a wry grin. With war about to break, all allies would be welcome, including Estreen. And afterward, when Ottemar and his forces had broken themselves on the unbreachable defences of Medallion Island, Tennebriel would dance to Eukor Epta's tune, not her mother-in-law's, for the assassin had already been primed for Estreen's death.

As Eukor Epta prepared to have his message sent to the northeastern isles, a slight frown creased his brow. In all this planning and manipulating, an art of which he was proud, there was one factor that he could not control as he wished: this power in the north. He had used its undoubted presence to obfuscate his own motives, but what real strength did it have? Cromalech had raved about it to Ascanar, almost as if in a fever. Could any of it be truth? Or the things Wargallow had said?

Whatever this power was, it could shatter Goldenisle, that seemed true. The Remoon Dynasty would be ended, and the Trullhoons would be as crippled as the Crannochs. There would be a new force here, centered on those of the Blood. They would rise to inherit what was theirs, and little would be able to resist them.

22
Utmourn

BY MID-MORNING the sea mist had not dispersed, keeping Utmourn island wrapped in a white blanket, sealing it off from the remainder of the Chain as if it were no more than a remote isolated islet, far out in the ocean. Darraban's ships had come into the harbor under the steep cliffs, far to the north of the eastern arm of the Chain; Utmourn had long been Trullhoon land, and Darraban had assured the Heir and his company that this would be as safe a place to plan their campaign as any other he could think of. Although the mist was chill and brought with it a sense of unease, like some bad omen, they were glad of the secrecy, the time to consider the future. Already word had come that the Empire prepared for war, and a few Remoon families had sailed north, asking that they be permitted to side with Ottemar: this had been granted.

Inside the large tent, Ottemar sat with Wargallow and Orhung, joined now by Darraban and his sons and by Rannovic, whose Hammavars were already beginning to settle with the Trullhoons after the sea battle in which they had literally fought beside one another. The rift of the years was already closing.

Darraban stretched out a map across the rough wooden table, and they could see the complicated pattern of islands that stretched north from the central point, Medallion, most southerly of all the large islands.

"You'll not find a better chart than this," said Darraban. "No sailors in the Empire have more accurate maps than the Trullhoons. There's not an island we haven't charted."

Wargallow nodded politely, recalling the charts of Ratillic, the map-maker of the east, whose mountain owls had spied out the world for him under Kirrikree's guidance. "This is Medallion?" he said, tapping the coastline of the Empire's largest island.

"Aye." Darraban began to describe its coastal features. "From the northern point here, the Spike, right down the east to this point here, Knuckle Point, run the great cliffs, four times as high as the puny cliffs we climbed on this island. The sea below these eastern cliffs is dangerous, and there's nowhere safe to bring a ship in. If we did, we'd never get up the cliff face. A few good men could, perhaps, for it's been done, but it's no way to land an invading army. From the north down along the northwestern coast there are more cliffs, but not so inhospitable. However, they are easily defended and there are a number of forts there. There is also an excellent beacon system, and if we attempted to climb the cliffs, we would find ourselves facing a concentrated defense which could easily sweep us away, even though there will be a fine balance of numbers."

Ottemar and Wargallow studied the map carefully, seeing in their minds the difficult terrain that Darraban was describing. Medallion Island was like a huge inverted dish, its middle almost entirely scooped out where the sea had rushed in to form the inner waters. Each of its forbidding coastlines was not only rugged, but precipitous, the entire island raised up like a vast plateau. Only these immense cliffs, Ottemar knew from the legends, had saved the island from complete inundation.

"The western coast," Darraban went on, "is as formidable as the eastern one. There is this chain of islands running parallel to it, and the currents that interact are far more treacherous than the seas of the east. Again, the cliffs are perilous, not as high and sheer as the eastern cliffs, but there is an added hazard: they are crumbling, riddled with chasms and channels. A nightmare for any ship trying to land men. Even the boldest of the fishing vessels don't venture in here, though the harvest would be spectacular.

"As the coast runs south and then turns, it becomes even more impossible, with hundreds of tiny islets and rocks, arranged like fangs. The water is very deep, the swells terrible, and there are numerous rock shelves that would rip the bottom out of any ship foolish enough to try to get close. Lastly, the south coast, running back up to Knuckle Point. We call these islands that run along it the Teeth, for good reason. The full force of the ocean strikes against them from the south, and it is unlikely that any ship has ever sailed between them and come out again. To attempt to scale the cliffs of the coast here would be madness.''

Wargallow nodded thoughtfully. ''What you are saying is that the island is impregnable, at least from the sea. And there is no other way to reach it.''

''The only way to Medallion Island's heart is through these narrows, the Hasp.'' Darraban tapped the thin stretch of water at the center of the northwestern coast, which had been aptly named, for it looked as if it could close and lock the island. ''And of course, the cliffs that overlook the channel are more heavily fortified than any other point on Medallion. Those fleets that have sought to force entry in the past have been reduced to nothing. There must be a thousand wrecks beneath the deep waters there.''

''How deep is the Hasp itself?'' asked Wargallow.

''It has never been plumbed.''

Ottemar was shaking his head. ''We cannot risk attacking there. It would be suicide.''

''I agree,'' said Wargallow. ''Tell me,'' he added, turning from the map to Darraban. ''How are the ships of the Empire currently deployed?''

At once Andric leaned forward and presented a scroll. Darraban glanced at it. ''This is the latest report. It seems that they have all been drawn in. Very few ships are outside the inner sea.'' He scowled at something else in the writing and darted a glance at Andric. ''What is this? Is it accurate?''

Andric nodded, and beside him his brother, Rudaric, also nodded.

''What is it?'' said Ottemar.

Darraban looked annoyed. ''Estreen! Mother of the Crannochs. *She* is now in this business.''

''Estreen!'' said Ottemar. ''But she has been lost in exile since the War of the Islands, sixteen years ago.''

Darraban shook his head. ''No longer. She is with the others, and it looks as though every outlawed Crannoch is back in Medallion waters. They have joined the banner of Tennebriel, and well they may. She is one of them!''

''How will this affect the issue?'' said Wargallow.

Darraban snorted derisively. ''Hah! Crannoch vermin! We sank them before, we'll do it again—''

''Father,'' said Andric, ''don't dismiss them too easily. They are a better fighting force than you give them credit for.''

Darraban turned and was about to snap something curt to the youth, but instead he nodded. ''Aye, aye, you are right to correct me. It was a bloody affair and many good Trullhoons went to watery graves. If the Crannochs are beside Tennebriel, they'll not be a rabble.''

''So where are they all?'' said Wargallow.

''In the safest place,'' grunted Darraban. ''The inner sea. Eukor Epta can send his forces wherever they are needed to defend Medallion. If we go for the Hasp, we would be lucky to get a handful of ships through. And they would be sent to the bottom as soon as they got into the inner sea. The old harridan herself will be waiting for us.''

''So we can't get in to them,'' said Wargallow, almost to himself. ''But by the same token, none of them can get out, not if we have our ships positioned close to the opening of the Hasp. Is that possible?''

Darraban grunted assent, but did not look impressed. ''The sea outside the Hasp is as calm as it ever gets anywhere in the Chain. We could anchor there easily enough. If any craft did attempt to come out, we could take it. But we are hardly likely to tempt them to such folly!''

''What were you thinking?'' Ottemar asked Wargallow, knowing that to underestimate the Deliverer was often fatal.

''We had hoped for a swift settlement of our differences with the Empire, for our real fears are that Anakhizer will strike. But I feel sure that he will be watching us now, waiting to see how the war resolves itself. He won't do anything until the war is over, by which time he hopes both forces will be so weakened as to be an easy conquest for him. He has plenty of time and can afford to wait. Then so can we.''

''Wait?'' said Darraban. ''For what?''

Rannovic, who had been thoughtful throughout the discussions, was also puzzled. ''What would we gain, Wargallow?

We could probably take every other island in the Chain, make the Crannoch isles our own, but without Medallion, we would have achieved no real victory."

"It is clear we have no chance of storming Medallion quickly. Any invasion we make will have to be thought out carefully. Darraban, you said it has been known for men to climb these impassable eastern cliffs. We may have to send men up them, day by day, month by month. Men enough to go to the forts above the Hasp. If we can win those forts—"

"You forget the other forts," said Darraban. "There are many of them scattered around the mountains and along the coasts, no matter how inaccessible. They are there to watch the seas, to warn of coming fleets. But now they will be watching the cliffs, not expecting us to attempt them, but careful to see that we don't. If we send as much as a handful of men up them, and I do have men who could climb them, they would be met with steel. I despair of success by that means."

"Even by darkness?" persisted Wargallow.

Darraban grinned in spite of his frustration. "You've not seen the cliffs, so I'll forgive your enthusiasm! They would be a nightmare by day. By night! Suicide. Oh, it may be that two or three very gifted men could do it, but I doubt even that."

"We have to take those forts," Wargallow said.

"If there's a way," said Ottemar, "we'll find it."

They nodded in agreement, but already were slipping into a sombre mood. The Empire looked secure, unbreakable. As they sat around the map, listening to the distant roar of the sea on the cliffs far below them, Sisipher entered the tent. Her face clouded when she saw the sobriety of the men at the table, although Ottemar and Rannovic both smiled and stood as she came to the table. The others rose more slowly, though not from lack of respect.

"You have not solved the riddle," she said.

Ottemar shook his head. "If we could rely upon the floating plants of Xennidhum, it would be easy. But here—"

She took him to one side, aware that Rannovic in particular watched her closely. But no one interfered, none of them sure what her precise relationship was with the Heir, though all sensed in her a power not to be meddled with. Even Orhung, who had again become like a man asleep or in a drugged trance, became alert when the girl was near him, as if he fed on her energy and gave back to her his own strange power.

"Leave them to discuss it and come with me," Sisipher told Ottemar.

He needed no second bidding and excused himself, leaving the others to puzzle over the map and other charts. Only Rannovic watched them leave and go into the cold outside air. If anything, the mist had thickened and made the sea invisible, although its whisperings seemed in some way to bring it closer to them. Two armed men leaned out of the mist, eager to lend protection to the Heir.

"What is it?" Ottemar asked the girl.

"We must travel a short distance across the island. Bring the guards, though we're in no danger."

Ottemar gestured to the men and they fell in step behind him and the girl, evidently relieved. Overhead there was a flutter of wings and Ottemar knew that Kirrikree was close by. Sisipher led them along narrow paths that had first been made by the sturdy sheep of Utmourn, and then down through a gap between two bleak hills. It was a bare, treeless island, its slopes dotted with poking stones, broken with paths that crumbled if not trodden carefully. No one lived here now, although there were a few houses on its leeward shore which fishermen sometimes used as a base if caught by a sudden storm, as they often were in these northern waters. But it was not to these houses that Sisipher led Ottemar now. She took him down yet another steep track until they came to a dip in the hills, a sheltered spot that ran out toward the east, ending in a sheer drop to the cove below as if the land had broken off. Sisipher took Ottemar as close to the edge as she dared, knowing his fear of such places.

Silence had crept around them like a stalking beast, and even the sound of the waves was muted. Utmourn had almost come to life, and Ottemar felt like some crawling thing upon its back, feeling it breathe.

"There!" Sisipher pointed. "You see them?"

Ottemar squinted through the sea mist and saw another path, chopped out of the rich earth by wind and rain, cutting downward to the cove, itself clouded by the milky mist.

Coming up the path like moving stones were a number of small figures. Ottemar drew in his breath in amazement.

"Earthwrought!" He was sure of it, and as the little beings climbed upward, he knew he was right, recognizing their build, their features. "But how did they get here?"

"I called them," said Sisipher.

He turned to her, shocked, but then grinned. "Of course! But where were they? Below the sea?"

"Underground, to the north. It was their distress that I felt—"

"Sire!" came a yell from behind Ottemar and the fresh shock of it almost had him tumbling over the cliff to his doom. But he steadied himself, terrified by the drop. Sisipher gently moved him away. They both turned to see what had alarmed the guards.

Standing on the ridge that overlooked the hollow was a solitary figure, looming out of the mist like a lonely monolith. As they watched, it descended. The guards had their swords drawn, though both men were ashen with fear: the figure was huge.

Ottemar could hardly credit his eyes as the figure approached. "Aumlac!" he gasped, rushing forward. It was indeed the huge Stonedelver and Ottemar called to the guards to put away their swords. They did so slowly, flabbergasted, but they could see by Sisipher's face that there was no reason to be afraid.

Aumlac bent down and hugged Ottemar to his great chest, laughing as he did so. "Ottemar Remoon!" he boomed. "I have found you. And you, mistress." He released Ottemar and bowed to Sisipher.

"But *how?*" said Ottemar, gripping the big man's arm in delight.

Aumlac smiled, but it was evident now that something disturbed him deeply. He pointed with his stone club. "I came with my companions, the Earthwrought, and with others of my people, who are not far from here. We have traveled under the earth."

"From Rockfast?" gasped Ottemar.

Aumlach paled at the word, but nodded. "You must hear the tale at once."

"Of course. Bring your companions. All of them! We have encamped not a mile away. You are with friends here."

Aumlac turned and shouted back to the ridge. At once a number of Stonedelvers appeared, and again the guards blanched, but made no move. In a moment several of the Earthwrought had crested the cliffs, as easily as lizards, and Sisipher ran to them, delighting in their company. Most of Aumlac's people preferred to keep out of sight and Ottemar sensed that there were many of them hidden by the hill, a thought that concerned him. He led the way back to the camp, wanting to talk to Aumlac about so many things, but finding it somewhat hard to begin. There was a weight of sorrow upon the big man and in his eyes a coldness.

There was great consternation as Aumlac and those of his companions who had chosen to come with him this far came before the men of the Trullhoons and Hammavars, but as Ottemar and Sisipher looked so easy in the company of the Stonedelvers, no swords were drawn. Wargallow was the first to greet the party and he studied Aumlac with open interest.

"A Stonedelver," he said. "I have heard of your people."

"And you are Wargallow of the Deliverers," replied Aumlac. "We have heard of you."

"There are many things to discuss," said Sisipher, aware of the growing tensions. "Shall we begin at once?"

Aumlac's men sat down peacefully at a nearby fireside and gradually they were approached by men eager to learn their story, and to speak to the tiny Earthwrought. Content, Sisipher led Aulac into the tent where the plans for war were being drawn up. He sat cross-legged on the floor, apparently relaxed and unmoved by the number of men here. Darraban and his sons and Rannovic seemed to have lost their tongues, and Ottemar chuckled at this. "Never fear," he told them. "Aumlac is as good an ally as we have. He would be the first to defend us."

"Let no man here doubt it," nodded Aumlac gravely. He saw then the silent figure of Orhung, who had not moved and who kept in the shadows of the tent. For a moment it seemed as if the Stonedelver would challenge the Created, but he looked away, thoughts elsewhere, even though Ottemar had seen the doubts in the huge man's eyes.

"I remain amazed, my friend," said Ottemar. "How is it that you have found us, so far from your mountains?"

Aumlac sighed and his companions outside the tent stopped talking as if they had heard Ottemar's question. The weight of Aumlac's sorrow had become a tangible thing, and the silence of the Utmourn closed in once more, bringing with its mist a premature winter chill.

"Give them your tale," said Sisipher, her own eyes mirroring some deep sadness she had not spoken of.

"Very well," nodded Aumlac. "I will begin where we departed from the village of Westersund." Ottemar had already given an account to Darraban and the others of his incredible flight from Drogund's citadel and of Rockfast and beyond.

"We made our way back across the mountains, but as we did so, we realized that there was great turmoil around us. Skyrac and his brethren flew to us with news of the Ferr-Bolgan. They had not subsided, and the caves under the earth disgorged more of them than a dozen men could count. Rockfast, we heard, was under siege. We hastened there as quickly as we could, and it was so. We could not climb up to it. The Ferr-Bolgan, normally so afraid of the light, had amassed in their thousands, and with them were the herders, scores of them."

"The Children," said Ottemar.

Wargallow suppressed a shudder beside him. This was the most evil news of all.

"The Ferr-Bolgan shook the very ground with the tread of their feet," Aumlac went on. "Their naked fists beat at the walls of the mountains. Their master was enraged by the escape of Ottemar Remoon. Already he had sent his minions to the citadel of the Hammavars, and we had had word that it was ripped stone from stone, the walls gutted, the men there either killed or sent seaward—"

Rannovic bristled "No one survived?"

"I am saddened to bring you this news, if you are one of them. Those of you who took to sea are all that are left. Your citadel is no more. The very rocks were pulled down to the sea beneath. The place is empty now," sighed Aumlac. "The fury of Anakhizer was dreadful. He unleashed it like a mountain storm. We could not have known what a vast army he has! The Ferr-Bolgan are as grains of sand upon the beach! Anakhizer must have imagined that Ottemar was still in Rockfast, for the Ferr-Bolgan spared no efforts to get in.

"Those of us who had come back from Westersund hid ourselves and watched the siege. Time after time the Ferr-Bolgan swarmed at the walls of Rockfast, and each time they were repulsed. The bodies lay heaped at the feet of the citadel, deeper than a man is tall, and yet they came again, goaded by the merciless herders. At last, during a lull in their assaults, I took my Stonedelvers through them when they were unprepared. Seven I lost, but we came to the citadel. The Stonewise and the Earthwise were preparing such powers as they could to defend the stone, saying that below us, deep in the earth, Anakhizer was uncurling some dreadful power. They could feel its heat, and around us the skies thickened like a pall. A storm broke over us of such magnitude that it split the very cliffs, sending avalanches of rock down into the canyons. Still Rockfast remained, its mountain secure. The Ferr-Bolgan withdrew briefly, but only while the evils below us began to gnaw upward.

"We watched helplessly as neighboring peaks turned scarlet with the fires of the earth and the stone began to run, molten like snow, leaving only the burnt stumps of mountains remaining. Rockfast held as the Stonewise and Earthwise fought this creeping power. We all felt it coming upward, the heat of the tormented stone. At last it struck at our very heart, and the cracks began to shatter our walls. As they did so, and as the walls parted, the Ferr-Bolgan came at us like a breaching sea. Bloody and ferocious was the battle, and for every one of them we slew, another three took the gap. Many a good friend I saw trampled beneath them.

"Luddac, our ruler, fell, for all the mighty strength of his arm. And when Ianelgon, Earthwise of Rockfast, was pulled down to his doom, we knew that the citadel was lost. Einnis Amrodin gathered the strongest of us to him and we fought our way out through the crumbling walls, unable to believe that Rockfast was dying, but it was so.

"Yet still the Ferr-Bolgan came up through the cracks in the earth. As we beat them back and took refuge on yet another high place, they left us to concentrate their spite on Rockfast. We saw it glowing then, like a tower fashioned from molten rock, and as we watched, the flames danced, peeling back the living stone to reveal the heart. Slowly it sank earthward, sliding down into the darkness below like a blood-red river, a scarlet grave, and in the mind of each of us was the terrible sound of its screams. Above us Skyrac and his eagles flew, maddened at the loss, shrieking, diving impotent.''

As he told his grim tale, Aumlac had let his tears flow openly, his face streaked with them. Abruptly he wiped at them, raising his head. ''There was nothing left for us but to die, or flee. Einnis Amrodin, drained of his powers, was magnificent then, for about him were the last of the Earthwrought and a few hundred Stonedelvers and their families. They wanted to fling themselves upon the enemy, defying them to the last life, but Einnis Amrodin would not permit it. His will would not be defied, though I wondered where he found the strength. He ordered us to disperse. He would go west, back into the high, cold wastes of the Slaughterhorn range, and he would take all who would go with him. His flight began at once.''

Ottemar and Sisipher had also shed tears at the Stonedelver's story, and it was a while before anyone spoke. Wargallow realized just how deeply the girl, and now Ottemar himself, were tied to the men of earth and stone.

''You didn't go with him?'' said Ottemar, breaking the silence.

''No. I knew I must flee Anakhizer and his armies of death, but I swore before them all that I would not be made a fugitive for the rest of my days. I would fight them, if not that dreadful day, then another. I spoke of Goldenisle then, and of its Heir, a man of honor, to whom I owed my life.''

Ottemar looked away; he had not spoken of saving Aumlac's life when he had given the story of the flight from Westersund, although Sisipher had mentioned it. Aumlac related the story in full now.

''So you see,'' Aumlac ended, ''I have returned to repay what I owe. I convinced a small party of Stonedelvers and their families and some hundred of our stone-brothers, the Earthwrought, that we should leave Teru Manga, come deep below the earth, and seek the Chain. It was difficult to escape the Ferr-Bolgan, but a madness was upon them as they as-

saulted Rockfast and its ashes. We came through their outer
ranks and fled. The journey under the earth is easy for the
Earthwrought, and between us we made progress that would
perhaps baffle you.''

"You came from Teru Manga?'' said Darraban incredulously.

"It is no lie,'' said Sisipher. "As we will soon see.''

Aumlac nodded. "Aye. We had no idea where Ottemar
would be, but we knew he would be in the Chain. Once here,
we would find him. Skyrac wished to remain with me, though
his people have all flown to the heights of the Slaughterhorn.
As it was, when we came not far from the northern islands
of the Chain, Skyrac and Kirrikree met each other. Soon after
that, Sisipher heard us below the earth and called.''

There were sharp intakes of breath at this, but the girl was
smiling. "No doubt our enemies will call me witch for this.
But I am able to understand the Earthwrought, even from a
distance. It is a gift I have been given, with it I heard the
Earthwrought and sensed their distress. Kirrikree told me
where they were and I called to them, in my own way. Thus
the birds led them here to Utmourn.''

"Under the sea itself?'' gasped Rannovic. "This is like a
legend from before the Flood.''

"It is easy for us,'' said Aumlac. "Whereas we do not
travel on water well. It was the Flood which almost destroyed
my people.''

"Well, it is a joy that you come to us,'' said Ottemar. His
brief smile became a look of sorrow. "Just as your news is
a painful tragedy. I shall not forget Rockfast, nor the life that
was there. Those fools in Medallion should hear this tale! It
is there in the north that we should be gathering.''

Rannovic nodded, turning to the huge figure. "This talk
of power makes me very uneasy, as it does my people. I have
seen something of it myself, and guessed there was more to
Teru Manga than we had seen. Now you tell us that such
things do exist and that your own people use power.''

"I once doubted its existence,'' said Wargallow. "But no
longer.''

Andric spoke up. "This power brings its own reward, so
it seems. I think it unwise to trust it, even in the hands of

one claiming to be an ally.'' He turned from the level gaze of Aumlac only to meet the calmness of Sisipher's.

He reddened at once.

"You are right to question me,'' agreed Aumlac, and Andric was visibly taken aback, as was his father. "I am not of your kind, nor are the small ones. But think of your own quarrels: how long ago did you take arms against each other?''

Rannovic grinned. "We cannot argue, Andric. The Stonedelvers may not be Trullhoons, but we would be mad to refuse them.''

"If it's power you fear,'' said Wargallow, "you are not unreasonable. But it is the misuse of power we must fear. Power such as Anakhizer would use. Power such as Eukor Epta desires.'' He turned to Aumlac. "What you have told us confirms our worst fears. Anakhizer has only begun his onslaught. Earlier today I was foolish enough to suggest that we had no need of haste. I fear now that we have little time at all.''

"Then show me your enemies,'' said Aumlac. "My people will seek their lives as you do.''

Wargallow smiled. "You have traveled far under the earth. Will you travel further?''

"If Ottemar asks it.''

"What are you thinking?'' said Darraban, knowing already that the Deliverer missed nothing.

"I am thinking of my talks with Sisipher's father, Brannog, who has become a king among the Earthwrought. He told me of the marvelous feats that the little people can perform below the earth, how they can pass through stone, just as your people can, Aumlac.''

"Even so,'' nodded the Stonedelver as if confirming no more than that his people could breathe the air.

"Can men follow you under the earth?'' asked Wargallow.

"They can. I made many paths for Ottemar and Sisipher under Teru Manga, and the stone there is corrupt in places.''

Darraban suddenly banged his fist down. "Aye! If you can do this, and travel so far below the sea, then—''

"He can take us into Medallion Island,'' said Wargallow. "There's no need to have men scale the cliffs like ants.'' He pushed the map toward Aumlac. "Can you understand this?''

Aumlac nodded. "A map. I cannot read the words, but this is land, and this must be sea. But I have no need of this! I will know the land when I am under it. I will smell the sea. What do you wish of me?"

Wargallow sat back with a sigh of relief, smiling at Ottemar. "Just one thing, Aumlac. For the man who saved your life. The Throne."

And for the first time since entering the tent, the Stonedelver smiled.

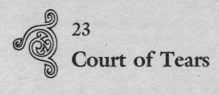

23

Court of Tears

TENNEBRIEL'S EYES WERE CLOSED, her face serene as the girl pulled the comb through her sleek hair, but Tennebriel's mind raced. Here, in the splendid chambers of the palace set aside for her, the Regent now, she was no less Eukor Epta's prisoner than she had been on the island. Apart from her two handmaidens, both new to her, she saw no one, other than the face of a guard at the door as he admitted the girls or let them leave. Her situation had become unbearable.

She opened her eyes and smiled at Nerine, who blushed shyly. She must be at least two years younger than Tennebriel. "When I am Empress—" began the older girl.

"But mistress, you *are* Empress!" cried the girl, carefully combing.

"I am the Regent. It is not the same thing. When I am Empress, I will reward you well, and Imarga. You have both been very kind."

"It is our duty, mistress."

"I have many enemies already," Tennebriel went on. "Some may even try to prevent me from taking the throne. It is why Eukor Epta has me locked away here like a prisoner."

"Not a prisoner, surely, mistress!"

"For my own good, he tells me."

"Well, mistress, it is true that he seeks out your enemies. Imarga and I both know that some of them have already been executed. There is a special place, the Court of Tears, where they have died."

"Where is this place?" said Tennebriel, showing an immediate interest.

The girl blanched, fearing indiscretion. "Here in the palace—"

"Have you seen it?" Tennebriel sat up, gripping the girl's arm.

"Why, yes, mistress, but—"

"Describe it!" Tennebriel snapped, then realized how close she was to revealing herself, her true fears. "Go on," she said more reasonably. "It interests me."

Nerine was frightened by the sudden change of mood, the fierceness of Tennebriel's gaze; the grip on her arm had been unexpectedly strong. "It is not far, mistress. Imarga and I sometimes creep along the corridors to a place where there's a tiny window overlooking the Court. It is closed in, with no trees, no seats, nothing. Just rings set in the paving stones where they chain the prisoners. There are only a few narrow windows, as if no one wants the prisoners to be seen. Usually they are killed quickly, with the sword."

Tennebriel relaxed her grip, realizing she was hurting the girl. "You have seen this done?"

Nerine's eyes dropped. "I am ashamed to say so, mistress—"

"You need not be. In such a place as this you must be glad of a little excitement. But tell me, have there been any recent executions you've seen? Who has died?" she asked, almost casually, though her heart thundered.

Now that she knew Tennebriel was not about to chastise her, the girl was more eager to speak. "In the last three days I have seen several die. Two of the men were Imperial Killers."

"Cromalech's men?" As she asked it, she wondered if the girls would sense her growing fear, her terror for her lover's safety.

"Yes, mistress. And Imarga saw a man die who wore the eagle of the Trullhoons. There is talk of war with them, and some say that Darraban is a traitor and will not support you. Ottemar Remoon is alive and plots your downfall."

Tennebriel nodded seemingly absently, but then became attentive again. "When will you go again to this Court of Tears?"

"Perhaps today, on our way back to the serving halls, mistress."

"And will anyone be executed today?"

"I expect so. More die each day as Eukor Epta's hunt becomes more thorough."

"I want to see this place. Today."

Nerine paled, almost dropping the comb. "But, mistress, how—?"

"Where is Imarga? Cleaning the bedchamber? Fetch her, quickly!"

In a few moments both girls stood before the Regent, trembling, their heads bowed. Nerine was the shorter of the two, with cropped, brown hair, while Imarga was as tall as Tennebriel, her own hair straight and dark. Tennebriel beckoned her forward and walked around her as if examining a piece of rare pottery.

"Take your dress off," she told her, and the girl obeyed at once. Tennebriel began undressing. She had a fuller figure than the girl, but in other ways they were not dissimilar. "Don't shake so, girl, I'm not about to harm you. I just want to take a brief walk." She grinned as she pulled Imarga's simple dress on and gestured for the girl to don her own. "There, a good fit," she said. "With a little more work, perhaps I can pass for you, and you for me."

Nerine was giggling, trying to cover her mouth with her hand.

"Well?" smiled Tennebriel. "Can you smuggle me out with you? We can be back in an hour. No one will know the difference. The guards won't notice, will they?"

Nerine straightened up. "We might get away with it, mistress."

Imarga looked frightened. "Oh, mistress, if you're found out—"

"I'm the Regent, aren't I?" Tennebriel laughed. "And I'll say I forced you. You won't be punished, I promise, Imarga. In fact, you'll both be rewarded."

The girls exchanged glances, smiling nervously. If the Regent was so eager to see the Court of Tears and its evils, it would be better not to deny her.

"Come on," Tennebriel told Nerine. "Get the empty plates and tray for me. I'll have to keep my head down."

Shortly afterward, Nerine knocked on the door for the guards and a key was turned. The door opened and Nerine smiled up at the guard who let her and her companion out into the corridor. There were two of the men, both armed, stiff as posts, and their expressions never changed. They motioned the girls away and locked the door again. Tennebriel kept her eyes on the tray, her head bent, and her face turned away enough so that she could not be closely inspected. Neither guard challenged her, but as the girls moved down the corridor, one of them eyed Tennebriel's back with interest.

"That one has a shapelier backside than I'd realized. I fancy I ought to have a word with her after this duty."

The other shook his head. "You'd be a fool to try. Remember who stationed us here."

While they spoke, the two girls had turned off the corridor and Nerine led them along several others, careful to see that they were unobserved. The palace here was old, the stairs and passageways narrow and dark. After some time they came to a short flight of dusty stairs, going up them like mice. Nerine put her fingers to her lips and Tennebriel nodded. Their feet made no sound on the bare stone and they slipped like shadows to the place where a bar of sunlight sliced through the only window in the corridor. Nerine had to stand on tiptoe to peer out of the slit, then turned with a nod.

"Soldiers!" she whispered. "Something is happening."

"Very well. Go back to the serving quarters. Leave me here for an hour, and tell them below that Imarga has been retained by me for the morning. We'll go back later."

Nerine wanted to protest, but she had little choice. After a moment she bowed, took the tray and slipped away as silently as she had come. When she was out of sight, Tennebriel went to the window. Outside she saw the Court of Tears. Several guards stood stiffly to attention. Fennobar's men, she thought, for they were not in the livery of Imperial Killers. She watched them for several minutes, and then other figures came into view from a door to her left. It opened from another part of the palace and through it now came two Administrators, though their faces could not be seen. After them came other soldiers, and between them were two men in chains. These had been stripped and wore no more than loin cloths. The men were taken quickly to the center of the tiny courtyard and their chains made fast to the rings in the paving stones.

Neither prisoner spoke, both standing proudly, seemingly unafraid as they gazed up at the blank walls of the palace, where ivy had once grown, but had died. There was dried blood on both men, who looked as if they had been badly mistreated. Tennebriel could not tell who they were, but one of the Administrators spoke. The words were said harshly, so that the walls of the courtyard caught them and flung them back.

"You have heard the charges made against you in the Hall of the Hundred. You have admitted fealty to Ottemar Remoon, the traitor. You have heard the sentence pronounced."

"Do your worst!" snarled the first of the men suddenly, like some beast cornered in a slaughterhouse, smelling its own death. "We will be avenged!"

The Administrator stood back and waved his hand. Two of the soldiers stepped forward abruptly, and to her horror, Tennebriel saw them plunge their naked blades into the prisoners. It was done expertly: the cuts were precise and the men fell to their knees together. Moments later they lay prone in widening pools of blood, spasming briefly before becoming very still. The Administrator clapped his hands and the bodies were unshackled and pushed to a corner of the courtyard like so much grain.

There was very little movement for a moment and then more guards entered the courtyard. This time they had a single prisoner, and as soon as Tennebriel saw him, her heart leapt and she wanted to scream. It was just as she had feared, the reason for her coming here. She had guessed that Cromalech had returned to Medallion and had been taken. She had been right.

They chained the First Sword to the central ring. He was naked, not even allowed a loin cloth to cover his genitals. Yet he had no marks on him and looked more healthy than the two other men had. He had seen their bodies, but his expression did not change and he stood proudly, whatever terror beat inside him. His feet were in the blood of the dead men and he shifted as he felt it, but he would not show fear in front of his tormentors.

Tennebriel felt a scream coming and put her hand to her

mouth to prevent it. Like a bird before a snake, she could not take her eyes away from the spectacle. Now a third Administrator came from the door, this time wrapped in black robes with a hood pulled over his head, his face obscured. He seemed to be taking a long time over proceedings, going to the bodies to glance at them, then circling back around the courtyard before coming at last to stand before Cromalech. Tennebriel could not see the man's face, and if he spoke, this time she could not hear.

Below her, Cromalech felt the darkness closing in on him. For a while, in his cell, properly fed and not ill-treated, he had thought there may be a chance that Eukor Epta had listened to reason. Again and again he had told Ascanar's men that Wargallow had been right to fear the north, but still Eukor Epta had not sent for him. Here, in this cold place with its stink of death and its freshly flowing blood, he felt his failure like a wound. But he would not break, nor would he beg for mercy for himself. These men here were no more than puppets and nothing would move them. His executioner stood before him.

"Have you prepared yourself?" said the man in the hooded robes.

Cromalech caught a glimpse of that face and drew in his breath, taken aback. At last! It was the Administrative Oligarch.

"You have come to hear me after all," said Cromalech softly. "I promise you, Wargallow was right. Whatever our differences, you must hear what is in the north—"

"Goldenisle has nothing to fear from the north," said Eukor Epta. "Only the perfidy of the traitors within."

"You must listen to me!" Cromalech hissed.

Eukor Epta drew out a long, curved blade and gripped it with both hands. "Before you die, Cromalech, you will listen to me. You have taken something from me. I have heard the truth of your ambition. You have abused the girl, have forced yourself upon her!" The words were as cutting as the steel he held. "Only know this. When she takes the throne, it will not matter to anyone else. But it will matter to me. Did you think, you vermin, you could so easily corrupt her mind? A simple child, who would give you all you wanted, her hand in marriage, was that it?"

"Simple?" breathed Cromalech, but closed out the thought. It had been Tennebriel's triumph. But he saw before him the reason for Eukor Epta's hatred. The mask had fallen, and the man without emotion had shown what all men have within them. There could be no reasoning with such a monstrous jealousy.

Eukor Epta's face became empty again. "She will make a superb Empress, with my guidance. I wanted you to know why you are going to die." He said no more, choosing that moment to bring the blade up in its terrible killing sweep. Cromalech felt the cold steel bite into him, the awful sting of it and then the tearing agony.

"TENNEBRIEL!" he shrieked, his voice crashing around the walls of the courtyard, and for a moment he thought there was an echo from somewhere deep in the castle, as if his lover had answered him. Eukor Epta stood back, releasing the blade. Cromalech's hands grasped the haft and he sank forward, head dropping, resting at the feet of his executioner. Eukor Epta had heard the agony of a lover in that cry; he barely resisted the urge to kick out at the head, turning instead and walking briskly to the door.

Tennebriel's mouth opened wide, but nothing came out. She sank back from the vision of horror, her back thudding into the wall behind her as she slithered weakly down it. In a moment she was convulsed with sobs, her body shaking uncontrollably. She wanted to scream, to shriek, but could not. Turning away, she tried to rise, but her legs would not support her. Eventually, using the wall, she did get to her feet, clawing her way to the window. The soldiers and the Administrators were gone, as were the two executed prisoners. But the corpse of Cromalech remained, bent over as if in prayer to some forgotten god.

Tennebriel's tears splashed on to the stone of the sloping sill, trickling through the dust. She slipped again to her knees, her body racked. Again and again she saw that awful sweep of steel, and heard her name yelled aloud, the walls amplifying it like thunder. He had loved her as he had always vowed! Even though she had sent him away in search of the impossible. If he had denied her, he could have saved himself. Why had he not done so!

She got to her feet, angry now, the storm of her fury beginning far down inside her, its energy about to give her a terrible new strength. She wiped away her tears. She had glimpsed the face of the man who had held the blade, and she held the image before her now as she ran.

The object of her blazing hatred had removed his executioner's robes and went now to another part of the palace, a place where only he and his most trusted followers were allowed to set foot. As he made for the room where he intended to draw up his plans for the defense of Medallion, one of his men came out of the shadows, his face white. The man looked to be badly shaken, almost terrified, something entirely unexpected in him, for he was a man Eukor Epta knew to be hardened to his cause.

"Your pardon, sir. There is a visitor, but I cannot say how they came here."

"Who is it?"

"A woman, sir. I think."

"Give me your sword." Eukor Epta took the blade and dismissed the man, but seeing his evident terror had made him wary. He went to the door of his room and pushed it open gently. This place was well below the palace levels that the officals used and he feared no trap here. If someone had come to visit him it was almost certainly one of his many agents. He entered the gloom. A single oil lamp burned, set upon one of the wide writing tables. He went to it cautiously, seeing no one.

"If you have come to see me, show yourself. I have little time to spare you. Say your piece and go."

The silence that fell was absolute and Eukor Epta scowled at it, refusing to be intimidated. In a way it was as though the world had receded. For a moment he felt suffocated, as though the walls had closed in, tunnel-like. He gripped his sword more tightly but already wondered if it would be of any avail against whatever had come here. Surely none of his enemies could have reached this place. He had been far too careful.

At the far end of the room there was a deep alcove set in the wall, a deep space where he kept many old records of the city. He felt himself drawn to this place now and as he stared into its darkness, he saw a shape there, the source of the mystery. Bending to the lamp, he lifted it so that it brought

the figure into fuller view. At once he set the lamp down,
stepping back with a gasp. He found it hard to accept what
he had seen. This must be an illusion.

The figure shuffled forward, but how was that possible?
For it was Ullarga, the dead woman, whose body had been
cast into the pits under the old city. She could not possibly
be alive! Eukor Epta held his sword out, wanting to call his
men. As the shape came into the edge of the light, he saw
that it was her, though changed.

"You hear me, Eukor Epta," came a voice like ice, hissing
through broken teeth like a wind from far away. "You see
this thing that I use?"

"Who are you?"

"I am power, Eukor Epta. A poor demonstration, but a
useful one. You understand power, you who are of the
Blood."

At this reference, Eukor Epta stiffened. Stiff he held up his
blade, but how could he use it against such a thing as this?

The voice changed, became less crude, as if not dependent
on the ruined vocal chords of Ullarga. "You know Ullarga
is dead. But I wanted you to see how I can move her yet."

"Who are you?" Eukor Epta repeated holding down his
fear.

"Anakhizer. Oh, I am not here, nor even near your islands. But I am watching them, and your enemies. They are
closing in on you. This war is of great interest to me."

"How is that?"

"I should not like to see the Remoon on your throne. He
already knows how I would serve him and those who follow
him."

"And if he is defeated?"

"A far better solution. Yet you and he are well matched.
Victory will be won at great cost to the victor. It would be
bad for you if you had to face a second invasion, and one
more powerful than the first."

"You feel it necessary to taunt me with this?"

"You seek power, Eukor Epta. The old power that runs in
the blood of your own kind. You can have it, but there is a
price. There are certain powers that I, too, am seeking, and
they are beyond the scope of the things you desire. I can give
you what you seek. I can help you to restore the people of

the Blood to what they were. All I desire is that you deliver the rest into my hands. Aid me, Eukor Epta, and you will have more power than you know of. I will give you your empire to do with as you wish.''

What treachery is this? Eukor Epta thought to himself. This evil from the north is real enough, but I would be a fool to give way to it.

''Let me help you destroy your enemies,'' said the voice, now that of a calm, rational man. There was no mistaking its depth of power. ''As an act of faith, I can show you how this can be done. Have you a map of the island?''

Eukor Epta said nothing but he took a scroll from one of the desks and spread it before the ghastly figure of Ullarga, holding its edges down with a number of heavy books. Medallion Island stood out clearly in the lamplight.

''Where are the ships of Empire?'' said the voice, and when Eukor Epta did not answer at once, the corpse pointed with a shrivelled finger at the inner sea. ''Here! And with them is the Crannoch fleet, eh? Old Estreen herself, eager for a piece of the throne. And your army is within the city.''

Eukor Epta knew that the power before him could not be deceived. ''I have men deployed in the mountains and in the forts at the Hasp.''

''And your enemies are without, already anchoring their ships beyond the Hasp in calm seas.''

''If they try to come in, they will fail. My defense is too strong.''

''Of course.'' The finger withdrew from the light. ''But there is a better way. Let them come in. Defend convincingly, but let them in to the inner sea.''

''And let them put us to the test? In such confusion, either side might triumph. Why toss away such an obvious advantage?''

''Tell me if I am mistaken, but do you love the Crannochs anymore than the Trullhoons, or the Remoons?''

''The Crannochs are the Regent's people.''

''Who is she? A girl who will fight you and what you stand for once she is Empress.''

''I will control her easily enough.''

''You think so? You think her a simple girl?''

A sudden wave of darkness came at Eukor Epta then, the

darkness of fear and of doubt, and as it broke over him, light followed it. Something ominous gleamed in that light.

"She has a mind to match yours," came the voice. "She has hidden it well from you. I have watched her with the eyes of Ullarga, my toy. I have drawn from the old crone such images!"

Eukor Epta heard again the death-cry of Cromalech, the shout of love.

"You are unwise to trust her, Eukor Epta. She and Cromalech were lovers. And he did not lead her on. She welcomed his embraces."

Eukor Epta forced himself to remain calm. "Perhaps so," he said, his mouth dry. "She has no reason to turn from me."

"So you say. But hear my suggestions out. Let your enemies into the inner sea. When the battle is engaged you and I will destroy them all."

Eukor Epta looked stunned, studying the map for an answer to this bold statement. "How? I do not have enough men to achieve such a thing. And I'll not let any creatures of yours into the city."

"Men? No, but we'll use the sea. Your enemies will drown."

A deep evil had crept into the voice now, the evil of ages, and in it Eukor Epta could hear the remote sounds of the sea, of that long forgotten Flood, when the island has almost disappeared beneath the waves. "How?" he said, his voice a whisper.

"You know well enough the old city beneath the island. And you know of the great spells that prevented its flooding: even now they hold and keep out the sea, which by natural laws should flood the city. I will lend you power and between us we shall release those ancient spells. The sea will pour in under the city. The ships in the inner sea will be sucked down to their doom—Ottemar Remoon and his allies, along with the Trullhoons, Hammavars and Crannochs."

"And Fennobar's fleet?"

"You will not need them. And when it is over, your own men, those of the Blood, can despatch any fortunate enough to survive. Medallion Island will be yours, as will the Empire. Tennebriel you can chain to your throne."

Eukor looked at the map, thinking hard on what he had been told. To release the ancient spells! But it could be done. And all that he had been offered would come to pass.

"And then what?" he said, looking up but seeing only the vague outline of the old woman.

"I'll not trouble you again. You will be left alone. My only condition is that you remain in Goldenisle and do not attempt to interfere in any plans I may have for the rest of Omara. Is that so small a price?"

"I confess I have no other ambitions," said Eukor Epta coldly. "I wish only to restore Goldenisle to those who own it. The outside world is barbaric and of no interest to me. You are welcome to it. But why are you offering me support? You must know I will question your motives. We are neither of us naive."

The voice chuckled. "When you have lived by deceit, it is hard to avoid seeing it in every glance. But I wish to see Goldenisle's threat to my own interests removed. If Ottemar wins the throne, in a few years he will be sending out whole fleets to harrass me. I can deal with them, but I do not want such distractions. By aiding you I gain two things: a respite from a potentially long war, and, I hope, an ally. You would be left alone, but even so, there may be further ways we could help each other. You'll not find me ungenerous, Eukor Epta. So, you had better decide, and do it soon."

"How should it be done?" Eukor Epta said to the darkness.

"Gather your faithful and begin the working to remove the spells. I will add power of my own. You will know when to begin."

Eukor Epta looked again at the map. He had never made a sudden decision in his life and had always been measured, careful to ensure that every detail of his planning was perfect. This would be a sudden change, like a rash fling of the dice. He was no gambler. Medallion was secure, and he did not need this alien help. But the prize to be gained if he took it! To wipe away all his enemies in one move. To restore those of the Blood! Anakhizer's logic was acceptable and his quest for power reason enough to offer Eukor Epta such bait.

Eukor Epta nodded slowly. "Very well. I will consider this thing."

"Decide quickly. I will be prepared." As suddenly as it had come, the voice was gone. Like an empty sack, Ullarga's corpse fell to the floor. Eukor Epta stood over it, bringing the lamp to its dead face. He drew back in disgust.

Outside, he found several of his men waiting for him, all afraid of the room. "There is a corpse in there. Take it below and burn it. Do you understand me?"

"At once, sire."

"Good. Forget what you have seen here." Eukor Epta strode past them and climbed the long stairs that led to the upper palace. He made his way to the corridor where Tennebriel's guards were standing stiffly erect outside her door. He must clarify this situation with her swiftly. He would see just how simple-minded a bitch she really was. How could he have been so stupid as to think her retarded!

"Is anyone with her?" he asked the guards tersely.

"No, sire. The handmaidens left some while ago." The guards let him in and the door was locked behind him. He could not see Tennebriel at first, but then found her stretched out on a couch, asleep with her back to him.

Cromalech's whore! he wanted to shout, but calmed himself. Carefully he touched her shoulder to rouse her. "Tennebriel," he called, and the girl stirred. As she turned to face him, her mouth opened and she gasped.

He jerked upright, face clouding with anger. "What are you playing at, girl!" he fumed. "Why are you wearing that dress? Where is your mistress?"

Imarga began to cry at once, hiding her face, terrified. "Oh, sire! She made me do it! She made me!"

"Where is she?" he snarled, gripping her and dragging her to her feet brutally. His hand slashed across her face.

"She wanted to see the Court of Tears—"

His eyes narrowed mercilessly, his voice turning to ice, dropping so low she almost missed the words. "She *what?*"

"It was Nerine! She told her she could watch the killings. She was bored. It was only for a short—"

Eukor Epta flung the girl aside and stormed to the door, hitting it so hard with his fist that it shook. At once the guards opened it. Eukor Epta swept past them and down the corridor. A startled Imarga came to the door and gazed after him, her face scarlet where his hand had caught her.

"What is it, girl?" snapped one of the guards.

"Idiot!" shouted his companion. "This is a handmaiden! Where is the Regent?" But as he said it, he recalled vividly the figure of the girl he had admired earlier.

Eukor Epta found the corridor that led to the window over-looking the Court of Tears. The footprints in the dust were clear enough. Two girls had been here. On the sill he found the dried pattern of Tennebriel's tears, and he read them prop-erly. She had seen! Seen him strike the blow that had killed her lover! Whatever plans he had concerning her were de-stroyed in that moment. She was no fool, and she had re-turned Cromalech's love. As Eukor Epta traced the tear lines with his finger, the puzzle began to fall into place. She had plotted against him from the first. She had sought to steal Ottemar for the same reasons he had!

And now she would be ablaze with hatred. Eukor Epta saw the footprints that led away into the palace. Very well. Let her run. That was over.

He turned back. This decides me. I will summon those of the Blood. We will begin the working and call up the power of the ocean.

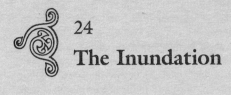

24
The Inundation

THEY CAME UP out of the earth in the highlands to the north east of Medallion Island, overlooking the inner sea and across to its western bay where the city nestled under the towering cliffs. Even from here they looked huge. Aumlac and his Stonedelvers and the Earthwrought had been true to their words and had made a way under the stone, using their staffs and their strange powers, burrowing like human moles. The men of Darraban gaped in amazement at the freshly made passageways. Darraban himself had returned to his warships and with Rannovic and the Hammavars was taking the fleet to the sea outside the Hasp, ready to sail into the inner sea at the given moment. He was also waiting for the arrival of the ships of Ruan from the east. Wargallow and Ottemar had decided upon a simple plan that would rely on surprise. They would come around behind whatever forces guarded the Hasp and set upon them, anticipating that they would overrun them with numbers unless something went very much amiss.

As the invaders blinked in the sunlight of early morning, watching the mists lifting off the sea below, they prepared themselves for battle, trying not to think of those who would fall this day. Aumlac's people were resting and the big man sat apart from them, studying the higher reaches of the Heights of Malador wistfully, as if they held certain secrets for him.

Ottemar and Wargallow joined him. "We owe you much for this," Ottemar told him.

Aumlac chuckled deep in his throat. "Aye, perhaps. But

did you not save me from the sea? Even so, there is a boon I would ask of you, sire.''

''Of course, what is it?''

''When we have rid this island of the darkness that sits here and of the powers that crawl below it, perhaps my people could make their home here, in Malador—''

''The freedom of the island will be theirs,'' said Ottemar.

''Stonedelvers dwelt here before, many years ago.'' He frowned for a moment, then brightened. ''The sooner we begin this day's work, the happier we shall be.''

As they spoke, Sisipher was with Orhung, looking out from their own dizzy perch at the city in the mists. Orhung, ever silent, his mind unfathomable so that Sisipher wondered if he was thinking or if he was in some way asleep, still enduring the undersleep partially, now seemed far more alert. His usually empty expression had been replaced by a deep frown. The girl sensed that she had moved something in him, some hidden power, just as he had been the catalyst that had jarred awake her own buried abilities. He both attracted and repelled her because of this.

''What is it?'' she asked him.

''I cannot tell yet. But I sense terrible evil here. As we came to the place below us where we began our climb upward, I saw through the thick strata of stone to the barrier, the wall of spells set against the sea below and inside the island. Aumlac knew it was there also. He did not seek to penetrate it, but chose instead to climb over its arc.''

''Who set this wall there?''

''Powers that go back far into the history of the island.''

''Are they still alive?''

Orhung did not answer at first. ''Perhaps,'' he said, having made some evaluation. ''Something is at work here that I cannot see. And there is something beyond us, near to the forts defending the Hasp, that is not as it should be.''

Her growing empathy with Orhung disturbed her most when he said such things for she had also sensed unpleasantness near at hand.

Ottemar appeared beside her with a grin. ''The men are rested and anxious to go on. We'll make for the forts at once. Now listen, Sisipher, I want you well away from the fighting. Orhung—''

"I'll be where I am needed," she said bluntly and their eyes met.

He grinned more widely. "Yes, I know you will. But be careful."

"Ottemar," she said softly. "It isn't going to be as simple as we thought. There may be a trap." She explained Orhung's misgivings.

"I see," he grunted. "Then we'll take great care."

In silence their column of Stonedelvers, Earthwrought and warriors moved over the lower slopes of Malador, dropping ever downward toward the open area above the cliffs of the Hasp where the eastern fort was perched like a guardian above the narrow channel to the open sea.

After two hours they reached the rocks high above the fort, able to find ample cover in their jumbled confusion and hiding from watchful eyes. They gathered to make their final plans. In the distance, on the open sea, they could make out the ships of Darraban and Rannovic cutting through the waters, quickly closing on the island. Beyond them, turning from the east, went more ships and Orhung confirmed with his uncanny sight that they belonged to Ruan.

Wargallow spoke to the leaders, including Andric, who was here to represent his father. He had wanted to be at sea, but Darraban had insisted that some of the Trullhoons had to swell the land forces and that Andric would have the responsibility of commanding them. Reluctant at first, now that he had seen the Stonedelvers at work, Andric had warmed to his duty.

"Darraban will sail into the Hasp and draw the sting of the two forts," said Wargallow. "Once the fighting begins, we will go down to this eastern fort and take it. In the confusion, Darraban's leading ships will sail through the Hasp, keeping well to this eastern wall. The efforts of the defenders in the western fort will not be enough to keep the fleet out."

There came a muffled shout from beyond them and one of the watch could be seen pointing. "They're coming in!"

Andric had difficulty keeping his men quiet, now that they could sense an easy victory, and with the fleet moving so swiftly. But Wargallow was watching Orhung and the girl, aware of their growing symbiosis. He had seen Sisipher in the past when she had been in such a mood as she was now, as if she saw things in the air that others could not see, evil forces that hung like vapor. Discreetly he joined her.

"This is a simple enough venture," he said beside her and she looked startled by him.

She shook her head. "I don't know—"

Orhung had stiffened abruptly, but he was still far more alert than usual. He took from his belt his rod and Wargallow could see that it had a faint blue glow which began to pulse. Orhung closed his eyes and stood like a statue carved from the naked rocks about him. Sisipher shuddered, then emitted a gasp.

Wargallow took her arm to support her and she did not flinch. "What is it?" he asked.

She shook her head, her eyes closed tight against something. At once Ottemar was with them. "A few more minutes and they can strike." He saw Wargallow holding her. "What's the matter?"

"Beware," said Wargallow. "Hold back the men a moment—"

But even as he spoke it was too late. With a great cry, the Trullhoons rose up as one and poured over the rocks, the Stondelvers joining them, and within minutes they were racing down upon the landward wall of the fort.

Orhung opened his eyes, pointing with his rod. "There are barely two score men in the fort, and no more than that in the one across the channel."

Ottemar whirled to look, but could see nothing. "What do you mean?"

"There is no defense," said Sisipher. As she spoke, the Trullhoons were shinning up the walls of the fort like apes, yelling their battle cries to crush their fear, and although a few defenders tried to keep them back it was as Sisipher said.

Wargallow's face had clouded. "This cannot be right!" he snapped. "The Hasp is open—why?" Then his face changed. "Can it be we have unexpected help? Otarus! Has he arranged this?"

Ottemar clapped his hands. "This is marvelous! Look, Darraban's leading ships are already below us. They'll be through in minutes." His delight vanished as he looked at Sisipher.

She was shaking her head violently. "No! Don't let him, Ottemar. Don't let him do it!"

Ottemar rushed to her side and automatically put an arm around her, pulling her to him. She clung to him as if drowning. "Who? Who is doing what?" he shouted.

"Orhung!" cried Wargallow, and all eyes were on the Created, who held his rod before him. It blazed now with its blue light.

"It's him," Sisipher breathed in Ottemar's ear. "I realize now. The power in me that keeps returning, blazing up. It comes from Orhung."

"But how?"

"He belongs to the Sorcerer-Kings. It's their power. But it is akin to the power of the Hierarchs placed in me, and draws it out."

"But you used it up at Xennidhum—"

"Did I?" she said, her eyes filled with angry tears. "Am I free of it?"

"Then what's happening?" Ottemar pleaded. "You must tell me!"

"Orhung sees something evil at work. And he is going to reveal it. Through me." She shuddered again.

Ottemar swung round and screamed at Orhung. "Leave her! Leave her, or I'll cut you down!"

Wargallow barred his way. "Be reasonable!" he hissed. "Don't try to touch him, or you'll die. That rod—"

Sisipher moaned and dropped to her knees. Her eyes closed tightly. The fighting in the fort below seemed far away, almost like the sounds of children at play.

"I can *see*," whispered Sisipher. "The gift, the telling, it is with me again." And beyond her, Orhung had turned to point his rod at her head as if pouring from it the power she spoke of.

Wargallow knelt beside her. "What do you see?"

Ottemar also knelt, protesting, but Wargallow was adamant. "We have to know."

Ottemar's anger rose in him, but he waited.

When Sisipher opened her eyes, she was calmer, and it was clear that she was not looking out upon the view that the others shared. She saw instead the landscape of the future. And it appalled her.

"The wall of spells," she said. "It is being lifted."

"By whom?" snapped Wargallow.

"Those of the Blood. They have gathered in secret to perform the ritual. I see them dance."

Wargallow and Ottemar stared at each other. "It is what Otarus spoke of," said Wargallow. "Yet those of the Blood want to keep their old ways, their old city. If they remove the spells that protect it—"

"The sea is coming in!" cried Sisipher, hands clasped to her face in horror as she saw it before her. "The sea! It floods the city under Medallion Island. And the ships—"

Ottemar gasped and turned to look down across the waters. Already the first of the Trullhoon craft were through the Hasp and into the inner sea. There were no ships coming to meet them. The entire fleet of the city was berthed in the docks. "The ships!" cried Ottemar.

"They'll be sucked down like leaves—" began Wargallow.

"Then it's Eukor Epta," said Ottemar. "He has betrayed us all."

Wargallow leapt up. "We must stop the fleet coming in! At once!"

Sisipher again closed her eyes and sank back against Ottemar. He held her tightly, caressing her hair, speaking gently to her. As he did so, Orhung lowered his rod and seemed himself to come out of some dream. Wargallow had seen and shouted to him.

"This way! We have to stop them coming in! Do you understand?"

Orhung nodded and leapt down from his rock as if nothing had happened. He joined Wargallow and they went as quickly as they could to the fort.

Ottemar and Sisipher were left alone on the hillside, except for the Earthwrought who closed in nervously, afraid for the girl. Her eyes came awake and she struggled up. "A dream," she murmured.

"Are you all right?" He kept his arms about her.

"A little dizzy. But the ships—"

"It's not too late to stop them."

"Orhung—"

"Gone ahead." He helped her to her feet.

"He's doing it. Reviving me. I don't want—"

"Then I'll stop him. Believe me, I'll stop him if I have to push him over the cliffs. Listen to me, Sisipher." His grip on her arms tightened. "I acted like a fool before the stairs of Xennidhum. I offered you something that I had no right to—"

"That was long ago, Ottemar. And you were possessed—"

"I am my own man here. And I will have my say. I would throw aside this Empire, this unloved throne, if you told me to do it. Before your people I say this. I would choose a single ship and sail with you again, far away from this chaos—"

"You cannot!" she said, but with no anger. "The Empire turns on you. You are its pivot. You must rule here."

His eyes held her for a long time, then he threw back his head and laughed. "Aye! Become Emperor. And take another war to the north."

"You have to, just as I have to use my unwanted gift. We have no choice.

He turned to her again. "Then sit beside me. I offered it before out of fear, madness, whatever it was, but this time I offer it to you out of love."

Still she did not pull away, but there were fresh tears in her eyes. "There are things yet you do not understand—"

"Then *explain*. Nothing will turn me—"

"I have learned things that I was not meant to learn about myself. You know that my gift for telling has been passed down to me by my mother and by her mother and so on back to the time that it was first implanted by the Hierarchs—"

A great shout from the fort snapped both their heads around.

"We must go there now!" she cried. "I will explain when we have more time. But we must go quickly."

"Very well," he grunted, angered, but in agreement. "But you won't deter me!" They raced down to the fort as quickly as they dared with the Earthwrought beside them. The gates had been pushed open and once inside they were confronted by a grim sight. The defenders of the place had been brutally cut down, though there were far more of them than they had thought.

"But there are hundreds of them!" gasped Ottemar as he surveyed the bloody carnage.

Aumlac stood before him. "My lord, most of them had been butchered already when we got here. The rest are dead, too, killed by our attack, though there were no more than forty of them."

"I don't understand—"

Wargallow came down from the battlements. "It's a trap!" he snarled. "To draw us into the inner sea. Once we are in, the old city will be flooded. Every ship in the inner sea will be sucked under. Fennobar, Darraban and the rest. They'll all perish. Only Eukor Epta's chosen will survive."

"The working has already begun," said Aumlac. "Orhung knows it. The wall of spells is beginning to weaken."

Ottemar raced up the ramparts. "How many ships are in?"

"A dozen," said Wargallow. "Darraban himself led them."

Andric stood close at hand, a look of horror on his face. "How can we turn them back?"

Wargallow studied the cliffs. "We must seal this channel. Close it up so that no more ships can get in. It's not so wide, though deep. Well?" He turned to Aumlac. "Your people move stone, cut through mountains. Surely you can turn this cliff into a landslide that will seal off this channel?"

Aumlac's eyes widened as if looking on the work already done. "It would take time—"

Andric rushed at Wargallow. "What of those already inside! My father! How do they come away?"

"They must get ashore," said Wargallow.

"Where?" snarled Andric. "There is nowhere to land save in the laps of the defenders. With just a few ships, they would be cut to pieces. We have to get them out!"

Orhung spoke dispassionately. "There is no time. Already the wall of spells is falling. The first of the waters has breached it."

Aumlac shrugged. "Then we'll not stop the flood. We cannot move the cliff in a day, nor enough of it to fill the deeps below us."

"With my help, it will be possible," said Orhung.

"What do you mean?" said Wargallow.

Orhung was gazing at the waters below, as though at a future landscape forming. His hand clutched the rod of power tightly, as if he fought to control a serpent that would writhe free of him. "I have been given the power of the rod," he said."

"The Sorcerer-Kings," nodded Wargallow. "It is because of the rod that Anakhizer sought to destroy the Created. Because you had the means to destroy *him*. It is the truth, isn't it?"

Orhung nodded. "I will not deny it. My one goal has been to confront him and use the rod upon him."

"Is it enough?" said Aumlac.

Orhung stiffened as if hurt by the words. "It is. And yet Anakhizer is powerful. I have wondered—perhaps he will turn the rod against me, against us all."

"Wrest it from you?" said Wargallow.

"I do not control it. It controls me, as with the girl." I dare not tell them the complete truth, he thought. That unless I reject them and their needs and think only of going on to confront Anakhizer, I will be defeated. Such ordained single-mindedness cries out my apartness from them and makes me the slave that I am. Aye, slave.

Something within him, an ember perhaps of remote humanity from the rulers of Xennidhum's far past, flared up at the thought. Dare I risk facing Anakhizer as anything less than a machine, an extension of this metal weapon?

Wargallow spoke urgently. "Orhung! Speak now. You said you can help. How?"

"I can unleash the power of the rod here, if you desire it."

"How?"

"I will move the cliffs. Close up the Hasp. But if I do, the power of the rod will be lost to us all."

Wargallow answered first. "But Anakhizer will have lost it, too. Very well. It has to be done. If we lose our fleet, and that of Fennobar, Goldenisle will be lost also."

"Fennobar!" cried Andric. "You speak of saving Fennobar?"

Wargallow stood within a few feet of the youth, eyes blazing. "When we have taken the city, we will need to rebuild it. There will be no executions of any prisoners. We need men, Andric! An army, an Empire. We have to make the survivors capitulate. Just as the Hammavars came to terms, so must Fennobar."

"There is no more time," said Orhung.

"So begin!" said Wargallow, and Ottemar nodded. Whatever powers Orhung held in check had to be spent now.

"You must all leave this place," said the Created. "Go back up to the Heights." He said nothing else, instead turning his back on them and studying the channel of the Hasp below him. I have no right to declare myself human, he thought. Nor should I have the right to defy the will of those who made me. But I will not turn from the people of this world. Omara will be safer with the rod's power dissipated. There are other powers here now, stronger maybe than the raw powers of old. Let them bring Anakhizer down.

Andric let out a sudden curse and rushed for the walls. Before he could be stopped, he had leapt off them, his plummeting body swallowed in an instant by the drop.

Down in the fort, many of the Trullhoons had seen what he had done and they raced in a body for the steps. Wargallow confronted them with an easy wave. "He is a rash buffoon!" he shouted. "But his father has to be warned. We could think of no way, and so the fool has taken it into his head to act for himself, for us all. He'll swim to your master. The fall will not harm him."

Some of the Trullhoons looked nonplussed, but when the tiny figure of Andric was seen at last, they gave a great cheer, and in the end it was their enthusiasm that swayed the others.

"Come!" called Ottemar to all the assembled men, Stonedelvers and Earthwrought. "We must go up to the highest ground, and quickly." Keeping Sisipher close to him, he led the exodus from the fort, back to the hills, leaving the solitary figure of Orhung standing on the battlements before the plunge that was the Hasp. Aumlac and his people and the Earthwrought split off from the retreating party and arranged themselves in a formation that faced the lone figure, waiting for its command.

Orhung turned once, then back again, so that no one above could see what he did. Aumlac suddenly came racing up the rocks to join Wargallow and Ottemar, a look of deep concern on his face. "Lords, there is much evil in this place. We feel it below us now, just as though we stand above a volcano. The anguish of the stone is deep. There is more at work here than the power of those of the Blood. Anakhizer has also sent power, filling this evil working to its limit.''

"Then Eukor Epta has made an ally of him!" said Ottemar. "But how has he achieved this? How could the people of the city allow it?''

"They are all to be sacrificed," said Wargallow. "That is my guess. Anakhizer feeds upon these lives, as many as he can take. Otarus was right. Eukor Epta is visiting on the Remoons and the usurpers of Goldenisle the same flood that they visited upon the original inhabitants. An ironic revenge.''

Orhung's tiny figure was suddenly bathed in a flash of bright blue light and there was a distant rumble under the earth, as of thunder. In a moment a huge cloud of dust rose up, and as it began to engulf the watchers, they heard the song of the Stonedelvers through the splitting of rock and the grinding of stone. Huge sheets of the cliff face in the Hasp peeled off and toppled into the channel below as Orhung released whatever full powers he had. The promised landslip began and in the noise and confusion, all sight of the inner sea was lost.

The sound of the landslide went on for many minutes, drowning out the Stonedelvers chanting, and as the dust finally began to clear, the watchers above could see that the western wall of the Hasp had also crumbled like paper, great chunks of it slithering into the waters below. The fort that the men of Ottemar had recently taken was gone, along with half a mile of cliff wall, as had the equivalent across the channel. The Hasp had been closed, but of Orhung there was no sign.

"Have we lost him?" said Ottemar.

"It was not a sacrifice I would have preferred," said Wargallow. His face bore no trace of emotion, so that those who saw it thought him colder and more remorseless than ever. Yet inside he wanted to shout his anger at this passing, this cruel sacrifice. "But I would not expect to see him crawl away from such destruction.''

"Destruction which pales beside what follows," said Aumlac, who had rejoined them with his people. He was pointing with his stone staff at the distant city.

Even as they looked, they saw the great swirling whirlpools

beginning out in the middle of the inner sea, drawing to them any ship that came close. Darraban had passed through the channel with a dozen of his finest ships, and the watchers could see now that the ships of Empire had been released from the docks; Fennobar himself had come out to meet the challenge of his enemy, no doubt completely baffled by the appearance of the Trullhoons. While the cliffs of the Hasp had been turned to rubble, the two fleets made for each other like blood-hungry war dogs, and they came together in the center of the inner sea. Fennobar's ships outnumbered Darraban's and the Trullhoons were not aware that the way had been closed behind them.

Andric, swimming as quickly as his strong arms could thrust him through the water, felt the abrupt drag of water beneath him and long before he could reach his father's ship he was pulled down by the plunging waters as they burst through the ceiling of the wall of spells and gushed into the deep halls and streets of the ancient city. In the dockyards the tide raced up and smashed at the wharves, punching out huge piles of stored grain and produce, drowning countless onlookers. The lower streets of the city were flooded by the sudden surge, and as the waters below crashed around inside the vast empty shell that had been the old city, the walls cracked like the side of an egg, the roof above splintering and caving in. Whole streets dropped down into the watery cauldron in an instant, and the noise rose like the shouting of a dozen enraged gods. Power poured into the chaos, shaking the earth, the entire island, as if it would be torn from its roots and remolded like so much primal mud.

Darraban and Fennobar were locked in a frightful contest of arms, their men hacking at each other, oblivious of the danger about them, when an abrupt surge of water took them all under the waves, dragging ship after ship to its doom. Rudaric, whose ship was the last to pass through the Hasp before its walls collapsed, saw the warring ships ahead of him sink down in a single rush, and before he could turn his own ship for the rocky shoreline, he, too, was stricken by the sea. A huge backwash took the prow of his craft and twisted it around as a giant would have, flinging the ship contemptuously on to its back. Not a man survived, Hammavar and Trullhoon alike, and in a moment they had all been swallowed by the waves. Elsewhere in the seething inner sea, Crannoch ships suffered the same nightmarish end, pulped by the waves before being dragged down.

Beyond the Hasp, in open sea, Rannovic and the first ships of Ruan drew together and watched the collapse of the Hasp in horror, knowing that ships had been buried under the amazing rockfall. Rannovic screamed for his leading craft to steer clear, and they turned up the coast, although there was nowhere to land. Instead the entire fleet had to hold off, anchoring in open water. They could do nothing but wait, numbed by what had happened. The sun faded; thick black clouds gathered like an audience, lowering down on Medallion's peaks. Rannovic looked stunned, sure that the fall of the Hasp was the work of Medallion's defenders.

Ottemar watched the destruction of the fleet on the inner sea with horror. Not a ship survived it and in the city he could see the chaos, as buildings crumbled like toys and the waters raced up the lower streets. Some of the smaller islands were engulfed, and one of the tower islands, a long needle of rock, toppled and was not seen again.

"Where can he be?" breathed Wargallow beside him.

Ottemar knew who he meant. "High ground," he muttered. "Just as we are."

"Kirrikree will find him," said Sisipher and at once she turned to search the crags where the great owl was waiting, not anxious to come any closer to the appalling destruction below. The others said nothing as she communicated with the bird, and in a while she turned back to them. "He will search."

"We've lost a dozen ships, no more," said Wargallow.

Ottemar scowled at him. His coldness staggered him at times. "You see this as a victory?"

Wargallow snorted. "We've lost good men. The Trullhoons have lost their ruler. The Crannochs are drowned, many Remoons, too. This is war, Ottemar. You have not seen the end of it."

The sea still tossed as if in the throes of a hurricane and the packed clouds darkened overhead. Ottemar fought back the urge to be sick. "Am I to live with this?"

"You cannot ignore it. Not while Anakhizer lives. But he

has failed here. He has lost Goldenisle. You will have your throne.''

Ottemar nodded absently, hardly aware as Wargallow went to the others, already preparing for what must follow, the journey to the ruined city. When the flooding was over, the Hasp would have to be reopened. Ottemar again found himself with Sisipher. They walked away from the gathered men, his arm around her. She, too, was thoughtful, dazed by the frightful scenes they had witnessed.

''It will soon be over,'' she told him. ''The seas will settle. When we find Eukor Epta—''

He turned to her. ''What are these things I do not understand?''

She looked away. ''Why must you ask?''

''Because I love you. You must have known it for a long time. At first it was infatuation. I wanted you as other men have, and you knew it. As Kirrikree knew it. I felt your scorn then. But not now. You don't loathe me as you did. I felt that under the Slaughterhorn, when we traveled with Aumlac's people. I knew then what I wanted. You, beside me in Goldenisle. I told you, I would give it up—''

''Goldenisle is Omara's only hope!'' she said suddenly. ''Why do you think Anakhizer has spent so much time trying to destroy it and hunting you down? Because if you take the throne, you can make the Empire into the weapon he fears, just as he feared Orhung's Werewatch and tried to kill them all.''

''Yes, I know all that—''

She smiled. ''Then don't speak about deserting! Your place is down there.''

''And yours?''

She looked away. ''You won't live for ever.''

Her words completely baffled him. ''What does that mean?''

''Not only must you take the throne, Ottemar, but you must secure it. The Remoon line must go on. Marry a Trullhoon: Darraban has some comely nieces—''

''What are you talking about!'' he laughed, grabbing her hand, but she pulled it away, troubled by something.

''I'm not joking.''

"Neither am I," he said seriously. "I will not marry a Trullhoon, however comely they may be."

"Nor can you make me your Empress."

"No one would oppose me."

She nodded, still unable to face him. "But I cannot give you children."

He stared at her profile for a long moment, then to her surprise he laughed, and it was not forced. "No? Is that all you have to say? That you cannot give me children? Not that you could not love me, or because of what has happened—"

"Ottemar, stop this—"

He gripped her, turning her to face him. "If you love me, it is enough! I will rule, I will make Goldenisle strong, even if I cannot have a son to follow me. That is not important to me."

Tears began to fill her eyes. "I know what is important to you," she whispered, stroking his face. "You think I cannot feel your love for me?"

"You think I could not love you enough?"

She shook her head. "You fool. It is too much love that I fear from you. You make me a goddess and put me before everything."

"Yes! Before my life," he laughed.

"And I would return your love, Ottemar."

He sucked in his breath as though she had doused him in icy water. "Then—"

"I could have a child. As my mother did, and as her mother did. And it would be a girl, just as the Hierarchs decreed it."

His face clouded. "What do you mean? *Decreed?*"

"It is the *gift*. As it is passed on from mother to child, it takes from the mother her strength. Within a few years of the birth, the mother dies. It is as though the Hierarchs did not want their secret shared. Only the child who carries the secret survives—"

"But you ended that! You woke Naar-Iarnoc as they wished. There is no need to go on through you—"

"Even so, I possess the gift yet. Orhung has taught me that. And it will pass to my daughter. So I can give you a child, Ottemar Remoon, and she will make a fine Empress to succeed you. If it is what you truly want, then I will give it to you."

He looked aghast. "And have you die within months! No!"

She sighed. "Then you understand why I cannot sit beside you on the throne."

He nodded. "It is you that I want, just as I have said."

"And your Empire must have an heir."

He turned away, silent for a long time, but then gripped her gently. His face lit up suddenly. "But you do love me?"

She, too, smiled. "I who detested you, who despised you. Yes, Ottemar."

Above them there came a flutter of strong wings and in a moment the great white owl, Kirrikree, came floating down like a ghost to sit upon a nearby rock.

"Has he heard our words?" said Ottemar, flushing.

She smiled, never more beautiful, he thought. "No, but he already knows." She listened to the bird for a moment, her face changing.

"Eukor Epta," she said, as if pronouncing a curse. "He is found."

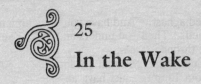

25
In the Wake

TENNEBRIEL KEPT RUNNING until she was out of breath, turning this way and that along corridors that meant nothing to her; they threaded without end through the palace. She was aware that in some rooms that she passed were people, but none of them rushed out to stop or hail her. Higher up into the maze of the palace she went, until at last, exhausted, she flung herself down in a wide chamber amongst old furnishings and drapes that clouded her in dust. She wept bitterly, until she fell asleep, curled up like a child in a place seldom visited.

Hours later she woke, her legs aching, and sat up. At once she remembered it all and felt a stab of misery. But she steeled herself to bring herself under control. She had no real plan, no idea what she should do, although she knew she must somehow get away from the palace, from the city. She could not remain here, but how to get out?

More carefully now she left the echoing chamber and, finding another long corridor, travelled along it until she approached a window. She could see through it that she was high above the main sprawl of the palace, in that old part of it that backed up against the very foot of the huge cliffs that formed the western wall of the city. It would be impossible to find a way up those cliffs. The window was too small to climb out of, but she knew that this would have to be her means of escape: a larger window. She would have to get on to the roofs.

For some time she explored the corridors, until she turned a corner and almost walked straight into the arms of an Administrator. He was as startled as she was and she was able to twist away. But there were armed guards with the man and they quickly overtook the girl and brought her, kicking, before him.

"What are you doing in this part of the palace, girl? Serving girls are not allowed away from—" the man's face altered. He reached for Tennebriel's dusty hair. She turned away only to have one of the guards grip her by the neck and transfix her. The Administrator tugged at her hair and it fell loose. The man gasped, but controlled himself at once.

"So, Tennebriel. My master is looking for you, girl."

Tennebriel spat but the guard only tightened his grip so that she winced in pain.

"Spare your struggling, girl," said the Administrator coldly. "Bring her this way!"

He turned without giving her another look, as if she were no more than a serving girl, and walked away down the passageway. The two guards roughly pushed her after him, and she felt the closing in of despair. They reached a long stairway that led up and began ascending, and as she climbed, Tennebriel gave up hope of getting out of the palace; this could not be the way to safety, even if she got free of these men.

As they climbed, a door opened behind them and the two guards turned, startled. Tennebriel also looked back. Out of the doorway a number of men had stepped, all armed with short swords and with their faces masked by thin steel helms. The Administrator saw them and shouted a challenge, but the men said nothing, padding up the stairs like huge cats, equally as menacing. At once the two guards pulled out their blades.

"Keep away from this place!" snapped the first of them, but there was little conviction in his voice. Moments later the masked men swung their blades and a frightful contest began on the stairway. The sound of ringing steel shook Tennebriel's ears and her nose filled with the reek of sparks. One of the guards fell, a sword ripping into him, and as he died the Administrator grabbed at her wrist and tried to pull her up the stairs. With a yell of fury she swung round and twisted him off balance, so that he tumbled past her and into the back of the other guard. Tennebriel watched in amazement as the masked men cut both of them down in the confusion, kicking their bodies aside as they came on up the stairs. One of the men stood before her, mindful of her hands and the nails she showed him.

"Stay back!" she hissed.

The man laughed from within his mask. "A fine way to treat those who have rescued you."

"Who are you?"

"Never mind that. Why were you their prisoner?"

Confused, Tennebriel shook her head.

"Come with us. There are other Administrators about, and more will come soon."

"What are they doing here?"

"There is war. Quickly!"

Tennebriel did as she was told. Whoever these people were, they were not Eukor Epta's men. They led her through the door from which they had emerged, and there were more corridors beyond, dusty and disused, thick with cobwebs. Beyond them was yet another old chamber, carved from the rock and lit by torches. Once inside it, the men bolted its door. Tennebriel found herself beside a table, and on its other side sat an old man with a long white beard.

"Who are you? What is happening?" she snapped.

The man stood up and studied her. He did not have the stamp of cruelty on his features that so many of Eukor Epta's men seemed to have, the dispassionate, fixed gaze, but even so he looked stern.

"We found her with one of the lesser Administrators," said the man who had brought her. "He was taking her, by force, to the place where the others have gathered."

"I recognize you," said the old man. "You are the Crannoch girl!"

"I am the Heir to the throne, the Regent!" she answered haughtily, hoping to impress them.

The old man shook his head slowly. "Regent you may be, but the throne is not for you, puppet of Eukor Epta."

Tennebriel's eyes blazed. "Puppet! Not to that filth, nor to any man."

"Perhaps not. But did he not intend to put you on the throne?"

"Yes. And use me—"

"Ottemar Remoon is alive," said the old man. "Even now he is preparing to come here and take what is rightfully his."

Tennebriel nodded. "I know it. And you serve him?"

"I do. I am Otarus, High Chamberlain of the Law Givers. It is the law of Goldenisle that Ottemar Remoon should be the next Emperor. Do you contest it?"

The girl shook her head, seemingly very tired. "I do not. Let him have what is his. I have only one wish and that is to be free of this place and that murderer."

"You speak of Eukor Epta?"

"Yes!"

"Has he abandoned you?" said Otarus, surprised.

"I can't say what his plans for me were. But he has lost me, I promise you. I will swear it before whatever powers you wish. Bring him to me and I will open him for you."

Otarus frowned deeply, both at the venom in the girl's tone and in surprise at her broken alliance. "Do you know that your aunt, Estreen, is waiting in her ship in our harbor, together with many Crannoch ships? Can you pretend that you do not know this?"

"Estreen?" said the girl, evidently shocked. "Why?"

"Brought here by the Administrator."

She laughed scornfully. "Of course! To be reinstated once I was on the throne."

"Estreen has waited many years for this moment. She will not give up the throne as easily as you have. Will you swear loyalty to Ottemar Remoon and all the others who rally to his flag?"

Tennebriel straightened. Cromalech was dead, and she realized that if she could have brought him back, she would have cast aside the throne and all that went with it. Power meant nothing if it could not give her the only thing she desired. "I spit on the flag of Eukor Epta," she said. "And if the Crannochs have chosen it, then I spit on them. They have let me languish all my life. Yes, I will swear loyalty to Ottemar Remoon. Before all of Goldenisle. Let him be Emperor."

Again Otarus was surprised, but he could see the determination in the girl's face. Something had happened to her to make her so adamant in her rejection of the throne and her people. But he believed her. "Very well, Tennebriel, consider yourself under my protection. You will need it, for there are men here in this palace who would cut your throat if they knew what you had said before me."

Another door opened and a white-faced man entered, dressed in the robes of the Law Givers. "Otarus! It is as we feared! The Administrators have all left the city and gone up into the secret places of the high cliffs. Eukor Epta is with them and they have sealed themselves in. They left a trail of dead behind them. And word has come from our men in the undercity that the wall of spells is disintegrating!"

Otarus gripped the table as if he had been speared. "The wall? Then it is the worst news! Eukor Epta intends to kill us all and spare only those of the Blood. We must evacuate the city. Get everyone up into the mountains, do you understand me! No matter who they are. Everyone below us, Crannochs too, is marked for death by the Administrator."

"Those from Skerrin, sire?" asked one of the masked men.

"Them, too. Wargallow told us we will need every man in the days to come. Eukor Epta is the enemy of us all. Him and whatever darkness it is he serves. Go on, all of you! Spread the word like fire." He spun on Tennebriel. "Come with me, Tennebriel. The city is in grave danger and may not survive what has been unleashed."

Perplexed, but not prepared to argue, the girl let him guide her through the door and away, and this time the armed men at her back were no threat, but a comfort to her. They all began a long and arduous flight through yet more old rooms and corridors cut from sheer rock and then up an endless stairway which made her guess that they were in the heart of the mountains behind and above the city. As they climbed they felt the ground shake, and more than once they were forced to stop and cling to the walls as if an earthquake had started. Far below them they could hear the roaring as of a subterranean storm.

A clear moon, bloated and sharp, looked down upon Medallion Island now as if sating itself on the vision below. As the sun had fallen beyond the western rim of the ocean, the last of the terrible tremors had ceased and the appalling working of power had come to its conclusion: the inner ocean had again settled in its bed, but the land that ringed it had changed, the whole island rising up from the water like some impossibly vast leviathan. The city of the Remoons had been flooded up to a third of its height, only for the waters to recede, leaving utter chaos behind them. Docks, wharves, houses, barracks, shops, all had been turned to rubble, and the pattern of streets had been swept away as if it had been no more than markings on a beach erased by the ebb and flow of the tide. Behind and above this destruction, the remainder of the city had fared little better, many of its taller buildings collapsing and shattering others. Great holes had appeared where the deep ceiling of the lower city had fallen in. There had been an exodus in search of higher ground, but countless thousands had been taken by the flood waters.

The inner coast of Medallion was not as it had been, for as it had risen up, so had land that had previously been under water become exposed. The old city that had been protected from flooding for so long had been drowned as the sea rushed into it, but then it had risen up, the waters again pouring out from it. Now the younger city perched on top of a great mass of weed-choked rock that pushed out from the inner sea, a mad god's fist, reducing the area of the inner sea by two thirds. Anakhizer's power had flung the old city up above the sea level where it had first been built before the Flood centuries before, a monument to his evil will. Of the numerous ships that had gone down, none were found. Darraban and Fennobar had perished as they fought each other, as had Estreen and most of her Crannoch faithful.

In the highlands above the city, the scattered survivors looked down on the moonlit water in confusion and despair: Trullhoon, Crannoch, Remoon and members of every minor house on the island. None of them now lifted a hand against each other, their horror at what had happened being too great. Whatever else Eukor Epta and his fanatic brothers of the Blood had achieved, they had not brought about an internecine war, for the fighting was over.

Ottemar, Sisipher and many of their followers had come at last to the highlands overlooking the city, where Kirrikree had first seen the men of Eukor Epta emerging. Already they were being hunted like animals, few of them escaping, for they had exhausted themselves in their bizarre working of power. Eukor Epta himself was, however, not to be found.

* * *

Even as Ottemar looked down in disgust at the madness far below him, Eukor Epta looked down at the changed coastline of Medallion. He made his careful way down through the layers of weed and sharp rocks, seeing the distant torches, knowing that his faithful were waiting. When he came at last to the water's edge, some two hundred feet or more below the former low tide line, the rowing boat was still usable when he found it. He had left the secret tunnels of the high cliffs and taken the escape route he had marked years before, one of the many secrets of those of the Blood, a retreat from the city they had once made. It led through the walls of the island to this western coast. As he rowed the leaking boat across the waters broken by sharp rocks, he saw the silhouette of the light sailing craft, anchored in the center of the channel. It was kept here, constantly manned, in case he ever needed it. He left nothing to chance.

The moon watched his solitary figure, and if it could have read his thoughts it would have been surprised by the lack of emotion there. Eukor Epta knew that he had been defeated, but he had almost achieved his goal, the destruction of the Remoons. This power, this so-called evil in the north, had not perished. It had been useful and it had given much, but it was far from spent. Ottemar Remoon may have eluded the trap, and he may well take the throne, but at what a cost! He would be ripe for conquest if Anakhizer could recover quickly.

Eukor Epta tied his boat to the larger ship and climbed up its ladder to the rail. The power he had tasted! It had been an elixir, flooding him, and although his fellow men of the Blood had been exhausted by the ritual, almost burnt out, it had been an incomparable pleasure. He would taste that power again.

He dropped softly to the deck and looked around him in the moonlight and torch glow. All was silent, but the men at the oars were ready, seated in place as if eager to be gone from here. Their spirits are low, Eukor Epta thought. Then I'll give them something else to think of.

"North and west, to the farthest of the Crannoch isles," he called, making for the steps up to the deck above. "We have allies there. Keep clear of the inner shores, though, for there'll be Trullhoon dogs waiting for scraps to feed on.''

No one replied, and Eukor Epta was surprised that there was so little humor in these men. They had been chosen carefully. None of them owed allegiance to anyone but him. Most of them had been criminals, men happy to stab back at an Empire that had given them nothing. He turned and studied their backs. It was only then that he realized something was amiss. Slowly he walked back down the lower deck and came abreast of the first line of oarsmen.

The man on the end sat with his eyes open, gazing fixedly ahead of him. The Administrator scowled at him and struck him gently on the shoulder with his fist. ''Hurry, now! Row!'' he told him. ''We'll not be taken. No stinking cell for—'' His mouth opened in surprise as the man lurched back, his head lolling to reveal the deep slash that had been made in the throat.

Eukor Epta went to another man, this one slumped over his oar, and pulled him up. He, too, had had his throat cut. There were some dozen oarsmen on this small craft: each one that Eukor Epta went to sat stiffly at his oar. The Administrator looked at them all; all were dead.

''If you intend to put to sea,'' said a soft voice from above him, ''you must row this craft yourself.''

Eukor Epta pivotted and saw at once the outline of the man who stood on the deck above, leaning on the rail as if nothing had happened here. No one else was visible, though Eukor Epta knew of no one man who could have done such grim work among the oarsmen. Slowly the figure above came to the stair and descended. Eukor Epta reached under his robes and slipped out his sword, watching the moonlight dance across its twin edges.

''Wargallow,'' he breathed as the figure left the stair and faced him.

''I have been expecting you,'' said the Deliverer. There came a sudden movement behind him and Eukor Epta lifted his sword at once, but it was no man that stood there. Instead he saw a white shape, its wings outspread, and the wide, staring eyes of a huge owl. He had never seen such a bird before: even the eagles of the Trullhoon islands could not match it.

"This is Kirrikree,' said Wargallow in an almost conversational manner. "It was he who found your ship. We guessed it belonged to you. Getting over the rim of the cliffs and climbing down to the coast here was a dangerous business, but Kirrikree acted as my eyes."

Eukor Epta looked about him casually. He had one hope, which was to leap into the sea and swim for land. But Wargallow must have surrounded him with his men, although they were very quiet. They would, Eukor Epta knew from experience, be the best. Someone like Wargallow would have seen to that.

"Are you looking for my men?" said the Deliverer. "There are none. Kirrikree and I are alone."

Eukor Epta's heart lurched. Alone! He did this to my men, *alone?* "And what is it you want of me? he asked calmly, deciding that this black-garbed man must want some favor, some price that he would not ask before his own masters. Would he betray them for power? That must be it!

"A little information, no more."

"In exchange for my freedom?"

Wargallow smiled, but it was a grim smile, and one that had no warmth in it. "Not at all. You are to die along with your men."

Eukor Epta remained outwardly impassive.

"Tell me first," said Wargallow, "why have you betrayed Goldenisle?"

"Betrayed! These are the lands of my people, those of the Blood. The Remoons and these others are invaders. They do not even belong to Omara, their ancestors spawned in Ternannoc! You have confirmed this yourself. What right have any of you to these lands?"

"And the Stonedelvers, the Earthwrought? Their blood is the blood of Omara. They are no less Omaran than your kind."

Eukor Epta looked surprised. "You have Stonedelvers with you?"

"Descendants of the men who once lived in the Heights of Malador."

The Administrator recovered himself. "Then they should have stood beside those of the Blood, and not fought against us!"

"With Anakhizer? A Hierarch from Ternannoc? Whom you were foolish enough to think your ally."

Eukor Epta laughed coldly. "You underestimate me. You think I would have become his slave? No more than I was a slave of the Remoon pigs! I merely used Anakhizer and his power. You have seen it—"

"It wasn't enough. And where is he now? What is his strength?"

Eukor Epta moved forward carefully, silent as a spider. If this fool really was alone, he would take him. "He is far from here. In time he will be strong, Wargallow. Far stronger than Goldenisle. You have merely put off your own execution. It is a pity you chose to support the Remoon. A man of your insight, a man who knows the potential of power, could have done far better for himself. Why concern yourself with Goldenisle?"

"Why, indeed? As you have?"

"I sought to give it back to those who owned it, to see justice done."

"Yet you now desert them."

"The gamble failed. I am no philosopher, but I have no desire to throw myself into a useless cause. There is no power here now. We risked it all and lost; it is drained. Those of the Blood will no doubt be hunted like wolves by your new Emperor. I'll not linger to watch their misery."

"So you go north."

"I do not understand you. Once you were a Deliverer, sworn to rooting out and destroying all belief in such things. But you have found it in the east and now here. It pervades all Omara. It is there to be used, not denied."

"I accept its existence, and the Deliverers who travel Omara also have to accept that now. But you cannot use it as you would wish, because it will use you. The prospect of having power is, I agree, compelling. But the power that leaks into Omara has only one aim. To devour."

"Those that oppose it—"

"Korbillian, who taught me the truth of power, compared it to a disease, spreading across Omara, killing it. A disease has no mind to take servants. It merely runs its course, ravaging the body it has possessed or dying in the process. There is no mercy, no reasoning. The power now in Omara will destroy it. There is only one answer to it.''

''Oppose it?''

''Exactly. I am no philosopher either, Eukor Epta. Nor do I claim to be an example to other men, a prophet, a man of honor and solid reason, ethical and just. But I have a mission. I believe in it and I make sacrifices for it. Not all my allies agree with my methods, which is why I am here alone. Ottemar Remoon, whom you so despise, is a man of pity. He will not wantonly kill your people. He might even have spared you.'' He stepped closer toward his prey and from out of his sleeve came the twin blades of his killing steel. ''I will see Omara purged.''

Eukor Epta lunged with his sword, but the steel came up in a blur and sparks fled from it. Again he chopped at Wargallow, but the man moved with incredible speed. Eukor Epta had seen good men in Goldenisle, for the army picked well and made notable warriors out of its soldiers. Eukor Epta had always kept himself in peak fighting condition, training with the adepts of the Blood, who were faster in their reactions than most other men. But no man Eukor Epta had seen before moved as Wargallow moved. Like a wraith, he shifted out of sword reach, his deadly arm hissing through the air, too quick for the eye to follow. There would be no more talking.

Twice more steel rang against steel and the sparks danced in the night. Wargallow allowed his opponent to take the offensive, weighing the skill of the Administrator. He knew at once that he was a superb swordsman. A sudden thrust caught his robe and tore through it, but he twisted his flesh aside, slightly unbalancing his opponent. He used his free hand to punch hard at the Administrator's exposed neck and the man tumbled back with a gasp. Wargallow ducked down and in one swift motion cut at Eukor Epta's legs.

The Administrator felt the awful bite of the steel and went down. Wargallow stood over him. His boot came down hard on Eukor Epta's wrist, pinning it to the deck. Eukor Epta drew upon the last vestiges of power within himself, mentally screaming for Anakhizer to help him, but Wargallow read this in an instant. Without a word he leaned forward and made a final cut. Eukor Epta saw nothing, and as he tried to speak his words were choked off by the blood that ran into his throat. His head sagged forward and as Wargallow stepped back, he knew that he had made a clean kill.

As he wiped his blades he heard movement behind him and swept around, killing hand ready, but it was only Kirri-kree, taking to the skies as if he had looked long enough on the scene below him. Wagallow watched as the bird flew upward, framed by the rising moon, and he wondered if the owl would have preferred to see him die.

A cough made him turn back to his victim. He stared down in horror as Eukor Epta forced his head up. Blood ran from the neck, soaking into his clothing, a black stain that widened as the Deliverer watched. The dead eyes moved, searching him out. In a moment Eukor Epta sat up, and as he tried to speak, blood frothed on his lips.

Wargallow drew back, disgust and fear filling him with a coldness that threatened to numb him.

"A fine killing," gasped the voice, and at once Wargallow knew that it was not the Administrator who spoke, not some last reserve of his power. As he pulled away to the stair, the fallen man tried to get to his knees, stumbled, then rose. But he was *dead*.

"Oh, yes, Wargallow," came the rasp again. "Your enemy is slain. But you are far too dangerous an opponent for *me* to leave alive."

Wargallow understood now. He looked about him, searching for the easiest means of getting off the ship, for the creature before him could not quickly pursue him, for all the power that Anakhizer was pouring into it. Yet as he looked, Wargallow saw the shapes climbing over the rails of the ship. He had not seen these creatures before, but he knew who they were: issiquellen. Scores of them. They meant to surround him and tear him limb from limb, or give him to the thing that now staggered before him.

Wargallow leapt up the stairs, grasping one of the firebrands that had been set there and hurling it back. It burst in a shower of sparks on the deck and at once set light to part of the rail. The issiquellen held off for a moment, but Wargallow could see there were others clambering over the back of the higher deck. He readied his killing hand. He would make them pay dearly with his life, for there would be no escape; it had been, ironically, a trap of his own making.

As they began to close, he heard his name called from out in the darkness. It was a sharp cry, and he couldn't say where it came from precisely, until with a shock he realized it was from above. Glancing up, he saw that Kirrikree had returned.

"Kirrikree!"

"Lift up your arms," the bird told him, and with a fresh shock, he realized he could *hear* the bird. But how?

"I hear your voice," he said, bemused.

"All men would hear me if I so chose. Hurry! Raise your arms!"

The bird came down, seemingly vast, and as it did so, other shapes swooped with it, including the largest eagle Wargallow had ever seen. The issiquellen, sensing what was happening, rushed in. Other eagles dived at them, ripping at them with deadly talons, creating havoc. Even so, it took all Wargallow's nerve to put his trust in the birds above him and raise his arms. He felt the grasping claws of the birds on his left arm and heard the clash of claw and steel on his right. The first of the issiquellen came for him but he swung his feet upward and crashed a boot into its chest.

His weight would be too much, he knew at once, but suddenly he was swung outwards, his heel catching the head of another of the issiquellen, spinning it aside. Then he was over the sea, dropping. His heart thundered in his chest as he heard more of the sea creatures breaking surface.

"Up! Up!" he cried.

"Pull, Skyrac!" came Kirrikree's urgent voice, and Wargallow heard another sharp voice call a reply. He came close to the sea, but then it was as if a blast of wind struck him. More claws caught at his arms, digging painfully into his flesh, and he was lifted higher, away from the clutching death below, outlined now by the blazing stern of the ship. Before him the cliffs loomed, as if about to slap him from the skies. But he was lifted higher, out of danger.

"I assumed you had abandoned me," he said aloud.

Again he heard the voice of the owl, hardly able to believe it. "Once I would have abandoned you and Guile without a second thought. But I know your mind, Simon Wargallow, better than you think. And I prefer you as an ally."

Wargallow grinned through his pain at that. He let the feeling of unease fall away below him with the sea and instead exulted in his new knowledge. Above him he felt the response of the great birds as they gloried in their mastery of the skies.

Epilogue

OTTEMAR HAD SET UP HIS CAMP in the mountains above the city, and had sent word to all those who had fled the city that no one should return to it until it had been properly examined and there was no further danger of flooding or collapse. Aumlac and his Stonedelvers were the only ones allowed down into the ruins, for they had promised to repair what they could and at least make parts of the city safe. Gradually, in small groups and large, the refugees came to the Remoon banner and accepted Ottemar as their ruler. He had sent out word that there would be no persecutions, no political executions. The war was over almost as soon as it had begun.

During the afternoon, Ottemar sat on a great rock, looking down at the inner sea and the fantastic changes there. There were armed guards beneath his rock and he knew that from now on he would never be far from such men and could never take for granted that his life would be safe on his own. As he sat alone, glad of the respite from the day's talks, he thought of Sisipher and what she had told him. What did he care about an heir? One could be found, even if not sired by him. He was not Quanar's son, so why shouldn't some cousin or nephew of his own someday succeed him? No doubt Sisipher would argue and talk to him of duty and so forth, but he would not be moved. He would marry her! He smiled to himself, hearing her again admit to loving him. Him! After the open contempt in which she had once held him.

A call from below broke his chain of thought. "I told you I had no wish to be disturbed for an hour at least!" he shouted back, but he could see over the lip of the rock to where a number of figures were waiting for him. One of them was Wargallow.

At once he leapt down from his perch, slid down the rock and landed with a bow no more than a few feet from the Deliverer. He clapped him on the arm but saw him wince. "Eukor Epta?"

Wargallow looked exhausted, his face pale, his eyes ringed with darkness as if he had not slept for many days. His left hand was bandaged and there was dried blood there. Even so, he grinned. "Dead. How I found him and how I came back is a long story and it must wait. There are others here you must meet at once."

Ottemar turned and recognized the old man who came forward. Otarus bowed deeply.

Ottemar shook his hand warmly. "You are the Law Giver!"

"At your service, my lord. You have our support. We are ready to hold an official ceremony as soon as you desire it and here if need be. All Goldenisle recognizes you as the Emperor."

"And the Administrators?" said Ottemar, with a glance at Wargallow.

"Many have been captured, the rest are dead or in hiding in the higher mountains. The power they used in their ritual is no more. In time, they will all be brought before you," said Otarus.

"Good. See that none are slain."

"If it pleases you, sire, there is another I would wish you to meet."

Ottemar nodded. "It seems I am not to rest today, then. Very well, bring him forward."

"It is a girl, sire."

Ottemar frowned, again turning to Wargallow, but the Deliverer remained expressionless. In a moment Ottemar found himself facing a tall, dark-haired girl whose beauty surpassed that of any other girl he had ever seen. He sensed that every man here studied her, but she held herself with great dignity her back straight as a rod, her face almost arrogant.

"This," said Otarus, "is Tennebriel, whose father was Vulder Crannoch, and whose uncle, Colchann, was the husband of Estreen. Tennebriel is the Regent, made so by the

Hall of the Hundred before it was known that you were alive.''

"Yes, I know my family tree," said Ottemar with a grin. He turned to the girl and it was difficult not to be disarmed by her haughty gaze. "I understand there was some dispute as to whether I should be Emperor, alive or not," he said to her.

"That is true," she nodded. "Eukor Epta had other plans. He has had me locked away since I was little more than a babe in arms. He took me for a simpleton, thinking to control me. And he meant to put me on the throne in your place. If this war was waged in my name, it was not at my bidding.''

"I accept that. And do you accept me now as Emperor?"

Tennebriel inclined her head regally. "I do. And I speak for the House of Crannoch."

"Then I will let it be known that the Crannochs are welcome in my own house, as with Trullhoon and Hammavar.''

Otarus looked greatly relieved at this and was about to make some comment when another figure came forward. It was Sisipher, and as she approached Ottemar, he knew that she could not match the beauty of the Crannoch girl, but even so, in his eyes she was more desirable than a dozen such beauties. He wanted to embrace her before everyone.

"My lord," she said to him and he grinned at her use of the title, the first time, he thought, she had spoken it. "The unification of Goldenisle is essential in the aftermath of this disaster below us."

"Of course—"

"We are all glad that the struggles between the Houses of Crannoch and Trullhoon are over. You, who are the son of a Remoon and a Trullhoon, can do much to strengthen your Empire."

What is she getting to? Ottemar wondered. None of this was rehearsed. Why should she wish to stand before those assembled here and make such a formal speech?

Otarus also looked puzzled. "What do you mean, my lady?" Already he had great respect for the girl.

"It is clear from what has happened in this war that the Crannochs were not to blame. It would be unreasonable to say that Tennebriel led them in rebellion. Eukor Epta led us all into darkness."

"Quite so," Otarus nodded.

"I have seen forward to brighter days," she said, her voice dropping, and Ottemar felt himself tauten. A sudden sense of foreboding overcame him; he felt his mouth go dry. He could not meet Sisipher's eyes, though she looked straight at him.

"What have you seen?" came a soft voice. It was Wargallow who had asked, his brow furrowed.

"Nothing clearly. But it leads me to venture a suggestion, if the Emperor will permit it."

They waited for Ottemar to recover himself, as he seemed disturbed. "What? Oh yes, if you must. I'm sure I'll need much good advice during the coming months."

Sisipher turned to the dark-haired girl beside her, the incomparable beauty. "There is no better way to repair the broken trust between the Houses of Empire than to offer Tennebriel of the Crannochs your hand in marriage."

There were gasps of indrawn breath from all around the circle of faces. Wargallow's face was the only one that wore no expression. He merely watched Ottemar, seeing the ill-concealed anguish there. Ottemar could not speak.

Otarus cleared his throat, diplomatically interrupting. "Well, this is hardly the time or place to discuss such matters. But I am sure we must thank Sisipher for such a thought—"

Tennebriel's face did not mirror the anxiety of Ottemar's but she had not smiled. "A bold suggestion," she said. "And one for which I was not prepared. I had expected the sword—"

"Too many survivors have," said Sisipher. "Which is why I have spoken out. What I have said was well meant. What better solution for Goldenisle? And from such a union it may well be that a son of the three Houses would spring—"

"I think that is enough," said Ottemar, his teeth almost clenched. He could not look at her and did not see the tears forming in her eyes. "There will be a time to discuss such things. But not here. Otarus, I would be glad if you could dismiss this meeting. I will retire for a short while and rejoin you later."

"Of course," bowed the old man.

Ottemar began to walk up the slope, away from the group.

He called out sharply for Wargallow to join him and as he did so, Ottemar asked for a report from the Stonedelvers.

Sisipher watched the two men move up into the grove of tiny trees, closing her mind to the pain she had brought upon herself. Above her, Kirrikree looked down, but he was silent.

When Ottemar and Wargallow were out of earshot of the others, the Deliverer faced the Emperor. "I understand your pain, Ottemar. I need no special powers to read it. But Sisipher is right."

"*I'll* decide that!"

"You have already done so, I think."

Ottemar glared at him, his anger rising now. "Am I or am I not Emperor?"

Wargallow smiled ruefully. "It is what we have striven for. But you cannot marry Sisipher, no matter how deeply you love her."

Ottemar's anger looked as if it would overflow into a rash act of violence, but instead he suddenly deflated. "Is it so obvious?"

Wargallow shook his head. "No, but I have seen it in you." And the owl told me, he wanted to admit, but Kirrikree had made him swear not to reveal that he had been admitted into the owl's thoughts. "It is Sisipher's love for you that makes her turn from you. If you made her your wife, you would have to watch the Crannochs always. By marrying Tennebriel, you bring them under your banner, and they need that badly, after the years they have spent atoning for the stupidity of one youth and the fury of a king."

Ottemar cursed. He looked back through the trees, but already the group below had dispersed, leaving only a few guards. "She has never ceased speaking to me of responsibilities and duty."

"Then add sacrifice to those," said Wargallow.

Ottemar was about to say something harsh in reply, but something in the Deliverer's look, now focussed far away, prevented him.

"We have become a strange company," said Wargallow. "And we don't have time to spend on ourselves. It's a little late to change that now." He smiled at some private thought.

"What amuses you?"

"I told Eukor Epta I was no philosopher. I may have been wrong."

Ottemar smiled with him. "There'll be a time for that. But not yet. Now is the time to be hard."

Wargallow inadvertently looked northwards, but he turned away, his eyes settling on the exposed steel of his right hand. The blood was gone from it and it shone as brightly as on the day it was made; it looked almost hungry for its new baptism.

APPENDIX I

I THE GOLDENISLE SUCCESSION
(To the death of Quanar, 3588)

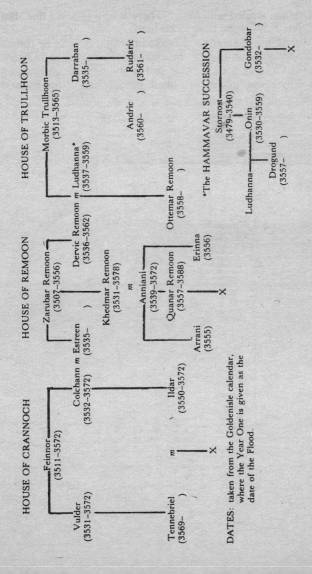

HOUSE OF CRANNOCH

Feinnor
(3511–3572)

Colchann m Estreen
(3532–3572)   (3535–   )

Ildar
(3550–3572)

Vulder
(3531–3572)

m ─── X

Tennebriel
(3569–   )

HOUSE OF REMOON

Zarubar Remoon
(3507–3556)

Dervic Remoon
(3536–3562)

Khedmar Remoon
(3531–3578)

m

Anniani
(3539–3572)

Quanar Remoon
(3557–3588)

Arrani
(3555)

Erinna
(3556)

─── X

HOUSE OF TRULLHOON

Morbic Trullhoon
(3513–3565)

Darraban
(3535–   )

Ludhanna*
(3537–3559)

Rudaric
(3561–   )

Andric
(3560–   )

Ottemar Remoon
(3558–   )

*The HAMMAVAR SUCCESSION

Stornost
(3479–3540)

Onin
(3530–3559)

Ludhanna

Drogund
(3557–   )

Gondobar
(3532–   )

─── X

DATES: taken from the Goldenisle calendar, where the Year One is given as the date of the Flood.

II THE GOVERNMENT OF GOLDENISLE
(At the time of Quanar's death, 3588)

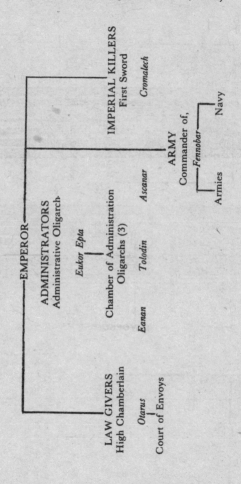